A Plague of Shadows

Bloodborne Pathogens, Volume 2

C. René Astle

Published by C. René Astle, 2018.

This is a work of fiction. Similarities to real people, places, or events are entirely coincidental.

A PLAGUE OF SHADOWS

First edition. October 13, 2018.

Copyright © 2018 C. René Astle.

ISBN: 978-1-7751591-3-1

Written by C. René Astle.

Also by C. René Astle

Bloodborne Pathogens
A Scarlet Fever
A Plague of Shadows

Watch for more at www.creneastle.com.

Thank you to my family for your lifelong support, to my friends for being patience beta readers and sounding boards, and to those who read and reviewed the first book - you gave me the motivation to finish this one.

CHAPTER ONE

MINA WAS ON THE HUNT for a creature of myth and legend. A nightmare made real. A beast that could rend her flesh from limb, leaving nothing but unidentifiable gore behind. She was searching for a gargoyle. And she wasn't happy about it.

As she sighed into the indigo night, her breath misted the air. She'd already dealt with the gargoyles, or at least de-fanged them when she'd killed Luca, their maker...and hers. Mina's lips tightened as she pushed the memory of Luca's blood seeping over her forearm back into the dark recesses of her mind. Dropping her hand from the handle of her holstered gun to her thigh, her fingers tapped out a syncopated rhythm.

Ahead of her, Bee led the way, stopping at every intersection of alley and laneway to look both ways before crossing. Mina dutifully followed her so-called mentor, though she hadn't been subject to any training sessions lately.

"There's been no sign of them since Luca died," she whispered. *Since I killed him*, she added to herself, and something in her gut twisted, a memory trying to surface, maybe. She kept the thought to herself, keenly aware how the others had been standoffish the past days.

Bee looked back at her, the whites of her eyes flashing against her deep brown skin as she put a finger to her lips with her free hand, requesting silence. Then she turned to inspect each path that led out from the intersection, still overly cautious, before leading them straight across as she'd done at all the others. Mina glanced upwards, as much out of boredom as anything else, though she told herself the gargoyles crept along rooftops as easily as cobblestones. As did vampires such as the Necrophagos, the wicked counterpart to the Athanatos that'd taken her in. They were as much a threat as any gargoyle. But there was no sign of anything, except the impending rain that was forecast.

As Bee halted yet again, Mina tapped her toe on the asphalt until the woman gave her a harsh glance. Stopping her foot, she gazed at the pavement instead, letting her sixth sense creep out along the maze of side streets – her blood sense as she'd come to think of it. The sense that made her different from the others, according to Jack, allowing her to hear the music imbued in the creatures that surrounded her. But there was still nothing. There was no music in her blood but Bee's metallic percussion unlaid with a deep twang.

There's been no sign of the gargoyles since I took out their maker, Mina repeated to herself as Bee started moving again. *Since I killed Luca*, she reminded herself. Again, something convulsed in her gut, and again she kept the thought to herself, recalling the looks the others had given her when they'd found out she killed her sire. And the sly looks they'd given her since, sideways glances when they thought she wasn't looking. *But vampires kill each other all the time, and I'm a vampire.* Mina's jaw clenched. She didn't see why there was such a taboo about her killing Luca, maker or no – after all, she stopped the gargoyles.

There've been no gargoyle attacks since I killed Luca, she repeated, making it a mantra while ignoring the writhing in her intestines, as Bee paused yet again.

A PLAGUE OF SHADOWS

"What's the hold up?" Mina asked, her hushed voice sounding sibilant in the silence of the alley.

Nonetheless, Bee turned to glare at her, eyes narrowed as they homed in on Mina. The woman pressed a finger to her lips. "Ssht!" She peered down the shadowed passage to her left for a long second, then returned her gaze to Mina. "I thought I heard something," she said, her voice so low Mina had to strain to pick out the words.

"I don't —" Mina stopped herself from saying 'feel', recalling Jack's exhortations that her blood sense was unnatural, even for vampires, even for the dracul she now was. She had to remind herself of that – she was twice-bitten, no longer dhamphir. She shook her head to pull herself out of her navel-gazing. "I don't hear anything," she continued, keeping her voice pitched low to match Bee's. "You know, this would be more efficient if we split up."

"You heard Dar," Bee whispered. "We stay together." She turned away and crossed the intersection. Mina spared a thought for her warm – and, more importantly, dry – bed as she sighed and followed.

Then she stopped in the middle of the small crossroads, canting her head to the side, her ears twitching. Slowly she shifted it to the other, trying to tease out what had raised the goosebumps on her arms, as her hand crept to the handle of her gun. Ahead, realizing Mina was no longer following, Bee turned back to her. Mina flicked her gaze to Bee as the woman opened her mouth to speak. Mina held up a finger. Bee scowled but was silent. Mina's eyebrows drew together, then she shook her head and joined Bee.

"What was that about?"

"I thought I heard something. But it was just the wind." Mina indicated for Bee to lead the way again. But as soon as they reached the next corner, Mina realized that it hadn't been the wind.

"Huh," Bee said, as they stared at the body covered in cuts while at the same time being as desiccated as an Egyptian mummy. "I don't think it was gargoyles."

"NOPE, NOT GARGOYLES," Jack said as he crouched next to the dried-out corpse, turning it gently with a piece of rebar he'd found nearby. Mina squatted beside him, while Bee and Dar stood back, Dar leaning against the far wall, Bee peering over their shoulders.

"Disease?" Mina asked. "But he's a vampire." She pointed her finger towards the fangs that were exposed by the taut lips while trying not to look at the ravaged face.

Jack swatted her hand away. "We heal. Doesn't mean we don't get sick. There are things that can infect us. Heck, for all we know, we're created by something tainting our blood us."

"*Very* few things can infect us." Dar shifted away from the wall. "All of them evil."

Jack stood up. "Well, I don't think it's disease, anyway, cut up like that."

Mina glanced back at the body. It was as if the rain itself had become shards of glass, leaving a web of fine lacerations over his skin. Except it was clear the cuts continued under the vampire's clothes. Quickly looking away again, she stepped over to join the others. "Is he someone you know?"

A PLAGUE OF SHADOWS

Bee and Jack started to shake their heads until Dar gave a sharp nod. "A revenant. One we couldn't save. He refused to even live by the minimal rules of the Necrophagos."

"A revenant?" The space between Jack's eyebrows crinkled as he glanced over his shoulder before returning his attention to Dar. "Like Lin."

"Not quite like Lin. A little more wild. A lot more raving."

Jack arched an eyebrow though Mina could understand Dar's point – Lin was mad but Mina wouldn't call her riddled speech raving exactly. "What's he doing here?" she said out loud. "I thought they lived in the woods and wild places."

Dar shrugged. "Something he shouldn't have been doing, it looks like." His head swivelled to peer at the end of the alley.

Shortly Mina heard what he had: a rumble of metal and mumbling. A form appeared in the opening, one she recognized. *Mike.*

"Speaking of raving," Bee said. "Time to go before we're conscripted to be an audience?"

Mina snapped her head around to scowl at Bee while Jack nodded towards the dead form. "What about him?" he said.

Dar's gaze slid sideways. "He's already dissolving into dust."

Surprised, Mina looked at the corpse. Sure enough, the body was disappearing, turning into a puddle of mud.

"Ashes to ashes, dust to dust." Mike's voice tumbled along the cement walls. Mina turned back to him as his sharp gaze flicked from the disintegrating corpse to her. "And death to death."

"Too late," Bee said, her tone waspish. "Raving's here."

Mina started to say something but let it out in a sigh instead. He was batty, and there was nothing she could do or say to help. "Have a good night, Mike," she said, keeping her voice quiet.

"There is no good night anymore. The angel of darkness comes to pave the way." He stepped closer despite the cat weaving between his ankles, and his voice became hushed as he glanced around. "Right hand of Night, the Herald comes, a whisper on the wind."

The hair on Mina's neck stood on end, and she edged away. He leaned forward as the cat jumped up on the cart, reaching its front leg up to paw his chin.

"But the whisper becomes a shrieking chorus, a howl of wolves. It says the Herald seeks the blade that will slice the vault of Hell." He reached to stroke the cat, and the cat responded by pressing its head into his palm. He scritched it under its chin. "Look out for old friends," he said, still looking at the cat.

Mina gave a lopsided smile. "I'm trying," she said as much to herself as anyone.

But Mike looked up , his eyes actually focusing on her. "Old friends become new enemies when Night comes."

Mina tried to come up with a response to that, but nothing came to her.

"Time to go?" Jack's hand was on her elbow, and he lifted an eyebrow in question.

Mina nodded and turned to follow him. Glancing back as she reached the alley the others had gone down, she saw the cat watching her with its golden eyes.

CHAPTER TWO

NOT ENOUGH. The shadow seethed as another drop of icy rain sliced through him. *Still not enough juice.* He needed more life than the street rats and alley scum provided. Dank alley scum steeped in sewer sludge. A tremor ran through his insubstantial form, as much of a shudder as a thing made of mist knitted together by terror could produce.

He was weary of this spectral existence. And he should have been corporeal long before now. He should have been dining on fine wine and finer blood rather than the viscous bodily fluid of the waste of society. He should have felt satin and silk against his skin, instead of the slice of sleet passing through him. His hope that sucking the life from a supernatural creature would help had been dashed – but the one he'd found was an emaciated skeleton of a vampire, unable to feed him when it clearly hadn't fed itself in too long.

Vampires. The word slithered through his mind. He wished he could spit it out. They always had been inconstant servants, despite Night's fondness for them. And lately they'd been more than unreliable – they'd been treasonous. First Luca, using the power *he'd* given him then betraying him to settle his own petty grievances.

Then the woman, Luca's creation, killing Luca. The shadow sighed, an exhale of longing almost. Luca would have had enough life to give him the flesh he needed, the body he craved. And she had stolen that from him.

A rustle sounded down the alley. A rat. Not a shifter nor an apparition, just a plain, old rat. But every little bit helped. Soon he'd be able to consume enough, and then he'd feed on the woman and her friends and her family and any creature in the city he took a fancy to.

The shadow descended as the rat scurried and squeal. But it was too late for this rat.

CHAPTER THREE

AS A DROP OF SLUSHY rain slid through her hair, across her temple and down her face, Mina scowled at Bee who led their little gang through the deserted streets. She couldn't really blame Bee for the weather, though she was the one who'd argued that they needed to be out here hunting now non-existent gargoyles for the second night in a row. And once again, Mina brought up the rear, where Bee had stuck her, away from the action. If there were any action to be had. Up ahead, Bee held up her hand again, her sign to stop, not speaking for fear of drawing attention to their passage. Mina snorted as she piled in behind them.

Bee hadn't even argued that they needed to pursue whatever could turn a vampire into shoe leather, her focus on the gargoyles that had been defanged and declawed, if not killed outright, at Luca's death. But Dar had agreed with Bee, despite the grumblings from the conclave.

"Why are we out here again?" Mina asked, not bothering to keep her voice low. Bee didn't respond. Instead, she started walking again, crossing the intersection, continuing straight, Adeh and Astrid following her lead. Mina huffed and followed the others, half tempted to holster her gun so she could tuck her freezing hand inside her jacket. It wasn't the cold that got to her as a vampire; it was the damp.

At the next crossroads, she stepped up behind Astrid, who glowed in the dark with her pale skin, though her black hair and oxblood leather jacket almost blended into the darkness. Astrid glanced back at her but didn't say anything, instead turning to follow Adeh, flipping the sai in her hands to point back towards Mina. A comment about being careful where she pointed those things crept to Mina's lips, but she let it go with a shrug.

She stepped into the intersection and paused, peering down the alley to her left, trying to tease shapes out of the darkness. But other than the occasional glint of damp asphalt, there was nothing. All she heard were the sounds of the city beyond, muffled by the buildings around them. She finally gave in to temptation and holstered her gun, unclenching her frozen fingers then followed after the others with a frown as she tucked her hands up under her jacket. They continued on like this, leapfrogging over intersecting alleyways, until they were at the rendezvous point, where they were supposed to meet Jack, Dar and Sha.

But there was no one there when they arrived. Bee took the opportunity to do some recon down one of the offshoots while Adeh and Astrid checked weapons and ammo clips. Mina leaned against the brick wall, tapping out a tech trance rhythm against the black denim of her jeans. A minute into this, she froze mid-beat.

A pebble had fallen into water somewhere down the alleyway to her left, but any hint as to what had dislodged it was lost in inky blackness, even with her unnaturally acute vision. Then she spun her head the other direction, at a scuffling on her right. As her eyes adjusted to its lighter shade of gloom, she started to pick up threads of music as three figures formed out of the darkness: Jack, Dar and Bee. She let out the breath she'd been holding.

"Where's Sha?" Adeh asked.

A PLAGUE OF SHADOWS   11

"Here." Mina's gaze shifted back to the left, as Sha – Alisha – stepped out of the night.

"You were supposed to stay together," Bee said, as she pushed past Jack and Dar, coming to stand beside Mina.

"Yes, General." Sha gave a mock salute. "Nothing bad happened, see?" she said, tipping her head to the side, arms wide.

Bee frowned at her before turning back to Jack and Dar. "Anything?"

Dar shook his head, running his empty hands through his flopped over hair. "Nothing."

"Maybe the gargoyles really are dead," Jack said, glancing at Mina as he holstered his gun.

"Maybe," Dar said. "I just don't trust things that come easy."

Mina glared at him. "It wasn't easy."

He stared at her for a moment as Mina's cheeks got hotter. "No, I don't suppose it was," he finally said. "Maybe it is time to call it a night."

He turned to lead the way out of the warren of alleys and side streets. The others followed, one by one, until only Mina and Jack were left in the intersection.

"Give him a chance," Jack said, his eyes glinting in the faint light. "He knows more than you might think." Then he too followed the others. Mina watched him leapfrog Astrid and Adeh to walk beside Dar.

"'Give him a chance,'" Mina muttered, her throat tight. "What about giving me a chance?" She breathed deep and shivered, as a breeze lifted the hair at the back of her neck, then followed the rest of them, glancing behind her now and then, just in case some rat tried to sneak up on them.

NEARING THE NEXT INTERSECTION, Bee slowed as always to check the crossing path was clear in both directions. It seemed like Bee was blinded by the darkness, it took so long. Cold seconds passed, ticked off by drops of rain from the wires above. Mina spent the time flipping her dagger and catching it. She let out a heavy sigh, expelling all the air in her lungs so loudly Astrid turned to glare at her, a frown on her alabaster face. Mina scowled back, canting her head, as she breathed deeply and exhaled again, almost masking a rustle ahead, past the intersection.

A rat? She smiled, then that turned to a frown as she cast her gaze around, looking for the source of the sound, as a shimmering cascade of dust fell from the eaves just past Bee's head. Mina slipped the blade back in its sheath and drew her gun. *On a roof?*

Blood buzzed in Mina's ears as a rush of adrenalin coursed through her system. Without conscious thought, she pulled her gun from its holster. Scanning the rooftop and the alley, checking for any other source of danger, her eyes passing over the others – no one else looked up, no one else saw the threat. Her pulse beat against her eardrums and her nerves made her skin tingle. Ahead she saw a shadow form on the rooftop. She sprinted forward, using a fire escape like monkey bars to launch herself past Astrid and the others, landing cat-like in the next intersection, coming to a stop in front of Bee. Sliding to rest against the far wall, kitty-corner to the others, she took a steadying breath then aimed at where she'd seen the shadow, firing off three shots with barely a breath between them. The shadow disappeared, and a shower of splintered cement rained down on Bee's head.

A PLAGUE OF SHADOWS

"Argh!" Mina charged at the wall, intent on climbing it with her bare hands. Instead, she found her forearm locked in Bee's iron grasp, the woman scowling at her.

"What the hell do you think you're doing?"

Mina pulled her arm away. "There was something up there." She gestured to the rooftop. "I saved you."

"It was probably a pigeon, disturbed by all your huffing and sighing." Bee let go of her arm. "And if it wasn't, all you've managed to do is scare it off."

Mina breathed in deeply through her nose, stopping herself from huffing at the last second, she let it out in a long, slow exhale. In the quiet, she heard another sound she'd missed before. Her eyebrows drew together.

"It wasn't a pigeon!" Sha said from the back, her voice tight, and too high.

Mina's mouth twitched, the smile at the fact that she was right turning to a frown at the low, heavy sounds of a funeral dirge in her blood. Before she could shout a warning, blinding flashes of gunfire filled the night, followed by the scent of blood.

"Run!" Adeh's deep voice boomed.

Mina tried to push towards the action, to help whoever had screamed, but Bee shoved her forward. "If he says run, run." Mina realized she had no choice in the bottleneck of the alley, and took off down the narrow lane, clearing a path for the others to follow. As she ran, her stomach churned, worrying over the thought of who had been hurt. *Killed.*

She slowed at that thought, stopping to catch her ragged breath. It was only then she realized that she was alone. And where she'd heard that sad, low, trudging drone before.

"Gargoyle," she whispered to the night.

JACK SKIDDED TO A STOP beside a tipped-over chunk of eroded stone. His hands on his knees, he panted, taking in great lungfuls of fetid air. They'd made it to the muster point, a patch of sculpture and muddy grass that had once been the home of St. Alban's church and its small cemetery.

I need to run more, he thought as he canted his head, listening for sounds of attack, but all he heard was the sound of his own heart thudding in his ears. This was nominally neutral ground, claimed by the dead that were buried there, but that claim grew more tenuous as the buildings grew ever higher around it.

He glanced up as the last of them leapt over the tilting wrought-iron fence. Sha collapsed back against the unrecognizable statue that stood in the centre of the small park, dark streaks on the hand she pressed against the striated wounds on her torso and blood oozing from a gash on her abdomen. Her normally almond-hued skin was ashen. Dar placed both hands into a headstone, leaning over as he caught his breath. Jack stood up, his eyes tensing as his gaze passed over the others.

"Where's Mina?" he asked.

Dar cocked his head, then looked from Jack to the rest of the small group. Adeh, Astrid and Bee glanced at each other, then Bee shook her head and shrugged. "She ran when we ran."

No Mina. Jack's roiling stomach dropped, then he strode across the small park, heedless of the graves he was treading on, stepping past Dar. But Dar laid a heavy hand on his shoulder, stopping him cold.

A PLAGUE OF SHADOWS 15

Jack turned to stare at his mentor and friend, then yanked his shoulder out of Dar's hand. "We have to find her."

Dar looked down at the headstone. "We have to get to safety, regroup." His brown eyes, dark in the night, turned to Jack. "You saw what that was back there." His jaw tensed as he looked away again. "We have to protect the conclave."

"She's a member of the conclave." Jack looked from Dar to the others. Adeh and Astrid avoided eye contact. Sha's eyes were closed, her breathing thready. Bee just stared at him, her lips tense.

"She is." Dar nodded slowly.

After a long moment of silence, Bee spoke. "She's also a big girl who can take care of herself. Unusually well for a dhamphir." She crossed her arms over her chest.

Jack canted his head as he parsed Bee's comment. "What? You think she's different, unusual?"

"You know she is," Bee said. "Faster, stronger." She went silent, as if challenging him to contradict her statement.

"Maybe she's strange. News flash, we all are. But for all we know, what makes her different might also make her more vulnerable."

"Or more dangerous." Bee dropped her hands to her hips, close to the hilts of her daggers. "After all, she's already a dracul."

"So are you and I."

"But not after such a short time."

Jack's jaw clenched as he tried to work out a retort for that. Instead, it was Adeh's soft voice that spoke.

"Whether or not she's different, she's a member of the conclave." He stepped up beside Jack. "I'm with him."

Jack looked at Dar, whose brown eyes shone as he glared at the two of them, his lips thin.

"I agree," another faint voice said. Jack turned to see Sha standing, her bloody hand leaving a dark print on the statue.

Astrid came to stand beside Bee, looking at Sha with an arched eyebrow. "You're injured. You need a healer before you bleed to death."

Sha looked down at her arm, and the blood that oozed between her fingers to drip onto the ground, as if it didn't belong to her. "I'm a vampire, I'll heal."

Astrid pursed her lips, then shifted her gaze to the others. "What's to say Mina's not dead already? Should we endanger all our lives going after one person?"

Dar sighed and hung his head. "Fine, we go."

"What? That's not—" Astrid started.

Dar held up a hand. "We go. You don't have to join us. You can see Sha safely back to the Sanctuary."

Astrid stared at him for a second, her thick eyelashes flicking. "Nah, Adeh can do that. He's got a crush on Sha, anyway. Give them some alone time while we find this wayward vampire."

Impossible though it was, Jack swore he saw Adeh's deep brown cheeks flush, despite the cover of night.

"ENOUGH!" DAR SNARLED. His head throbbed, and irritation grated over his skin. Jack and Bee went silent. Astrid was clearly unhappy with the enterprise, given the frown on her lips, but she was at least keeping her displeasure to herself.

A PLAGUE OF SHADOWS 17

Dar glared at Bee and Jack, his hard eyes flicking from one to the other like a whip. His lips pressed into a thin line and his nostrils flared. With his blood pounding in his ears, he forced himself to take a deep breath, then continued, keeping his voice even as a blade. "How does your bickering help us find Mina? You've been at each other since we left St. Alban's. All you're accomplishing is bringing attention to us."

Dar returned his gaze to the crossroads, turning his flushed face to the darkness, grappling with his anger. He released his hands, finger by finger, from their clenched fists.

"Sorry," Bee said, her voice not reflecting contrition. Jack retreated to his usual taciturn self.

Dar tilted his head to the side, cracking his neck. "I don't need your apologies...." He closed his eyes and breathed in through his nose, opening his nostrils wide and filling his lungs. There was a scent on the wind, something his heart knew but his brain refused to process. Whatever it was sent shivers up his spine. He shook his head, trying to clear it. "Never mind. We're all on edge."

"Some of us more than others," Jack said, his voice low. Dar glanced at him over his shoulder. Jack's dark eyes shone in the night, his face hard.

Dar turned away from his stare and breathed in again through tense lips and a clenched jaw, sucking the cool air slowly.

"This way." He nodded his head towards the left. The others followed his gaze, peering into the unlit lane.

"You sure you want to go down there?" Jack asked.

Dar flushed as his ire rose again, so soon after tamping it down. "Are you sure you want to find Mina? This is your quest after all. But, as you say, she is strange." Dar arched an eyebrow as he peered at Jack.

"I didn't—" Jack stepped towards him, pulling his shoulders back. "She's just a bit different, and more than a little headstrong. It could get her into trouble, left to her own devices."

Dar's hair stood on end as his skin bristled. He lowered his centre of gravity. "Yes, I noticed your pet project has a tendency to wander off," he said, his voice low.

"She's not—"

"Disobeys orders. Puts us all into danger."

"Enough," Bee said, stepping between the two and into the laneway Dar had indicated. "Bloody men and their pissing contests," she muttered as she walked away. Astrid sauntered after her, a look of amusement replacing her frown.

Dar's eyes followed them. He breathed in and out slowly. He felt Jack's eyes on him.

"I just have a bad feeling about all this," Jack said, his shoulders sinking a fraction of an inch, before he stepped past Dar to catch up to the women in the lane.

Dar looked at the ground, his hair flopping over his eyes. "I know, I do too," he said to himself. *About a lot of things*, he added silently before heading after him.

CHAPTER FOUR

PIETRO COUGHED HARD into his elbow, a cough that hunched his shoulders and worked his abdominal muscles. It was followed by a worrisome rattle. The cold had started as a tickle in his throat a few weeks ago. Since then, it had ebbed and flowed, lingering on and on, all the while sapping his energy. He was glad the long day was over so he could go, wrap himself in a warm blanket and drink some spiced tea, spiked with some of his mother's special medicine: brandy.

"Ah, I know it's here," a rough voice said from the dark lane beside the church.

Father Pietro glanced in its direction then back to the door, his hand on the key in the lock. The thought of warmth and brandy gave him pause, then he sighed, his sore shoulders slumping as he turned the key and slid it into his pocket. Then he made his way down the stairs, his knee clicking with each step.

"Rain soon," he said to himself, rubbing the palm of one hand over the knuckles of the other. He didn't need to look up at the dark grey, looming sky to tell him the forecast. "My knees are better at predicting the weather than that woman on Channel 6," he muttered.

Pietro looked into the lane, dimly lit by weak security lights on the church wall; he noted that some of the bulbs needed replacing. Ten paces along, an old man in a worn but clean winter jacket rifled through a pile of old newspapers.

"There was a message here. Now there's none." The man picked up a jumble of papers, tearing them as he shifted them from one hand to the other.

"Michael, what's the matter?" the priest asked.

The old man shook his head and waved his hand. "I tell them, I tell you, I tell them," he said, not looking at Pietro. "There's only Mike, no Michael. No Michaels anymore. I am not the messenger, just the medium."

"Sorry. Mike." He took a step toward the old man, who bent to his task again, muttering about a knife. A new motif that worried Pietro; Mike had always seemed harmless but his rants the past month had taken a darker, more strident turn. But they'd never involved weapons, not that Pietro had heard. He glanced around, as if answers would appear out of the darkness. Some concern niggled at the base of his brain, but he couldn't pinpoint what until he saw a rat, further along, scurry for cover from Mike's ravings. "Mike, where's your cat?"

"Hunting. Out hunting for vermin. The vermin. Always looking for evil creatures while I hunt for answers. Together we find the truth." Mike shook his head, pulling his faded blue toque down over his ears. "But there is no truth anymore, only the message."

"What are you looking for? Maybe I can help." Pietro took a step closer, but Mike pulled away.

"No, you don't know what the knife of darkness looks like. No one does." The old man tapped his temple. "But I know, I've seen it." Mike got down on his knees, lifting soggy, dirty pieces of newspaper. "It was here. Dark blade of the Even Star, piercing the heart of the Sun."

A PLAGUE OF SHADOWS

Pietro frowned, and rubbed his hands together, before tucking them under his armpits. The threat of snow had passed, but the night was still cold. He crouched down beside Mike, reaching out, placing his hand on the man's shoulder. "Come with me, I can get you a warm bed, some food."

Mike shrugged his hand away. He always refused shelter. Pietro sighed; he might need to dig deeper to get the man the help he needed.

"Aha, see." Mike extracted something from the pile. He jabbed a finger at a scrap of newspaper.

All Pietro could make out were words with more letters than any word should have. Nothing about a knife.

"Can I see?" Pietro reached for the crumpled paper. But Mike clutched the scrap to his chest.

Pietro retracted his hand, moving it back to Mike's shoulder. "Okay, I don't need to look. Won't you come to the shelter, just tonight?"

Mike shook his head, then looked at the sliver of dark clouds visible above them. "I need to watch. The Herald descends, and the servants of Night fill the air." Mike clutched at Father Pietro's arm. "Don't let them take the day," he said. "Don't let the sun fall." Mike let go of his arm, then turned to pat the sodden pile of cardboard and newspaper. "Now, where's that cat?" he muttered.

Pietro stood, his knees protesting. He looked down at Mike for a long moment before turning and walking back to the front of the church. At the end of the alley, he glanced back at Mike. "Are you sure...?"

The man's eyes finally met his. "You? You shouldn't be out here." He tilted his head, his eyes shining in the weak lights. "Beware the crow that enters on silent wings."

Father Pietro sighed, suddenly very weary. Then he turned towards home, his feet leaden and his heart heavy, his shoulders convulsing as the cough returned.

MINA STOOD FROZEN, peering down the small lane she found herself in, until the darkness resolved into a value study in shades of grey. Unsure of whether to go forward or go back, she didn't move. She couldn't hear any more gunshots. Nor could she hear footsteps or screaming. She couldn't even hear the skitter of normal city critters in their nocturnal scavenging.

She closed her eyes and opened up her sixth sense, reaching out for the others. But she couldn't hear them: the heavy tones of a funereal dirge filled her blood. She shook her head to clear it. But the sound remained. Her human ears picked up a soft hiccoughing from the nearest rooftop.

She tipped her head, shrinking from the sound, not wanting to believe what her ears heard, when footsteps behind her interrupted her concentration.

Mina spun around, dagger in hand, as a voice reached her out of the darkness.

"There you are." The words held a remnant of a long-ago Irish lilt. Still, it took Mina a second to process, her fingers tight on the hilt of her blade.

"Astrid. You scared me half to death."

Astrid stepped out of the shadows, an eyebrow arched at the irony of that.

"You know what I mean." Mina slid the dagger into its sheath. "Where are the others?"

A PLAGUE OF SHADOWS 23

"We got separated, out looking for you." Astrid shrugged a shoulder. "They're in this warren of alleyways somewhere." Astrid's gaze travelled up the wall to her left, across the narrow patch of sky, then down the other side, gun still in her hand. "And now that I've found you, we should find them," she continued, her voice lowered. Her feet shifted, preparing to turn back the way she'd come.

But in that second, Mina's heart dropped into her stomach as a whoop cascaded through the alley and a shadow coalesced behind Astrid. A set of razor-sharp talons went into the woman's back, coming out the front where Mina could see them glistening.

"Gargoyle," Mina whispered, as Astrid's warm blood sprayed over her face, another taloned hand tearing into the woman's throat. Mina grabbed her gun, despite her shaking hands. Her aim was wild though, and she only hit the creature's shoulder. But it pulled its claws out of Astrid, and advanced towards her instead, blood dripping from its hands. Mina forced herself to take a calming breath before firing again, being more careful with her aim this time. The creature snarled at her as the bullet tore into its right pectoral, still wide of the heart, but that was enough to cause it to retreat into the darkness.

Mina slid to a crouch beside the other woman, pressing her hand to her bleeding torso. Warm blood seeped over her fingers, but even in the weak light, she could see that there was no life left in the woman's eyes. She might have healed from the multiple stabs to the abdomen, but not from having her head half ripped off.

A skittering of shadows passed over her head, and Mina pressed herself back into the wall, under the overhang of darkness cast by the building, wiping her bloody hand on her bloody jeans. The deathly tune grew louder.

"They're dead." Mina's lips formed the words though barely a sound escaped her. She didn't move for long minutes, waiting for the dirge to fade into the night. Then she slumped against the cold, brick wall, and slid down to rest on the grimy asphalt of the dank alley.

All tension drained from her sore muscles, and she felt empty. She let her head flop sideways, to where a shadow flitted at the edge of her vision. But there was nothing there, no vampires, no gargoyles, just a fog of fear and the burden of death. She pressed her eyes closed, willing away the image of Astrid being rent through by the gargoyle, her blood gushing out of her. She rubbed her fists into her eyelids, pushing away the memory of the stake sliding so easily into Luca's chest, his heart popping under the slight pressure. She opened her eyes and rubbed her hands on her jeans, blocking out the smell of blood oozing between her fingers. But it was no good. The memories were imprinted on her senses, on her muscles, on her nerves.

She tilted her head back, gazing up at the sliver of sky, as wracking sobs reached up from her gut and passed through her raw throat. She brought a fist to her mouth, biting it to choke off the sound, pulling it away as she tasted Astrid's blood on her lips. A pang of unwanted hunger shot through her.

She looked at her bloody hands, mottled grey in the shadowed alley. She'd killed a man...vampire...thing. *Luca, I sought him out and killed him.* She'd killed him with the hands she now let fall onto the icy damp asphalt, not caring what else might be mixed with the blood. It wasn't the same as shooting a creature with a gun, separated by however small a distance. Or even stabbing a gargoyle intent on ripping her throat out. She'd intended to kill him, and she had. And it hadn't change anything, she thought as a whooping sound echoed in the night, underscoring this realization. *And Astrid is dead now because of me.*

Because I'm a killer. A cold-blooded hunter. Worse, a parasite that lives by siphoning life from others. Her stomach clenched at the thought of feeding, her nostrils filled with the odour of blood. She ran her tongue across the teeth between her canines.

What kind of monster am I? Mina let her head hang and spoke to the shadows. "I'm a vampire. A killer."

SEEMA SLUNK DOWN THE alleyway, weaving through piles of soggy boxes and overflowing garbage cans. The hair on her neck stood up, her tendons strung like zither strings on her limbs. Examining the shadows instead of watching where she was going, she stepped in a puddle of icy water. She scowled and shook off the unctuous liquid.

God only knows what's in that water. She wanted to clean herself off but knew now was not the time. She shook her leg again, the shaking travelling up her spine and into her ears. The temperature had dropped, and snow was starting to displace the rain. But that wasn't why she was out of sorts. She knew that much even if she didn't know the cause. Something just set her teeth on edge. She sniffed the air, cocked her head from side to side. A scent in the snow tugged at her memory. Something sweet and sour and sickly all at once. Something that didn't belong there.

A shadow to her left twitched, and she jumped right. Her heartbeat raced through her veins, but her senses soon told her it was a rat. An ordinary rat. Normally she would have thanked the gods for such a gift, a plump and juicy morsel. But tonight was not normal. Tonight her stomach jittered, the meal she'd eaten earlier burbling uncomfortably.

So Seema left the fortunate rat alone. She needed to get back to Mike, to protect her protector against the deepening night.

Slinking along the alley, she kept close to the brick and concrete wall to her right, not wanting to be startled by another rat. Or something worse. To her left, the passage widened, allowing glimpses of a busier street and the sky above. Grey clouds reflected the lights of the city, casting the sky in a nauseating orange and skewing her internal clock.

Seema picked up the pace, wending her way back towards the square. There was a whisper in the wind, like something she'd heard before, though she couldn't make out any words. Tickling her whiskers, it told her something wicked this way cometh. All of it spoke of things better left slumbering in the abyss.

She rounded the corner.

And stopped short.

A body lay in the alley, its blood congealing on the cold asphalt. She craned her neck, trying to discern the manner of the wound without getting any closer. Failing that, she breathed in, inspecting the air for a hint as to the killer.

She crept closer, inch by inch, keeping as much distance between herself and the body as possible while still getting close enough to examine it. One lesson she'd learned the hard way – never trust a corpse to stay dead. She couldn't smell any nascent putrefaction; this death was recent. But she did catch a scent she recognized. Disbelieving, she got close enough to see the face. The skin was ghostly pale, and the slack mouth revealed an im-

A PLAGUE OF SHADOWS

pressive set of canines. Cautiously, she sniffed the dark pools that had formed between the ridges of buckled pavement.

Vampire. She skittered back against the wall and glanced left, right, up. But she saw no sign of the creature that took down the vampire.

She stepped gingerly forward again, one careful step after the other. This bloodsucker she didn't know. She inched closer and sniffed. Over the stink of alley, blood and entrails, she smelled something else.

Seema spat. *Gargoyle.* The odour of mildew and rotten earth they left behind on their kills had filled her nostrils too much of late. She huffed to clear her nose of the metallic tang of blood mixed with rotting garbage.

Then something shifted in the shadows and Seema jumped, her ears twitching. But she didn't run. Another lesson learned: it was running that let the predators know where you were. Instead, she crouched low, and let her eyes absorb the dim light. A breeze stirred, carrying a whiff of another smell, one more familiar to her. Of spice and warmth and kindness. She breathed in deep, taking in that scent. Her whiskers twitched. This time it was mixed with blood. *Could this be the killer?* The thought caused her supper to burp in her unsettled stomach. It seemed out of character if the owner of the scent was who she thought.

She was torn between investigating and going home to curl up for the night. She looked out to where the alley opened onto the welcoming square. Already she could feel the warmth of being nestled close to a beating heart. She glanced back down the dark alley, devoid of even rats. Huffing out a breath of air, she turned away from the square and towards the limp form, ignoring her mother's voice in her ears saying something about curiosity and cats.

Sidling up to the body slumped against the brick wall, she moved sideways, hackles up. She got close enough that she could clearly smell it through the reek of garbage and unidentifiable detritus. Through the blood that splattered its clothes and hands.

This was the source of the scent she associated with warmth and caring, not with a killer. The new vampire, the woman who had been kind to Mike.

The one who was different.

CHAPTER FIVE

THE GREY SHAPE, MORE a coalescence of shadows than a creature of flesh, clung to the wall. Hovering somewhere between solid and vapour, he flowed along, cloaking himself in the pools of darkness. Rain was not his friend. Despite being a ghost of his former self, the puddles betrayed his passing. The fat drops didn't know whether to swerve around the void he created in the night or to try to pass through it. If only he had his rightful strength, the weather would have done as he commanded.

Angelos had tried to order the raindrops away from him, but they hadn't listened. The voice he'd used to mesmerize the weak-minded Luca was abandoning him; already it was hoarse, little more than a whisper, and becoming more gravelly every passing hour. In his present state, he could barely charm a rat, let alone a gargoyle or a golem or a sacrificial lamb. He struggled to keep in check the various creatures he'd called upon in Night's name, and hadn't yet been able to claim a body for his own. How was he supposed to pursue the life and death task she'd set for him, without having her powers? A tingle of pain coursed through him at the thought of what failure would mean, threatening to dissipate his nebulous form into the night.

He let out a low growl. Words had power in and of themselves; they could be weapons. When he could speak the proper words, in the right intonation, people had no choice but to listen. He needed to act soon, before the voice Night had given him was gone completely, leaving him with little power and no chance of success.

Angelos snarled. He needed flesh, a physical form so the words would reverberate with power. Which meant he had to find both a voice to steal and a body to house it in.

He tested the edges of the shadows that enveloped him, probing them, pushing them outward ever so slightly until one ran into the next, allowing him to cross the chasm of light. Once across, he followed the shadows again, turning into an alley overhung with fire escapes and air conditioning units, creating a surfeit of shade from the taunting moonlight and judgmental stars.

He sighed, letting go of the tension caused by the insufferable light. A body would help protect him from that too.

He slid along the brick wall. As he approached the end, he realized that his path of shadows might have led him falsely. The alley opened onto a large square. Opposite, a church spire rose behind a cage of scaffolding.

The oppressive building was illuminated by an obnoxious number of lights, as was the square in front of it, even though it was empty at this time of night. He tried to warp the darkness around himself, hoping to ease his passage to the other side, and allow him to skirt the holy ground. Pulling the threads of his being together, he stepped one foot out of the alleyway.

"The Night comes."

Angelos froze. His gaze swivelled to his left, scanning for the source of the words. A pile of rags and newspapers, clumped against the wall beside him, shifted in the stillness.

"The Messenger heralds the Darkfall."

He turned full-on to the owner of the voice that spoke words so near the mark. The jumble papers morphed into a form: an

A PLAGUE OF SHADOWS 31

old man swathed in tattered clothes under a blanket of cardboard and newspaper. Angelos held his breath as he appraised the man, pulling shadows to himself. The man smelled of stale sweat and must, the eternal scent of the homeless and destitute. He waved his hands, clad in a surprisingly decent pair of gloves, moving them through the air in random motions as he continued to mutter.

"Where's that darned cat?" The man moved his hands around, patting his pile of cardboard. "Ah, right, I told her to hunt. She's hungry, even though she doesn't complain." The homeless bum frowned. "I promised to take care of her, so I sent her away. No food today. And coffee's not for cats." The man glanced through the air, his eyes passing over the shadow. "And best she's not here when Night comes."

The man waved towards the church, its facade lit by floodlights. "And the night is not safe for man, but maybe for beast."

A crazy old man. Angelos sighed, releasing tension he hadn't realized he was holding. The man's gaze swivelled towards where he lurked, his nebulous form pressed against the wall.

"Night comes, but I can see shadows in the darkness. Night will fall, but not before her Messenger."

Angelos stiffened again, and took a silent, sidling step towards the man, ignoring the pain caused by the streetlight.

"The blade is found. The vault cracks. But Night is fickle," the man said, looking up at the silver and grey clouds. "She may find a new voice for a new world."

Angelos dared another step closer. The man stilled, then turned to dig around in a bag beside him, as if he had stopped ranting and was looking for something. But Angelos knew better.

"Are you crazy?" he said, his voice rasping in his ragged throat. "Or prescient?"

The man stopped digging in his bag and looked at a space a few inches in front of Angelos. "I hear the Herald, but I heed it not," the man said, returning his attention to his bag.

"But do you fear me?" Angelos asked. "As long as you fear me, I don't care if you listen."

The man stilled and looked forward. "It is a false instrument that Night plays falsely."

"What riddles do you speak, old man?"

"The vault of hell is cracked, but the gates are barred. The heart of the sun is hidden." The man shook his head. "Yet the message is heard by beast wide and far."

"Enough," Angelos hissed, taking another large step so he loomed over the man.

"Night falls, but the Herald's voice is weak." The man tilted his head up and looked right at where Angelos stood, but his eyes didn't focus. "Will the day break before the prison of Night is unlocked?"

Angelos looked down his nose at the old man. Under the dirty clothes and piles of newspaper, a strong heart still beat. He could see the young man that this old man used to be: broad shoulders, strong jaw, deep voice. He could steal that voice at least, if not the decrepit flesh.

"You're as good a sacrifice as any, I suppose." The grey ghost descended on the man, lacerating exposed flesh. The man barely had a chance to call out, a formless petition to life, and there was no one around to hear.

A slurping sound squelched out from the pair, then Angelos stood up. He felt a fullness, a flush. Looking at his hands, they

A PLAGUE OF SHADOWS 33

were slightly more opaque, though he could still see the cobblestones through them. He tried a simple spell, to shatter the street light, but nothing happened. It was not enough. He needed to cloak himself in flesh to give his voice power, and this one life had not been enough. He was still a shadow of his former being. Not that he was entirely disappointed, looking down at the pale form of the old beggar man, whose wide, empty eyes stared back.

"I wouldn't have wanted to be you."

A clang sounded over his shoulder, and Angelos spun around, pressing himself against the wall beside the body.

"Hullo?" A man in a black shirt and white collar scanned the square from the doorway of a small building next to the church. But no hue and cry followed.

Angelos knew that all the man saw when his gaze swept over him was a pile of newspaper under an extra heavy overhang. A puddle of darkness in a pool of shadows.

CHAPTER SIX

THE PRESENCE THAT HAD been lurking in the shadows crept towards Mina. A small voice in the recesses of her mind told her to run. But she didn't listen, drowned as it was by louder voices of guilt and dejection. Her arms and legs tried to force her to move, but she ignored them too. Instead, she sagged back against the wall, closed her eyes and waited for whatever was descending upon her. Her punishment for failing to kill the gargoyles.

A tentative shape formed out of the shadows, peeling itself away from the darkness to become a small point of light in her mind's eye against the imposing mass of the wall. She remembered her vision of the gargoyle that had almost killed her, its features imprinted against her closed eyelids in pinpricks of vicious light. She was pretty sure this sixth...or seventh sense was no more normal for a vampire than hearing music in the blood of others.

Whatever it was, the light of this shape was less harsh than the gargoyle, softer, and smaller too. It inched forward, its feet almost silent on the wet asphalt. It had a heartbeat, rapidly pulsing through its veins, and it had a blood song –– a high-pitched string instrument. She sighed a little tension away, but not enough. When the fuzzy edge of the shadow touched her pinkie finger, she jerked her hand back, to rest it against her bloody thigh,

A PLAGUE OF SHADOWS 35

Apparently, she still had some instinct of self-preservation. *Very little*, she thought. *Better Luca had sucked me dry.* She tried to open her heavy eyelids and failed, despite what she saw in her mind's eye was the shocked look on Astrid's face as the talons had torn through her. *I should be lying there instead of her.* Something soft ran across her hand, soft with sharp edges. Since death didn't seem to be coming to claim her, she forced her eyes open. Struggling to focus, she tilted her head to look at the shape.

"A cat?" The creature took a step back and looked at her, in between glances over its haunches. Mina reached her leaden hand out to pet it, and it pressed its arched back into her palm, before skittering around to peer into the darkness to their right. Mina stroked it again, absentmindedly wondering what it was so interested in. When she reached the tail, she stopped, causing the cat to turn around and rub its muzzle, followed by the rest of its body, against her arm, leaving a trail of orange fur.

"Do I know you?" Mina asked, half expecting an answer when the cat peered at her with its golden eyes. She scritched it under the chin. "Be a good cat and fetch me a dose of ibuprofen and a vodka chaser," she said, her reluctant lips forming a half smile. Then she remembered that would just make her ill...more ill. The cat pulled away, crouching to press its belly into the ground. Mina's heavy hand fell to the cold pavement without the warm body to hold it up.

"Sorry," she said, her head lolling to the side. A low, moaning growl emanated from the cat's small body, filling the alleyway. "Grumpy cat," she whispered. "It was just a joke."

Its hackles raised, the cat hissed. But not at her.

Mina froze, returning to her senses and picking up what the cat was reacting to. Arching its back, it jumped towards her.

"There's something out there, isn't there?" she whispered, her voice hoarse. *Something headed our way.* She peered into the darkness, where she could make all manner of creatures out of the nebulous forms and random glints of light. But it wasn't some unknown creature that made her stomach churn and her blood sing a thrumming song.

"Gargoyle." Her breath barely past her lips, but the cat still twitched. "It's back." She pressed into the wall, pondering the night, a part of her thinking she deserved to be rent into pieces to make up for Astrid's death.

"Ow!" A pair of golden eyes glared at her, and Mina looked at her hand where blood welled up from two tiny pinpricks, almost like a miniature vampire's bite. She sucked at the wound and glared at the cat. It continued to peer at her with those fiery eyes, its tail-end wagging as if getting ready to pounce.

"Right," Mina sighed. "I might deserve death, but you don't." In one scrambling move, she lurched up, heavy limbs forgotten, and grabbed the cat. The animal scampered up over her shoulder, using all four sets of claws to gain purchase. Mina bit her lip to keep quiet as she nestled the cat into her jacket and turned her attention to figuring out which direction to run.

MINA CHANCED A GLANCE over her shoulder as she approached an intersection of laneway and alley. And almost fell flat on her face, or flat on the cat nestled in her jacket, as she stumbled over buckled asphalt. Catching herself against the wall, she paused for a second to catch her breath and get her bearings. Her jangled nerves played havoc with her sense of direction. She

A PLAGUE OF SHADOWS

looked back the way she'd come then down the path ahead, trying to decide where to run next.

A rapid purr vibrated against her chest, accompanied by an even faster heartbeat. She'd snugged the cat, skin and bones under its striped fur, into her jacket as she'd fled the gargoyle. The cat kneaded her shirt, digging in with all its claws but not piercing the skin underneath, as it tried to wriggle its head up a bit to peek out her partially unzipped jacket.

It ducked back in as a spattering of dirt and gravel fell on Mina's head, trickling down her shoulder onto the ground. She pressed herself against the cinder block wall, wishing she could disappear into it, and craned her head up, trying to catch a glimpse. A grey hulk crouched on the edge of the roof four floors up, looking out over the intersection of lane and alley. Mina stopped breathing, and the cat stopped purring. The gargoyle's head moved side to side as it scanned the paths that led from the junction. Mina's heart jumped when it looked down their alley. Either it didn't see them in the shadows by the wall or wasn't interested since it took off down the one heading left.

Mina inched her way to the intersection. She glanced right – the overshadowing buildings seemed to open onto a well-lit space. She peered into the left lane, trying to see where the creature had gone.

A whoop cascaded towards her from that direction, echoing through the alley.

"Decision made," she whispered, creeping around the corner to the right, sliding along the wall. "Not that way." The cat seemed to agree as it recommenced its purring, more slowly this time. A mimicking chirr rippled through the air from the direction they'd just come. Mina transitioned to a jog, her feet landing lightly on the wet pavement.

The chirr was answered by a whoop much closer by.

Mina's heart tripped and she broke into a run, hoping that there was some safety to be had, in the middle of the night, in the open space ahead – St. Frank's square, her inner map told her, her sense of direction coming back online.

She skittered to a stop as she entered the square, the lights piercingly bright after the blanketing dark of the alleyway. She realized that the square didn't mean safety. It was deserted, with no backup or protection in sight. The spire of St. Frank's peeked out from scaffolding on the other side but these days its holy ground didn't extend much further than the sign. Mina spun around trying to decide which way to go but froze as her scan brought her back around to face the alleyway. She heard the soft chuff, and her eyes drifted upwards.

A gargoyle sat perched on the building next to the alley she'd come out of, its talons wrapped around the edge of the roof. Its eyes, entirely black, stared down at her.

Mina's breath caught in her throat, and her hand moved towards her holster, but with her jacket zipped up tight around a cat, she couldn't reach the grip of her gun. She had a pair of knives in sheaths in her boots...which were currently covered by her pants.

There was nothing in the square to stop the creature descending on her from its perch, no crowds, no Athanatos, no holy ground. But it stayed put, rocking back and forth on its haunches. Mina took a probing step backwards, keeping her eyes on it and her hand on the wall to guide her way. The cat nuzzled

A PLAGUE OF SHADOWS

its head into the crook of her neck. Not daring to look down, she could only assume that it was checking out the gargoyle as well.

With a soft clicking of talons on stone, another gargoyle joined the first. It chuffed quietly and crouched beside its fellow. This one craned its neck, sliding it one way then the other, twisting it back and forth, up and down, its nostrils flaring and ears twitching.

What are they waiting for? She continued her slow backward progression, one foot at a time, until her footstep landed on something soft and squishy.

She stopped mid-step, and tried to look up and down, forward and back simultaneously, an impossible feat.

Then she felt sharp talons pierce flesh. The cat scrambled over her shoulder, digging its claws into her skin. Using her shoulder as a springboard, it leapt, landing on the papers she'd stepped on, its light footfall barely making a sound.

The cat yowled. A low, guttural sound from the depths of its bowels. Forgetting the gargoyles for a second, Mina turned to look down at the cat. Its back was arched and tail puffed. It continued its howling, its whiskers pulled back.

"Shhh! Cat, quiet!" Mina hissed as she tried to approach it, but it skittered to the other side of the pile of newspaper. She reached her hand towards it. That's when she saw the face staring back at her with dead eyes.

The scream building in her chest was drowned by a pulse of adrenalin as another sound started behind her.

"What is that infernal racket?" a voice said.

The cat jumped back, as did Mina, before she settled into a crouch, her hand sliding to her hip, poised to grab her gun, now that she was no longer wrapped in cat. Her heart beat so fast it threatened to explode. She blinked, realizing she knew the owner of the voice: Bee, flanked by Dar and Jack.

Mina placed her hands on her bloody knees and breathed deeply, trying to slow her heartbeat. She raised her hand, finger pointing at the roof behind the trio.

"Gargoyle," she said, in between gulps of air.

They looked up at the creatures, stepping back as she had done. The gargoyles gazed down at them before slowly peeling themselves away from their perch and heading into the night.

"Where are they going?" Jack asked.

"Why don't they attack?" Dar added, before sliding his gaze to her. "And why are you covered in blood?"

Jack stepped up to her, his chiseled features softening. "Are you injured?"

Mina's cheeks grew hot, and she shook her head, looking at the cobblestones, not trusting herself to speak past the lump in her throat.

"Astrid?" Dar asked. With a slight inflection at the end, it was halfway between question and statement.

Rather than answering, Mina nodded then crouched beside the cat, which still howled but more quietly. Its deep, rapid purr had returned. She reached out and placed just her fingertips on its head. This time the cat crouched low, its ears back, but let her touch it.

"What the hell is wrong with that thing?" Bee said as she glared at the cat and Mina, arms across her chest. Mina felt the weight of the silent accusation in that gaze.

"It's injured," Jack said, coming to crouch beside Mina. The cat jumped to her other side, away from the others.

A PLAGUE OF SHADOWS

41

When Mina picked it up, its muscles tensed but it didn't resist. She nestled it back in her jacket, where it started kneading her torso.

"It's not injured, that's Astrid's blood," she said, glancing at him. "The cat belonged to him." She nodded at Mike's dead body, half hidden under crimson-tinged newspaper and cardboard.

CHAPTER SEVEN

SEEMA SKITTERED AROUND the corner, sliding on the polished floor, overshooting doorway at the top of the stairs. She scrambled back to the midnight blue opening and fled down into the darkness, not seeing any other means of escape. She needed to get out of here, away from these vampires. *Athanatos or not, they won't understand.* But the only exit she knew of was the one through which she'd entered the den of bloodsuckers, ensconced in Mina's arms. And it was blocked by the conclave chattering about Mike's death – 'what killed him, why kill a bum'.

As if they have any idea. Mike wasn't a bum, and her home was out there with him – or had been. Patrolling the streets, the back alleys, the rooftops, watching the goings on at the church with Mike. She paused halfway down the stairs. But Mike was gone. He'd saved her, and she'd failed him. He'd been raving about Night and her messenger for weeks, but she hadn't listened. Disbelieving the unbelievable, despite Mike never being wrong before. But there'd been no signs and, however much she hated to admit it, Seema had started to believe what people said, that he'd fallen prey to a disease of the mind.

But I was wrong, and now he's dead. Her eyes flicked about in the low light as her tail twitched. All that was left for her was to avenge his death. She started down the stairs again, more slowly.

But what can I do as a cat? She imagined herself big and fierce like a tiger, but all that accomplished was making her lose her

A PLAGUE OF SHADOWS

43

footing and slip on the step. Thankfully there was no one around to witness the lack of grace unbecoming of a feline.

At the bottom of the stairs, she came to a jarring stop and spat at the shadows, the fur on her neck standing on end. But these shadows were empty. No demons haunted them. No painful memories. She sniffed the air through parted lips, whiskers twitching as she moved her head from left to right, up and down. No direction smelled like outside, and nothing smelled like home. Nothing smelled like Mike. But one direction held a thread of something familiar and comforting. She followed the trace of scent halfway down the hall and nudged at a door not quite latched. She nosed the door again and was rewarded with it opening onto a small room.

Crouching low, Seema scanned the area, her keen eyes picking up details hidden by the half-light. She picked her way through the clothes that were strewn across the floor, ostensibly tossed in the direction of the basket in the corner or aimed at the half-open armoire. The desk against the left wall was scattered with pencils and markers, the bin beside it filled with crumpled sheets of paper. More were fanned out on the floor, all variations on a theme – a mask of some fierce creature, large teeth, large eyes, large horns. She glanced up to the drawing of a flower that hung over the desk. *Hibiscus syriacus.*

Rose mallow. It had been her mother's favourite.

Seema checked behind the door. Nothing hid there. She looked under the bed. No monsters were lurking. She backed into the door, bumping it shut, then jumped up onto the unmade bed, where she curled up beside the pillow and nestled against the wall, her eyes on the door. After a few minutes of vigilance, during which nothing attacked, she half closed her eyes, only to be confronted by images of Mike's mangled body. She chirred, wishing the images away, willing the pain away. But she couldn't forget him. He'd saved her, taken care of her when she couldn't have cared less. From that moment, she'd vowed to always do the same for him. But, in the end, she hadn't kept her promise, even if it was one made to herself rather than him. She turned towards the wall. All the threads of memory were jumbled up in her mind, and Mike's thread pulled at another, unravelling the barrier to her past.

More loved ones, tortured and torn asunder. Simply because they existed. They were anathema. Haram. Forbidden. Unwanted in whatever language was denouncing them.

And now the scent in the air told of an old evil descending. Night was coming, Mike had said. Her eyes tensed and her whiskers flicked as she lifted her head. *What sucks the life out of a man, down to the last dregs?* She realized she knew: a creature of shadow wanting to be made flesh. *The Herald is already here. And if the Herald is here, lurking in the shadows, he can be stopped. Before he ushers in Night.*

Seema needed to leave, to find the First Angel of Night, and figure out a way to stop him with her small cat's body, claws her only weapon. She pawed at the sheets, said claws catching on the fabric. Starting to purr as a nebulous, unfocused plan of action formed, she settled into the soft pillow.

Vengeance, she thought. *But first a catnap, and then maybe a bite to eat.*

A PLAGUE OF SHADOWS

SEEMA STRETCHED HER striped limbs, from the tips of her toes to the ends of her whiskers. She rolled over and started kneading, keeping her claws in, and purring.

But something was off. The body was not soft enough. Her heavy eyelids resisted her attempts to open them when she sensed a shadow descend towards her head. Her muscles contracted, preparing for flight, as her whiskers twitched, until she realized it was a hand, one that scratched her chin and rubbed her belly. She tensed again – the hand was too small, the air too clean, and she was in a bed too warm.

Seema forced her eyes open and examined the person that was looking at her. Mussy, black hair framed the woman's face, a face where the eyes were warm, and a corner of the lips lifted in a lopsided smile. Mina, they'd called her. Seema closed her eyes again and pressed her chin into the woman's hand, glad for a minute that she was not alone with only her memories to keep her company.

Engrossed in the attention, it took her a minute to realize that the woman was speaking.

"What do you think about that?" the woman said, pausing in her petting. Seema lifted her head. "Should we find you something to eat?"

Because vampires keep kibble lying about? Seema stared at her, purring nonetheless. *Maybe rats.*

"They must have some real food around here." Mina swung her legs over the side of the bed and wriggled them into a pair of black skinny jeans that had been lying on the floor. "For the familiars. Rhys." The woman picked up the phone from the bedside table, a frown pulling her lips down as she looked at it. "Still nothing," she mumbled.

No news is good news, Seema thought as her eyes tracked her movements. Mina put the phone back down, then picked up a hoodie and sniffed it before shimmying into it. Seema's nose waggled at that, sniffing disapproval. Then she remembered how she'd lived for the last...too many years to count...in forests, on ships, on the streets. *It is not for us to judge another*, a voice in her head said. It sounded suspiciously like her father's, but that couldn't be – she'd lost her father's voice long ago.

Lost in her thoughts, she found herself ignominiously scooped up into Mina's arms, and together they headed into the dark hallway. Part of Seema wanted to protest being carted around like a kit, but she told that part to shut up, and nestled deeper in the warmth of the woman's arms.

Mina carried her up into the large open space they'd come into the night before, with the star-spangled, stained-glass roof. Seema glanced around, casual-like, making note of potential exits. She couldn't let her present comfort (or lack of opposable thumbs – infernal doors) prevent her quest to find Mike's killer and make him face his justice. At the far end of the cavernous space, a vampire stood at the main door, a woman from somewhere south of the great desert if Seema had to guess. Tall, imposing, watchful, she stood with her arms crossed. Her black eyes sparkled as she peered at the approaching Mina, barely sparing a glance for Seema.

"Mina. We need to continue your training."

Mina looked down at Seema rather than the woman and shrugged. "Yeah, it's just been busy, you know, with things."

"Yeah, I know the things." The woman's expression didn't change. "Just because you killed your maker doesn't give you a free pass."

Mina's head jerked up. Pressed close to the woman's chest, Seema heard the heart beat a little faster. "I know," Mina said after a moment's pause, nodding. "But first I was looking for some food?" She shrugged, jostling Seema. "This one might be hungry."

"Mmm, the descendants of Bast can be voracious eaters." The woman stepped closer, and reached out slowly, letting Seema sniff her before running her hand over her head and down her back. "There'll probably be something in the kitchen."

"The kitchen?"

"Downstairs, past the bathrooms." The woman gave a crooked smile. "Familiars and guests have to eat something."

"Right. Thanks."

SEEMA SAT ON THE COUNTER as Mina opened and closed cupboard doors. She liked this room. The late afternoon sun slanted into the window wells, sending spears of light across the counters. It was empty now except for her and the vampire, but a table in the corner held a half-done jigsaw puzzle and a newspaper folded open to a crossword. An afghan was thrown haphazardly over a chair as if the occupant had just gotten up to turn the kettle off and forgotten to come back.

"Aha!" Mina said, pulling a can out of a cupboard. She turned to look at Seema, her eyebrows raised. "Tuna?"

Seema padded over to her, craning her head and licking her muzzle.

"I'll take that as a yes."

Seema rubbed against Mina's elbow. A little encouragement to the proper behaviour never hurt.

"Now I just need to find a can opener." Mina started to pull open drawers.

"It's in the drawer to the right of the stove."

Seema spun around into a crouch at the sound of the low voice. She appraised this newcomer, her back arched. *Not a vampire, this one. A familiar?* Mina smiled at the man over her shoulder, a fire sparking in her eyes. *Ah, he was food then.*

He came up behind Mina. She swayed into the hands he placed on her hips. *Obviously well-acquainted food.* Her mother would have tsked. But Seema didn't judge, given the dalliances strewn through her own past.

"I have to work, but I'm free later," he said, his lips close to Mina's ear, but being a cat, Seema heard every word. And realized she didn't like it one bit. Mina could help her in her quest, but not if she were fraternizing with this human.

"Give me a ping when you get off," Mina said as she dumped the contents of the can into a bowl. "You can help me find cat kibble."

The man reached a hand down to Seema. She hissed, and skittered back, almost falling off the counter, her fur standing on end.

Mina placed the bowl in front of Seema. "It's okay. He's a friend."

"Something more than a friend I hope," he said with a crooked smile. He placed his hand in front of Seema's nose and made that annoying sound through his lips that people made when they wanted her to like them. "I won't bite."

A PLAGUE OF SHADOWS   49

Seema breathed in through parted teeth. Maybe not a vampire, but there was something off in his scent. Still, she deigned to let him pet her, then she set to devouring the tuna, her ears twitching as they talked.

"Will do," he said, dropping his hand off Seema's head and onto the counter. "Though you may be busy."

"How so? I just have a cat to babysit and training with Bee to avoid."

"And track down what's been leaving desiccated corpses around the city?" the man said, his hand coming absentmindedly to Seema's head again. Her ears twitched, surprised to hear the vampires knew of more than one body left in the same state as Mike's had been.

"You heard?" Mina went to the sink and turned on the water.

"I've heard, along with some other interesting rumours."

Seema sensed Mina go still. She turned her eyes to the woman but kept her nose in the bowl, ears perked up.

"Such as?" Mina asked as she grabbed another bowl from the cupboard and filled it with water, not looking at either her or the man.

"There's another new vampire."

Mina breathed, and Seema saw her shoulders relax. "Is that all?" She placed the water bowl beside Seema.

Seema stopped eating as silence filled the room. The man stared at Mina for a half a minute before responding. Seema joined his appraisal, realizing where his thoughts travelled.

"You were the first newly made vampire I'd met in all my time as a familiar."

"So?" Mina shrugged. Seema's tail twitched -- two new vampires and the Herald.

The man continued. "I've been a familiar since my brother's death ten years ago."

Seema looked at the man with new eyes. Maybe they both knew this Mina was unusual.

"I thought you were going to say there were more gargoyles," Mina said, looking at Seema rather than the man, her voice quiet. Seema watched her shoulders slump. "Killing Luca did nothing."

"I wouldn't say nothing." He leaned in close to Mina, placing his lips on her forehead.

"What do you mean?" She pulled back a step.

"I've heard rumours about that too. There've been fewer deaths in the last few weeks." He shrugged. "At the very least you saved some innocent lives."

CHAPTER EIGHT

"YOU'RE STILL AVOIDING me."

Mina ran face first into Bee as she rounded the corner in the dark basement hallway. The cat squawked as it jumped out of her arms, its claws conveying its chagrin at being squished.

"Hmm, no," Mina said, tracking the cat as it took off down the hall while cursing herself for not paying more attention to her surroundings. She reached out to grab it, too late despite her enhanced reflexes, and started after the animal. "Cat!"

Bee placed a hand on her shoulder. "I assume the cat's been fed and can fend for itself for a while." Her grip was light but the intention incontrovertible. Mina's shoulders sagged. Bee's other hand came to rest on Mina's other shoulder and turned her towards the staircase. "If Dar can spare us both from patrol, with Astrid dead and all, it means your training is important. I don't know why you're so keen to avoid it."

"It's not the training I'm avoiding, it's the pain in the ass," she muttered under her breath with a smirk at her cleverness as she glanced at her phone – still no message from Cam. After a few seconds of heavy silence, she glanced up and flushed. Bee regarded her with one eyebrow lifted.

"Excuse me?" she said, her arms crossed over her chest.

"From being knocked on my ass," Mina clarified, silently cursing vampire hearing. "Repeatedly."

"Hmm, you've nothing to worry about today then." Instead of heading up the stairs, Bee opened the door leading down into the bowels of the building, towards the shooting range.

"I've already learned how to shoot," Mina said, stopping at the top of the stairs as the cat returned and wound itself in and out of her ankles.

"No, you learned how hopefully not to kill yourself or, more importantly, any innocent bystanders," Bee said without looking back. "Shoo cat," she said, nudging the cat away from her feet. "That's not the same thing."

Bee continued down the dimly lit staircase, and Mina knew she had little choice but to follow. Mina's steps slowed when the other woman passed the door to the left that led to the shooting range.

"Besides, tonight is two steps back, learning what you should have learned before picking up a gun. There is a proper order to these things." Bee stopped at a mahogany door on her right, inlaid with a four-pointed star out of some lighter wood. As she placed her palm on the access panel, the door slid open and a light turned on. Bee took a deep breath, letting it out in a long sigh. "The wonderful world of projectiles."

"I've already learned about – oh." Mina's mouth dropped open as she took in the room. The walls gleamed, glistened, sparkled, as the light fell on all manner of burnished metal. Several martial arts dummies populated the room; wooden ones were dispersed throughout while straw ones, each marked with smaller targets at various heights, stood at attention at the end of the room.

Bee walked down the far wall, her fingertips trailing over the diverse weapons.

A PLAGUE OF SHADOWS 53

Mina followed, wondering how some of these things could be thrown without the wielder losing a finger. "But why even bother, when we can just use a gun?"

Bee froze, then slowly turned to her. "Why bother? Why does an artist learn to mix colours from the three primaries?"

Though the question was clearly rhetorical, Mina answered anyway, glad to be in a subject area where she was the expert, having lived and breathed it for so long. "So they can learn colour theory."

"Wrong," Bee said, walking back to her, carrying some small blades. "It's because sometimes that's all you have. I thought you'd already learned that lesson." She held one blade in her hand, the point between her fingers. Mina made to take the handle, but she shifted backwards as Bee spun around and sent the blade into the furthest target. Dead centre.

"Besides, they're more innocuous than guns or swords, slightly easier to sneak into places people might get tetchy about weapons." Bee laid out a series of said weapons on the pommel horse beside her. Mina recognized a few – short knives and a series of stars that looked like props for an old Asian action movie. But most of them she'd never seen before, including a couple of small rings, a smidge too big and a lot too sharp to be bracelets.

"But are these really going to be deadly?" Mina leaned against another horse, waving her hand at Bee's array.

"Watch and learn," Bee said, picking up the first set of blades. In a blur of movement, she danced her way between pommel horses and sparring dummies, while throwing one projectile after another at a wooden form on the far side of the room. Each one lodged deep into a target that was a lot more resistant than flesh.

As Bee collected the blades, Mina spared a second to glance at her phone. Checking for a response from Cam was becoming an unhealthy obsession. She sighed and stretched her neck. Instead of a message from Cam, there was one from Dale: they needed to go to the lawyer's office again.

"Am I boring you?"

Mina blushed as her eyes flashed from the screen to Bee. "No, sorry. I'm just worried about my roommate." Bee leaned against the pommel horse, casually flipping the knife in her hand. "Ex-roommate," Mina corrected.

"The sooner you're dead to them, the better."

"So I've heard." Mina slid her phone into her back pocket. She watched Bee toss and catch the knife repeatedly. "What did you do, you know, when you were made?"

"What do you mean, what did I do?"

"Well, how did you deal with your family?"

"I'd been taken from my family years before." Bee casually sent the blade flying into the forehead of a target halfway across the room, then reached for another. "Though I think they were happy to be rid of me. I wasn't like the other girls." The muscles on her arms tensed and flexed as she continued.

"You must have had friends, or something. People who wouldn't have understood the whole vampire thing." Mina picked up a couple of the knives, throwing one at the dummy. It sunk into one of the eyes marked on the target.

Bee threw another knife, this one going wide. Mina paused, waiting for Bee to answer but her teacher stayed silent. Mina threw the second knife, lodging it in the target's other 'eye'.

"I killed them."

A PLAGUE OF SHADOWS

Mina glanced from the target to Bee. Her mouth opened, but she said nothing.

Bee looked steadfastly at the target. "I killed them, then I killed the ringmaster."

Bee threw another knife, this one landing in the heart of her target. "I would have killed myself if a good man hadn't found me and showed me there was still light in me, even if I couldn't live in the sun."

Mina picked up another knife and threw it, this one lodging just below the other two. "Was that Dar?"

Bee laughed. "Dar?" She shook her head. "No."

"Who was it then, who found you?"

Bee shook her head again. "That's a long story, deeply buried. One day I may tell you, but today is not that day." She stood up and indicated the tray of weapons. "Try the stars."

Mina did as she was told, throwing the stars one right after the other until there was a smile on the target's face.

"Hmph. You are a strange one," Bee said. Mina's stomach twitched; she'd been different all her life, but here being different could get her killed. She glanced nervously at Bee, whose lips quirked into a smile...or a sneer. Whichever it was, it quickly disappeared, and her tone was flat when she continued. "Showing off will get you killed one day. Or someone else around you." Her left eyebrow lifted, as if in challenge.

Mina kept her lips pressed together as she started down the room to collect the projectiles. She got a step and a half away before an arm snaked around her neck and pulled her back. Her sound of surprise was cut off, turning into a duck-like gak. The point of a knife pressed against her side, just below her ribs.

"What the fuck?" she said, her voice breathy.

"Close quarters combat," Bee said, turning the hilt of the knife up as she released Mina, presenting the blade to her, her face expressionless. "These are laced with silver, so the cuts will hurt and heal slowly. If they don't fester."

"And you say I'm the strange one." Mina took the knife. "You know what, it's not the pain in the ass I hate most. It's a knife in the back."

CHAPTER NINE

DAR WATCHED RHYS, WHOSE bookish ways and treasure trove of knowledge had earned him the nickname the Librarian, through half-closed eyes, as the man's long fingers click-clacked away on the keyboard of his laptop. Rhys' apartment was 5 degrees warmer than normal yet the man was wrapped in a thick wool sweater, worn at the elbows and frayed at the wrists. Dar's eyebrows drew together: despite Rhys' apparent chill, a sheen of sweat still coated his upper lip.

As Dar watched Rhys' fingers, the sound of the typing was superseded in his mind by that of Nocturne Op. 48 No. 1, the slow, melancholy tones of which had lured him into that dark room in Oxford.

The song had always tugged at him whenever he heard it. Even so, he'd tried to ignore it all those years ago, and block out the memories it raked up. But he'd been unable to resist the ache Rhys' fingers had drawn out of it on that day.

If he had known what would come of entering that room, would he have been able to turn away, could he have tried harder to resist? Or would the lure have been even stronger?

A familiar melancholy twined through Dar's stomach, a constant companion he could sometimes ignore if he had something else to focus on. He never understood how other vampires avoided it, watching the world from the outside, as their mortal friends and lovers, enemies even, flickered in and out like a flame in the night.

Through his half-open eyes, he saw the young man he'd come upon in that room, completely ensconced in the music he created, unaware of the predator who'd found him. The urge to feed had been almost unbearable, even now Dar's gums ached at the memory. But the music had forced him to stillness, eyes closed in the dark.

Unfortunately, there was no music now that would stay the savage beast.

"Penny for your thoughts."

Dar's eyes flicked open, his irises contracting, as his teeth ached to sink into Rhys' neck. In a split second, Rhys' look of expectation turned to trepidation. Dar sucked his breath in then shook his head, slowly, still half lost in a dreamy languidness. He pushed his tongue against his teeth, his fangs pressing into his bottom lip. "Just thinking," he said, his voice thick.

"Obviously," Rhys said, looking at him sideways. "I do have some experience with your moods." The man turned towards him, tented those magical fingers, then pressed the index fingers to his lips, waiting for an answer.

"Wondering what's leaving a trail of corpses more reminiscent of Egyptian mummies than the recent dead."

"Hmph. If you say so." Rhys arched an eyebrow but continued. "No idea yet."

"What about why we still have gargoyles to contend with if Mina slew their maker?"

Rhys separated his fingers to flip through the pages of the book that sat beside his laptop. "*Primum mobile*, perhaps."

"Sorry?"

A PLAGUE OF SHADOWS   59

"The first cause. Maybe Luca was not properly their progenitor. Or, perhaps, *doctrina imperfectus*."

"My Latin's a little rusty."

"I think this theory of the Created dying at the death of the Creator is flawed. It's always seemed off." Rhys leafed through a few more pages. "For one, there would be far fewer vampires if it were true of your kind, as you well know." His blue eyes met Dar's and held them. "And why should it hold true for any of the other preternatural beings if not for you?"

Dar conceded the point with a nod.

"Though I think it's just the three gargoyles, at the moment, anyway," Rhys said, then sighed, his shoulders falling heavily. "And we have bigger problems to worry about."

"What do you mean?"

"I've been doing some calculations, death rates from being torn asunder or consumed before Luca's death versus after. There's been no increase in carnage. In fact, there has been a decrease."

"That heartens me to hear," Dar said, eyebrows arched. "However, I was more wondering about the part where we have bigger things to worry about."

"If you'll bear with me." Rhys ran his hands across the pages of the book, then up and down his corduroy pants. Dar tracked every move, every wrinkle, every spark of static, curious to know what Rhys was avoiding saying. He let silence hang in the air until Rhys couldn't stand it anymore.

"The decrease in carnage suggest that something is controlling them," Rhys finally said, his head tilting to expose his neck.

"Maybe they've been weakened by Luca's death after all." Dar's fingers gripped the arms of the chair.

"Possible, but no. They'd be feeding more to recover their strength. I think they're being controlled, or at least coaxed into good behaviour. And there are very few things that can do that. Luca thought he could. He was wrong."

"He seemed to be doing alright, until the end."

Rhys shook his head. "No, I think it was never him."

"If not him, then who? Matteo? He didn't seem pleased with the powers his son was playing with."

Rhys placed his fingers on the keyboard as if to start typing.

"Rhys, darling, what are you not saying?"

"It's Night." Rhys stared resolutely at the screen.

Dar glanced at the window, where he could make out the feet of people walking by in the darkness. "Yes?" When the silence grew long, he looked back at Rhys, who had turned his steady gaze to Dar.

"Not that night. Night, capital N."

Dar stopped moving. His heart stopped beating for a second before thudding heavily in his chest, echoing in his ears. He shook his head. "That's not possible," he said, enunciating each word as if that would somehow make it untrue.

"If I've learned one thing from living at the shadowy edges of your world all these years, anything is possible. However much we might wish otherwise."

"Night was banished. Imprisoned in a cage of nothingness, no darkness, no company. Bound in a void outside the known universe. Never to see the light of day, or the moon, or the stars again."

"Every cage can be broken."

"But how?"

A PLAGUE OF SHADOWS 61

Rhys became the Librarian. "I've been doing some digging. Apparently, there are words to be said. Rites to be performed." He turned the laptop towards Dar, the screen too bright in the dimly lit room. A sketch of a wavy-edged knife, a scanned page from an old book. "And a sacrifice to be made: 'Blood will have blood, and Night will rain from the sky.'"

"So what? Luca always intended to make our Mina, so he could kill her?"

"Maybe." Rhys cocked his head, scrunched his lips. "Maybe not. If I'm any judge of character, I imagine he meant to kill Matteo, and Mina just happened. But the thing is, the outcome would have been the same if Matteo had killed Luca, also a very real possibility. The sacrifice would have been made."

"Pitting father and son against each other."

Rhys nodded. "A tale as old as time. Our Mina was just an easier sacrifice."

"Or so Luca thought." Dar paused as a dark thought wormed into his brain. "Are you sure Mina was an accident?"

"What do you mean?" Rhys glanced at him, his eyebrows drawn together.

"She killed him," Dar said. "A young, untrained vampire against a dracul. She killed him, and, if what you say is true, opened the door for Night to return to Earth."

"Are you suggesting Mina knew what would happen?" Rhys looked at him, his eyebrows shifting into incredulity.

Dar just shrugged in response, squirming under Rhys' judgment. More than once, he'd served as Dar's conscience. And too often lately all Dar could think about when he looked at him was the sweet-salty taste of his blood, seasoned by time and the yearning of memory.

He turned away to look out the window again as a shiver passed through him.

DAR SLOWED AND LOOKED around. He found himself surrounded by skeletal trees, dead grass and pale stone rather than the life of the city. The cemetery had crept up on him unawares.

It wasn't good to be so wrapped up in his own thoughts that he couldn't see what was right in front of him. Or sense what lurked behind. He pulled his hands from his pockets, and slid his left hand to his right hip, under his jacket. He tilted his head down, chin to shoulder, as his fingers found the handle of his short sword, then he turned around to face his stalker.

"Hello, old man." Matteo stood, his hands behind his back, where Dar couldn't see any weapon they might hold. Not that Matteo wasn't weapon enough on his own.

"Why are you following me?" Dar asked, his fingers itching to pull out his blade. Instead, he forced himself into stillness and waited.

"Why do you think I'm following you? Maybe we're just two old friends who happened upon each other in the graveyard in the middle of the night." Matteo brought his hands out, palms forward, and shrugged his shoulders in a movement feigning human unconcern.

To Dar, it looked like a puppet master had jerked the strings of his vampire marionette a little too hard. Although he wondered how long before others thought the same of him, he sim-

A PLAGUE OF SHADOWS 63

ply stared at Matteo without speaking, and without removing his hand from the hilt of his sword.

"So I was following you," Matteo said through tense lips, his eyebrow arching. "Have you heard the rumours?"

"Rumours? You mean the ones that say there's another new vampire?"

"What new vampire?" Matteo said as he glanced away, but as Dar watched the twitches and quirks on Matteo's face, he realized the man knew more than he let on. After a second, the nosferat had smoothed his countenance and looked back at him with eyes narrowed. "I'm referring to the rumours of Night."

"I know a little," Dar said. "What do *you* know?"

"Why should I tell you?"

"To keep me from asking more about a new vampire." It was his turn to lift an eyebrow. "Besides, you brought it up, stalking me here for a reason. And there's no gain for you in the coming of Night."

Matteo splayed his long fingers over his chest. "You always knew the way to my heart. Maybe we're more alike than you pretend."

"By 'heart' you mean that lump of charcoal buried under avarice and ill-will?" Dar half turned away, his hand dropping to his side. "I've no time for games, Matteo. Either tell me or don't."

"What is there to tell? The voices in the shadows chatter about the coming of Night." Matteo cast his gaze around at the drizzling grey sky, before returning to look at Dar. "But Night has not come. And so I can turn my attention to new pursuits."

Dar let out a hard laugh as he took a step to the left, watching Matteo mimic his movements with his own leftward sidle. "You don't know that for sure. None of us knows what form Night might take. Unless you've dealt with Night in the past."

Matteo's thin lips pressed together, almost disappearing. "I think we'd know if Death incarnate walked the earth."

"Evil enters with a soft caress and a silver tongue." They were both silent for a moment, then Dar continued as a horrible thought started to accrete at the back of his mind. "And something is leaving bodies with every bit of vital fluid sucked out of them. Unless that's your doing."

"As you say, what would I gain?" He glanced up at the sky, his voice quiet when he continued, almost as if he were talking to himself. "What sucks the lifeblood out of the undead?"

"Not your gargoyles?"

"You should know better than that." Matteo's head swivelled back to look at him. "To think you can trap me with words."

"But the gargoyles are still a real and present danger."

"Mmm, yes, killing Luca accomplished nothing." Matteo's black eyes glinted in the moonlight, as Dar stepped sideways.

"It caused their trail of death and dismemberment to diminish." Dar sighed. "But it's still enough to be noticed by the mundane world." He ran his fingertips along the mossy top of the nearest tombstone, where the icy core at the heart of the raindrops was starting to settle. He glanced at Matteo. "Your son's grave mistake has exposed us all to those who love to hunt us. Again."

Matteo was silent as the coldness crept between them. The stony set of the nosferat's jaw told Dar he'd gone too far, but he no longer cared.

A PLAGUE OF SHADOWS 65

Matteo's eyes slid sideways before coming back to Dar. "One for which he paid. At the hands of your newest recruit. How is she, by the way?"

Dar tilted his head. "Why do you care?"

"She's my kin, blood and bone," Matteo said with a thin smile that dropped again right away. "My son's slayer."

"She survived killing her maker."

"Hmm, so did I." Matteo exposed his fangs as he took a step towards Dar, getting closer in that one step than he would have if he were human. "As you very well know, some of our most cherished beliefs turn out to be false."

Dar held his ground, refusing to listen to the nibble of fear in his gut. "But it might explain why the gargoyles still live," he said instead, though his hand shifted back to the hilt of his sword. "Are you seeking vengeance?"

Matteo didn't answer.

"Because that would be an act of war," Dar continued. "A breaking of the truce."

Matteo's face split into a horrid smile, full of fangs and malice. "One man's vengeance is another man's justice."

Dar's eyebrows pulled together in question. "When did you start caring about justice?"

"As I said, now that I no longer fear the descent of Night I have time for other pursuits," Matteo said, tenting his fingers in front of his chest. His smile turned into a sneer and his eyes sparked with cold malice. "The truce is already broken. By the one who killed my son without my blessing."

Dar's lips tightened, but he stayed silent.

"The offer still stands," Matteo said, his voice deepening, smoothing out. "More so now that Luca has been taken care of."

Matteo stepped closer, his long fingers lifting as if to touch Dar's face. "Think of the power you could have if you came to me. You could live a life free of that nattering guilt. Take what you desire. Slowly, savouring the sweet ichor that flows through their veins."

Dar's throat tightened, and his stomach twisted in yearning. He clenched his jaw, forcing himself not to say yes. He tortured Shakespeare instead. "I think thou dost...insist too much. What are you worried about?"

Matteo ignored the question. "All it takes is one bite," he said instead, glancing away before returning his dark eyes to Dar. "Or a little more time."

"I'd rather die," Dar said, his voice low and hoarse.

"I'm sure that can be arranged."

Dar's hand tightened around the hilt of his sword.

Matteo raised his hands, palms open. "Save your energy. You'll need it for the fight to come. As the man said, cry havoc and let slip the dogs of war."

Dar remembered how much he hated Shakespeare sometimes as the nosferat slipped into the night.

CHAPTER TEN

"FORGIVE ME, FATHER, for I have sinned." Dar slid into the pew beside Father Pietro.

The priest looked askance at him. "You've never been one for confession, Dar. What brings you to haunt me at this ungodly hour of the night?"

"Is what I say bound by the seal of the confessional?" Dar focused on the priest's hands as he spoke.

"Are you going to murder someone?" Father Pietro asked with a dry laugh that turned into a phlegmatic cough.

"Would that change things?" Dar shifted his gaze to the cross as the silence beside him grew deeper.

"No."

"So you're bound?"

"You're not Christian, Dar." Dar heard a rattle in the priest's chest as he sighed between sentences. "But what you say to me is bound by the seal of *my* confessional."

Dar hung his head, looking at his palms. "I'm haunted." He glanced at Pietro's knees, then turned his head, chin still close to his chest, to look sidelong at the old man. "By evil thoughts, wicked desires, and unwanted hungers."

Pietro pulled his gaze away from the cross to Dar. "So what's new?" he said, his eyebrows raising in amusement, before falling when Dar ran his hands over his face.

"I'm serious," Dar said, his voice raspy, as if the words travelled over sandpaper.

"I see that." Pietro turned more fully towards him. "Something's changed?"

"Yes," Dar said, his knuckles white as he gripped the pew in front of them. He breathed deeply and shook his head. "No."

"Which is it?" Pietro reached a hand out but pulled it back before touching him. Dar gave thanks for small mercies, since he was strung tighter than a violin. He cracked his neck, trying to relieve the tension. All that accomplished was causing a spot of pain to bloom behind his ear.

"You don't understand. It's not a change, it's a subtle shift, a malignant growth. Barely noticeable until the knife twists in the gut and the bloody parasite takes over."

"It is a man's own mind, not his enemy or foe, that lures him to evil ways," Pietro said.

"You're quoting Buddha at me?"

"Wisdom can be found on many branches." Pietro clasped his hands together.

"And what did Buddha know of vampires?"

"What do *you* know, really? It's not like there are vampire scientists studying vampire biology. Or vampire psychologists." Dar watched Pietro look down at his own hands, which trembled slightly, before turning to him. "How do you know you're not building a beast that doesn't exist?"

"I have the evidence of my own eyes over a thousand years."

"There is that." Pietro gave him a small nod. "However, *my* eyes tell me we often see what we want to see."

"You think I want to look at Rhys and see my next meal?" Dar hissed.

A PLAGUE OF SHADOWS 69

"Or we see what we've been told to see."

"It's not just what I've been told," Dar said, his throat tight. "The voices in my blood whisper terrible things to me when I'm around him. I feel it coiling like a snake inside me, and I need to stop it. For the sake of others, if not my own." Dar looked at the cross. "'Destroy the seed of evil, or it will grow up to your ruin.' How's that for a quote?"

"So what are you going to do? Have you considered that these voices lead you falsely?"

Dar sighed and ran his hands through his hair. "We've had this conversation before." He looked up at the altar. "I want to make sure the conclave is taken care of if something happens to me."

"If something happens to you, or you do something to yourself?"

"I'll kill myself before I harm Rhys." His voice was ragged to his own ears. He ran his hands over his pants before clasping his hands together and leaning his elbows on the pew. "Will you judge me harshly if I do?" he said into his hands.

"I'd think after all this time that you'd know me better than that. I cannot give you my blessing, but I will also not burden you with my judgment. Or burden myself for that matter."

"What about your god? Am I bound for an eternity of hellfire and damnation?"

Pietro laughed, a short huff that ended with a wet cough into his elbow. "I expect if you're damned for the manner of your death, you're already doomed. But I'm not a great believer in hell."

"Despite seeing so much evidence of evil?"

Pietro nodded slowly. "I still see the light that shines even in the darkest of nights."

"But something wicked this way comes." He really did hate Shakespeare.

"Mmm, Night, so Rhys says." The priest's gaze was fixed on the stained-glass vista, always backlit by hidden lights.

"You've talked to Rhys? What else did he have to say?"

Father Pietro looked at him, with a half smile. "Bound by the seal of my confessional."

"I suppose I deserve that." Dar grasped the back of the pew in front of him. "So what do we do?"

"What we always do. Be a beacon towards a safe harbour and protect those who cannot protect themselves from what creeps in the shadows."

"Like the man who was killed in the square."

Father Pietro nodded, his shoulders sagging with a sigh. "Like Mike. If I had known what would happen, I would have been more insistent that he come inside for the night."

"You can't always protect those who refuse your help."

"No, but he was rambling, raving." The priest's lips pulled into a frown. "About night coming and a knife. I didn't think much of it at the time."

"A knife? Strange." Dar clasped his hands together, as if in prayer. "What did he say?"

"Hmm, let's see." Father Pietro closed his eyes. Dar watched his face as he thought. "'Dark blade of the Even Star, piercing the heart of the Sun.' Still makes no sense."

"No." Dar laid a hand on the priest's shoulder as he stood. "But then the world isn't making a lot of sense these days."

The priest smiled at Dar and shook his head. "I have some praying to do."

"You have a shadow," Dar said, barely turning his head to indicate the large space behind them. "Do you want me to deal with him?"

Pietro sighed. He was well acquainted with this particular shadow: he'd already smelled Father Mark's soap, carried on a waft of cold air when the young man had entered the sanctuary. He shook his head. "No, but head out the side door, will you? I don't think our new priest likes your kind."

Dar raised an eyebrow, his lips forming a reluctant smile. "And what kind might that be?"

"Punked-out foreign homosexual infidels." The priest smiled at him.

Dar spread his arms, his lips stretching into a grin. "What's not to like?" The smile waned as quickly as it had come, but it had felt good. He rested a hand on his friend's shoulder for a second, before heading out the side door.

PIETRO CHOSE TO IGNORE his overbearing shadow, at least a minute longer. He walked to the altar and knelt on sore knees, noticing as he did that the altar cloth hung askew. Crossing himself, he let a half-formed prayer for Dar's soul and Rhys' safety flicker in his mind, like a candle sputtering to life. He tried to shape it in the old language, but his words were lumpy and uneven. Still, he expected God would understand.

He heard Mark walk up the aisle, his clipped steps echoing through the vaulted space. Pietro's prayer turned to Father Mark, a wish that he would do no harm to the flock and maybe even some good. And, finally, he came to himself, asking that God give him the energy he needed to be patient and understanding, even though his energy was so lacking these days.

Mark stepped into the halo of light beside him and stopped. "What was that?" he hissed, his words like a lash.

Pietro paused in his prayer but didn't turn away from the cross or the altar to look at Mark. "What do you mean?" he asked, suppressing the tickle that crept down the back of his throat and into his lungs.

"Look at me," the young man demanded. Slowly, Pietro did as he was asked, turning his head as he wiped a fleck of spittle from his cheek. "That creature," Mark continued, pointing in the direction Dar had gone. "You let that thing in here, others as well, with their tattoos and piercings and inappropriate attire. Did you think I wouldn't see them? Or did you think I wouldn't realize they are the Wicked, and you're corrupted?"

"Give us a hand, will you?" Pietro held out his hand for the young priest to help him up, as he'd done in the past. Mark cringed, a sneer on his lips, and took a step back.

Pietro sighed and drew his hand back. Placing it on his knee, he got slowly to his feet. "There are many people who come seeking solace and sanctuary." He stepped towards the altar. "I let them all in."

"They are not people, those parasites on life." Mark followed him up the steps. "I talked to an elder of the Brothers. I know."

A heaviness settled in Pietro's gut at Mark's obvious knowledge of what Dar was and his mention of the Brothers. He knew too well the sect Mark spoke of. If they'd gotten their claws into the young priest, no wonder he was so angry. Mark's heavy

A PLAGUE OF SHADOWS

73

hand landed on his shoulder and let himself be turned around. A slight frown formed on his face but he looked at his junior priest calmly. "I've always been a believer in 'Judge not, that ye be not judged'. I know I have my own sins for which I will be judged." He pulled his shoulder out of Father Mark's hand. "However, I hope turning away someone – anyone – in need of counsel is not one of them." He laid his gnarled hands on the altar cloth, straightening it out. As he did, one of the candlesticks fell over, and he reached to set it right again.

"Don't you dare desecrate the holy with hands that have touched that devil." Father Mark pulled Pietro away from the altar, with intent this time.

Pietro's aching joints fought with his tired muscles to keep his balance; something in his left knee twinged, and he knew it would be unhappy tomorrow. He glanced at the cross. It seemed like one prayer would go unanswered, at least tonight.

"You should kill that creature rather than suffer its presence here," Father Mark continued. He stood up tall, towering over Pietro. "More than suffer it – be polluted by it," he said, spittle forming at the corners of his mouth, flecks landing on Pietro's face. "How can you break faith so flagrantly in the house of God?" he added, his face contorted into a grimace.

Father Pietro canted his head, a small, sad smile on his lips. It was unfortunate – Mark was handsome when his face wasn't twisted in hate. There had probably been a few women, or men, who'd been disappointed at Mark's choice of vocation. He sighed, which caused phlegm to bubble up in his lungs. He let the resulting cough take control of his torso; when it had passed, he turned back to the altar to set the candle upright.

"I said, don't touch those!" Mark pulled Pietro away again before he could put things right.

He looked at the young man, and a sadness pressed at his sternum and filled his throat until he felt he was choking on it. It wasn't the lad's fault that he was so angry, so judgmental. Pietro would have been that man himself if not for his teachers. He pressed his lips together, resolving to be a better teacher, live a better example. Walking around the altar, he checked the hanging of the cloth, until he came to face the young priest again. He opened his mouth to say something.

"Don't try to justify," Mark spat before Pietro had the chance to get a word out. "I don't want to hear your lies. Just think of all the unshriven souls that have passed through your confessional."

Pietro's heavy heart dragged his shoulders down. He rubbed his nose, between his eyes and sighed. If he was going to be a better teacher, he needed time to think, and to pray, on this conundrum of Father Mark. For now, he held up his hands in peace. "Let's talk about this tomorrow, shall we? When we've both had a good night's rest. At the moment, I'd like to set the altar in order then go to sleep." He stepped once again towards said altar.

In response, Father Mark shoved him, hard. "I said don't."

At that moment, Pietro realized he was too close to the edge of the stair. His foot shifted back to stop his fall but instead met empty air. His other ankle twisted as he windmilled his arms by instinct but some part of his brain knew, as he watched Mark's face turn from anger and hatred to shock and fear, that this was his last moment on earth. A smile pulled at the corners of his mouth as a wordless prayer for Mark's soul bloomed red in his heart.

A PLAGUE OF SHADOWS 75

Then pain exploded in a blossom of white, and everything faded away.

CHAPTER ELEVEN

MINA SAT IN THE CORNER on the floor, scritching the cat under its chin, as she waited to be hauled off by Bee into some new dungeon for more training. The cat craned its neck, allowing her better access. Mike's cat. Mike who was dead, and the cat seemed to know. It clung to her and hissed whenever anyone else came too close, like Brett in the kitchen.

The other vampires were in a heated, hushed discussion, minus Dar, who was still AWOL. The group stood in the middle of the Sanctuary, contained in a circle of muted light cast from the stained-glass sky above, arms crossed and jaws set. They'd stopped briefly when she'd come upstairs to watch her walk towards them, but returned to their debate after she slid to sit in the corner. She'd been letting their words wash over her like gentle waves on a warm ocean as the cat kneaded her stomach and purred.

Fewer attacks...another person dead...drained, not eaten...desiccated flesh. The cat shifted in her lap, and Mina looked down to see it staring intently at the vampires. Just then the door slammed open, blown by a wicked wind, and Dar entered, striding towards the assembly with a grim expression on his face. The door banged again as he reached the circle. They all swivelled around, bodies shifting lower, hands going to concealed weapons. There was a collective exhalation as Rhys entered, looking haggard, worn, old. As she watched a cascade of emotions

A PLAGUE OF SHADOWS

play out on Dar's face, Mina realized that he looked the same, in his own way.

She stood up, carefully cradling the cat in one arm. It clambered up to nuzzle at her neck.

"We have a problem," Rhys said. He glanced at Dar then scanned the assembly. "I've been delving deeper into the lore of the gargoyles. Perhaps deeper than I should have." His voice dropped low. Mina found herself leaning forward, as if to hear his words even though she could hear him well enough. "The gargoyles were the advanced army, the shock troops, of something much worse. They're the vanguard of Night."

Night again. Mina's breath caught even though she had no idea what he was talking about. "Ow." The cat's claws had dug into her back. The assembly turned to her, almost in unison. She shrugged, then repositioned the cat's paws.

"Night?" Jack said. "Really? That's just a legend, a bogeyman to scare those who walk in the dark. And there've been no trumpets announcing her coming. No fanfare from the wicked netherworld creatures."

"And what are gargoyles then, if not netherworld creatures?" Dar asked.

"Now then, no fighting on my account," Rhys said. "I can take barbed words and give them back, as you well know, Darius." Rhys coughed into the sleeve of his wool coat, then shifted his weight to lean on his umbrella as he pulled a handkerchief from his pocket.

"Though Jack has a point." Dar glanced at him before returning to Rhys. "The legends do speak of an angel of darkness announcing her coming."

"Yes, there is that." Rhys arched an eyebrow. "But who's to say that the harbinger of Night won't use whispers rather than trumpets. Has there been anyone new around? Any rumours of something new haunting our world?"

"The new vampire," Mina said, without thinking.

The group looked at her again. She gathered the cat more closely to her chest as her gaze shifted over the questioning faces of the others.

Rhys peered at her, his head cocked. Dar stood behind him, frowning.

"The new vampire," she said, looking around.

"New vampire?" Dar asked, his eyes peering at her through his thick lashes.

"Yes?" Mina said, her voice rising, turning it into a question.

"Where did you hear that?"

"Brett mentioned it."

Rhys gave her a small smile before turning back to Dar. "No, not a new vampire, even if the rumour is true. And not our Mina." Rhys paused. "Something more, well, nefarious or nebulous. Or more seductive." His hands clutched at the air as he spoke, as if trying to pull the image out of nothing, but he gave up. "I don't know. I just think you would know this thing if you came upon it."

"What is it?" Mina said, taking a step towards the others, closer to the ring of light.

"A creature that lurks in the shadows, listening, watching, waiting."

Mina arched an eyebrow as she stepped into the circle. "That doesn't really give us a lot—" The cat interrupted her with a hiss, the fur on its hackles rising.

A PLAGUE OF SHADOWS

"No." Rhys cleared a frog from his throat. "I don't have a lot of details." He looked at her with a furrowed brow. "If the gargoyles are the portents of Night, this thing is its herald."

A low rumble arose from Mina's chest. She glanced down at the cat she had clutched there.

"I don't think it likes you, Rhys," Jack said, his gaze dropping from the man to the cat. Its growl turned to a purr as Mina stroked it, but its tense muscles didn't relax.

Rhys stared hard at the cat. "Where did you find that thing?" he asked, his voice even but his eyebrows pulled together.

"I know she's scruffy." Mina scratched behind the cat's ear. "She just needs some good food and a little TLC."

Rhys stepped forward. The cat hissed, and he stopped.

"Don't take offence," Mina said. "She doesn't seem to like anyone."

"Except you," he said. "Besides, I'm not offended. I'm curious." He took another cautious step towards them. The cat pressed into Mina's chest but didn't hiss again.

"She belonged to Mike," Mina said. Looking at Jack, she continued. "The man we found dead."

"The old bum?"

"The old man," she said, her voice sharp. "Bled dry, desiccated."

"Desiccated," Rhys said, his forehead lifting.

Mina nodded, and the cat tried to press even deeper into her, its chin nuzzling her neck. She stroked it, then paused.

"The last few months—" she started. She looked around at the assembled vampires. "Whenever Mike saw me...." She glanced from Jack to Rhys. "Whenever he saw me, he talked about night." The others eyed her. She looked down at the cat.

"I thought he'd just finally lost it, though he'd never seemed so, I don't know, 'off' before."

Rhys took another step towards her. The cat eyed him but stayed quiet.

"What do you know?" he asked.

Mina shrugged. "Nothing."

"Oh." Rhys glanced at her then nodded to the cat. "I was talking to the cat."

"Huh, if only cats could talk."

He stepped closer, coming to her shoulder, peering at the cat's face, causing it to squirm in her arms. "Hmmm, I think this one can." The cat hissed and pressed away from him. "It just chooses not to for some reason."

"Talking animals?" Mina arched an eyebrow. "Another thing about this world that I don't know?"

He looked up at her as he reached out to stroke the cat's head. It tensed but let him. "Well, yes, but this thing you do know. We talked about it."

"I think I'd remember talking cats."

"You see these marks on her head?" He scratched the cat's chin, causing it to purr and lift its head. "Werekind."

The cat's golden eyes went wide and it dug its claws into Mina's skin, trying to climb onto her shoulder. "Ow! Stop that." She grabbed hold of it and looked it in the eyes. "No claws, remember?" She wrapped her arms around the cat, feeling it shiver with tension.

"And if I recognize these correctly, she's not just any werecat."

Mina looked at the markings on the cat's face. Dar came beside Rhys and place his hand on the old man's shoulder as he examined the cat.

"You're not serious?" Dar said.

"Dead serious."

"Would someone care to enlighten the rest of us?" Jack said.

"Aarashi 'Seema' Sen," Rhys said.

"The last of the Bengali?" Bee said, approaching. "This scrawny thing?"

The cat ignored all of them, choosing to lick its paw and use it to clean its head.

Rhys glanced at Bee, forehead lifting. "You know a bit about the history of other creatures, I see. Good."

"But they're all dead," Jack said. "In the Great Purge."

"The actual wording in the history texts is 'lost', she was lost in the last purge by the Brothers of Light." Rhys shifted from them to the cat. "You were lost, not dead. And now you've been found."

At that, the cat hissed again, then scrambled over Mina's shoulder, thankfully keeping her claws to herself this time. It...she took off down the stairs into the bowels of the Sanctuary, too fast for even the vampires to react and catch it.

Mina looked from the disappearing cat to Rhys. "If she's a werecat, why hasn't she turned, you know, human? Why doesn't she talk to us?"

Rhys shrugged. "I don't know, but if what you say is true, she may be the key to unlocking the riddle of Night."

"YOU TALK ABOUT NIGHT as if it were a person," Mina said to Rhys, as she crouched to look under the chest of drawers that stood just outside the kitchen, even though she knew the cat wasn't there. But the search distracted her from her own thoughts: killing Luca for nothing, causing Astrid's death, being a bad friend to Cam. She wondered again why Cam wasn't talking to her. *I have to start stalking her soon*, Mina thought. *And then I still need to 'die'.* Jack hadn't followed up on their conversation, but she was sure he hadn't forgotten it. She sighed as she stood up; the bramble of worries always caught up with her.

"Not a person, exactly," Rhys said, oblivious to her internal monologue. His voice was muffled by the closet he had his head stuck into, though the cat wasn't there either. "An entity."

"A nightmare," Jack added from where he stood, arms crossed, leaning against the frame of the kitchen doorway.

"A very evil entity, though I'm sure she doesn't see herself that way." Rhys shrugged, pulling his head out of the closet. "All heroes in our own stories, and all that."

"I don't care how she sees herself," Jack said. "If Night is coming, we need to prepare for war."

"Armageddon more like," Rhys added, his light tone at odds with the words. "But understanding Night may be the key to defeating her."

"Or the key to your unmaking, thinking you can understand a creature like Night. Looking into the abyss, and all that." Jack stepped past them, heading down the hall. "The cat's not here."

"I'm sure there are those who say the same about you." Rhys peeked his head into a half-open door. "How can you understand a bloodsucker?"

"You all seem to know what this Night is. Care to enlighten me?" Mina asked as she followed Jack, stopping to look into a nook under the stairs. "Here kitty kitty," she added, even though she didn't sense the cat.

A PLAGUE OF SHADOWS 83

"She was one of the first angels," Rhys said. "The greatest, some fragments of old texts of ancient poems say. The most powerful. The most beloved."

"Doesn't seem very angelic, from your reactions to her."

"Well, she was also one of the first to fall. Being beloved, being granted the keys to heaven, that wasn't enough for her, so the stories say. She didn't want to use someone else's power for someone else's purposes. She wanted her own power so she could do with it what she willed. She went so far that even some of the other Fallen turned against her." Rhys pursed his lips to make smooching sounds as he popped his head behind a tapestry. "She took it upon herself to become the Admiral of the Ninth Circle."

"Ninth Circle?" Mina's head swam as these enigmatic pronouncements were piled onto her own worries.

"Of Hell," Jack said as he led them further down the hall, towards the stairs. "I tell you, the cat's long gone."

"What?"

"Maybe it has secrets it doesn't want exposed. We have no idea why the purge took place."

"No, I mean Night, the Ninth Circle of Hell," Mina said, not bothering to keep the irritation from her voice. "Always more riddles. I've had enough to last a lifetime."

"You're talking to the wrong person if that's the case." Jack leaned against the railing and crossed his arms again. "Rhys loves them." His eyes twinkled, and a smile threatened to appear at the corners of his lips.

Rhys gave him a frown before turning back to Mina. "The ancient histories are written in riddles, fragments of riddles from dead languages." He sneezed into the elbow of his tweed jacket, paused to see if another sneeze was coming, then continued.

"The oral poetry of pre-history, eventually written down after years of an epic game of...how do you say it...broken telephone. All speaking of a world no one wants to believe exists. Deciphering them is, at best, a near thing." He opened his mouth as if to sneeze again, but the moment passed, and he turned to Jack. "This 'cat' may have crucial information in her feline brain, if she was a familiar of the dead man's." He tipped his head to the side, his eyebrows waggling as some thought passed through his brain. "I wonder if she knows how he died? It might help us understand what we're dealing with. What leaves a trail of desiccated bodies but no other trace?" He shook his head.

"I don't think she knows since she was with me," Mina said. "It wasn't gargoyles?" she added, though she already knew the answer.

"Oh, no, they rend their kills limb from limb, not leave them dry as a mummy." He waved a hand, and his serious face changed in an instant, brightened by a smile that brought out the crow's feet around his gleaming eyes. "Just think, if she really is one of the Bengali Were...the things she must know." He lay a hand on Mina's arm, his enthusiasm almost infectious. A smile crept onto Mina's lips in response.

"Whatever she knows, I know she's not here," Jack said, starting up the stairs, before stopping to glance back at Mina. "And we have a rumoured new vampire to hunt."

Mina sighed – another worry to add to the list – and turned to follow when Rhys' hand came to her arm again.

"He may seem like a hard one, but he cares. They all do." Rhys' expression was soft but his eyes held hers. "They just aren't sure what to make of you yet." Letting his hand drop, he walked past her towards the stairs. "If you're off hunting vampires, it means it's time for all good folk to be in bed," he said more loudly, before heading up the stairs, leaving Mina alone in the dark hallway.

After a moment of indecision, Mina followed Jack and Rhys upstairs.

CHAPTER TWELVE

ANGELOS SHIVERED. IT was snowing again, and somehow he felt the slushy cold more keenly in his current ghostly form than when fully fleshed. But his discomfort didn't matter. He had a mission to complete: find the key to the ritual that would unlock the cage of Night. The keeper of his soul and the font of his power, she would not be pleased with the delay. And she was a harsh mistress.

And to fulfill his mission, he needed a body. He breathed in, little more than a whisper in the lee of the building, then exhaled slowly, deeply, mote by mote, as his frustration turned the breath into a growl. He'd returned to haunt the square where he'd sucked what life was left out of the old bum the other night. He needed a body. But not just any body: he needed one that was strong and hale, with a soul that was weak. However, people were cautious, wary of the shadows, skittering away. As if there'd been strange deaths in the darkness. The thought brought a lopsided smirk to his non-existent lips, which turned to a scowl. Either that or they were like the old man, sallow flesh and thin blood, already too dried out and decrepit to bother with.

And he wasn't the only creature seeking prey. Somewhere out there, on the edge of his perception, he could sense the gargoyles, hungry, hunkered down in dark places and yearning to be free of their bonds. He'd also felt the vampire leave the church earlier,

A PLAGUE OF SHADOWS   87

which had caused him to raise a ghostly eyebrow at how such a being was allowed on holy ground.

Now, in the deep dark hours after midnight, the square was empty, devoid of even the homeless who would normally find a home in its nooks and crannies.

Wrapped in his blanket of useless pondering, he almost missed the sound in the alley behind him: a door opening and closing, and the slap of soft soles on wet asphalt.

Angelos turned around. A priest. But not just any priest. A bloody priest. The metallic tang wafted through the air – he could smell the blood on the man's hands even from a distance. He pulled his coalescence of shadows together and heaved towards the man. A young, healthy, attractive priest. *Strong of body, weak of soul.* Angelos smiled. *As if an angel answered my prayer. Or a demon.* He crept down the alley along the far wall, away from the lights.

Ahead of him, the priest stopped at the crossroads where the alley opened onto a small road. The man looked down the road, his breath coming quickly and his heart beating rapidly.

Angelos swooped up behind him, pulling his tendrils into as solid a form as he could muster.

"Forgive me, Father, for I am about to sin." His voice was still rusty, but it was enough.

The priest whirled around, his eyes wide, as he grasped at the crucifix around his neck with a crimson hand and waved it at the shadows. "Please, I didn't mean to hurt him."

Angelos had no idea what the man saw as he glanced around the darkness. But Angelos knew what he saw: a murderer.

Perfect. He oozed closer.

"He was wicked." The priest reached out the hand not wrapped around the cross, trying to fend him off. But the fingers just sunk into a miasma of dark energy. The priest gave a startled, strangled cry and pulled the hand back to his chest. Blisters had formed on the fingers.

Angelos realized he needed to act quickly before the priest ruined his perfect form trying to fight him. He took a deep breath in, savouring the man's fear for just a second. Then, he sent needles of power into the priest, locking the two of them together in a rigour of pain and ecstasy. When the man tried to cry out, Angelos sighed into him, filling the man's lungs and choking off the scream. He settled himself into the priest's flesh and looked upon the beautiful night with real eyes for the first time in ages.

At last.

CHAPTER THIRTEEN

MINA'S FROZEN FINGERS clutched at the wire of the chain-link fence as she watched the scene in front of her, ignoring the droplets of rain that pooled in her eyebrows until they overflowed and dripped down her face. Her lashes were heavy with drops but she didn't want to blink for fear of missing some pivotal turning point.

Her stomach fluttered. She wasn't supposed to be here. She was supposed to be a few blocks over, closer to downtown, searching her section of a grid set up to find this rumoured new vampire. She was shirking her duty to her new so-called family to stalk her old one. She had followed Jack's lead in abandoning Rhys, who seemed quite happy to continue the search after an elusive werecat on his own. Whereas she was expected, as a member of the conclave, to do her part in protecting the world from evil; in this case, trying to lead a rumoured newly turned vampire to the light side of the dark. Spread thin already, each of them had been assigned a vast area to search. Alone, which allowed her to make a wrong turn, and, when she realized her error, to take a detour that led to this street that wasn't part of her large square of the grid. A shortcut, she told herself. It was an accident almost that found her on this path that ran by the school.

It had nothing to do with the text from Aunt June earlier in the day: *Maggie has a rugby game tonight. Swing by. Dale worries.*

90 C. RENÉ ASTLE

But now she stood at the edge of a muddy field in the thick rain that threatened to become sleet. Bright lights cast a wide halo around the bleachers and field but didn't quite reach where she lurked outside the sphere of humanity, a step away from the siren call of the blood that flowed under their skin. The creature inside had revelled at the potential orgy of feeding, making Mina nauseous.

It's been too long since I've fed. Mina pushed that thought away, not wanting it to infect her enjoyment of watching the kids play. Still, her vision swam with stars as she craned her neck, trying to catch sight of her niece through the rain and the mud and the other players. A skater punk with sallow skin and bloodshot eyes passed behind her, splashing through a puddle and sending icy water up her legs to soak through her jeans. Mina's eyes narrowed as she turned to glare at him. The wheels of his board clattered over the uneven surface, but he kept his footing. Her pulse quickened, and her teeth ached.

Just a nip, she thought as she tracked him down the dark path until he disappeared into the copse of trees that butted up against the school grounds. *A taste, a little lesson about not going into the woods alone at night.*

Mina breathed in sharply, checking herself and the monster inside. Her cheeks flushed, she forced her eyes back to the game. *Definitely too long.* Mina promised herself she'd take Brett up on his offer. *After the game.* She cursed silently and corrected herself, as another raindrop dripped off the tip of her nose: *After tonight's search is over.*

Mina knew she needed to leave, but she turned her attention back to the field for one last glimpse of Maggie. So much mud splattered the players that it was hard to tell which one was her

A PLAGUE OF SHADOWS   91

niece. Briefly, just after a pause in play, she'd been able to track Maggie by her heartbeat. Mina had never realized how unique each human pulse was until becoming a vampire. But now her niece's signature rhythm was drowned in the sea of percussion. Instead, Mina bopped up and down on her toes, weaving slightly from side to side as she tried to catch a glimpse of number 11 under the muck, through the scrum of players.

There was a break in play that Mina didn't understand, but she glanced over to where Dale and Hana sat swathed in plastic rain ponchos with little Liam beside them. Even June and her new man were there, despite the rain. Liam was clearly bored, playing with some figures arrayed on the bench beside him, plus one in each hand. These two appeared to be having an argument of some kind, as her nephew moved one while making a face and saying something, then repeated the actions with the other. The argument escalated into a fight, as one arced through the air clutched in Liam's hand, headed towards the ground. In turning, her nephew's face shifted towards her and she caught a closer view of the figures – dinosaurs. Mina's eyes welled up, and she smiled sadly. She'd given those to him then spent hours playing with him.

Liam's gaze moved past her, then came back. His hand stopped its arc mid-air. His head tilted, and his eyebrows came together as Mina's heart stuttered.

"Which hors d'oeuvre do you have your eye on?"

Mina held her breath, recognizing the cadence and tone of the voice that had snuck up on her out of the night. She needed to stop letting herself get so wrapped up in her head that she couldn't sense the dangers around her. She glanced sideways, not wanting to look away from Dale and Liam, but not wanting the vampire beside her to see where she was looking.

Not just any vampire. She was too familiar with the blood song that trilled in her veins: discordant violins. "Emily." From what Jack had told her, the woman hated the name, choosing Em instead. "What are you doing here?"

"Not the same as you, I suspect." Em didn't look at her. Instead, she kept her gaze fixed on the field. "Looking for a bite to eat." She sighed, long and slow. "Too bad about the mud. I don't like grit in my food."

Mina glanced back at the bleachers. Liam turned to his father and tugged on his sleeve, dinosaur still in hand, and pointed towards where she was hiding.

"I was just walking by." Mina nodded in the direction the skater boy had gone, without really taking her eyes off the field. "Thought I'd take a shortcut."

Em glanced down the path before turning towards the field again. "You've been standing here an awfully long time for someone just walking by."

Mina's stomach clenched. Out the corner of her eye, she saw Liam say something to Dale, who shook his head, his lips moving in response. A part of Mina wished she was closer so she could hear what Dale said, but the other part wished she'd never come this way. She took a step back, further into the shadows. "I'm a fan of the game, what can I say," she said, her words crisp. She glared at Em. "Though you do seem like the type who'd prey on children," she continued. As she hoped, Em turned away from the field, away from the bleachers and stepped towards her. Mina glanced at her family over Em's shoulder.

A PLAGUE OF SHADOWS 93

"You should watch what you say. There's dark times ahead. And night makes us bolder."

Liam pointed again, with more conviction. Dale looked right at her. For a moment she thought he'd seen her, and her heart stopped beating. Then he shook his head and said something to Liam before turning back to the game. Liam frowned and turned to where she had stood a moment ago, staring hard.

Mina looked at Em. "If you want to fight, let's fight. Somewhere away from these mundane witnesses."

Em sneered, not quite baring her fangs, and leaned in closer. "I'm going to play with my food. I'll come back for dessert later." An image of Liam drained of blood, Maggie crying beside him, flickered through Mina's mind before she quashed it. She watched Em until she disappeared into the woods, then returned her attention to the field, as she despaired at the thought of becoming like Em. But the others said all vampires eventually succumb to the monster. The game was breaking up, and Liam was collecting his dinosaurs, no longer looking her way, perhaps deciding she'd been a figment of his imagination.

Mina stayed where she was until the crowd dispersed. With still no sign of Em, she pulled out her phone to call Jack.

"Have you found him, or her?" Jack asked, without so much as a hello.

"What? Oh, the new vampire." Mina shook her head. "No, I'm still looking. But...." She stepped back to let a family with two muddy girls pass. "We need to talk." Mina took a deep breath, realizing her next words meant saying goodbye forever, even as it meant keeping her family safe. "I need to die."

CHAPTER FOURTEEN

ANGELOS BREATHED DEEPLY, filling the lungs of this body with damp air. Tipping his head back, he revelled in the icy rain on his face. He drew back the wide shoulders, making himself even bigger, forcing the ebb and flow of humanity on the city street to go around him. This body he'd claimed wasn't the one he would have chosen if he'd had more time – too blond and too ruddy – but he could have done a lot worse. He could have been stuck in the shell of that old bum, for one.

He flexed the fingers and cracked the neck, getting a feel for the form. He eyed up a group of women who passed him, thinking of the other benefits of no longer being a shadow. They gave him a strange look, focusing below his chin, and he remembered the clerical collar. Not that that had ever stopped anyone. But he let them pass and turned into a small laneway off the main road. He had more important things to do. He needed to see a man about a blade.

The whispers that had roused him from centuries of slumber had carried a name and a place. He'd found the city; now he just had to find the man. He followed the narrow lane to a T, then turned into a smaller, darker passage, so overhung with buildings that even the rain didn't reach. Somehow frigid puddles still lurked in the darkness. He cursed silently as he stepped in one, his sight unaccustomed to these human eyes. He slowed as he neared the end of the small street, peering at the grimy window

A PLAGUE OF SHADOWS 95

filled with junk and the sign with three orbs, lit by a lamp that flickered overhead.

The sense of smell was muted in this human form – one of its disadvantages – but this was definitely the place, with the lingering aroma of sulphur under the reek of garlic. Angelos cocked an eyebrow. *As if an allium could repel me.*

Looking at the dirty glass, Angelos realized that it wasn't completely dark inside. Somewhere in the back a light shone, casting undulating shadows on the few patches of floor visible under the jumble.

Angelos turned the doorknob and pushed lightly. The door didn't give.

"Locked." Angelos formed this body's lips into a tight smile, then spoke words in a long dead language, sibilant in its sounds. With a soft clink, the lock gave way and Angelos entered the shop. An insistent beeping arose, and he scowled as he tried to determine where it was coming from. A shadow grew shorter as a form appeared from the back, an ebony cane in one hand. *Not a man then.*

Angelos took in the diminutive woman. She was at most 5 feet tall, even though she stood ramrod straight, barely using the cane carved with ornate symbols. Her hair was obviously grey under the wash of a shade of red not found in nature. She peered at him, her eyes sharp behind big spectacles.

"How did you get in?" She frowned at him, then looked over his shoulder. "We're closed."

Angelos pulled his new body up to its full height and stepped forward. "I've come to find a blade." Looking down at her, he added, "I'm told you have something special."

"I have nothing." She shifted back behind the counter, her lips still pulled severely downward. "Come back tomorrow."

"The whispers in the dark say you do." He sidled so he was between her and the door.

"Go away, or I'll get my son to kick you out." She feigned a nod to the back room as her free hand reached under the counter. "Day is the time for respectable business."

Angelos paused to look at his hands, turning them over in the dim light, before speaking. "You and I both know you're alone here. Except for me." He looked back into her narrowed eyes, letting his own gaze bore into her. "And I think we both know you don't run a respectable business." He gave her a smile and raised an eyebrow. "Why I'm here is best discussed at night."

She lifted an eyebrow of her own and slid her hand, empty, back out from under the counter. "Night time business, is it then?" Her eyes sparkled with understanding. "A night time blade."

"I hear you have it."

"What will you give me for it? I'm a businesswoman after all."

Angelos stepped forward, a sneer forming on his lips. The woman tapped her cane on his calf, and he found himself on his knees, throbbing pain in his leg, despite the light touch.

"This little cane packs quite a punch, young man," she continued. "And I know how to use it on louts like you, who try to force little old ladies to do something stupid."

Angelos forced himself to take a step back, realizing he was still weak in this body. "Wealth beyond the dreams of avarice?"

The woman opened her arms slightly and glanced down at herself before returning her gaze to him. "And what would I do with that when I'll soon be dead?"

A PLAGUE OF SHADOWS 97

"For your son."

The woman snorted. "Money I have. Life not so much. If you're looking for the item I think you are, come back tomorrow night." The woman turned and headed towards the back of the shop again. "And bring life with you."

Angelos sighed, reaching the end of his patience. He slipped up behind her, grabbing the cane first so she couldn't use it to defend herself, then looping the other arm around her neck. "I don't think you realize who you're talking to." It wasn't quite his voice, but it was getting closer, drawing on the wells of power given to him by Night. Yanking the cane from the woman's hand, he spun her around and pressed her up against the wall. His voice went deeper. "Give me the blade."

The woman shook her head as she clawed at the hand around her throat. Angelos relaxed the grip a little, giving her air to respond. Instead, she started to ramble off the words to some incantation. He squeezed again, even tighter this time, until her eyes went bug-like behind her glasses in her struggle to breathe.

"Answer my question and only my question." He loosened his grip slightly. "Where is the blade of the Even Star?"

"Citlal...." The woman coughed as his fingers constricted then released. She shook her head. "Not a spell. Even Star...citlalpol is at the museum." Her own fingers, claw-like, grasped at the air in the general direction of the counter. He let go of her entirely but stayed wary. At the counter, she pulled over a piece of shiny paper. Opening it, she stabbed a gnarled finger at the paper. "I knew it for what it was as soon as I saw it."

"Museum?" The word meant little to him, but he looked at the paper, trying to pick out what she'd been pointing at, when he heard a click. Looking up, he saw that her eyes shone, but not as much as the silvery thing she pointed at him.

Gun. He pulled the word from somewhere, though it was not a weapon he knew.

"But it will never be yours." Her finger tightened at the same time his hand clutched the cane more tightly. The crack was deafening as he slid sideways.

When it was over, Angelos picked up the paper from the museum, wiping off the smears of blood and brain matter on the woman's sweater. Absentmindedly, he did the same with the end of the cane as he scanned the paper.

He saw no blade of the Even Star, but maybe this museum held more secrets.

CHAPTER FIFTEEN

IVAN FELT A BIT NAUSEOUS as the bass beat of the club music pulsed through his bones. The swirl of humanity caused his skin to itch. He didn't like being amongst so many people when he couldn't fight them or feed off them. And they'd been expressly forbidden to do either tonight, all except the dhamphir. It had been a difficult choice for Matteo: take his pet project out on the town or force the gargoyles to bend to his will since they were more tolerant than obedient. In the end, the woman had won out. Not the choice Ivan would have made, given the currents of unease that rippled through the netherworld at the moment. A guard that wanted nothing more than to rend apart flesh, vampire or human, could be useful.

Ivan glanced towards where the woman stood. Camellia, Matteo had called her. He thought her more a girl even though she was older than his wife had been when she died. When the lights strobed over her face, he could see the flush on her olive skin. Through the mahogany curls that half covered her face, her hungry eyes devoured the man in front of her, his white teeth flashing against his dark skin in response to her attention. Matteo hovered like a ghost nearby, his face hidden by his fedora. Across the club, Em and Adam were supposed to be keeping an eye out for Athanatos or for dining prospects for the dhamphir. Even at a distance, Ivan could tell they weren't paying attention to anyone except the unfortunate fellow they'd marked for their own dinner.

Ivan's focus shifted back to Matteo, wondering if he was sparing any thought for other members of his conclave, besides his new pet. An unfamiliar feeling pulsed through Ivan's abdomen when he saw that the nosferat's deadly gaze had indeed homed in on Em and Adam. Ivan knew they'd pay a price later. But for now, Matteo's eyes returned to his dhamphir.

The woman glanced at Matteo, her eyes wide, then slid her focus back to the man she clearly and desperately wanted to suck the marrow from. Her need was clear to Ivan from where he stood, but Matteo was doing nothing to help her. The stranger's eyes narrowed as he glanced from Matteo to her, perhaps sensing some unnatural relationship there. Shifting on his feet, he mumbled something Ivan couldn't hear over the noise of the club and stumbled away. Ivan sighed and took a step towards her as an angry snarl threatened to reveal her fangs to anyone nearby. She was like a fumbling teenager, all the desire but none of the knowledge of what to do next.

"Let him go," Ivan said, laying a placating hand on her arm. She turned on him, releasing her snarl, and he saw the hunger in her eyes, and underneath it something else. A look he recognized though he'd never seen it. A human trapped in the mind of a beast, with no way out. He blinked at the unwelcome thought that passed through his mind: *can I excise the beast before it devours her?*

"Let her be." Matteo's iron fingers gripped his wrist and pulled his hand away.

"Let me show her." Ivan breathed in deeply, releasing his clenched jaw. "Let me show her, or we'll be here all night."

A PLAGUE OF SHADOWS 101

"Then we'll be here all night. She needs to learn to hunt if she's to be a hunter worthy of my pride." Matteo flicked his chin towards Em and Adam. "If you want to be useful, go babysit your cohorts."

Ivan paused, his stomach still upset. But he ignored it, unclenched his fists and turned towards the other two dracul. "Even a wolf teaches its cub how to hunt," he mumbled, his voice too low to be heard in the crowded club, he hoped. He'd never made a vampire, never would, but he knew that this was not how to introduce one into the world. Even his foul sire had taught him the ways vampiric.

As his gaze travelled through the press of people, his queasiness grew. He glanced around, feeling there were eyes watching him, but saw nothing other than half-doped humans. Stepping up to Em and Adam, he nestled himself between them and their prey. "Anything to report?"

Em glanced towards Matteo and the dhamphir, thunder in her eyes. "Are you being a good little lapdog?" she asked, turning back to him, frowning as the young man they'd been toying with took one look at Ivan then trundled off. "You scared away my dinner."

"Your entertainment more like."

"They're not mutually exclusive, you know." Her eyebrow arched, and Adam suppressed a smile. "What bug has crawled up your ass?"

"I could ask you the same thing."

Em leaned into him but looked at Matteo as she spoke. "Do you think you'll gain anything by doing as he asks?" She crossed her arms over her chest. "What has any of us gotten?"

Ivan frowned at her open rebellion. It wasn't like Em; she always hedged her bets. "Protection," he said, shifting so he could better scan the dance floor. Something feral nibbled at his senses, but he couldn't place it. Something almost familiar.

"Ha!" Em's laugh was harsh. "Like Luca? Killed by his own progeny? Matteo couldn't even protect his own son."

"Luca was playing with powers he couldn't control." Ivan turned his attention back to Em.

"Because Matteo didn't bother teaching him how to deal with powers beyond what was needed to beat other vampires."

Adam finally spoke up, his face turned to a scowl. "He has more powers than he speaks of and won't share any of it."

"Some of us don't want that power," he said, his voice flat, not really paying attention to the words he said. The sense of something wild whirled in Ivan's gut. It was like something from fireside stories told on a cold winter's night from long ago, but he still couldn't place it. He grabbed Em's arm, as he'd done a hundred times before in battle. "We should go."

"Don't tell me what I should do," she spat, pulling her arm from his grasp.

"Don't you feel it?" The words were clipped by his tight jaw.

"Feel what?" Em said, then her eyes narrowed as her head cocked to the side. "There's something here besides us."

"Something...." Ivan paused, not sure how to label the thing he felt.

"Different," Adam said, glancing around.

"Powerful," Em said, her voice lifting in a question, as if more curious than scared, as her eyes scanned the club. "Wicked," she added, her tone husky. Then she returned her attention to Ivan, a savage smile on her lips. "You're right, we should go."

THE BASS POUNDED IN Mina's ears, while the thrum of a hundred heartbeats pulsed through her veins. A woman jostled her, and Mina turned to glare. Something fluttered under her sternum at the sight of the woman, with her neck exposed by her low-cut top and high-piled hair. Mina clenched her teeth tight together and forced herself to look away. *I know I'm hungry...thirsty...whatever. I don't need a reminder*, she grumbled at the beast inside. Scanning the faces in the club as if they were a series of warped, strobe-lit mugshots, she saw no sign of Jack. With her own pulse drowned out by the enveloping music, she couldn't sense his blood song in the crowd. But there was something nearby that set her fangs on edge. She tapped her thigh off-beat to the music.

Maybe it's just hunger. Or maybe I'm worried about Cam. Her roommate – ex-roommate – still wasn't answering her texts. Coincidentally, Jack had asked her to meet him here, at the club she and Cam had frequented the most when they needed some relaxation and stress relief.

The club where I met Luca. The one who made me this monster...without asking if I wanted it. Maybe her agitation was just an echo of memory from her past life.

She quashed that useless thought and scanned the faces again, from one side to the other, then swung her head back so quickly sparks flew across her vision. She squinted into a miasma of fake fog and flashing lights. For a moment, the crowd had parted, and she swore she glimpsed a face she knew.

"Cam," Mina said.

"Hey, that can be *my* name, don't wear it out," a voice slurred in her ear. A droopy face with half-closed eyes stepped in front of her, those eyes trying to focus enough to mentally undress her. "Second thought, you can wear me out any time you want." The man took an unsteady step closer, invading her space.

Mina's eyes narrowed. "I'm not that hungry," she said. With a shift of her body, a step of her foot and a twist of her wrist, Mina repulsed his advances, sending him reeling into his equally drunk cohorts.

"Fucking Asian anime babes." He stepped closer, trying to cop a feel. "All sexy lines and no action."

Mina grabbed the hand that tried to grab her, bending the index finger back further than biology wanted. "If you try to lay a finger on me again without asking, I'll break it." She gave him a vicious smile, not caring if her fangs were showing then turned back to where she'd seen Cam.

But the moment had passed, the crowd had closed in again. Mina growled, feeling an urge to send her knuckles into the man's throat. Instead, she took a deep breath, suppressing the thought, and assessed the club and her options: find Jack or look for Cam.

She sighed. *It probably wasn't Cam anyway.* But if it was, maybe Mina could force her to talk to her, face to face.

Mina stepped onto the dance floor and was soon swallowed up by the pulsation of inebriated, intoxicating humanity. Standing on tiptoes, bracing herself against the sweaty bodies, she scanned the crowd looking for her roommate – former roommate, she reminded herself again.

A PLAGUE OF SHADOWS 105

A glimpse of cascading curls and long eyelashes. A sliver of red lips and russet skin. But with so many people, Mina didn't know if she was seeing Cam or a figment of her imagination.

"Hey." A hand landed on her shoulder.

"I said I'd break it." She drove her elbow into the form behind her before stepping away and twisting around. "I'm not...."

Her response was cut off when she found herself face to face with Jack, wrapped in an embrace that trapped her arms at her side.

"You're not what?" he said, his lips a breath away from hers. "Not paying attention and letting a vampire sneak up on you? Or not being very discreet by picking a fight in a crowded club?"

"Sorry," she said, arching an eyebrow. "I thought you were one of the drunk yobos who've tried to feel me up while I was waiting for you."

He kept his embrace tight for a long second, his dark eyes looking at her through the shaggy hair that fell over his face.

She reached up, breaking the embrace, and swept the hair behind his ear. "You need a haircut."

He let go and stepped away. "So you've accepted that it's best to die?"

"I don't know about best," she said, her eyes roaming the club, on the off chance of spotting Cam, but she was becoming convinced that she hadn't actually seen her roommate. "But necessary. Can you help me?"

Beside her, the air moved as Jack nodded.

"The whole conclave can, and the sooner the better. But right now, there's more pressing business to attend to."

Mina thought her death was pretty important and was about to say so when she felt something new. A sensation that wasn't quite a sound. As if strands of darkness were vibrating in her veins. It flickered in and out, making her head spin.

"Do you feel that?" Jack said. Now he was the one scanning the crowd.

"Feel what exactly?" One glance at him, and she could tell that he didn't feel what she did. His expression was curious, not concerned. Mina's sense swept the club. She sensed the bass and the treble, the heartbeat of the dancers, and the tendrils of black, like India ink in water.

"The hum of a vampire nearby," Jack said, interrupting her thoughts. "But off-kilter, untamed."

Mina shook her head to clear the inky wisps. With Jack so close, she realized she could still hear his song if she focused: wooden and brass percussion. "I hear the techno, I hear the crowd, I hear you." She stopped and looked at him, her lips parted.

He glanced at her, his lips forming what could be taken for a smile or the start of a question. "Right I forgot, you're different," he said, then turned away, his eyes trawling the crowd. "I wish I could tell you what your music sounded like," he said, his words almost swallowed up by the noise of the club.

"I hear...wait." Mina grabbed his hand. She cocked her head to the side and looked at the floor. "I hear cellos and windchimes, but...catawampus." He turned towards her as she looked up at him. "I think I hear the new vampire," she said, stepping off into the crowd, dragging him with her by the hand she hadn't let go of.

Mina and Jack were thrown against each other as they made their way through the crowd, jostled like driftwood on a tumul-

A PLAGUE OF SHADOWS 107

tuous river. Eventually, they managed to get to the other side only slightly worse for wear.

"Ow," Mina said, glowering over her shoulder as she picked up her foot and rubbed the toe. "Wearing heels is a privilege, not a right," she said, but the offending heel-wearer had disappeared into the mass of bodies.

Jack studied the crowd again as Mina turned toward the dimly lit hallway in front of them. She remembered this hallway. It led to a propped open door which opened onto the area out back where staff and sweaty dancers could go to have a smoke and cool off. *Or meet a man with amber eyes.*

And that door was just swinging shut.

"This way," she said.

"How—"

Not pausing to explain, she grabbed Jack's hand again and led him down the hallway. They tumbled out into the alleyway, just as a group of people rounded a corner onto a side street. The last person – vampire – glanced their way. Its mask slipped for a second, revealing the skeletal visage of a nosferat.

"Necrophagos," Jack said from over her shoulder, his voice hard. He started running towards the corner as Matteo slipped out of view.

"Stop," she said, but he either didn't hear or didn't listen. Mina took off after him, her stomach unsettled. A new sound filled the air, which also carried a whiff of something rotten to her nostrils.

Jack turned the corner and slid to a stop, hands at his sides. Mina drew up beside him as the sound grew louder, a deep and oozing organ music she hadn't heard before. A tendril of decay crept into her nostrils, so strong she glanced around for an overflowing dumpster.

"Matteo." Jack's lip snarled, and the name came out as a growl. Mina placed her hand on his back and followed his gaze. The side street was empty. She felt his deep sigh more than heard it, as the lethargic organ music vibrated through her bones, sending her teeth chattering. She didn't want to be in this alley.

"We need to go."

"Dammit," he said, turning towards her, running a hand through his hair.

"Don't worry about him. We can deal with Matteo another day. He's a monster we know." She breathed deeply, glancing left and right in the deserted street. The smell had disappeared. *Just garbage carried on the wind*, she thought, choosing to ignore the fact that there wasn't even a breeze. The music had also dissipated, but the nausea remained.

"Matteo might be more a monster than you think," he said. "Besides, you felt the new vampire, yes?"

Mina nodded, her eyes closing as comprehension dawned. "Where there's Matteo—"

"There's that vampire." He turned in a circle in the intersection. "But we're too late."

But Mina only half heard him. The organ music had been replaced by another dirge. One she knew too well. "I hate to say it, but I think we have a bigger problem."

Jack turned to her, his eyes crinkled in a question. His lips opening to say something but whatever he meant to share was forestalled by the soft churr descending from above. Mina let her eyes slide up while trying to keep stone-still otherwise, her mus-

A PLAGUE OF SHADOWS 109

cles tensing with the effort. A grey bulk crouched where there hadn't been one before.

"Gargoyle," she whispered.

CHAPTER SIXTEEN

"GARGOYLES, PLURAL," Jack said, his gaze over her shoulder, above her head. But Mina focused on the direction they'd come from. Towards the deadly organ music that had disappeared but left her blood vibrating. She accepted there was no wind to carry that fetid stench down the alleyways, nor waft the odour of wet wool that now settled around her, making her want to gag. The source was close by. She strained to pick out any sound, a huff of breath, a soft padding of feet, a sniffling of nostrils.

Jack's arm reached behind her, dispelling whatever half-formed questions tumbled around in her brain, and guided her until they stood back-to-back. Whatever she'd sensed behind them, assuming it wasn't a figment of a fearful imagination, was overshadowed by the gargoyles above.

Mina canted her head, looking up at the gargoyle above her with the barest movement. It stared back at her as it used one of its talons to pick its teeth. Jack inched a step towards their right, in the direction of open ground. Mina followed his lead. The creature stopped picking its teeth and looked at her with shining eyes.

She stopped moving, adrenalin spiking through her veins.

"What's up?" Jack asked.

"It didn't like that." She moved her hand to reach for the gun nestled in the holster against her back. Inconvenient but it

A PLAGUE OF SHADOWS   111

seemed not to set off bouncers, police and other normals. She started to draw it, careful to keep her finger off the trigger.

"Fuck," she said, pulling her hand away from her gun.

"Shh," Jack hissed.

"I don't think we need to be quiet," she said, her voice almost normal. The creature above her reached its taloned hand over its shoulder to scratch its back while keeping its eyes on her. "They know we're here. And they're waiting." She realized the truth as she said it. Jack's head move against hers.

"Point taken," he said, his voice still low. "So that's what the swearing is for?"

"No. I just realized my gun's loaded for vampires, not gargoyles. Silver hollow points, not liquid lead."

There was a second of silence from behind her. "Fuck," Jack said.

She felt his hand retreat from his back. "You too?"

"Me too."

"The bullets still have some lead." Mina shrugged. "Enough to sting?"

"Enough to piss them off." Again his head moved against hers though Mina couldn't see what he was looking at. "What are they waiting for? It's giving me the creeps."

"You wish they would attack?" She shuffled another step to the right, and Jack mirrored her movement. A piece of something was dislodged from the roof, clattering its way down the wall before plunking into the puddle at her feet.

"I don't think they want us to leave. We may need to fight them here." His deep breath expanded his shoulders. "With what is the question."

"I have throwing knives," she said. "From Finn, inlaid with intertwining silver and lead. Not enough to seriously harm either a vampire or a gargoyle, but enough to slow one down. If you hit it in the right spot. They're against my back." She groped behind her for Jack's hand and guided it to the sheath snugged against her lower back, pulling her shirt up with her other hand. Goosebumps raised on her exposed skin as his cold fingers sought out the hilts of the short blades. Then the fingers were gone, the knives still there.

"What gives?" she said.

"You need them."

Disgruntled by his chivalry, Mina bit her tongue. His weight shifted, allowing icy air to come between them, chilling the sweat on her back.

"There's a piece of pipe against the wall," he said. She felt him lean to the left. "If. I. Can." There was more skittering from above.

"I have more knives, in my boots," she said, dropping her voice back to a hoarse whisper.

"What?" Jack stood upright and pressed against her. "What's with all the knives?"

Mina rolled her sore shoulder, the stiff tendons crackling as she did. "The latest training with Bee was throwing sharp pointy things. Repeatedly." She slowly raised her left leg, sliding the blade on the outside out of its sheath. She repeated the process with the right.

Jack's hand found her back again as she pressed against him. His other hand joined it as he drew a couple of the short, light blades. "You any good?"

Mina recalled the bladed smile she'd given the target then she shrugged, deciding this was not the time to discuss her un-

A PLAGUE OF SHADOWS   113

usual skills or Bee's comments about her strangeness. "Good enough." She let loose a blade that sank into one of the gargoyle's hooded eyes, releasing a howl from its belly that ricocheted along the walls of the alleyway. The thing with poison as a weapon is that it took a while to work, especially when it was just inlaid metal. She heard the clatter of a blade tumbling down the wall behind her. Only one, so one of Jack's throws must have hit its mark.

"Run!" Jack grabbed her wrist with one hand while reaching out to snatch the pipe leaning against the wall with the other.

Reluctant to turn her back, she nonetheless followed his lead, though not before sending her second blade into the gargoyle's thigh. She'd been aiming for its head when Jack pulled her away.

A series of thumps let her know that the gargoyles had landed on the asphalt behind them. At that moment Mina realized it was impossible to extract a weapon from footwear while running. She glanced over her shoulder.

"Don't look, just run." Jack pushed her in front of him. It took her a couple of seconds to realize that he was no longer behind her, by which time she was halfway to the street. She pulled up and turned around.

Jack stood still, hands lightly grasping the metal pipe, facing down a gargoyle with a knife in its eye and blood running down its thigh. Mina would have placed even money on Jack winning that fight if it weren't for the other gargoyle between her and him.

Both of the creatures took a step towards him.

"Jack!"

He glanced over his shoulder. "Go."

Mina's stomach clenched. She grasped the last two blades from her boots. Fear gnawed at her insides, and the first blade flew wide, barely missing Jack.

The closer gargoyle peered over its shoulder at her. She loosed the second knife. This time it hit home, piercing the gargoyle's back between its shoulders. It reached around and pulled the dagger free, scratching its back with the tip of the blade. It still didn't turn to attack her. So she started towards it. Then both of the creatures went into a crouch and looked down the alleyway past Jack, their heads bobbing. With a rumbling growl and a snarl, they clambered up the wall onto the rooftop and fled into the night, leaving a trail of dark blood, but taking with them that smell of wet dog.

Mina ran to Jack, who still stood holding the pipe. His face reflected the surprise she felt at being alive and in one piece.

"What do you think that was about?"

He shrugged his shoulders, dropping the pipe. "I have an idea, but I think we both need more guns."

IVAN FROZE IN FRONT of the cemetery gates. He stood just beyond the copse of trees near the fence, almost at the far side of the holy-unholy ground, blessed but full of death. But it wasn't the death that had stopped him – he and Death were old acquaintances. No, it was the hairs on the back of his neck standing on end, though he couldn't pinpoint why. Up ahead, Em and Adam crossed the threshold and turned onto the street leading to the mansion, guiding and guarding the girl that stood between them. Given their comments in the club, he wouldn't have

A PLAGUE OF SHADOWS   115

trusted them to do the job. They seemed as likely to attack Matteo's pet as protect her, but it wasn't his call. He glanced back into the cemetery, at the nosferat, who looked even more a phantom surrounded by gravestones.

Matteo had also stopped at the edge of the markers, his bony hands clasped in front of him and his head cocked to one side, as if listening. Instead of joining the others, Ivan turned to Matteo, his eyebrows pulling together in question.

Somewhere in the distance, on the far side of the graveyard they'd so recently crossed, a snarling howl rose above the rooftops, clear to his undead ears.

Gargoyles. Ivan was beginning to recognize the sound. His shoulders heaved as he took a deep breath in through his mouth and pulled them back. His exhale formed a damp cloud in the night. He breathed in again, this time through his nostrils, filling his chest with icy air.

Ivan caught a whiff of something feral and musty, aroused and hungry, somewhere much closer than the gargoyle. It was a scent he knew.

"Werewolf," he whispered, the word escaping his lips. It was implausible, in the middle of the city, since the Wolves kept to the wild nowadays. Besides, there was an unwritten rule: they kept away from the vampires, and the vampires from them. It hadn't always been that way; they had the same prey after all. His arm pulsed with tension as his hand sought the handle of his gun. He wished he had his broadsword – he knew from experience that it could take the beast's head clean off. He wondered how it had got in: cemeteries were technically holy ground. Though there was always something unholy enough lurking in them to invite a vampire in. Maybe it was the same for other creatures.

Just beyond Matteo, a hiccough of a breath fell in the silent night and a tendril of rot snaked through the air into his nose. Ivan's blood throbbed slowly against his eardrums. It was a sickly-sweet aroma that told him Death was near at hand. The scent stirred the well of memory, dredging up dark, chaotic images.

Forcing himself to focus, Ivan's intestines fluttered as a stillness formed around them, like the absence caused by a master predator stalking his prey. Also something he was familiar with, having been both hunter and hunted.

Ivan stayed half-turned towards Matteo, watching him in his peripheral vision while he kept an eye on the copse of trees in front of him, where the scent of wet dog emanated from. Matteo kept his face forward, shaded by the brim of his fedora. Still, Ivan caught a glimpse of full-on nosferat around the edges, a spectre of death reanimated. Matteo had dropped the glamour he'd worn in the club. Apparently fearful of something, but not the wolf.

"What do you want?" Matteo asked. Ivan was startled to hear a voice break the oppressive silence. Something shifted in the trees, but it didn't show itself. He adjusted his stance so he could better watch both the stand of trees and Matteo. The nosferat tilted his head to the side but still faced Ivan. Ivan took a step forward; there was no use pretending they didn't know that something skulked in the shadows behind Matteo.

Matteo shook his head, barely a twitch, but Ivan took his meaning and stopped. Instead, he peered over Matteo's shoulder, as a man emerged from the night. An unexpected one, with a

A PLAGUE OF SHADOWS   117

face he knew, albeit in passing. *The young priest*. Ivan canted his head, his eyebrows furrowed, as he tried to make sense of it.

The sodden, half-dead grass behind Matteo squelched, turning to rot as the thing stepped closer, keeping its silence.

"I have no patience for games anymore," Matteo said, as he turned to face his stalker. "Either kill me or tell me what you want?"

"You shouldn't utter such a challenge to the night unless you're willing to stand before the darkness," the man said, an odd echo to his voice as if the words rumbled around in a stone crypt before emerging from his mouth.

"And what do you know about the darkness?" Matteo asked.

Ivan thought that was entirely the wrong question to ask a creature of shadows, but Matteo just stepped forward, sliding to the right, keeping a wise distance between the man and himself. His movements were mimicked by their stalker, eddies of disturbed air contorting the fog at his feet. Ivan held his breath against the odour of death – decay masked by an old lady's perfume – as Matteo took another cautious step, circling his adversary.

Ivan inched forward but paused at a rumbling growl to his left. He glanced at the shadows over his shoulder. He'd forgotten about the werewolf. When no attack followed, he forced himself to look back at Matteo and his stalker, all the while very aware of the feral presence over his left shoulder.

Though, in that moment, Ivan realized he was more afraid of man than beast. The figure wore the form of a man, and not just any man. But even cloaked in the skin of that young priest, he didn't feel human. He obviously wasn't one of the usual things that rattled around in dank graveyards. Ivan was well acquaint-

118   **C. RENÉ ASTLE**

ed with those. But he still felt familiar to Ivan, raising his hackles and stirring up buried memories of the dead. The man-shaped thing was the exact semblance of the priest: as tall as Ivan, 6 feet plus, with Teutonic blond hair and a ruddy complexion. He even wore the black suit, black shirt and white clerical collar. The only thing that didn't fit was the intensity with which his eyes watched Matteo.

"I know that Night is coming," the man finally said.

"I've heard that before in my long years," Matteo replied, rolling his shoulders back. An innocuous shrug to cover his readying of the stiletto blades under his cloak. At last, Matteo's circling put the creature between him and Ivan. "So far Night has failed to make an appearance. Perhaps still locked in her prison of darkness."

A muscle in the man's jaw ticked. "So you know of what I speak." The man tented his fingers in a mockery of Matteo. "But this time, her Herald is already here, calling all her creatures to make ready the way."

"How do you know that?" Matteo asked. A breeze travelled through the cemetery, snaking between the gravestones and up Ivan's spine, causing him to shiver. "Have you heard the Messenger's call?" Matteo continued.

Goosebumps raised across Ivan's skin, and suddenly he knew the answer, and knew that that was definitely the wrong question to ask.

"I *am* the Messenger," the man said, standing taller, as the air became frigid. "So I ask, are you with me or against me?"

"Angelos," Matteo whispered, stilling.

Viznyk, Ivan mouthed the word, the werewolf forgotten. He realized why he had a sense of familiar foreboding, even though

A PLAGUE OF SHADOWS 119

the Messenger had cloaked himself in a different body all those years ago.

"Some call me that." The man shrugged a shoulder.

"What should I call you?" Matteo asked.

"If not lord and master?" The thing inclined its head. "Angelos will do."

How quickly can I lodge a blade in that creature's skull? Ivan thought. He shook his head to clear that idea away – he wasn't sure if any of his weapons would kill it, or just anger it. So he stayed still, instead watching as Matteo pulled himself tall. He heard the gate squeal behind him, as the others returned. The sound caused the creature possessing the priest to turn halfway around, so his shoulder was facing Ivan. Ivan stayed as he was as he sensed the trio behind him come closer. The stranger looked over his shoulder, the man's eyes narrowing. It was a barely noticeable tightening of the muscles around his eyes, but it made Ivan shift, not wanting to be the centre of his attention. Out the corner of his eye, Ivan saw the girl step away from Em and Adam. He placed his hand on her arm, stopping her from going closer to the vipers' dance between Matteo and this man.

"You still haven't answered my question," Matteo said. "What do you want?"

Angelos trained his gaze on Matteo again, causing his head to twist at an unnatural angle. "I want the gargoyles."

Matteo's lips pursed. "I think you've already stolen my army."

"I can't take from you what was never yours." Angelos cocked his head and peered over Matteo's shoulder.

"So what do you want then?"

The creature smiled. Then he raised his right arm and pointed at Ivan. Ivan's heart dropped into his stomach. Then he realized Angelos wasn't pointing at him. His gaze slid to Matteo's dhamphir as Angelos confirmed his suspicions.

"I want her."

Ivan watched as Matteo became still as a corpse, his lips thin. Ivan sidestepped so he was between the creature and the girl, forcing her to take a step back. She lacked any sense of self-preservation in her current state.

"What if I say you can't have her?" Matteo said, taking a step towards the creature in priest's clothing.

Angelos barked a hoarse laugh. "What if I say you can't keep her?" The emissary turned around to face Matteo and the desolate cemetery, obviously not worried about having Ivan behind him. Ivan's fingers clenched, wishing they had a sword.

The breeze stirred, and Matteo shifted, turning his head. Ivan grimaced as he watched the realization rise on Matteo's ghostly face that there was something else amongst the tombstones. The old man was slipping if he hadn't realized yet that there was a beast out there.

Werewolf. Ivan's lips moved but no sound came out. He clutched the hilt of the dagger at his back. But it wasn't made for werewolves. Neither was the ammo in his gun, lacking the hide piercing rounds. Werewolves that skulked around the cities were scavengers that avoided vampires. Or died. But if this one was hanging out with the priest, Ivan was sure it didn't fall into normal.

A shift in the shadows amongst the gravestones caused Ivan's fingers to twitch. Matteo sniffed the air, then opened his long jacket, revealing the rapiers at his side. Ivan shivered. If Matteo was preparing to draw weapons, the situation was bad.

A PLAGUE OF SHADOWS   121

"Kian." Matteo looked at the whisper of movement in the trees. A snarl rose, travelling through the gravestones. "It's been a long time since we crossed paths."

"Not long enough." A tall, muscular woman stepped out from the trees. She rubbed her hand over the right side of her face where a long scar puckered the skin. "But maybe it's time for a rematch." The sides of her head were shaved, the hair along the top shaggy. Despite the chill, she wore a simple T-shirt and jeans that showed off the branding on her forearms.

This was not a wolf Ivan knew, which worried him all the more. Apparently, Matteo was worried too. Ivan watched as he stepped back, turned and sidled sideways, extricating himself from between Angelos and the werewolf.

Angelos mirrored his movements until they'd swapped positions again. Ivan and the girl stood to one side of Matteo, with the werewolf opposite. A rumble rose in Ivan's chest as he glared at the wolf, his lips pulling down into a deep frown. The keening bay of a werewolf pack preparing to descend on him echoed through his mind, so loud it almost seemed real, even though it was just a memory. His face flushed as he felt the heat of the wolf cub's warm breath, spitting a mixture of its blood and his own onto his face as it exhaled, his dagger driven into its side. A lightning bolt of pain coursed through the invisible scars on his back, where he still felt the heavy paws of the she-wolf, pushing him into the mud, preparing to tear him apart.

"Enough." Matteo took another sidling step sideways. "The night grows light. The sun is about to rise." He buttoned up his jacket. "You may have taken my gargoyles. But you won't have her."

"I will if I can take her." Angelos glanced at the dhamphir.

"What makes you think you and your pet dog can take her from me and my...." Matteo glanced over his shoulder. "Me and my army." He spread his arms wide before returning to clasp them in front of his abdomen. "Besides, why would you want an unschooled, weak, nothing of a vampire?"

"Why don't you want me to have her?"

Matteo shrugged, an awkward jerk of his shoulders. "I'm her maker. What will the other vampires say if I just let her go?"

Angelos snorted. "I hardly think you're the type to care what others think. If you did, she wouldn't be half starved. Just look at her, you can see the bloodlust in the pout of her lips, the hunger in the set of her jaw."

Ivan glanced sideways and had to admit there was some truth to what he said.

Matteo didn't respond, so the man continued, casting a predatory look at the dhamphir. "Though I can see why you might want to keep her."

Matteo looked at the woman, who stood with her arms hugging her chest. Ivan could smell her need, as she glanced from Ivan to Matteo to Angelos. Her eyes shone, without fear, without question. Only with hunger. Although he'd never made another vampire, even Ivan had to agree that Matteo had done poorly by her.

"All the more reason I should keep her." Matteo took a step back. The priest shrugged, making no move towards the girl. "Besides, you still haven't answered my question."

"Hmm, what question is that?" Angelos slowly shifted his gaze from Camellia to Matteo.

"Why do you even want her?" Matteo moved backwards again.

A PLAGUE OF SHADOWS   123

Angelos regarded Matteo for a long moment, his blue eyes sparkling, though he did nothing to stop Matteo. Ivan shifted back towards the gate as well, sure the question would go unanswered. Then the Herald spoke, his voice rich, carrying through the shadows that dwelled amongst the gravestones, causing Ivan to pause at the threshold of the cemetery.

"For Night, of course."

CHAPTER SEVENTEEN

SEEMA COWERED, TRYING not to move while huddling into an even smaller ball behind the grey stone. She'd made a mistake. Not as big a mistake as when she'd left Mike alone to fend for himself. This time only *her* life was at stake. But maybe bigger than when she'd run away from home all those years ago.

She'd realized leaving the vampire's lair had been a mistake soon after she'd fled, and yet she hadn't gone back, tail between her legs. Instead, she'd wandered the streets, her pride forcing her on, despite getting drenched by the rain and feeling increasingly ill at ease. Increasingly ill full stop.

Cats aren't known for admitting their mistakes, preferring to pretend they always meant to do whatever stupid thing they've done, a sibilant voice from long ago said.

I'm no ordinary cat, she replied to the memory, jutting her jaw out. Though right now, she wasn't sure. If she'd admitted her mistake, she wouldn't be, at this particular moment, crouched against an icy stone which provided little shelter from the wind, and even less from prying eyes, trying to make herself small. Trying to seem very much like an ordinary cat.

Snippets of conversation reached her from the other side of the stone.

'Gargoyles.' If she'd admitted her mistake, she wouldn't have prowled the desolate alleyways and shadowed rooftops all on her lonesome, in search of creatures long lost to the minds of men.

A PLAGUE OF SHADOWS 125

There was a pause in the voices. The tension she felt from the far side of the stone caused the hair at the nape of her neck to stand on end.

'Dhamphir.' But then, if she'd admitted her mistake, she wouldn't have picked up the unknown scent of a new vampire, sharp and astringent. This was one she hadn't come across in her nighttime prowls though the smell was annoyingly familiar.

'Angelos.' If she'd admitted her mistake, she wouldn't have accomplished what she'd left the den of vampires to do – she wouldn't have found Mike's killer, cloaked in priest's clothing. She sniffed the air. The sickly-sweet aroma was the same even though the scent memory was mingled with the copper tang of Mike's blood. Her small heart beat out a staccato tattoo, sounding as if it was announcing to the world 'here, here, tasty tidbit here'. She pawed at the mossy ground before willing herself to stop and listen as the dialogue continued. One word, in particular, pricked her ears.

'Night.' No, if she'd admitted her mistake, she wouldn't have heard the Herald talk about Night. And she knew with every bone in her body, from her frozen ears to the tip of her puffed up tail, that it was the Herald on the other side of the stone. A shiver ran through her, and she crouched closer to the ground, as if she could disappear into one of the graves.

Again the conversation paused, and Seema glanced around, realizing how exposed she was if any of the things that lurked in the cemetery determined she wasn't an ordinary cat. She nestled down in the damp grass next to the grave marker, willing herself invisible as a gust of wind blew through. As it died down, she heard a sound to her left. Lifting one paw pad at a time, she shifted, canting her head, craning to sense what was there. She sniffed. She saw nothing, but the wind carried a scent to her, one she knew all too well, burned into her sinuses in ancient, pointless turf wars.

Werewolf. She almost let a low growl escape before she checked herself as a twig snapped on her right. She peeked around the gravestone.

The others were leaving the cemetery, the vampires backing out through the far gate. But the creature that possessed the priest stayed where he was, just watching.

"You're not going to take her?" the werewolf, human at the moment, asked the priest, turning towards him, letting Seema get a look at her partially shaved head.

"Not yet," the Herald said. "He can keep her until everything else is in place. I still need the blade."

The Herald turned to head out of the cemetery the way he'd come, and the woman followed him like a good dog.

Seema gave the pair enough distance that the wolf hopefully wouldn't scent her, then she trailed them, block after block, down to the river. Down to an abandoned warehouse.

A low purr crept into her belly of its own volition. If she'd admitted her mistake, she wouldn't have been shivering in the cold as she peered through a broken window at a nest of gargoyles. As if she needed more proof they weren't all dead.

CHAPTER EIGHTEEN

HIGH ABOVE JACK'S HEAD, a raucous timbre of rain fell against the stained-glass windows. There was little morning light at this time of year, and even less with the blanket of clouds, so the Sanctuary was a deep ocean blue. Over the sound of the rainfall, Jack caught the soft padding of stocking feet across the floor, followed by the thumping of a pair of shod, heavy human feet. From his shadowed perch, he saw Mina's head appear as she glanced into the narthex, though it was clear she was distracted and didn't see him. His eyebrows pulled together. *Strange she doesn't seem to hear me with her odd senses.*

He closed the book he'd been reading, the philosophizing on finding serenity no longer holding his interest. Mina stepped into the space, followed by Brett, his hand on her back.

Jack frowned. She was spending too much time with one familiar, getting too attached. Worse, letting him get too attached. He should encourage her to feed off other familiars and set Brett free. The man had a life outside of being a familiar, friends and family, a home. His own bed to sleep in.

When they reached the door, Mina turned the knob slowly and inched the door open on its well-oiled hinges. Brett wrapped both arms around her and pulled her close, nuzzling her ear, seemingly oblivious to the wind and the rain. And Jack.

"Go," Mina said. "Before I get hungry again." She turned him around and gave a playful shove out the door. After watching him for a few seconds too long, she took care to close the door as softly as she'd opened it, turning the knob, pressing it to the jamb, releasing the handle. Shutting out the weather, she laid her head on the wood. "Besides, you look tired," she whispered, the smile falling from her face.

"You shouldn't get so attached." Jack stood and stepped out of the shadows, bare feet silent on the cold floor, then leaned against a pillar, his arms crossed over his chest.

Mina spun around, her eyes flashing to him. "I don't know what you mean," she said, crossing her arms in a mirror of his posture and leaning against the door.

He laid the book on the shelf beside him and stepped towards her. "You've been spending a lot of time with him."

"So, we get on, what's it to you?" She raised an eyebrow as she slid her gaze up to meet his, her dark eyes shining.

He peered at her, keeping his face smooth. "Nothing."

She shifted her gaze to look past him. "When I'm with him, I don't hear any music in my veins, my blood doesn't vibrate. He feels normal." As she took a step towards the nave, she continued in a whisper. "Besides, if it's nothing, it's none of your business." She edged around him, seemingly intent on moving into the larger space of the sanctuary.

Jack placed his hand on her wrist as she passed. "It's just...."

She stilled and looked at him, or at his left shoulder anyway. Jack's eyebrows twitched as he tried to think of what he meant to say, but he was distracted by the throb of her pulse just below the skin.

"What?" she said, her voice softening.

He shook his head. "For one, you don't know his story. Has he told you how he came to be a familiar?"

"None of us truly know another person's story. I don't really know yours." She looked from his shoulder to his jaw. "Other than you were made by a vampire named Lin, who's now a crazy revenant."

Jack's jaw clenched, but he tipped his head, conceding the point. "But you do know I won't grow old and die on you." He heard Mina swallow and felt her warm breath on his cheek when she exhaled.

"You won't grow old." Her dark eyes peered into his. "But you might die on me." She opened her mouth as if to say something more, but he beat her to it, afraid of where this conversation was going.

"Speaking of death, we still haven't talked about yours."

MINA'S HEART JUMPED when the door swung open, banging against the wall. As she stepped back, Jack let go of her wrist, leaving the memory of his fingers on her skin.

Bee stood framed in the doorway, one hand on the doorjamb, the other on her side, the last of the grey daylight silhouetting her figure. Sweat sheened her forehead and a grimace twisted her lips.

"Father," Bee said, her voice raspy. She took a couple of deep, audible breaths, then continued. "Father Pietro."

"What the hell is going on?"

Mina turned to see Dar come out of the dark stairwell, wearing hospital pants and a T-shirt, running his hand through his lopsided mohawk, sections of which stood out at right angles to each other. She'd never seen him so unkempt and dressed down.

Her eyebrow arched. As he walked through the open space, the wall sconces brightened of their own accord in response to the drop in ambient light as night fully descended outside.

"No need to bang doors at this early hour." He twisted his neck side to side then rubbed his face as he yawned. "The sun's not even set yet. And some of us didn't get to sleep until well after sunrise." He closed the door gently behind Bee, shutting out the weather, as she stepped into the Sanctuary.

"What about the priest?" Jack asked.

They all turned their focus on Bee, whose normally lustrous skin was dull. "He...he's dead."

Mina's mouth opened. Jack's eyebrows drew together. Dar stood up straight, eyes opening wide.

"Dead?" Jack said. "How?"

Footsteps sounded behind them, and soon Adeh joined them at the door, followed by Simon and the familiar Nicole.

"I don't know." Bee shook her head, lips tight. "But I think he was murdered."

"Why?" Dar asked.

"What are you talking about?" Adeh asked.

"Father P." Bee shrugged. "I was just walking by the church. There were police, an ambulance. A woman crying." She glanced over her shoulder. "Then they brought out a black bag."

"How do you know it was the Father then?" Nicole asked. Mina watched as Simon side-stepped an inch closer to the familiar.

"Vampire, remember?" Bee said. "I could smell him – eucalyptus and mint – even across the distance, through the body bag and the blood." She glanced around at the growing circle of the conclave.

A PLAGUE OF SHADOWS 131

"But why do you think it was murder?" Mina asked, worrying at a thread on the hem of her shirt.

"It would have to have been a brutal accident for there to be that much blood."

"Possible though," Dar said.

"Gargoyle, do you think?" Simon suggested, his large hands grasping his elbows. "It seems they'll attack whatever."

Bee shook her head. "He was in the church."

"Do we know they can't cross a blessed threshold?" Jack asked. The gathered group looked at each other, no one having a ready answer.

"We hope so," Dar said, raising an eyebrow. "So far they haven't come in here."

"There could be other reasons for that," Adeh offered.

"Could it have been one of Matteo's band?" Mina asked, even though she knew from her own experience they couldn't enter the church. Unless someone had invited them. Mina thought back to the night she'd met Father Pietro, when Jack had found her after the priest had invited her into the church, then called Jack without her knowing. She recalled how, when she'd crossed the threshold to the Sanctuary uninvited later that night, the world had shrunk to a pinprick then disappeared into blackness. Father Pietro had said he was protecting her, though she didn't believe him at the time. And then she'd never thanked him. But her life had been somewhat chaotic since waking up in the Sanctuary. That thought brought her back to the present. "Or some other vampire? The new one, maybe?"

"No," Dar said after a minute, as he ran his fingers through his hair trying to coax it into shape. "None of them can cross that threshold, both blessed and guarded by Father P."

"But he was always inviting in disreputable souls," Jack said, his eyes staring steadfastly at Dar, with an undercurrent Mina couldn't quite catch.

Dar shook his head. "He invited in lost souls. There's a difference."

The group lapsed into an uncomfortable silence, broken only when a gust of weather blew through the Sanctuary as the door opened again, banging against the wall as the wind tore it out of the opener's grasp.

"Sorry," Rhys said, as he leaned into the door to close it. Stepping into the Sanctuary, he glanced around at the assemblage. "So you've heard then?"

Dar nodded, glancing at Bee.

"I saw him," she said. "Or sensed him, rather."

"Gargoyles?" Rhys asked, shaking out his umbrella.

Dar shook his head. "We've been going over—." He stopped and stared at the door for a second, his eyes focusing on something not present. "Father Pietro." His voice lifted up in a question even though there was none asked.

"Yes?" Jack said, his narrowed eyes peering at Dar. "He's the one who died."

"The homeless man, the one we found desiccated," Dar said. "He spoke of Night."

Mina straightened her spine, leaning into the circle. The word drew her in like a moth to a light.

"Do you mind connecting the dots for the rest of us?" Rhys asked.

"Sorry," Dar said, reaching up to scratch the side of his head. "Father Pietro talked about Night. Rather, he shared something the man had said before he died. It still makes no sense." He

A PLAGUE OF SHADOWS 133

paused before going on. "Dark blade of the Even Star, piercing the heart of the Sun."

Mina's eyebrows pulled together at a thought that flitted through the back of her brain. But when she tried to catch it, she was distracted by a tickle on her bare ankles. She glanced down. The cat had come back, possibly sneaking in with Bee or Rhys. Now it circled her legs, weaving in and out, its tail twitching in agitation as it rubbed its wet fur against her shins.

"I might be able to add to that," Rhys said.

Mina bent to pick up the cat, but it danced away.

"I've searched and scoured and googled," Rhys continued. "I've called in favours and extended credit. Looking for clues on the nature of Night, and how to defeat her. Or, better yet, how to stop her coming at all. This is all I've found." He pulled a slightly soggy printout from the inside pocket of his coat. "The pitch vault of Hell," he intoned. "Sundered by the blooded Blade—"

"Do you think that's wise?" Mina asked, her eyes widening.

"Hmm?" Rhys looked up from his piece of paper.

"Maybe it's a spell." Mina shrugged, aiming for nonchalance as she looked over his shoulder at the paper, despite the queasiness in her stomach. The cat started pawing at her leg.

Rhys looked back at the words, in some squiggled script Mina couldn't even begin to read. "No." He shook his head. "I shouldn't think so. There'd be a ritual to go with, I'm sure."

"How sure?" Dar asked.

Rhys looked over his glasses at Dar before shifting his gaze to Mina. Then he coughed to clear his throat and continued. "The pitch vault of Hell, sundered by the blooded Blade, the prison of Night unlocks, at the break of Day."

"Ow!" Mina yelped, and the others jerked back ever so slightly.

"What?" Jack asked, concern written on his face when she glanced up at him. "You're sure it's not a spell?" He glared at Rhys before returning his attention to Mina.

"Sorry, it's the cat," Mina said, her cheeks flushed. "She decided my legs were a scratching post." She looked down at the creature as it crouched close to the floor, bug-eyed, its tail puffed out to twice its normal diameter. "What was that for, huh?" The cat peered up at her then took off into the warren of the Sanctuary basement.

"I wish she would speak," Rhys said wistfully, his gaze following the path the cat had taken.

"I don't think your riddle helps us," Jack said, pulling Rhys' attention back. "Even if it's not a spell."

"No, I suppose not, but it's a piece of the puzzle. The thing about puzzles, you need to approach each one differently to figure them out." Rhys sighed as he folded the paper and put it back in his pocket, pulling out a handkerchief from the same pocket to blow his nose. "If only I could see the picture on the box."

Dar took a step closer to Rhys, laying a hand on his arm. "I think you all should get a bit more rest, if you can. Go back to regular patrols." His hand dropped to his side. "I have a feeling it'll be the last lazy night for a while."

"Walk me home?" Rhys said, looking at Dar. "There are dangerous creatures lurking in the dark."

Dar glanced at Jack, and Mina saw some unspoken message pass between them. Jack nodded his head, barely a millimetre, almost unnoticeable if she weren't a dracul, before Dar answered.

"Of course."

A PLAGUE OF SHADOWS

Mina sighed, realizing she'd have to save the puzzle of that weird triangle for another night. Tonight she had a morgue to visit.

CHAPTER NINETEEN

STARK NAKED, LIN PEERED at the development across the stream, the latest one to encroach on her forest, and shivered, more a gentle tremble of anticipation than a shudder of cold. She twitched and half-turned as a howl rose behind her, answered by another – voices she recognized but didn't know. Unwelcome creatures had started stalking her woods, sometimes man, sometimes beast, all disturbing her unrest. She scanned the houses, noting which ones had lights on, where people were more likely to be home. Despite the cold, the little creek still ran. She picked up a handful of snow and scrubbed her face, another handful to run over her arms, then her legs, her torso. She sighed. She'd forgotten how glorious it was to be clean. She'd left her filthy forest clothes behind.

Twisting her head at an unnatural angle, she cast one last glance over her shoulder, at the forest that had been her home for too many years. A few nights ago, snuffling through the woods in search of rats and voles, she'd stopped, looked up, sniffed. Cocked her head this way and that. Contorted her back and twisted her arms, trying to scratch an itch she'd never reach. And she knew something was different. The night sky had changed despite the clumps of ice that continued to rain down. The air smelt off, with a whiff of rotten flesh. The ground sighed, telling a tale of something that was wrong. Wonderfully, deliciously wrong.

Lin turned away from the forest, back to the houses. Houses that hadn't even been there when she'd made the woods her home. When she'd been cast out from polite society. Cast out by Matteo. Spurned by Dar. She peered into windows, then closed her eyes and let the hum of a hundred heartbeats overwhelm her. She'd forgotten what it sounded like to be surrounded by life. So much human blood. This is what had been stolen from her.

"Matteo must die," she whispered through chapped lips, her voice rusty despite having spoken more in the last month than the previous 10 years. "Speared by sunlight and silver, a festering end."

Lin stopped herself. "Enough speaking in riddles," she said to the night, her voice smoothing out, as she finished her ablutions. "It's time to take back my city. And maybe more." She stood and strode through the frigid water, over sharp stones to the nearest house with lights ablaze.

"OH MY GOD," THE WOMAN said, keeping the door mostly closed. Lin pulled her features into what she thought was a forlorn countenance, an emotion long forgotten. Shock, confusion and pity played across the woman's features in quick succession. "What happened, you poor thing?" the woman said, though the door didn't move.

Lin looked at the doorbell where her finger was still poised, the nail broken, then to the woman's shoes. Then she let her gaze meander up the woman's body. The corners of Lin's mouth lifted. She tried to stop them, to pull them down, but failed; she gave the woman a toothy smile. The pity in the woman's eyes was replaced with horror.

"That's it." Lin's voice was a purr, now that she'd filed off the rough edges of disuse. "That's the look I want," she said as she watched fear settle into the woman's eyes.

The woman tried to slam the door, but Lin was quick as a snake. She darted her bare leg, inured to any pain, into the gap, a pillar of stone between door and jamb. In a heartbeat, she spun the woman around and pulled her close, feeling the warmth of hearth and heartbeat against her naked breasts. Her right arm clamped around the woman's neck, cutting off the scream that was building there before the woman could release it. All that came out was a gurgle.

"Now, now, is that any way to treat a guest?" Lin whispered in her ear. Then she sunk her fangs into the woman's neck, sucking back the blood as quickly as she could, making room for more. Still, she wasn't able to quite keep pace with the amount the woman's rapidly beating heart pumped out, and blood oozed out the sides of her mouth and down her chin. She was as quiet as she could be, given how hungry she was, but still made small slurping noises, like a dog sucking the marrow from a bone. Her eyes rolled back, lids open, and a shudder passed through her.

A flicker of movement caught the corner of her eye. Lin tensed, pulling the woman to be a shield between her and the thing that came down the stairs near the door. A cat arched its back and hissed with its entire being. Lin let the nearly drained body of the woman slide to the floor and hissed back. The cat fled into the house.

"Smart cat," Lin whispered. "You were dessert."

"Melissa?" a man's voice called from down the lighted hallway. "Who's at the door?"

"Now that sounds like a better second course." Lin closed the door behind her, carefully turning the knob, then looked down at the woman's body. "You look like you have good taste."

AFTER FEEDING ON THE husband, who had, to her frustration, resisted satisfying other hungers long dormant, Lin luxuriated in a deep, hot bath. It was a reminder of her ancient, human life. She excoriated her soaked skin, softened by the warm, soapy water, abrading it until it was pink and the water grey.

Stepping out of the tub, she walked over to the closet, drying herself as she went, dripping water across the wood floor. She assessed the woman's wardrobe: she did have good taste.

Sated and satisfied, Lin pondered what to do next. A whisper of change rustled through her veins, telling of a new power...no, an old power come to Earth. But either way, a paradigm shift. It was a shift that could restore her to her rightful place...or take her even further.

But how to find this power, how to get from this place to where I need to be. This world was different from the one she'd left. Voices buzzed in the air, cameras were everywhere, capturing misdeeds and misdemeanors. The vampires were different from the ones who'd abandoned her. In her day, vampires hadn't exactly lived openly, but they had ruled the night, forcing the inhabitants of the netherworld and its fringes to do their bidding. Including driving them anywhere they couldn't walk on their own. Lin had never had to learn how to operate one of the infernal machines that could carry her quickly to the city.

She was ruminating on this conundrum as she pulled on some pencil thin jeans of dark denim when she stopped and canted her head. A rumble downstairs, a tremor that travelled through the wall, along the floor, up her legs. Peering out the window between the blinds, she saw the back end of a car disappear below her.

A voice mumbled something even her unnatural ears couldn't make out, followed by the caterwaul of an unhappy cat – so far the creature had eluded her grasp, hellish thing. Lin buttoned up the jeans and shrugged the skin-tight turtleneck on over the lace bra, then slipped down the stairs in bare feet.

She crept forwards with silent, tiptoeing steps, towards the figure that had dropped itself on the sofa. She stopped, one foot hovering off the floor, as the person moved. Lin held her breath, waiting to be discovered. Instead, thumping, tuneless, toneless noise emanated from all around her. Her lips curled in a snarl as she reached her arm around the person's neck.

LIN DIDN'T KILL THIS one, the son, judging by the photographs: he knew how to drive. He would take her to the city. She dragged the boy out to the garage, though as tall and broad as he was, 'boy' was hardly accurate. He must be almost out of his teens. When she was still human, he would have been a man with a wife, maybe children of his own, ripe for the plucking. But times had changed, now even vampires might frown on her if she plucked him.

A PLAGUE OF SHADOWS 141

"Open it." She pointed at the vehicle with her finger, the woman's rings glinting in the low light. Despite feeling flushed and lush after her feeding, her hand was still pale against the black leather jacket. She let go of him, and he fell to the floor, the blood from the punctures on his neck dripping onto the grey concrete. She hadn't killed him, but she had weakened him.

"Open it," she repeated, back-handing the man across the face. A bruise was forming on his jaw, where she'd kicked him when he fought back, upon seeing his parents' bodies. To his credit, he hadn't screamed or collapsed. No, instead he'd lashed out, trying to drive his shoulder into her waist. She'd propelled herself straight through his grasping arms, catching herself, planting her hands on the marble, before doing a round-off and landing to face him. But he was already up and ready to take another swipe at her. Which she didn't have the patience for. That's when she'd kicked him, sending him sprawling. She landed on top of him, grabbed his hand and wrenched it behind his back. Just like that, she'd sunk her fangs into flesh for the third time in an hour.

But this time she'd been able to restrain herself, her hunger tempered. She'd pulled out before the end, only taking a few sips. Then she'd leaned forward and whispered in his ear, barely hearing her own voice above his thrumming heartbeat.

"Do you want to live?"

His jaw pulsed, but he didn't answer. She wrenched the arm she held further up and pressed her knee deeper into his back.

"I said, do you want to live? Not a rhetorical question."

"Fuck you," he spat, as he tried to buck her off.

She grabbed his hair in her free hand and slammed his face into the marble.

"If you'd been more genteel in your response, I might not have done that." She ran her lips along his jawline and nipped his earlobe. His Adam's apple bobbed. "One more time, do you want to live?"

He'd been still for a second, then nodded. Unfortunately that didn't mean he was now cooperative.

"For the last time, open it."

CHAPTER TWENTY

"SO WHAT DO YOU THINK of our riddle?" Dar asked, his hands stuffed in his pockets. The tip of Rhys' umbrella tapped a rhythm on the sidewalk.

Rhys didn't say anything for a minute. Dar wondered if he'd heard him. Then Rhys spoke, without looking at Dar. "The riddle." He sighed. "It is a puzzle. Two pieces of a puzzle."

"Two pieces?" Dar scanned the empty street, glancing at rooftops. "Your riddle and that of the homeless man, do you they go together?"

"How can we know if two pieces of any puzzle go together," Rhys said. Dar felt Rhys' eyes slide towards him. "We can only try and see if they fit."

Dar clenched his jaw, pulling his lips tight over his fangs. He glanced over his shoulder to see if they were still being followed. He let out a sigh of relief – his shadow still trailed them.

Rhys continued. "They both talk about a blade. And images related to Night, if not Night herself. The Even Star likely refers to the first of her Generals, said to have wielded a blade of pure darkness that consumed the souls of those it killed."

"The Evening Star," Dar said, nodding slowly. "Not the Morning Star? Not Lucifer?"

"Oh no, that's a different tale entirely. The Even Star is said to have betrayed Night and used that blade to seal her prison, in hopes of buying his way back into the light."

"What happened to the Even Star?"

Rhys shrugged. "Quite likely he, or she, never betrayed her in the first place. Just a tale told by the victors to discredit their enemy: her own lover, so horrified by the extent of her evil, locked her in her cage."

"How can you imprison Night?"

"In a vault of nothingness. Her own personal hell. Empty of light, empty of darkness."

Dar's breath caught. "Empty of souls to feed on. Her madness would have nothing to feed on but itself."

"Now you're starting to understand."

"Not really." Dar laid his hand on Rhys' back and leaned closer. "The riddle still makes no sense."

"The blooded blade is obvious enough, I should think. There will be a sacrifice."

"There haven't been enough already?" Dar ran his fingers through his hair, dislodging icy raindrops. "And how do you pierce the heart of the sun?"

"With a shard of night? A blade of a star?" Rhys shrugged. "I have no idea. Maybe the heart of the Sun is some other artifact." His steps slowed as they came to an intersection even though the street was empty. "But we use these words for all sorts of things. It's not necessarily literal." Rhys' voice pitched lower. "My heart, my sun, the poets say of love."

Dar breathed deeply, ignoring the ache of his gums at his straining teeth and the ticktock of Rhys' heartbeat. "Rhys," he said, his own voice rough.

They stopped in front of Rhys' apartment. Rhys turned to unlock and open the door. Dar laid a hand on the cool brick and leaned close.

"Am I invited?" he said, whispering his words over the grey stubble of Rhys' jaw.

"You're already allowed in." Rhys placed a hand on his chest. "But I think you and I both know that would be a bad idea." He nodded over Dar's shoulder. "And it's getting late. You should go home, or wherever it is you go. Take Jack with you. He gets cranky if it's too long between fights."

Dar glanced over his shoulder at their stalker. He'd forgotten Jack, even though he'd asked him to watch him as he walked Rhys home.

He turned back to Rhys. "You'll continue to investigate?"

"Of course. I'll call you if I learn anything." Rhys nodded and took a step backwards into his hallway. "In the meantime, maybe talk to that young familiar, Sam. He has connections in a world I don't, and he's nearly as smart as I am." Rhys graced him with a smile that caused half his heart to lurch and the other half to die.

"WHAT'RE YOU DOING HERE?" Hana shrugged into her lab coat as she hurried Mina down the long hall and into a small office crammed with four desks covered in teetering piles of paper.

"Dale said you were working." Mina tried to keep the defensiveness out of her tone.

"Yeah, not 'til later." Hana pulled her long, black hair back into a severe ponytail. "This is a nighttime job. The dead don't sleep."

Mina's cheeks flushed even though she knew Hana meant the dead in the morgue. "Right. So about the dead...." She hesitated, not sure how to frame her request. She rubbed at her nose; even though the occupants of this part of the hospital were dead, it still reeked of blood and necrotic flesh.

"What do you want?" Hana stared at her, hands on her hips.

"You look like Mom when she was disappointed."

"Well, you only seem to come by lately when you're asked, or when you want something." Hana clipped a badge to her jacket. "So what do you want?"

"It's not me. It's a friend."

"What does your friend want?"

"He's dead."

"Oh." Hana's lips opened as if to say more, but Mina continued before she could, afraid she might lose her nerve.

"Well, he wasn't so much a friend as someone without any friends to look after him." Mina stuffed her hands in her pockets and examined a spot on the floor. Looking back up at Hana, she pulled her nerves together. "He died a few nights ago. Killed. I wanted to know how."

Hana glanced at the door. "That's highly unethical."

Mina shrugged and scratched her forearm. "Yeah, forget I asked."

"Why do you want to know, anyway? It's a bit macabre."

An image of Mike's avuncular face came to mind. She stopped, her hand on the doorframe. "It's just, well, nobody cares. They think he was just a bum who got on the wrong side of someone."

"The homeless man?" Hana asked, her eyebrows pulling together.

"You know him?"

"I know the case." Hana looked over her shoulder and pulled the door almost shut. Lowering her voice, she continued. "We've all been talking about it. Complete and utter exsanguination."

"Huh?"

"Total blood loss. And I mean total. Eventually, when someone dies from blood loss, their heart stops pumping, and blood loss slows. Not in this case. The blood was gone."

"But...." Mina stopped herself before saying that there had been a lot of blood, focusing on a spot on the floor. She glanced up at Hana again. "But that's horrible. How would something like that happen?"

"No idea." Hana shrugged. "Why do you think I don't talk about work much?" She shifted to stand with her arms crossed, and Mina saw her sister-in-law's cheeks flush and heard the trip of her heartbeat.

"Sorry."

Hana turned around and shuffled the papers on the nearest desk. "Somebody needs to speak for the dead." An awkward silence followed until Mina shifted her stance. Hana looked at her. 'I know...you need to go. But come by. Dale worries."

Mina nodded, and then left, walking back along the corridor of the dead, remembering she needed to become one of them to her family.

SEEMA STREAKED THROUGH the waking city. Every building had its hidden entries and exits, and she'd found a hole big enough she could slip out of the vaulted mausoleum of a building the Athanatos called home. Dodging pre-dawn delivery vans and garbage trucks, she made her way back to the warehouse by the river.

The blade of the Even Star. It had been a very long time since she'd heard that spoken of, even longer since it was done in anything more than whispers. *Do these humans know of what they speak?* Even the words held power, deep and inky and stealthy, like the nighttime river waiting to pull you down into its depths. She paused as a spine-rattling, body-shaking shiver passed through her.

A weapon that could slice a soul from its body, leaving both alive, if one could call it that: the body an empty shell to do Night's bidding and the soul trapped in the blade, giving it strength it fed to Night.

Seema started walking again, without a destination. She'd heard rumours of the blade from her ancient great-grandfather when she was a kit sitting at his knee as he lifted his face to the sun, gazing at the sky with eyes that could no longer see and absorbing the warm rays into gnarled bones. But the adults around her had dismissed the tales as the ravings of a senile, old man, as they turned and whispered amongst themselves, their faces pale in the shadows. Seema shook her head to dispel the fogginess of memory. What she remembered from the old man's stories was contradictory. It was a piece of the vault of Night, splintered off by one of her followers. Or by Night herself as she tried to resist being imprisoned. Or it was the lock to her prison, keeping it sealed like a linchpin. Or it was the key to opening her cage.

Seema crept along an alley, keeping to the dark side, though there wasn't really a light side at this time of day. Whatever the blade was, it boded evil. And Mike had known, if she had listened. She hadn't paid attention to him in the last weeks of his

A PLAGUE OF SHADOWS   149

life, but she cast her memory back, trying to remember what he'd said. She went back even further, peeling away the safeguards she'd put between her past and her present. *If there's the Evening Star, maybe there's the sliver of the Moon. And the blade of the Sun. A triumvirate of deadly power.* She sighed. According to her history lessons, the blade of the Sun was lost, along with that of Night. But the blade of the Moon...Seema growled and stopped her ramblings. *I have none of these, nor hands to wield them.*

She huffed into the cold air. She wasn't kitted out for a quest. Once again, she cursed her cat-sized body. She spat and hissed and imagined herself a tiger. *Not a tiger, a tigress.* She growled, baring her teeth. *No, not a tigress but a human warrior with long, curved swords in each hand.* She arched her back and yowled, then collapsed as the tension left her. It was no use, she remained cat-sized and handless. She was no tigress, not even a human warrior, just a cat whose only weapons were her claws.

Coming to a crossroads, she glanced left to make sure the coast was clear – there were unnatural things that hid in the alleys. Then she turned right, intent on heading back to the Sanctuary, where a least one of its residents was happy to have her around, and live the rest of her life as a cat. Looking around to get her bearings, she realized she was in St. Frank's square. Mike's favourite haunt. Outside the church of the kind priest.

Seema sat down and stared at the spot where Mike had died...where he'd been murdered by with the Messenger of Night. Her whiskers twitched, and her tail flipped back and forth. She knew then she couldn't just abandon the fight, weaponless and clueless as she was. She would go on, for his sake, do what she could as a cat, and hope an answer presented itself.

She knew little of dark magic, but for Night to break her bonds, the magic would need to be dark indeed. A sacrifice was needed. The prescribed ritual, whatever it was, would need to be performed just so. At the right time: maybe at dawn, or at dusk, when the scrim between the worlds was at its thinnest. At the right place: a river bank maybe, or a cemetery, somewhere the worlds were close together.

The one thing she could do was find the blade of the Moon. She had no idea where to start. But she knew who might.

Angelos.

CHAPTER TWENTY-ONE

MINA EXHALED SHARPLY through her nose, trying to dislodge the scent of the hospital, and glanced at her phone. Still no answer from Cam. She'd tried calling and texting so much she felt like a stalker, but her messages went unanswered. She looked up at the building opposite. From here, she could see that there were no lights on in their apartment. Of course, there were lots of things Cam could be doing in there that didn't need light.

Bypassing the perennially broken elevator, she took the stairs two at a time. When she reached the apartment, she pressed her palms to the door and closed her eyes. No heartbeat, no breathing.

No Cam. Mina let her breath out and unlocked the door. She'd been hoping Cam would be home and she wouldn't need to figure out what to do next. She flicked on the light switch even though it was unnecessary. Something rustled under her foot as she stepped into the entry. Bending down, she picked up an envelope and tore it open: final notice of overdue rent.

The afghan lay folded on the back of the couch, almost as if it hadn't been moved since the night she'd gone to the hospital wondering what the hell was wrong with her. But they hadn't had a cure for vampirism. Her fingers disturbed a layer of dust as she ran her fingers along the top of the hand-me-down TV that her brother had given them, despite their lack of cable. Mina glanced into Cam's room. The bed was unmade, but that was normal and didn't signify that Cam had used it recently. The room smelled like a dorm and the floor was strewn with medical textbooks interspersed with a couple of bodice rippers. Still, the place felt lifeless.

Mina went into the bathroom with the now empty duffel she'd brought back from the Sanctuary. She tossed a bottle of face wash into the bag, then raised her hand to open the medicine cabinet. Her fingers stopped a shade shy of the mirror. She studied the face that looked back at her. Paler, smoother, more angular. Not the face she'd seen in the same mirror a month ago. Mostly it was the eyes; there was a hardness, a sadness. The eyes of a predator. A killer, even if a reluctant one.

Mina opened the cabinet door, swinging the mirror away with a little more force than intended. Studying the contents, she realized she didn't need any of it in her new life.

Closing the cabinet while avoiding the mirror, she went to her bedroom and stuffed more clothes, art supplies and a box of photos into the duffel. She crammed in a pair of boots then took a look around the room.

I need to come back again before my 'death', Mina thought, though she knew she'd need to leave most of it behind: you can't take it with you.

Looking at her bed, she had a yearning well up inside to crawl in, to pull the covers over her head and not come out for a couple of days.

"No, I'm on a mission," she said to the shadows. Sighing deeply, she dug through her desk for the cheque book she only ever used for rent, and wrote out three months' worth, to give Cam some time to find a new roommate after her 'death', then she slung her duffel over her shoulder and headed out the door, pausing to look back as she turned off the light. Her brows knitted together. *What should I do now? If Cam's in trouble, not just avoiding me, what would* she *do?* Her family was out of the question, and Mina knew few of her other friends. But she did know one.

"Maybe Sam knows where you are." A flicker of nerves passed through Mina's abdomen. Sam had kept the existence of this world of vampires, gargoyles, Were creatures, and who knows what else, from her. And now she was bound up in it.

AS SHE STEPPED OUT of the building, with the strap of the over-full duffel digging into her shoulder, her phone pinged that she had a text, but it wasn't the right tone for Cam, Sam or Dale. After a few seconds of debating, she dropped the bag in the middle of the sidewalk, causing cursing from those who had to go around her, and pulled out her phone. Looking at the message and the sender, she frowned.

Dar. Talk to Sam. Ask about blade rumours. She got that Dar was kind of her new boss, but that didn't mean she liked him ordering her around.

Relegated to messenger girl. She sighed. But it was where she wanted to go anyway, and there was no point in changing her plans just to spite Dar. She heaved the duffel back onto her shoulder and stepped into the crosswalk. The shop was closing soon, so she hurried as fast as her overladen bag would let her. But the butterflies in her stomach grew in size and intensity as she got closer. Part of her knew it wasn't fair to judge Sam for not telling her about vampires and werewolves and other creatures of the netherworld. She would have laughed in his face and asked what drugs he was on, despite knowing he'd never touch the stuff after what he'd been through with his father. Still, she'd shut him out since becoming a vampire.

Standing at the edge of the window, she looked through the glass, hidden by the notices of art installations, concerts and one-person plays. Sure enough, the shop was empty. Except for Sam, who was going through his pre-closing rituals.

He glanced up when the bell chimed to announce the door opening.

"Hey," she said, stopping at the threshold. "Am I allowed in?"

He stopped what he was doing to stare at her. "My shop's certainly not blessed. You can come and go as you please."

She stepped into the shop and dropped her duffel just inside.

He nodded at the bag. "Unless you're planning on moving in."

She shrugged a shoulder. "Transferring stuff from old life to new." She glanced at her hands as she rubbed them together. "So...how's things? Haven't seen you around the Sanctuary lately." She looked back at him, her cheeks flushing as she remembered her first exposure to vampire feeding. "Well, not since the one time."

"Anyone who wants to see me knows where to find me." He went back to sorting through a stack of papers. "If you're going to stay, mind locking the door?"

Mina did as he asked, also turning off the Open sign.

"Did you want a drink?" he asked.

Mina spun around. Sam had pulled out a bottle of Widow Jane and a pair of shot glasses.

A PLAGUE OF SHADOWS   155

He stopped, bottle in one hand, glasses in another, and raised an eyebrow. "A drink of a different kind could be arranged, though I might not be your poison of choice."

She gave him a half smile. "No, thanks. I already ate." She glanced at the bottle. "I don't think I've had anything to drink, other than...." She tilted her head. "Since the ill-advised consumption of bagel and coffee just after I was turned, when I thought I had the flu."

"Some flu."

"Yeah."

"Maybe just a taste?" He waggled the bottle. "It'd be a sad fate indeed if you could never wet your palate with a fine bourbon. And it would be cruel to make me drink alone."

"Maybe a smidge."

Sam carefully poured a finger for her and two for himself. He stuck his nose in the glass and sighed, then took a sip, coating his mouth before swallowing. She took a wary sip, waiting for her stomach to protest.

"No Paul? He usually works the late shift on Friday." Mina tried a bit more of the liquor.

Sam shook his head. "Fired him."

"Really? What finally made you snap?"

"You actually." He twirled his glass around and watched the legs flow back down.

"What, you were afraid I'd make him an appetizer?"

He tilted his head and smirked. "No, before I knew about you. He was a good tattoo artist."

"If you say so."

Sam raised his glass. "But not good enough to put up with the crudeness, the sexism, the disrespect."

"Do you have someone to take his place?"

"Since I don't suppose I can get you to moonlight...daylight, whatever." Sam poured himself another finger. "Do you know Nicole?"

"You mean Nicole Nicole? The familiar?" Sam nodded. Mina's mind flashed back once again to her first feeding as a vampire, to dark hair, red lips and smooth legs. She licked the liquor from her lips. "Yeah, kinda." She nodded, looking away from Sam as her cheeks flushed.

"So what brings you here?" he asked, putting the cap back on the bottle. "I don't imagine you were just walking by lugging that monstrous bag."

There were so many answers to his question that Mina settled on one she hadn't thought of until that second. "I need a totem, some kind of spirit tattoo."

"Really?" His left eyebrow lifted.

Mina made a face. "It's what all the cool vamps are doing."

Sam tipped his chin down to peer at her over his glasses.

"Okay, maybe I just think it's time for a new tattoo."

"And you trust me enough for that?"

Mina glanced at the wall of happy customers, then looked back at him. "I've trusted you with my flesh before, nothing to change that now."

"What are you thinking of?"

Mina shrugged. "Not sure."

"So that's not really why you're here then."

Mina slouched a little. "Dar also wanted me to swing by, ask you about a riddle."

"Time."

"What?"

A PLAGUE OF SHADOWS   157

"Riddles. The answer's always time."

"Not that kind of riddle. One of Rhys' riddles. And to ask if you've heard rumours from your less than human clientele."

"OK, shoot."

"Something about a dark blade unlocking the prison of Night. Wait, I have it in my phone." Mina reached into her jacket pocket.

"Don't worry about it." Sam shook his head. "I think I'd have remembered something like that. Though send me the riddle; I like puzzles." He put the papers he'd been sorting in the lock box. "But right now, I gotta go. I'm meeting someone."

"Really, who?" Mina smiled at him as she spun on her stool. She hoped he was becoming less unlucky in love.

"None of your business." Sam put on his coat and packed up his shoulder bag. "Not until I know he's going to become my business."

Mina stopped spinning, getting to the crux of her visit before he could leave. "I was wondering if you'd seen Cam around. She's not at the apartment, and she's not answering my texts."

Sam unlocked the door again and ushered Mina out, waiting for her to re-shoulder her duffel, before re-locking it behind him. "Sorry. If I see her, I'll let you know."

He wrapped his arms around her. "I'm glad you came by." Mina hugged him back, then watched him walk away. She pulled out her phone and frowned. Nothing. She looked up, wondering what next.

Her eyes fell on one of the flyers in the window. The travelling exhibition visiting the museum. Cam was a docent there, among her other type-A hobbies, with a particular interest in

Mesoamerican archeology. And, as Mina recalled, Mesoamerican archaeologists.

Mina started in the direction of the museum, then stopped and raised her arm to flag a cab. *Drop off the really heavy, awkward duffel first then go on the quest to find the missing girl.*

IN A DARK CORNER BETWEEN one dimly lit exhibition hall and the next, Mina paused, pressing herself back against the wall. She closed her eyes, shutting out the crowds. Despite being near closing time, the museum was still full of people pressing to see the green and gold grave goods of the travelling Mesoamerican exhibit before they were moved to the next museum in the tour.

Her ears twitched as she tried to tease out the heartbeats and the voices, searching the chorus for the sound of Cam. But there were too many people, all jumbled together. And she was thirsty again. She knew she needed to feed regularly, but it was still a part of her life she hadn't gotten used to. At least when Brett wasn't around to provide both entertainment and sustenance.

Her heart skipped a beat and her head spun as a couple pushed their way past her. She shrunk back even further, against the solid wall, into the dim shadows. The museum was Cam's place. Although Mina appreciated the artistry and technique behind the items on display, she preferred the art gallery, with its light, its tall ceilings, and its sleek lines.

Still, she breathed deeply, sucking in the unique scent of the museum, like a library but with less must and more arsenic. The smell of an old friend she'd neglected for too long, given her

A PLAGUE OF SHADOWS 159

favouritism for the art gallery. What her nose didn't pick up was any thread of lavender and rosemary.

She opened her eyes. She'd have to look for Cam the old-fashioned way. She moved into the next room, her steps unsteady as her stomach turned queasy at the crush of people. Every once in a while, she got up on tiptoes to see above the crowd as she skirted the edges of the room.

"Damn people," she muttered.

"Mina?" A hand landed on her shoulder. "Right?"

She coiled her muscles and spun her head to glare at the hand's owner. One hand grasped his, while the other went behind her, under her jacket, to the gun pressed into the small of her back that she'd easily gotten past museum security to her chagrin.

A middle-aged man with a broad smile, wide cheeks and a docent's jacket stood there, unaware of how near he'd been to having a finger broken at the very least.

"Cam's friend?"

"Right." Mina's muscles relaxed and her hand dropped to her side, but her nerves stayed on edge. "Sorry, I've forgotten your name."

"No reason you should remember me. But you, the pictures you drew of our Nike, with just a ballpoint pen, sitting on the floor in front of her. Well, that made an impression."

Mina canted her head, a shadow of a smile passing over her lips. "Thanks, I guess." She scanned the lines of people trying to peer over each other at the artifacts. "Hey, I was actually wondering if Cam was in. The woman at the front couldn't tell me." She ran her tongue along the top of her palate, trying to scratch the itch in her inner ear.

"Wouldn't, more likely. No, I haven't seen Cam all this week, sorry. I'm guessing she's busy with studying. I'm amazed she finds time to come here at all."

"You and me both."

"But look what she's missing out on." He swept his hands over the crowd. "Once in a lifetime, this. They discovered the tomb, expecting nothing, or worse everything jumbled by grave robbers, half gone, the rest broken. And then this, the New World's King Tut."

"Yeah, amazing." Mina paused a few seconds then held out her hand. "Look, thanks...."

The man took it and gave her another beaming smile. "Graeme."

"Graeme. If you see Cam, can you let her know I'm looking for her?"

"Will do."

Mina started to turn back the way she'd come, sighing at the thought of fighting the crowd again. She shrugged her shoulders and stuck her elbows out.

Graeme's hand fell on her arm again. "No, no, no. You've come this far. You at least need to see the crowning glory of the exhibit." He turned her towards the next room. Mina realized there was no way out without making a fuss, and this direction she'd be flowing with the crowd rather than fighting against it. She gave Graeme a crooked smile and headed into the room.

Before she even stepped over the threshold, she saw what all the fuss was about. A fearsome creature of green and gold rose in the centre of the room. Atop the form of a man sat the jade head of a jaguar – an elaborately carved mask. Cascading down the torso were alternating tiles of gold and beads of jade. Jade tiles

A PLAGUE OF SHADOWS 161

covered the thighs, giving way to golden greaves. It was a thing of beauty, if not practicality. Mina held her breath in awe and let herself be carried by the tide of people.

She gasped. Her hand went to her chest as her pulse quickened. Her breathing grew shallow. Though this room was as crowded as the last, the voices of the crowd became muted as they entered. As if they sensed what she did: something evil lurked here.

Mina glanced around but couldn't pinpoint the source of the sensation. She closed her eyes, canting her head, listening for a sound that wasn't there before. Nothing obvious bubbled to the surface. She twisted her head back and forth, thinking for a moment that she caught a whisper underneath the voices, but then it was gone. She opened her eyes again and scanned the faces around her. Whatever it was, it wasn't something she'd come across before. All her senses told her it wasn't a vampire. But her gut was equally certain that it was wicked.

But her gut had led her astray in the past. It had led her to invite Luca home. But nothing presented itself, and she decided the trifecta of worry, stress and hunger were causing her to imagine things. Then the crowd parted, revealing a dark object that glinted malevolently in the spotlights, as if sentient. The prickling sensation turned to needles jabbing in her spine, and a wave of nausea coursed through her.

The hungry object tugged at her, as if it wanted her near so it could swallow her body and soul. She examined it without stepping any closer even though it took all her will. A sluggish heartbeat pulsed from it, throbbing in her ears, then the whisper became a wail, as if all the lives it had taken were locked inside it.

It was a blade, wavy like a serpent, about the length of her forearm, pommel to tip, with another impression of a dagger inlaid in silver on the hilt. And it was black as night.

"Obsidian," Mina whispered. Despite every fibre of her being protesting, she knew what she was looking at. *The blade of Night.*

CHAPTER TWENTY-TWO

THE FACETED BLADE SANG a siren's song, drawing Mina in with its tales of long-ago feasts, of gorging on delicious, bloody death seasoned to perfection by fear. An inkling of raw power and brazen desire coursed through her blood like ichor, causing her head to spin and her skin to flush. Her lips parted, her stomach twisted, and she took a step forward.

The wall of people closed, blocking the blade from sight, cutting off its song. This left an echo of the voices that cried underneath the luring melody...and a sick feeling in her gut. Mina sucked in a ragged breath and rubbed her sweaty palms down her thighs. The wave of nausea, mixed with that dark desire, slowly abated but didn't disappear entirely.

The flow of people ebbed again, exposing her once more to the blade and its seductive song. Mina closed her eyes for a second to fight the heady dizziness that pulsed through her. Without the blade in sight, its music was muted to a whisper of wails that spoke of tortured histories. Her eyes tearing up, she forced them open so she wouldn't cry. Exposed to the anguished histories woven into the song, Mina found that the sick yearning passed, and now she just felt nauseous.

She hugged herself, running her hands down her arms. Stepping back into the shadows, she pressed against the wall, as far from the blade as she could get, and willed herself invisible to its malevolent influence.

She glanced at the faces around her, expecting grimaces of revulsion, or askance glances of trepidation at the very least. But most ignored it entirely as they jockeyed to get closer to the star attraction – the green and gold funereal armour. And those that did stop stepped right up to the blade, canted their heads as they read the interpretive plaque, and peered casually into its soul-searing facets. Mina took a half step forward, wanting to reach out and pull them away.

But they turned away of their own accord, switching their focus to the glittering armour. And Mina recognized that there was nothing she could actually do here. It wasn't like she could steal the blade, even if the thought of touching it didn't make her skin itch. She needed to tell the others, and let more senior vampires, with longer histories of being nefarious, figure out how to deal with this evil artifact.

She turned to go back the way she'd come, an effort of will given that the blade still called to her even as it repulsed her. But she focused on her revulsion and focused on the idea of getting back to the Sanctuary to tell the others. She wove her way through the crowd, looking ahead to find the path of least resistance.

Mina stopped so suddenly the person behind her bumped into her, when she saw a face she recognized through a gap in the crowd. Blond hair framing a handsome but bland face. *The other priest.* Father Mark, the one who'd worked with Father Pietro. He was standing at the transition between the two halls, staring through the crowd at the blade, his expression placid, seemingly as unaffected by it as everyone else. Except for his utter focus.

Maybe his holy orders protect him? Mina thought. *What's a priest doing at an exhibit of Aztec artifacts, and so soon after his col-*

league's death? Then she shook her head, reminding herself that priests were people too, and she had no idea what was going on in his mind.

Maybe he's into Mesoamerican archaeology. Or maybe, like Cam, he's into Mesoamerican archaeologists.

As she chided herself for her irreverence, she watched the priest get bumped by someone jostling to get a better look at the suit of jade and gold. His eyes passed over Mina's corner as he looked at the little grey-haired lady with her purple hat. Out of instinct, Mina pressed further back into the shadows. For a second, as his gaze flicked over her, his blue eyes turned black.

Eyes of obsidian. A shudder passed through Mina. If she looked into those eyes long enough, she'd be consumed by them, sucked into a morass of malevolence. Her head reeled, and her stomach clenched as she pulled herself along the wall towards the exit, the song in her blood sounding an alarm.

EVERY TENDON IN HIS body tensed, every muscle contracted, and every nerve tingled. It was like he vibrated. Yet Angelos stood stock still, caught in the rigours of pleasure caused by the mere sight of the artifact. He recognized a kindred spirit as soon as he saw it and knew he'd found what he was searching for. Or rather, he knew it as soon as he heard it: the sweet symphony of souls entombed in glinting stone. He could hear all the voices it had enslaved crying out. The old woman hadn't been lying in the end.

With this blade, he would give Night back her voice, with the correct words, the right ritual, and the proper sacrifice. He imagined how pleased she'd be when he freed her, quashing the thought of her wroth at being imprisoned for so long. A shiver ran across his skin, puckering the follicles into goosebumps. *But we've all suffered.*

A stooped old woman bumped into him, clumsily crushing his foot with her ridiculous cane as she pushed forward with the other sheep trying to get close to the shiny green and gold relics. He turned to glare at her, imagining all the things he could do to her to make her pay. His cheeks flushed. Then he looked up, remembering the people. He relaxed his face into blandness, letting go of his immediate desire for revenge, while holding the last image of torture in his mind, allowing it to placate him. Soon he'd be able to kill openly, but not yet. Still, he let his hand glance over her elbow as she passed, and a ghost of a smile returned to his features as he watched her double over, coughing into the handle of her cane. *Not enough to kill, but enough to maim.*

Kian stepped up beside him as he turned back to the blade, pretending to read the placard as he assessed the security.

"Do you want me to kill her?" Kian said, her voice husky with either longing or hunger, or some other emotion Angelos didn't care about.

However, he paused for a second at the thought, then shook his head. "No, we have work to do. Like figuring out how to relieve the museum of its dagger."

Just then the announcement came over the PA: the museum would close in 15 minutes. He took a half step forward towards the blade and its breakable glass case, then stopped, remembering the crowd. If only there weren't so many people, if there were just a handful, he could corral more magic from the shadows to muddle their minds. Or if he'd been flesh for longer, he could

A PLAGUE OF SHADOWS 167

cloak his voice in the richness of the dark and enthrall them. Or better yet, he could just set the wolf upon the sheep, and snatch the blade. As it was, he needed another plan.

He turned to the man in the blue jacket. "Excuse me, is there a restroom nearby?"

The man pointed. "If you go straight, then turn...." At that moment, a loud clanging started, causing Kian to bristle beside him, her head turning sharply, her hands coming to her ears. Angelos craned his neck in an attempt to crack it and relieve the tight spot on the left. He huffed, disgruntled at being subjected to the human frailty of this body he'd appropriated.

"Everyone, can I have your attention?" the docent said, raising his voice above the worried murmur and the raucous alarms. "I need you to exit in an orderly manner."

"What's wrong?" the woman with the ridiculous cane and absurd purple hat asked.

"Nothing," the man said. "Just some punk kids, happens sometimes, but we still need to go through the process."

Angelos took a step back, realizing the opportunity: he could find a dark corner and wait for the museum to clear. Then a hand fell on his shoulder. His eyes slid over to the offending fingers, and he envisioned it diseased and desiccated, festering, then rotting, then withering away until it was dust.

"Exit's this way," the docent said, taking his hand away as he pointed ahead. Away from the dagger.

The woman with the cane turned to Angelos, placing a hand on his forearm, the firmness of its grip belying her age. "Could you show me the way out? My old brain gets so turned about."

A bolt a lavender energy course through Angelos' arm, and he gritted his teeth under tight lips. "Witch," he muttered. Her eyes glinted as they peered at him, a look of innocence on her face. He could break her hold, or break her hand, but that might cause a scene he didn't want tonight. He glanced back at the object, snug under its glass enclosure. The dagger wasn't going anywhere.

"Come on, let's go," he said to Kian. The woman with the cane released her grip but trailed close behind as he and the werewolf followed the herd of sheep out the door. "I'll find her later and break her neck."

WALLOWING IN HIS FRUSTRATION, consumed with seething anger, it took Angelos a few minutes to realize that he was being followed. In the end, it was Kian turning her head and sniffing at the night air that alerted him.

Not good, to be so lost in my own head.

He slowed his pace, relaxed his shoulders, and opened his eyes and ears. And tuned into his sixth sense, the worm that niggled at his gut and wriggled through his blood.

Vampire. Though he wasn't strictly one of them, his blood still tingled when one was near, a pleasant effervescence. A gentle warning. He wondered what this one would taste like.

Female. The cadence of the heel strikes spoke of broader hips and a lower centre of gravity.

Dracul. She had enough sense to realize he'd slowed down, but not enough to realize the danger she was in. He saw Kian's hand slip inside her jacket, to her sacrum, where he knew a bowie knife lay.

A PLAGUE OF SHADOWS 169

"Why are you following me?" he said without turning, but his hand reached for the hilt of the short, curved dagger Kian had procured for him.

CHAPTER TWENTY-THREE

WITH AN INTAKE OF BREATH, the footsteps stopped, but that was the only sign that his pursuer heard him.

When no response was forthcoming, Angelos turned to face her. "When I ask a question, I expect an answer." He focused on the woman, and realized he knew her though he'd only seen her the once. He'd been preoccupied and hadn't gotten a good look. But it was her, the hair, the curves, the black leather.

"Is it enough to say you intrigue me?" she said, taking a step closer, her eyes glancing at Kian, who shifted to keep the woman in the best attack position.

He didn't answer her question. "How did you find me?"

Her shoulders lifted in a shrug. "I was out. Looking for vampires." She sighed, her lips pulling into a fake pout inviting him to ask her more.

He ignored the invitation. "That doesn't answer my question," he said instead as his mind mapped out the ways he could use her. A spy, a release, a sacrifice.

She shrugged. "I found you instead." Her eyes travelled down to the broken concrete, then returned to him. She tilted her head back an inch, exposing a part of her throat. "You crossed my path, and I decided you were a more interesting quarry."

"A more dangerous one." He didn't move as she took another step forward, shifting herself away from Kian. The woman knew enough to recognize a wolf in woman's clothing and be wary.

"Maybe I like a little danger," she said, an eyebrow raising.

"So you disobeyed orders to follow me?" He pulled himself up to this body's full height so he could peer down at her. "What does that say about your loyalty?"

"That it's earned." Her lips snarled as she spoke, then she stepped so they were toe to toe.

"You're intriguing yourself," he said, grabbing her arms. "What's your name?"

She tipped her face up and back, looking him in the eye as she pressed against him. "You can call me Em."

The priest's body responded. *Release it is.*

FROM HIS PERCH ON THE top floor of the abandoned warehouse, Angelos gazed over the water, towards downtown. The window where he stood was open to the night, the glass having been broken long before he'd found the place, and the wind tickled the fine hair on his legs, travelling up to his crotch and across his chest before lifting the blond-brown strands on his head. He wished this man had been less Teutonic, but slowly he'd remould this body into a more pleasing aspect, one that Night would appreciate.

A boat slued through the water. He tracked its path before returning to peer at the jumble of skyscrapers and old buildings. The museum was downtown. The blade was over there, in that constellation of light, shrouded in artificial brightness instead of its natural darkness. The object of his desire.

As if on cue, a moan rose behind him, drifting from his makeshift bed to the open window. His unexpected meeting with the vampire Em had temporarily slaked his human hunger, ameliorating his mood. And it had opened up some new possibilities to get what he needed for the Letting of Blood ritual, without shedding his own. Because the blade on its own was just a blade.

Although he ached to hold the dagger in his hand, to feel the power of the Even Star course through his veins and get that much closer to the heart of Night, it was safe where it was, under glass and layers of security.

He needed the vessel, which he'd found. But he needed to figure out how to procure it without marring it. Night would not be happy if it were damaged.

And then there was the sacrifice. That was still an enigma. The riddles were dense and unclear. But he knew not just any sacrifice would do. So he might as well leave the blade where it was for now.

A rustle rose behind him. Followed by a squeak.

Too bad she won't suffice as a sacrifice. Angelos turned around to where Em lay on the incongruous sofa that somehow still sat, clean and dry, in the otherwise empty space. Knees pulled to her firm breasts, back pressed into the arm, her golden hair cascaded over her shoulders and her skin glowed in the dim light from the window, glistening with perspiration from his vigorous exercise of her body, though surprisingly she'd held her own.

Not my type, but she'll do for now.

He looked from her to the creature that crouched beside her, sniffing at her. One of his exquisite gargoyles, the cause of her exclamation and current cowering. Its grey skin absorbed what little light there was while its eyes shone like two black stars in a

A PLAGUE OF SHADOWS 173

desolate night. And one hand held something that dripped on the concrete.

Angelos sighed and strode towards it. It pulled up and stepped back as he neared, towering over him by at least a head. He grasped the carcass, still twitching, from the creature as its lips tightened and its nostrils flared.

"How many times do I have to tell you: don't bring your kills up here." He turned and walked back to the window and tossed the thing – the rabbit – out. It splashed as it hit the water. Angelos noted that it had started to rain, the wet drops landing on his bare feet.

The creature chuffed a few times then slumped its shoulders.

"Where are the others?" he asked without turning. The gargoyle huffed as it stepped up beside him. Out the corner of his eye, he saw it jerk its chin towards the ceiling as a growl rose low in its throat. He heard a skitter of stones overhead. "On the rooftop?" Although the gargoyles had no trouble scaling walls and clambering over scaffolding, they were distrustful of stairs. Only this one had mastered the climb. The others needed to get over it.

Something I can help them with, Angelos thought, staring at the spot where the rabbit had entered the water. *Learn or die.*

"Go." Angelos stepped away from the window. "Bring them tomorrow night to the cemetery." The gargoyle cocked its head, eyes narrowing as the dull gears in its brain churned through the words. "Where I found you."

The creature nodded then loped off towards the stairs, stopping to stare at Em, who had stood up. Its growl turned to a purr, causing Em to pull her clothes to her chest.

"Those things give me the jitters," she said as she tugged her pants on, struggling to get them up over her sweat-sheened skin. Leaning against the window frame, he watched her as she bent to put her boots on. She dropped her bra and underwear onto the jacket at her feet then picked up her sweater, sticking her arms into the sleeves as she stood up. She was pulling it over her head when he stepped up behind her.

"Why are you getting dressed?" he said, running a finger down the side of her still naked torso, the hem of the tight sweater stuck at the top of her breasts.

She paused for a moment, goosebumps raising on her flesh, then pulled the sweater down. "I figured we were done. For now." She looked at him over her shoulder, pressing back into him. "Unless there's something more you wanted from me."

He smiled and twined a lock of her hair around his finger. "No," he said, letting the hair fall. He saw the look of worry before the fire rose in her eyes, her lips set in a hard line, and she turned to stride out of the room, stretching her long legs to their full extent. "But I do need your help with something." She stopped but didn't look back. He walked up behind her, taking all her hair in his fist, twisting it around his hand and pulling back. "I'd suggest not walking away from me until I tell you that you can go." When she didn't respond, he continued. "I need to acquire a vessel." He brought his lips close to her neck and lowered his voice. "And find a sacrifice."

CHAPTER TWENTY-FOUR

MINA PUSHED THE FLYER into Dar's face. She'd told him about the blade, and its haunted song, and all he did was stare at her, his ancient face unchanging. She'd shown him the flyer, but he'd barely glanced at it. So she shoved it at him.

"What makes you think this thing is the Blade of Night, or whatever Rhys called it?" Dar asked as he took a step back, an eyebrow arching. "What do you know that the rest of us don't?"

"Look at it," she said, her voice wavering. As he stared at her, an aftershock of nausea hit her just looking at the picture. She could see the glint of malevolent sentience she'd felt standing in front of it. She turned to the others, but they were all deferring to him...Bee, Adeh, Sha, even Jack. Rain dripped off her hair onto the paper. "If you'd seen it in person, you'd know." She lowered the flyer. "If you had felt it...that thing, it pulls at you, like it's sunk tendrils into your soul. It whispers to you, drawing you closer." Her voice dropped low. "Then it sings of torture and pain."

She blinked and shook her head, trying to banish the twisted melody. "Besides, he was there."

"Who?" Dar asked. "Matteo?"

Mina frowned, realizing this was another thing he wouldn't believe. "The priest."

"Father Pietro's dead," Jack said, his tone flat. A look passed between him and Dar.

Mina cocked her head. "Don't worry. I'm not seeing dead people. It was the other priest. The blond one." She squinted her eyes, as if trying to puzzle out some pattern in the wall over Dar's shoulder. "He looked different," she said, her voice falling almost to a whisper. She returned her gaze to Dar. "But it was definitely him."

"So? He was probably just enjoying the exhibit," Dar said, his tone even.

"Just into Mesoamerican archaeology?" Mina shook her head.

"Or—" he started.

Mina interrupted him. "That's what I thought, at first, but there was...something, I don't know, wrong about him." In her mind, she saw a pair of eyes shining like glass, dark as night. She looked around the group. Crossed arms and slight frowns met her. She crossed her own arms, pulling her shoulders back. "If you don't believe me, go see for yourself. That blade is evil, as much as a thing can be."

"Oh, things can be evil," Dar said. He was silent for a minute, gazing at her, as if judging her sanity. Her lips tightened, getting ready for a fight. Then without taking his eyes off her, he turned his head towards Bee. "Bee, this afternoon, go with her, check out this blade."

"I can go," Jack offered.

Dar shook his head. "No, I want you to go see Rhys." Another one of their inscrutable looks passed between them.

"Why can't you go see Rhys?" Bee asked, eying Mina. "Then he can go to the museum, and I can do something else...anything else." Mina glared at Bee, though the woman had turned her attention to Dar.

"I'm busy," he said, holding Bee's gaze for a minute before turning on his heels and walking away.

RHYS TOOK A STEP BACK when he opened the door. "Jack, I, I didn't expect you." He coughed into his elbow before peering around Jack as he wiped his nose with a handkerchief. "How can I help you?" He paused. "Is Dar alright?"

"He's fine...at the moment," Jack said, wondering if Rhys could read the hesitation in his words. "Can I come in?"

"Oh, yes, sorry." Rhys stepped back to make way. His grey cat hissed at Jack from its perch on the pile of papers stacked on top of the desk.

"Mina says she's found the blade."

"Really?" Rhys took his glasses off and cleaned them with the sleeve of his sweater.

"At the museum." Jack handed him the flyer Mina had brought, drawing his hand back as the cat jumped into Rhys' lap, keeping its eyes on him.

"Why doesn't Dar come and ask me himself?" Rhys gave the flyer a cursory glance.

"Too busy for an old man?" He went back to cleaning his glasses, alternating holding them up to the light and attacking them with the sleeve again. "I have a life beyond being his worn-out, decrepit research assistant."

"Unless you've gotten significantly older and more decrepit in the last few months—" Jack sniped, responding to Rhys' mood, then stopped as a worm of worry gnawed at his guts. "You haven't, have you?"

"Excuse me?" Rhys stopped cleaning his glasses and put them on to peer at him.

"Sorry, I mean, you're okay, right? It's just, your cough—"

"Why, are you afraid you'd have to search the interwebs yourself?"

"You know it's not the interwebs, right?" Rhys just looked at him over his glasses. Jack stared down at his hands and sighed, his shoulders heaving. "That's not what I'm afraid of." He met Rhys' gaze. "I'm afraid for Dar."

Jack waited for Rhys to respond, but the man held his breath for a long few seconds then let it all out in a sigh and slumped in his chair, releasing the tension Jack had felt since arriving. The cat kneaded Rhys' thighs; the old man ran his hand down the creature's back. "You and me both."

They sat in contemplative silence for a minute, the cat settling into Rhys' lap, having made its temporary peace with Jack. Rhys adjusted his glasses and peered at the flyer. "Hmm, I can go take a look at this thing." He glanced up at Jack. "I think we both know our Mina is different. Maybe she senses something no one else does."

Jack swallowed and clenched his jaw. "What do you mean, different?"

Rhys stared at him, an eyebrow raised. "You'd know better than I."

"I don't know what you're talking about," Jack said, forcing his voice to be even.

"If you say so." Rhys put the flyer down on his desk. "On to old news then, I've searched and I've delved. There's no way to stop the gargoyles growing their wings."

"Their what?"

A PLAGUE OF SHADOWS

"Their wings." Rhys took his glasses off and rubbed the bridge of his nose. "Obviously, it's only a matter of time before they grow, sooner if they have someone who knows a thing or two to help them."

"Wings." Jack sat in the chair opposite Rhys, his thigh muscles clenching to keep him upright as it tilted precariously.

"Eventually yes, unless you kill them before that comes to pass." The cat started to purr as Rhys stroked it.

"We're going to have to fight those things when they can fly?"

"If you can catch them. Flight will make them harder to corner."

"Thanks for that useful piece of information." Jack envisioned the members of the conclave – his family – surrounded by taloned gargoyles swooping down to tear them apart.

"But their wings could also be a vulnerability." Rhys ran a hand down the cat's back to the end of its tail, his eyes squinting in thought.

"How?"

"If you think of them like a bird or a bat." Rhys scritched the cat between its ears when it pressed its head into his hand. "For those things to even soar, the wings need to be light. Porous bones, easy to break." The cat lifted its head and Rhys rubbed under its chin. "But then they could have razor sharp spikes at the end of each one for all we know."

Jack looked into the cat's green eyes. "So we need a weapon we can use in close combat, preferably made of solid lead, so too soft, but that will break the wings off a creature that turns to stone while not harming innocent bystanders? Easy."

"Really?" Rhys looked up from the cat.

"No, I was being facetious." Jack stood up, which ended the truce as the cat hissed and jumped off Rhys' lap, up onto a shelf behind the man, keeping its eyes trained on Jack.

"Ah, right, it's sometimes hard to tell with you." Rhys got up and showed him to the door.

"Any ideas?" Jack asked.

"Go see the Smiths?" Rhys offered. "It is their area of expertise."

"I was hoping for something other than that." Jack groaned, thinking of Finn, the Smith's daughter and a force in her own right.

MINA LOOKED ASKANCE at the black blade as the crowd in the museum swirled around her. She clasped her hands behind her back, the nails of one hand digging into the knuckles of the other. This time she'd anticipated the song of the blade and braced herself against it. Or so she'd thought. Instead it was louder, its pull stronger. She closed her eyes for a second, rocking back and forth on her feet. Her mind screamed at her to jump over the cordon, smash the glass and grab the blade, then fling it against the tile and shatter it into a million pieces, heedless of what that might unleash. But another part at the base of her skull whispered at her to take it and drive it into the nearest beating heart, just to feel the warm blood pulse over her fingers, oozing with raw power. Her stomach roiled, and she glanced sidelong at Bee, trying to gauge her reaction.

"Obsidian blade from the tomb of...I'm not even going to attempt to pronounce that...circa 1450," Bee read from the plaque,

A PLAGUE OF SHADOWS 181

then stood up straight, looking at her before continuing. "Doesn't seem like anything special. Just a blade, though I've never seen an obsidian one before."

Mina slid her gaze from Bee to the dagger and back. "Don't you feel it?"

"Feel what?" Bee returned her attention to the plaque. "Says obsidian blades could take a man's head right off. Huh." She leaned towards the blade, her nose inches from the glass.

Mina placed her hand on Bee's arm. "Don't!"

"What? The alarm's not going off." Bee looked at her. "What's got you so squirrelly?"

Mina hesitated. Jack had already told her she had senses she shouldn't, and the others in the conclave were still standoffish after she'd killed Luca. Then there was Astrid's death. But she had to try. "You're telling me you really don't feel that?" Mina glanced around the room, a little dizzy, her vision splotched with crimson stars. Everyone there looked human, but then the priest had appeared human too, and she was sure he wasn't. "You don't feel nauseous?"

"I feel a little annoyed. Tetchy even. Definitely hungry." Bee glanced over her shoulder then leaned into Mina. "In case you haven't noticed, we're surrounded by supper. And I haven't fed in a while."

"But—"

"No buts." Bee's lips tightened, and Mina glimpsed fangs in the second of sibilance at the end of her statement. "Enough. I came, I saw. Maybe this thing is the blade of riddles. More likely it's not. For all we know, the blade of the Even Star isn't even a blade. The ancients weren't all that literal in their riddles. Rhys

C. RENÉ ASTLE

will come, he'll do his research, he'll tell us for sure." Bee turned away.

Mina was reluctant to leave the thing. She told herself it was because it would leave it vulnerable to theft by darker powers. "But don't you hear them?" she blurted out, laying her hand on Bee's arm.

"Hear who? I hear the crowd, I hear their heartbeats, I hear my pulse quicken in response." Bee looked at her askance. "I'm going to find myself a drink." She turned and headed towards the exit.

Mina opened her mouth to try again then stopped...Bee was not going to listen. The woman didn't like her, and certainly didn't trust her. *Maybe if I take the blade, I could show it to her up-close, let her taste its power.* Mina sucked in a breath, inundated by a sudden vision of Bee's blood oozing over her hands. They felt so warm the sensation compelled her to look at them. Bloodless. She sighed, and took a last look at the dagger, her eyelids sliding closed under the weight of all the blade's victims, their cries penetrating her skull like a knife. Or whispering to her like a lover. She forced herself to turn away and follow Bee.

The wails rose to a crescendo, trying to call her back. She ignored them until she got to the edge of the room, when the sound became so loud it felt her ears would bleed. She glanced over her shoulder. The crowd had parted, as if giving the blade a wide berth. Or avoiding the pair that now stood in front of it.

The priest, and he has a minion. As if feeling her eyes on him, the man's head turned slowly around. Mina knew she should move, make her escape. At least duck down behind the woman with the outrageous hat, but before she could act on that thought, he was looking at her. And she had no doubt he saw her

A PLAGUE OF SHADOWS 183

and knew that she'd seen him. He leaned towards his companion, keeping his eyes on Mina, and whispered something to the woman.

Mina was rooted to the spot, her heart still telling her to run but her body not responding, as the woman turned around. As Mina took in the porcelain skin and the ice-blond hair, she recognized a sound she hadn't earlier, another song underneath the wail of the blade. *Em.*

Em saw her too, and gave her a frosty smile, her eyes sparkling like snow on a sunny day. Finally, Mina tore herself away and hurried after Bee.

CHAPTER TWENTY-FIVE

VAMPIRE. Angelos tracked the path of the woman through the press of people, as she fought against the flow of the crowd. *But not like the one beside me.* His gaze slid towards Em. Her eyes were also trained on the woman, though her face was smooth, seemingly unperturbed. Except for the tick in her jaw muscle.

"Do you know her?" he said, keeping his voice laced with boredom.

Em flashed him a brittle smile and flipped her hair. "She's a nothing. A mistake allowed to live, an error made by someone deservedly dead." She stepped closer and lowered her voice into a husky whisper, her breath brushing against his cheek. "But I can take care of her for you, if you'd like."

Angelos ignored Em, peering instead at the place the woman had been standing. He couldn't pinpoint the difference he sensed between Em and her. *Something in the set of the lips? The cant of the hips?* He shook his head. *No, it goes deeper than that. Something in her blood.*

Exhaling, he turned to the dagger, the yearning to hold it in his hand so bad his fingers twitched. A pulse throbbed in the blade; it wanted to be used. He squinted at its glinting facets, lit by all the souls trapped inside. The people around him shifted, and he glanced back at the track the woman made through the crowd. *It's something in the eyes. A glimmer of hope, faith even. I can whip that out of her.* Angelos smiled at the thought.

"No," he said out loud, shaking his head again. Em turned towards him. Even though he hadn't meant it as an answer to her, he turned it into one. "She'd make a good servant," he said.

"Her?" Em said, arms crossed across her chest, lips thin, trying – and failing – to hide her annoyance, which annoyed him, but he decided to placate her since she was still useful.

"And if not that, then a good sacrifice." He almost heard the blade vibrate in its bloodlust at the last word. Relishing the shiver of her skin under his touch, Angelos took Em's shoulders and turned her towards the woman. "We follow her, we take her." Looking sideways at Em, he saw the smile spread on her lips. "Alive." The smile fell.

"Mother of fucking pearl, when will I get to kill her?" Em headed after the woman, her jaw set.

Angelos glanced at the blade, hovering his fingertips above the glass, feeling the energy pulse from it. "I'll be back soon."

A cough beside him made him turn. The docent stood beside him, a small, round man puffed up by a false sense of importance.

Angelos smiled thinly. "Beautiful, isn't it? As if the blade were made of night itself." He lay a hand on the man's arm then stalked off after Em, leaving the docent with a hacking cough as payment for his interruption.

SEEMA CROUCHED UNDER a poor shelter, her tail flicking from side to side. She'd crept under the bench to take refuge from the dogged, misting rain and the steady cavalcade of feet that trudged up the steps to the building with the neo-ancient facade. But it also proved a decent stakeout spot: no one sat on the damp bench, given the incessant drizzle, so her view of the building was unblocked. She glared at the entrance where Angelos had disappeared. She didn't want to stay put, fearing he'd found another exit; she didn't want to move, fearing she'd miss him.

So she stared, letting the occasional low growl turn into a snarl to vent her annoyance. Luckily, the square in front of the building was too busy for the freakishly large city rats to bother her tonight. At the thought of those vermin and the bugs they carried, the skin behind her left ear began to crawl. She twitched her ear, trying to dislodge the itch. That just spread it out; she lifted her back paw and, claws half out, tried to scratch it away. With her head cocked to the side, she noticed a familiar figure come down the steps, two at a time.

The girl Mina, who took me in. Seema straightened up. *What's she doing here?* Even as a cat, she knew anywhere Angelos prowled was dangerous.

Mina bent over and pressed her hands to her knees like she was going to be sick. Seema sank lower and crept to the edge of the shelter provided by the bench. The girl tilted her head back and took deep gulps of the cold air, letting the mist fall on her face.

Not normal girl behaviour, Seema thought, trying to cast her mind back to when she was that age, then realized she may never have been that age, unable to do the conversion between cat years and Were years and human years. Mina cast her gaze around as if looking for something. *She seeks the other one*, Seema realized. The one with the moves a sleek Siamese, who'd strode across the pavement a few minutes ago like she owned it.

Mina glanced back at the museum, then followed the route the other woman had trod, before turning right into a side street, rather than keeping straight along the same path.

Seema's tail flicked, her whiskers twitched and her paws kneaded the ground as she tried to make sense of a vampire, with senses almost as sharp as a werecat's, taking the wrong turn. *The girl needs tending, that much is clear, like a lost kit without its clan.* Seema looked back at the building. Angelos still hadn't emerged. As she crouched, debating, yet another vampire emerged, this one with muscles tense like a coiled adder, and followed in Mina's footsteps. Seema huffed out a breath of steamy air. *If the girl can't watch her back, I'll have to do it for her.* With one last glance towards the doors, Seema abandoned her shelter and followed the vampires, keeping low, as a shadowy weight formed in the pit of her belly.

MINA COULDN'T HEAR anything other than the dripping, splashing and squelching the city was prone to after a deluge of rain. The wailing of snatched souls was silenced. But she also couldn't hear Bee or her unique song of syncopated rain on metal. She paused, and the city seemed to pause with her, as if holding its breath. Except for the drip-drip-drop of water from eaves and overhead lines. One of these drops found its way under her collar and snaked down her back. She glanced around, realizing how deserted the side street was. Something skittered behind her, a hushed splish-splash, but she saw nothing in the street when she turned around to scan the way she'd come.

The street that she'd gone down so many times before took on a whole new hue, beyond her enhanced dracul night vision. The edges were both jagged and sharply defined, a sensation that left her disoriented if she thought about it too much. Tonight fear also coloured her vision. Nonetheless, she turned around, to forge ahead and take the quickest route to the Sanctuary, as she'd done before.

Then she froze as the drone of untuned violins rose around her, and a figure dropped into her path. Her dracul eyes homed in on the shape even in the dimly lit street.

"Em."

"Mina. Long time no see." Em took a step towards her, her high-heeled boots crunching on the gritty, wet asphalt, her hips swaying sensuously. But Mina wasn't fooled. She knew it was just the movements of a snake that could strike with blinding speed. "Without Jack to guard your back." Em arched an eyebrow as she stepped around Mina, coming up beside her. "And how's that luscious roommate of yours?"

Mina turned her head sharply to look at Em, then pressed her lips tightly together, not wanting to give Em anything she could use. Her hand twitched, unsure of whether it should be reaching for a weapon or getting ready to throw a punch.

"Oh I see, you don't know." The woman stepped back around in front of her, her gaze focusing sharply on her. "You might want to take better care of your loved ones."

Punch it is. Mina jabbed her fist at Em's jaw, but her punch was wild and weak. The other woman easily dodged it and moved to aim a knee into Mina's side. Mina drove her elbow down onto Em's thigh, doing little damage, but stopping the momentum of the woman's leg.

A PLAGUE OF SHADOWS 189

Em stepped back into a ready position, one foot behind the other, fists loose in front of her face, elbows tight to her torso.

"Leave Cam alone." Mina mirrored her movement, scowling at her as her stomach twisted.

"What if she doesn't want to be left alone?" Em smiled, then flicked her ponytail over her shoulder just before she aimed a kick at Mina's head. Her flexibility was impressive, but it wasn't the best kick to use on a vampire; Mina had plenty of time to step out of the arc of her foot, then duck back in to slam a punch into Em's right side. Or so she thought. As she came in for the punch, Em spun around, almost into the path of Mina's arm, and swept her leg out, swiping Mina's feet out from under her. At the same time, she drove her palm into Mina's back, sending Mina sprawling onto the wet asphalt.

"Oomph." The wind knocked out of her, Mina didn't have a chance to recover before she felt Em's knee in her back and her arm around her throat, choking off the return of air.

"You should pay more attention to your opponent's tells," Em said, tightening her arm. "Rather than thinking about your next move."

Mina hadn't been thinking of her next move; she'd been thinking about her friend. But all that came out when she tried to speak was a rough gak. Stars started to spangle across her vision, a rushing filled her ears, and she wondered if vampires could die from a lack of air.

"Enough." A multi-tonal voice replaced the rushing sound. Emily stopped throttling her, but her arms stayed around Mina's throat. Mina craned her head back to look at the new arrival.

The man looked from her to Em. "I said enough." Slowly Em's grip on her neck loosened. Mina stood up, rubbing where Em's arm had been.

"Who are you?" she croaked, trying to force her voice back to normal, and not succeeding. "You may look like the priest, but I doubt that's what you are."

The man didn't answer her question. "I'm here to make you an offer," he said instead, his eyes travelling over her face, then sliding down the rest of her, before returning to peer into her eyes. "I want you to join me."

"What?" Em's sharp voice cut through the night.

"And why would I do that?" Mina asked, shifting a foot back.

"Security and acceptance." He stepped up to her, and Mina took a big step back, right into Em. He reached out and tucked a hair behind her ear, and Mina shivered at the violation.

"Really? Not power, wealth beyond the dreams of avarice?" Mina quirked an eyebrow at him.

"Oh, safety in the times to come is worth more than a dragon's horde. I promise you a place under the aegis of Night."

"Hmmm." Mina canted her head as if thinking about his offer. "Trade freedom for safety? I'm not interested."

He stepped away, and Mina slid out from between the two, not expecting to get far. Still, her breath came easier as she inched down the street. Then it caught in her throat when he did indeed follow, though he motioned for Em to stay where she was. "You haven't heard the details of my offer. A place at my side, a member of my family, a child of Night."

"You said that already." Mina took another step back. "And what would I have to do, slaughter children, torture small animals?"

A PLAGUE OF SHADOWS   191

He scoffed, his eyes flashing. "Night has a bigger vision than that. You can be a part of it."

"I'm not interested in Night's vision."

He waved a hand at the slick walls. "So what, you stick with your Athanatos?" He stepped closer and his voice dropped lower. "When they don't know what you really are?"

Mina slowed, not wanting to hear what he had to say, but unable to resist. Only her eyes shifted as they flicked to his face.

"But I do," he continued. "I can sense an unnatural power in your blood. In fact, I'm disappointed that you let this one beat you." He gave a sharp jerk of his head towards Em, whose response was cut off when his eyes flashed at her. He returned his gaze to Mina more slowly. "I know that if they really knew what you were capable of, they'd fear you. I know you hear the wicked voices singing." He closed the distance by another few inches. Mina didn't move. "As it is, they'll never trust you."

"You know I tell the truth." He reached out to move another hair away. "You'll never be a part of their family."

In her mind's eye, she saw Jack's uncertain frown, Dar's narrowed lips, Bee's furrowed brows reflected in the false priest's eyes. She saw their questions and their doubts in his handsome face. But when she glanced at the eyes that stared at her, those images turned to ones of death and torture. Mina broke out of her trance and swatted his hand away. She saw the darkness flick over his eyes before he quashed it.

"You'll beg Night to take you before the end."

"I'll beg for the end before Night takes me. I don't want to be a part of her 'family.'"

"And what about your family?" His icy blue eyes caught hers again, flecked with sparks of cold fire, then he closed them. Mina blinked. "Your real family...what is it?" He canted his head then opened his eyes. "Liam? Maggie?"

A knife of ice pierced Mina's gut, a spasm of terror travelling up her spine into her chest. But she managed to swallow the gasp that formed in her throat before it escaped and confirmed his words. Instead, she slid her hand up her back, reaching for a weapon, any weapon. Her fingers touched on the hilt of a short blade, when she found her elbow pressed up, locking her arm, making her unable to draw the weapon.

Em's other arm wrapped itself around her throat again, when she hadn't even realized the woman had moved behind her. "Be polite when someone's talking to you."

Mina tried to drive her head back into Em's face but couldn't get enough range to make an impact. She thought briefly about falling forward, taking Em down with her, but realized as she shifted that that would likely just leave her with a dislocated shoulder. She gave up trying to kick Em and settled on driving her heel into the woman's foot, but she couldn't get much force behind that since Em was strong enough to lift her as soon as she moved.

"So I don't have a choice?"

The man opened his mouth to speak when a song of tinny percussion rose in her blood. He tilted his head, indicating he heard the sound too. He evaporated into the shadows, leaving Em behind. Em shifted as her heartbeat sped up. She forced Mina along with her, putting Mina between her and the far end of the small street. The tension on Mina's arm eased, then disappeared, as a pissed-off Bee strode towards her, a cat at her heels. Mina spun around to give chase, but Em had already fled around the corner, into the nighttime city.

CHAPTER TWENTY-SIX

"YOU HAVE TWO OPTIONS: I turn you or I kill you." Lin held the young man face down on the ground as he struggled, her hands tight on his arms, her knee in his back, her wiry muscles taut beneath her pale skin. He was built like a warrior, she'd give him that. *But I'm uncanny.*

He'd gotten her to the city, fighting her in bits and pieces the whole way, even after she broke his finger to show her resolve. Though he'd been more taciturn since she'd broken her own finger to demonstrate her healing powers when he'd tried to crash the car. But in the city, among people, a recalcitrant human was a liability, no matter how well-formed he was.

Lin's nose twitched as she sniffed the air. The graveyard reeked of the living and the dead, but underneath it all there was a tendril of something familiar, something ancient. Something evil. Her flesh itched and her blood tingled, and she knew: this was what had woken her from her forest reverie. She was so close; she just needed to focus on it rather than this not-yet-a-man.

She bent forward and whispered in his ear. "Time's up."

His head hit her nose. She heard a crunch of cartilage, and let go of his arms, her hands coming to her face. He took the opportunity to scramble out from under her. When she brought her fingers away from her face, they were covered in blood. Her blood. "Decision made," she said, followed by a snarl as she peered at him with wild eyes. The anger on his face was replaced by fear. She crawled towards him, like a spider towards its fly. For a moment, he seemed to forget that he could move. Then he shuffled backwards, his movements frantic. That's when she realized his fear wasn't directed at her: his gaze was focused over her shoulder.

Lin froze. She'd let herself get distracted and become vulnerable. Something powerful lurked behind her. *Always watch your back.*

"Do you always play with your food?" The voice was liquid smooth.

Lin flowed up to standing and turned around in one seamless motion. Face to face with her stalker, her eyes told her it was just a man. A man with caramel blond hair, an equine nose and full lips. A man that was a cross between Michelangelo's David and a Teutonic god. But still very much like a man. Her blood, however, told a different tale.

To her right, a twig cracked and a leaf crunched. She glanced in the direction of the sound and saw something she never thought she'd see. Her jaw dropped in a mixture of shock and awe. The creature's leathery skin was damp and glistened in the weak light from the distant street lamps. Its pointed ears twitched at every rustle and snap. Its long arms hung by its side, talons tapping its massive thigh.

A trill of fear rippled through her stomach, followed by a wave of wonder. "Gargoyle," she whispered.

She turned her focus back to the man. *Definitely not just a man then.* Her blood hadn't lied to her: this was not a creature born of woman.

He looked past her, an eyebrow lifting. "Your food's getting away."

A PLAGUE OF SHADOWS 195

She glanced over her shoulder, then took a couple of long steps back without turning around. Crouching, she reached down while still keeping her eyes on the man, not on his pet gargoyle, nor her captive. Grabbing the young man's ankle, Lin walked back to this new entity, dragging the boy with her. She gave a lopsided shrug.

"He's just a means to an end." There was movement beside her, but she forced herself to keep looking at the man. "You're why I came here."

"Me?" He canted his head.

Lin nodded. "You. And the one who sent you."

"You know who sent me?"

Lin tipped her head, as her captive struggled at her feet, his twisting accompanied by a growled curse. She let go of the young man's ankle, but sent a sharp heel into his stomach, winding him.

"And do you know who I am?" the not-man in front of her asked.

Her breath caught in her throat. She peered into his deep, dark eyes, like puddles of squid ink, no longer the blue they were a moment ago. She smiled. "You're the emissary of Darkness. The Herald of Night."

His words were drawn out one-by-one when he spoke. "If you know what I am, do you know why I'm here?"

Lin nodded, raising an eyebrow in invitation. "To break open the dark vault and let the reign of Night fall upon the world again." The grass and mouldering leaves by her feet squelched as the young man inched away. She ignored him.

"And what are you going to do with that knowledge?"

"Help you, of course." She gave him a tight smile, the blood from her nose drying on her skin.

The man canted his head, appraising her. "You can call me Angelos."

"The Messenger." She nodded, ignoring the strangled scream behind her.

The man smiled at her then looked over her shoulder and made a clicking sound with his tongue. "That's her supper," he said, his voice harsh as he strode towards the gargoyle that had sunk its teeth into the young man's throat.

Lin shrugged. She'd shared a meal with worse things.

"I APOLOGIZE FOR MY pets' behaviour," Angelos said as Lin stood up from her meal. "They need to learn some manners. Or else."

Lin looked down at the body of the young man and sighed. It had been a long time since she'd turned a man, and she missed watching them wake to their new life, tutoring them, and killing them when they failed to thrive. A twitter fluttered in the space above her navel at the thought. She glanced past the body to the gargoyle that was rubbing its back against a tombstone. "Maybe they just feel unsatisfied."

"Don't we all."

Lin turned back to him. "But for them, it's simple: they want to fly."

"Maybe, but they haven't grown their wings yet. The self-serving cretin who created them lacked intelligence."

"No." Lin shook her head, ignoring his tensing when she approached the nearest gargoyle. It slunk back. "Maybe they just need a helping hand." She made a purring sound deep in her

A PLAGUE OF SHADOWS 197

throat and held out a hand as she took another step closer. The creature snapped at her.

"No," Angelos said, his voice sharp like a whip. She ignored it; she was used to the sting of the whip. The gargoyle, however, cringed and stopped its snapping.

She stepped up close to the creature and placed her fingertips lightly on its back. Its muscles tensed and its bony shoulder blades flexed. It didn't snap again, and digits intact, she ran her hands down its torso, tracing the corded muscles, feeling the power coiled within. The creature chirruped, and Lin closed her eyes.

She felt Angelos come up behind her. Her lips opened as she ran her hands up the gargoyle's back. Her breath became ragged, snagging in her throat, and her hands stilled. The gargoyle cooed. She opened her eyes.

"Do you have a sharp blade?" she asked, turning to Angelos, keeping her fingers on the gargoyle's back.

Angelos stared back at her for a half a minute, then pulled out a short knife, hilt to tip about the length of his forearm. Its curved blade glinted silver even in the low light of the cemetery. "Will this do?" he asked. She assessed the one-sided blade, which he flipped repeatedly in his hand, as he looked at her with his head cocked to one side. Lin gave a sharp nod.

At that, he stopped tossing it and turned the hilt towards her. When she laid her hand on the hilt to take the blade from him, he didn't let it go. Instead, his other hand gripped her wrist, fingers digging into her skin.

"What are you planning to do to my gargoyles?"

Lin canted her head. "Help them grow wings, of course." She glanced around the graveyard. "But this will never do. We need somewhere more, um, sound resistant."

ACRID SMOKE HUNG IN the air, wafting in sheets from the pile of ash in the middle of the concrete floor of the warehouse. Angelos ignored the burning in his purloined mortal body's eyes and the tickle in his human throat as he watched this vampire named Lin. He was about to send out another spark to set her on fire, tired of this waiting. She stood by the circle of soot left by the fire twirling the dagger Angelos had given her in one hand, seemingly without conscious thought. With the other, she prodded the ash and bits of charred bird bones with a long sliver from the palettes they'd burned, as if she were looking for something. Or drawing something, he realized as he cocked his head, seeing it from a different perspective. He tried to make out the form taking shape, like two scythes crossed. Or a stylized set of horns.

The runt gargoyle shuffled forward from the shadow, sniffing at the corpse of an unused bird. Lin lashed out with the stick and hissed, sending it into the corner again.

She does have a way with them, Angelos thought.

Letting go of the stick, she lifted the hand with the blade, bringing the tip of her other index finger to the point. She looked at the blade and tipped her head, as if seeing it for the first time. A thread of blood welled up on her finger as she ran the blade across it. He could smell it from here. "Ow," she said, though her tone spoke of boredom, not pain.

A PLAGUE OF SHADOWS   199

"Sharp enough I imagine," Angelos said. He still wasn't sure about this unexpected vampire and whatever she had planned for his gargoyles. He beckoned to the runt. It crept out of the shadows towards him, skirting Lin's range, and the other two followed. Angelos whispered words in its ear. It stared at him for a minute with its murky eyes, making a sucking sound over its tongue. Then it turned to do as he bid. Though small, it was smarter than the other two. It nodded and chuffed at one of its fellows, then they both grabbed the third, and forced it down, face to the concrete beside the sooty circle.

"Show me what you can do." Angelos laid his hand on the hilt of his other blade. Lin peered at him for a second before stepping forward to crouch beside the prone creature. She placed one hand on the gargoyle's neck, while the other held the dagger backhanded, the spine of the blade against her forearm. Lin twisted so her blade hand was nearest the creature. The gargoyle shifted, as if sensing the blade's edge hanging over him. She looked up at the other two gargoyles then back at Angelos. He gave a sharp nod.

In a flash of metal, Lin drew the blade up the gargoyle's back, digging deep into the muscle on the left side of its spine, hooking the blade in under the shoulder blade at the end of its arc. The creature howled and surged against the restraining arms of its fellows. Black blood flowed down its back and over the blade.

Angelos tensed, ready to attack, but then took a deep breath, forcing himself to wait and see. Instead, he spoke a harsh word in a guttural language. The gargoyle mewled but stilled. Lin shifted the dagger to the other hand and quickly did the same procedure to the other side. That done, she placed the dagger, sticky with black blood, on the gargoyle's back and dug her bloody hands into the ashes. These she rubbed into the gargoyle's wounds, eliciting a whimper.

The sight of the large muscled creature whimpering at the hands of this slight woman put her in a new light. Lin stepped back from the gargoyle, hands and blade dripping blood onto the concrete floor and her leather boots.

"Next."

Anger burned in his gut as he took in the tortured state of the gargoyle. He shifted his weight, preparing to plunge his dagger into her chest as payment for her failure when a deep keening rose from the gargoyle on the floor. Its back heaved and bucked, tearing a twisted scream from its torso. Bones forced their way through the cuts Lin had made.

"Wings." Maybe he'd keep her around after all – she did have a way with them.

CHAPTER TWENTY-SEVEN

JACK EYED THE UNNATURAL feline as it twined its way around Mina's ankles until she reached down to pick the creature up with a fluidity of movement that spoke of years of training in either martial arts or dance.

First nestling up into her neck, the werecat then crawled onto her shoulder and turned its phantasmagoric, golden eyes on the rest of the conclave, pausing as they came to him, as if passing judgment. He stared back from where he leaned against one of the pillars separating the vaulted nave from the arcade, arm crossed, jaws tense. The creature looked away first. Jack smiled and shifted his gaze to Dar, who had absentmindedly ran a tanned finger along the cat's marmalade fur, as Adeh gave his report: no sign of this new threat Rhys had hinted at, no Herald shouting from the street corners. And no new vampire either, though the rumours persisted.

Jack's attention returned to Mina, who rocked up onto her toes, her mouth opening as she took a quick breath, then closing as she shifted back to her heels when Dar turned his gaze to Bee.

"What about the museum?" Dar asked. Jack looked at Bee, whose face was a mask of disinterest, though Jack knew it was just a mask.

"Noth—"

"I saw the Herald," Mina said, her words tumbling over each other in a cascade. She looked up from the floor, her cheeks flushed. "I mean I met the Herald, face-to-face."

Bee turned her head sharply to Mina, her eyebrows pulling together in a question. Jack stood a little straighter, his gaze shifting between the two women. The cat crouched lower, its paws kneading Mina's shoulder.

Dar stepped back so he could look at her straight on. "What do you mean?"

"I...." Mina's mouth opened and closed a few times, like a fish out of water gasping for air, as she fidgeted under the weight of all the vampire eyes now turned upon her. Then she pulled her shoulders back. "The Herald. He spoke to me."

"What did he say?" Dar asked, his voice flat, his words measured.

"How do you know?" Jack asked, glancing at the cat before returning his eyes to Mina.

Mina tore her gaze from Dar to look at him. "Because he told me."

"He told you?" Dar kept his tone neutral as he appraised Mina. Jack shifted a half step closer to her.

Her nostrils flared as she peered at Dar. "Yeah, when he offered me safety and security if I joined his forces."

"And what did you say to him?" Dar's voice was silken, his neck long as he pulled his head back. Jack stepped even closer to Mina while staying away from the cat.

Mina's lips tightened into a thin line before she answered. "What do you think I said?"

"Where did you meet this Herald?" Adeh asked, coming halfway between her and Dar, always the peacemaker.

A PLAGUE OF SHADOWS
203

"Outside the museum." Mina crossed her arms in front of her.

Dar mimicked her movements, adding an arch to an eyebrow. "The monster of myth and legend is hanging around the city streets, taking in some art."

"He's not a monster. He's the priest." Mina took a step back as the cat fluffed its tail.

Dar turned his gaze to Bee. "You saw this priest-turned-messenger?"

Bee slowly drew her gaze from Mina to Dar and gave a small shake of the head. "No. I saw no priest. And I saw no Herald."

Mina looked at her. "I tell you, the same priest was there again at the museum, the one from St. Frank's." Mina's cheeks turned red, though Jack couldn't tell whether it was a flush of anger or frustration. "Then I left to follow Bee." Mina nodded at the woman. "And then I was attacked," she added, her voice quieter.

"By the priest," Jack said, nodding.

Mina shook her head, the tightness around her eyes softening as she looked at him. "Em."

"Em?" Jack cocked his head.

"That I can vouch for," Bee said. "The cat found me." She nodded at the creature on Mina's shoulder, her eyes narrowed. "And dragged me back to Mina. Em left when I showed up."

At that, the conclave fell silent, the only sound the cat's rapid purring, as Dar appraised Mina, his gaze unblinking.

"Hmm. We can't discount any possibilities," he said finally, uncrossing his arms. "This priest—"

"He's not really a priest," Mina interjected.

"He may have an unnatural interest in the blade," Dar continued, before turning to Bee. "And what of the blade?"

Jack heard the breath catch in Bee's throat. "Nothing." She looked at Mina and shrugged. "Sorry, I felt nothing. I saw nothing. Just a dagger."

MINA FELT THE SCOWL written on her face as her lips pulled down and her shoulders lifted. She tried to reform her features into friendly disbelief. She failed. "You don't believe me? Why would I lie?"

Dar's eyes flashed as they worked their way over her face, as if searching for something. "I didn't say that," he said before looking down at his hands. "But you are still an unknown quantity." He glanced back at her. "Sired by a meddler in dark arts. Who you then killed. The only one of us to face a gargoyle and live to tell the tale. You're...unique."

Mina breathed in deeply, her back expanding and shoulders lifting. Dar moved towards her with a sidling, sideways step, perhaps cautious of her mood, causing Seema to hiss at him and leap off her shoulder.

"Now, I hear you've been shirking your training," he said, changing the subject. Mina glanced at Bee, her cheeks going red. "I think it's time I tested you myself, especially if Em can best you." He walked over to the nearest pillar and slid off his shoes, placing them neatly at the base, then glanced back at her. "Besides, it might help temper your mood."

She cocked an eyebrow and looked him up and down. She hadn't seen him use so much as a steak knife. And although he

A PLAGUE OF SHADOWS

was tall, he was slight. At the moment, she didn't care if her disdain was written on her face for these people who claimed to be her 'new family' but couldn't bring themselves to trust her.

Dar stripped off sweater and shirt. Mina mirrored his actions, right down to her tank top. With both of them exposed, she felt a little more nervous. Wiry muscles corded his arms and his chiselled torso tapered into a toned abdomen: Dar was cut.

The other vampires stepped back as he walked over to the arcade.

"What weapon would you like?" he asked.

"I don't care." Mina shrugged.

"The challenged gets to choose."

"Bo okay with you?"

In response, he picked up a staff and tossed it to her. She caught it in a fluid motion, sending her ankle back and slicing the staff through the air until the tip tapped her ankle. A little too hard. Mina forced herself not to wince or yelp. Dar walked back to the centre of the sanctuary and lowered himself into a wide-legged crouch, rocking from side to side on his heels as his hands came up in front of him in loose fists.

"Um, aren't you going to get a staff?"

"No." He started to circle her. "If you think standing agape with a stick at your side is the ready posture for staff fighting, I need to have a talk with Bee about her abject neglect of your training."

Mina pursed her lips and picked up the staff properly, holding it lightly in both hands.

"That's the way to show him," Bee said from the sidelines.

Dar stopped rocking and glanced over. The audience had stayed. "Isn't it past your bedtime?"

"No way, no how," Bee said, a smile on her lips. Leaning back against a pillar, she crossed her arms and settled in to watch.

"This is worth losing sleep over." Adeh pulled some bills out of his pocket.

"No betting," Dar said. Adeh made a face at Dar but put the money away. Dar returned his attention to Mina. He arched an eyebrow and gave her a small smile. "En garde."

He turned sideways to her, presenting a smaller target. Using her lessons from Bee, Mina watched, assessing her opponent. Hands curled into open fists, he ran the knuckle of his thumb across his nose and continued to shift back and forth. Like a snake charmer mesmerizing his charge. But Mina wasn't having any of it. She spun the staff around, aiming for a side strike under his forward arm.

The cheer from the sidelines died down when he managed to duck under the mid-torso strike. Mina brought the staff around, intent on driving one end into his chest, but he swayed back to avoid the jab, instead grabbing the end and pushing the staff back into her ribs.

Mina coughed, the wind knocked out of her, while Dar stepped back, into his infernal rocking. She rubbed her side and felt the bruise that would form, then set herself up again. Almost in time to raise the staff and stop Dar's foot from contacting her cheekbone. Almost but not quite.

Mina staggered sideways but was able to keep hold of the staff. As he came to offer her a hand up, she swung low at his ankles, knocking his legs out from under him. He managed to follow through on the fall, somersaulting backwards as she came in for the 'killing' blow.

A PLAGUE OF SHADOWS

But he moved like water, flowing out of range. So she swung the staff sideways, spinning to increase momentum. Mina felt a second of glee as the staff contacted his torso hard, causing him to wince. Then he promptly pinned it with one arm while sending the palm of the other hand into her chin. Mina's head snapped back, stars filling her vision. She shook them away, and when he pulled his hand back, she followed it, trying to head-butt his nose. But she was too slow, and he used her momentum against her, torquing the staff they both still held, twisting her and it until he had her over his knee, the staff across her throat.

"Do you yield?" he said, leaning his head down, his mohawk falling into her face, his brown eyes flecked with red as he peered at her.

Mina struggled, kicking her legs. She bucked, trying to twist out of his hold. She smiled as his eyes widened at the strength of the move, but then he pulled the staff tighter. Pinpricks of light filled her vision.

"Dar." Jack's voice sounded as if it were coming through water. "Enough."

"Do you yield?" Dar asked again, his voice hard and rough, the words like pumice stone. Mina tried to nod against the pressure on her neck as she let go of the staff and Jack's hand fell on Dar's shoulder.

Dar breathed in and out deeply, his eyebrows scrunching together, then he pulled the staff away, and helped her up, all in one liquid motion.

"Not bad." He nodded to her as she rubbed her throat and wiped away a trickle of blood from her cheek. The action over, the others dispersed in search of rest or refreshment.

C. RENÉ ASTLE

Dar tossed the staff to her without warning. As she caught it out of the air, not showing off this time, he walked away without another word, a frown on his face.

Mina stalked over to the arcade to put the staff away.

"'Not bad' is high praise from Dar, you know." Jack appeared from the shadows, towel in hand. "It was years before I got anything more than 'maybe you'll do better next time.'"

"Maybe he was just taking pity on me." Mina glanced at her watery reflection in the glass of the cabinet door.

"Dar doesn't tend to take pity on his opponents, and less so on his friends." Jack's voice was soft as he stepped closer.

"I don't know that I count as his friend."

"You count as family."

Mina let out a harsh laugh and glanced sideways at Jack. "If you say so," she said, turning towards him. She could smell sandalwood and soap as he touched his fingers gently to her chin and tilted it up. She looked into his dark eyes, which narrowed slightly as they assessed the marks on her face. The wet towel stung as he dabbed away the blood on her cheek. "It seems I'm always tending your wounds."

She tipped her head sideways. "Maybe some time you could kiss them better instead."

Her stomach fluttered as the rasping of terry cloth against her skin paused for a split second then continued. The flutter turned to a sinking sensation. She let go of the breath she'd been holding.

"Maybe I could." The hand with the towel dropped away from her face. But instead of her bruised cheek, he pressed his lips to hers. She rose onto her tiptoes and brought her fingers up to the hand that still lifted her chin. Then he pulled away, his

A PLAGUE OF SHADOWS 209

forehead pressing to hers. "But it's probably not a good idea to go down that road right now," he said, his voice low. His head pulled away and his hand dropped from her chin, but he stayed where he was, his dark eyes looked into hers for a long second.

Then he turned and walked away. Mina's jaw clenched, and she hoped she kept her growl of anger tinged with sexual frustration to herself.

CHAPTER TWENTY-EIGHT

RHYS WAS SITTING ON the cold stone bench as he waited for the museum to open, doing a cryptic crossword to pass the time, when he sensed a presence descend beside him, like an angel of death.

Long minutes of silence passed, broken by a few false starts at conversation. Rhys kept his lips pressed together and kept doing his crossword. A hand came to rest on his knee. His pencil stopped moving on his paper, and he looked at the appendage but not at its owner.

"Why did you send your errand boy instead of coming yourself?" he said, finally taking pity on his companion, but still not looking at him.

After a second of hesitation, Dar spoke. "I don't think Jack would appreciate being described as my errand boy."

Rhys folded his paper and clutched it in his lap. Dar's hand moved from his knee, coming to rest on the hand that held the paper. Rhys looked down at his own hand, veined and papery, and splattered with brown spots, next to Dar's, as smooth and even as when they'd met.

"The question still stands," he said as he looked up towards the museum. It was opening soon. "I am happy to do these things for you. Happy to turn my mind to your problems. Happy to watch myself grow old while you gad about as vibrant and attractive as ever. But I'd like the respect owed a lifelong friend, not a

A PLAGUE OF SHADOWS   211

servant." He turned his head away, to watch a homeless woman feed pigeons across the square.

Dar's hand grasped his, the grip almost painful, and Rhys felt Dar's irresistible eyes on him. It took a monumental will not to return the gaze.

Dar was silent for a second. "You are so much more than either friend or servant," he said, his voice hoarse. "I couldn't bear it if anything happened to you."

Rhys finally looked at him, but Dar had turned away. "Coward," he said, then softened his tone and laid his other hand over Dar's. "You're going to have to bear it."

"No."

"Time has never listened to the likes of us. Besides, we've had this conversation before. And now it's too late anyway."

Dar pulled his hand out from between Rhys' and breathed deeply through his nose. "It's not that," he said. "It's....If I did anything to you, I—"

"What are you talking about?"

Dar's eyes finally met his. His hand came up to rest on Rhys' cheek. "If I bit you, if I could no longer control the creature inside, I...." His warm, brown eyes glistened with unshed tears, a sight Rhys hadn't seen in a long time. Dar dropped his hand and looked down, resting his forehead on the shoulder of Rhys' wool jacket. "I have a hard time controlling it around you, harder than with anyone else. It's like it feeds off my feelings for you."

"This beast doesn't scare me. I'm afraid *for* you, not of you." Rhys shifted, his fingertips lifting Dar's face to his. "I fully expect my life will be stolen away slowly, breath by breath, heartbeat by heartbeat." He pressed his lips to Dar's, and Dar returned the gentle kiss. "I've made my peace with that, but I don't like the pain it causes you." Dar looked at him with a quizzical expression.

"Age is irrefutable," Rhys said in response, smiling sadly at him. "As is disease, oftentimes."

Dar's face turned ashen, and Rhys took pity on him. "It's okay," he added. "I've got a few years yet." He looked away, towards the museum, where the doors were finally open. He stood up, his aching joints protesting. "What was it you wanted to talk about? I don't imagine it was us growing old."

"Mina says she's met the Herald."

Rhys felt a wave of dizziness as he turned his head back to Dar. "Did she say who?"

"Do you really think she has?"

"Why do you think she hasn't?" He tucked his paper under his arm. "Her claim at least deserves investigating."

"Yes, but it seems unreal."

Rhys laughed, setting off a bout of coughing. Dar ran a calming hand down his back. "You forget, you're unreal." Dar gave him a slight nod and a half smile. Rhys turned back to the museum. "Well, I suppose I should go take a gander at this thing our Mina has found." He held out his hand. "Would you like to come with me? Get up to no good in a public place?"

"Just like old times?" Dar's face bloomed into a full smile, all the way to the rich brown eyes Rhys always lost himself in, and he reached up to take hold of Rhys' hand, as he stood up to join him. Arm in arm, they walked up the steps to the museum.

A PLAGUE OF SHADOWS 213

DAR STARED AT THE HEADDRESS, its feathers still holding hints of iridescence even after centuries swathed in damp and darkness. The gold band still gleamed. The bits of royal vestments were astoundingly well-preserved. The depth of the tomb had spared it from looters and hidden it from archaeologists until now, the sign at the entrance to the galleries had said. That and whispers of a curse on any who so much as thought of plundering its secrets.

"But I don't see how any of these can be the blade of Night," he said to Rhys, who had stopped a few paces back.

"It's not the 'blade of Night,'" Rhys said, placing his hands on Dar's shoulders and turning him 90 degrees. "It's the blade of the Even Star."

Dar saw what Rhys had stopped to look at: a small, black blade that shone in the dim light of the gallery.

"Though Mina's moniker of the blade of Night would seem more apropos," Rhys continued. "Obsidian."

"It's just a ceremonial blade. I expected something bigger, more, I don't know, evil-looking for the blade of Night." Dar laid a hand on Rhys' shoulder, revelling in this moment of old camaraderie.

"The blade of the Even Star."

"Yes, teacher." Dar looked at him with a lop-sided grin. Nearby, the docent shifted as Rhys stepped closer and hovered his pinkie finger over the encasing glass, drawing an invisible line along one edge.

"And why do you think it's ceremonial?" Rhys asked, in his rhetorical voice. "See that? Obsidian can be knapped to an incredibly keen edge. So sharp that they've done trials on using it for surgical knives."

Dar stood back for a second, watching the wonder transform Rhys' features, seeing the young man at Oxford again. Finally, he stepped beside him, turning to the blade. "Do you think Mina is right, could this be the blade of Ni...of the Even Star?"

Rhys squinted at him, pulling his head back. "Can't you feel it?"

Dar peered at the blade, then closed his eyes, scanning his senses. He felt the usual twitter of a hushed room deep in his bowels, the pulse of the heartbeats around him. He felt a slight nausea at being so close to Rhys. He felt the hairs on the back of his neck where the docent's eyes landed. None of which Rhys was referring to, he was sure. He shook his head, opening his eyes. "Feel what?"

"The smothering heaviness of death," Rhys said, his low voice hoarse. "Whispering tendrils of wickedness, an unquenchable thirst for blood."

Dar spun his head to look at Rhys, who continued to peer at the blade.

"Oh yes," Rhys said. "I think Mina is right: this is quite likely the blade we're looking for."

"So close? It seems an unlikely coincidence." Dar looked back at the blade which now seemed to absorb the light from its spotlight.

Rhys stepped even closer, causing the docent to fidget again. "So close and yet so far." He waved his hand at the case enclosing the blade. "And coincidence is just us not understanding the threads that drew us all to the here and now."

"Someone once said 'The warp and weft of past, present and future form an incomprehensible mesh.'"

"Sounds familiar. What pompous git said that?"

A PLAGUE OF SHADOWS

"You did, shortly after we met." Dar smiled, as Rhys glanced at him.

"I suppose I probably did. I was trying to impress."

Dar nudged as close to Rhys as he dared but turned his face to the blade. "If this is the blade, we need to get it out of here."

"How do you propose we do that?" Rhys said, his eyes sliding towards the docent.

Dar had no answer to that.

CHAPTER TWENTY-NINE

BEE THREW A HOODIE at Mina's sweat-soaked, prone form without looking at her, her eyes reading a message on the phone that had beeped just as she was taking Mina down with a strike to the calves. Mina had seen the move coming but her limbs no longer listened to her orders to get out of the way. As a result, she'd landed hard on her back, the wind knocked out of her.

"Get your shoes, get your jacket, and get armed," Bee said, pulling a T-shirt on over her own, less sweaty tank top. "We're going out."

Mina moaned. "Can't I at least have a shower?"

"I know how long that takes you, even without Brett to keep you company." Bee picked up her gun, snug in a holster that also held refills of ammo – one of silver and one of lead this time – and strapped that on over her T-shirt. Then she looked up at Mina. "No."

"A bite to eat?" Mina struggled into the hoodie which clung to every drop of sweat.

"Ha, even longer." Bee pulled on her trainers. "No."

"Ice my bruises?" Tonight had been truncheons, though Mina couldn't think of any occasion when that would be her weapon of choice.

"You're a vampire, you'll heal." Bee held out her hand to help Mina up.

"Bitch," Mina said, but any bite was taken out by a quirk of her lips. She took Bee's hand.

"Damn right." Bee shrugged her toned arms into a neon pink bomber jacket. "Get your stuff. Be back here in ten."

Mina was back in five, wearing her leather jacket and her shit-kicking boots with good ankle support and a practical heel. And heavy enough to add some oomph to a kick. She'd armed herself with her usual weapons of choice – a pistol and a series of four short knives ranging from the length of her hand to the length of her forearm, and added one the blades from Finn, etched with whorls of dull lead. She was actually looking forward to a simple patrol in the crisp night air, under the stars.

She cinched the last strap holding the blades snug to her hips tight under her leather jacket. "So boss, where we headed?"

"There was a body found in the cemetery across the river."

"Um, doesn't sound like a news flash."

"A fresh body. Not in a grave."

"Oh." Mina didn't think she'd enjoy this after all.

A RING AROUND THE MOON, the rustle of metal signs and the sweep of plastic bags along the street suggested that the night, although calm now, would not be for long. *So much for the stars,* Mina thought as she pulled her jacket tighter against the glacial wind as she followed Bee to the nearest subway station. But at the top of the stairs, she hesitated. She hadn't been underground since the night Luca had bitten her a second time, making her dracul. Shortly before she'd killed him.

"I know, the water makes me nauseous too," Bee said.

"Huh?"

"The water, broad rivers, deep oceans, makes me almost seasick. Does for a lot of vampires."

"Oh, I haven't been over the river since, you know, I was made." Mina dropped a token in the turnstile. "What causes it?"

"Don't know." Bee shrugged. "I used to love going out on the boats, you know. I'd run away from my mom and my sister. It was worth the hell I'd catch later to sit in the sun and watch my brothers fish."

"Maybe the thing that makes us, well, vampires, is allergic?"

"Hmm, maybe," Bee said, though her voice was still far away.

Sure enough, on the ride over the river, Mina struggled to not throw up. Sitting didn't help. The floor was too filthy to lie down on. Looking out the window at the expanse of water was the worst. Eventually, she settled for pressing her forehead against the cool plexiglass, closing her eyes and breathing deeply. But not too deeply...it was the subway after all.

OUT OF THE SUBWAY, Mina took a deep draught of the cold air, hands on her knees. "I had no idea."

Bee patted her back. "Seems it hit you hard. Don't plan any sea voyages until you get used to it. This way." She headed down a street that ran parallel to the river. Mina followed on weary, wobbly legs.

Soon Bee turned them inland. At the end of the street, a void of light met them. Mina could pick out the tendrils of the unique scent of death. Decay had started to set in.

"Who called you about this?"

A PLAGUE OF SHADOWS 219

"One of the familiars. She lives nearby. But so do the Necrophagos, so stay alert." They crossed the quiet street to the iron gates of the cemetery. Footsteps approached from behind them.

They turned in unison to see a woman with long black hair and a short black skirt.

"Nicole." Mina blushed in the darkness, remembering the first time she'd met this particular familiar: her first feeding. She was flooded by phantom sensations: the sweetness of the woman's blood on her tongue and the smoothness of her skin on her lips. "Hi."

Nicole's red lips formed a lopsided smile. "Mina, we really need to get together sometime."

"Seriously?" Bee looked from one to the other with raised eyebrows. "Where's this body?"

"Through here." Nicole led them on a winding path through the gravestones to a copse of trees. "I stopped here on my way home from school, leaving flowers for Grandma...her family has a mausoleum here from way back; otherwise I'd have to travel to hell's half acre and back."

"Nicole," Bee said. "Body?"

"Right, flowers for Grandma. Then I caught a whiff of something unpleasant. Blood and excrement, the start of decomposition."

"You're familiar with those smells, are you?" Mina asked, wondering what the glam goth woman got up to in her spare time.

"Pre-med, on my way to becoming a doctor," Nicole said. "I might not be a vampire, but I know the smell of untimely death."

"Why call us?" Mina asked, covering her surprise at Nicole's answer. "Not the police?"

In response, Nicole pulled back a curtain of branches to reveal the body of a young man.

"Oh." He had what Mina could only surmise were bite marks from a large jaw on his arms and his neck, and his jeans were torn. One foot was bare, the other shod in a basketball shoe. If Mina had had any blood in her stomach, she would have vomited.

"Gargoyle." Her voice was weak.

Bee crept over the body to look more closely at the man's face. Eighteen or so, Mina guessed. To her, he looked like one of the chiselled, all-Americans from high school. The ones she'd avoided as if her life depended on it; if only she'd known then what she knew now. The ones she'd imagined bad things happening to. Now, as she looked at him, seeming so young, even though he was only a few years younger than her, she felt sad.

Bee turned the boy's head to the side, exposing the fact that the back of his head was crushed.

"Bee," Mina hissed. "What are you doing?"

Bee looked at her, her eyes shining. "Take a look."

Mina took a half step closer and leaned as far forward as she dared. Two pinprick holes marked his neck. "Vampire?"

"And gargoyle."

"I have a bad feeling about this," Nicole said.

AFTER DROPPING NICOLE off at her brownstone, which wasn't anything like what Mina expected from the familiar –

A PLAGUE OF SHADOWS 221

mid-century modern rather than velour and tassels – she and Bee went back to the cemetery.

Threading their way among the graves to the stand of trees, Mina tried to make out the names and dates on the headstones, but many of the engravings were too eroded with age. She wondered if she'd be wandering through another cemetery in a few hundred years, only to find her own parents' names erased by time.

A sound up ahead drew her out of her morbid reverie. She laid a hand on Bee's forearm as she searched for the source. Bee turned her gaze from scanning the ground to look at her. Mina nodded in the direction of the sound, and they both loosened guns in holsters and blades in sheaths. Mina realized what she had missed in contemplation of the grave markers: a buzzing in her blood, a jumble of off-kilter melodies.

Vampires. Two women facing each other, flanking a man with his back to Bee and Mina. The women's voices didn't carry, but whatever conversation they were having appeared to be heated, judging from the expressions and gesticulations. Mina breathed in over her teeth. *Vampires, and something else.*

"Em," Bee whispered beside her. "I can't quite make out the other two." She ducked behind a gravestone, and Mina followed her lead.

"Other one," Mina said, keeping her voice pitched low. "The third's not a vampire."

Bee looked at her, an unspoken question written on her face, then peeked around the gravestone. She cocked her head to the side. "Isn't that...the other priest?"

Mina popped her head up, so her eyes were just above the gravestone. The man's face was now in profile. The world stopped for a second as she remembered the deep abyss when she met his gaze in the museum. She imagined herself invisible.

"He's not a priest anymore," she said as she dropped back down. "I told you...he's something else." She peeked again. "The other vampire, she looks familiar." Mina drew her eyebrows together and her mouth into a frown as she tried to pull up where she'd seen the woman before, but try as she might, she couldn't place her.

"So what do we do?" she asked Bee.

"What we're paid to do. We go bust some heads...or stake some hearts and shoot some poison bullets."

"I get the picture, though I'm not paid." Mina slid her gun out of the holster and double-checked that it was loaded with the silver-laced rounds, rather than lead. "The student follows the teacher?"

Bee gave her a look that said she'd pay for that, then started to emerge from behind her hiding place.

As Mina moved to follow, a sudden heaviness bore down on her, constricting her chest, making it difficult to breathe. She was barely able to get her hand onto Bee's shoulder.

"What—?" Bee stopped when the night sky became even darker and a whoosh of wind stirred the half-dead vegetation around them, as if it were being buffeted by helicopter blades. Bee crouched again, and they both looked up.

"What the hell?" Mina said as she watched grey forms descend from above, pitching, yawing and flapping like ducks trying to land. "Gargoyles."

"Flying gargoyles," Bee said, looking up at the creatures. "Change of plans: we get the hell out of here. Let the others know they need to look up. Way up."

CHAPTER THIRTY

LIN GAZED SKYWARD, mouth agape.

"That's not so impressive," Em said, ending the moment of as. Lin flashed her an angry look at her, but the woman didn't notice. Her arms crossed, her gaze was trained on the gargoyles, who pitched and yawed their way down from a rooftop on the other side of the cemetery with a few courageous, clumsy beats of the wings.

"They're just fledglings," Lin said, her eyes narrowing as she looked from the beautiful beasts back to the ghastly Em. "How would you be, if you'd suddenly sprouted wings? Other than dumbstruck." She took a step towards Em, grasping at the hilt of her dagger as she did. "Maybe I should see if I can make you grow wings."

Angelos tensed beside her, though whether at Em's imperious tone or her threating stance, she couldn't tell.

"So they'll learn to properly fly?" he asked, making his voice sharp as a knife.

She forced herself to relax, to shift back and shrug, to seem unperturbed. "I'm not an expert on gargoyles; they were legends even before my time. I suspect they'll always be a bit more duck than hawk." She stepped towards the nearest one. It shied back but, after snorting out a huff that steamed the air in front of its nostrils, it let her approach. She ran her fingernails along its scapula and the skin along its spine, alternating rough and smooth. "But yes, they should grow into their wings. And I imagine even a gliding gargoyle descending on you from above is a terror to behold." She flicked her gaze up to Angelos then back down, so he couldn't see the vision in her head. The gargoyle started up a purr deep in its belly at her ministrations.

Angelos stepped up beside her and laid his own hand on the creature. The soft vibration stopped. "If you have no experience with them, where did you learn the trick of cutting them open?"

"Dragons, of course," Lin said. She drew her hand along the humerus and the radius, cooing to coax the gargoyle to unfurl its wing.

Angelos jerked his head to look at her. "Dragons," he said. Lin didn't let her smile reach her lips. She was full of surprises, but apparently he didn't like to be surprised. "Of course," he continued, returning his gaze to the gargoyles. He stepped away and just watched as she ran her hands along the leathery skin and bony structure of the gargoyle's wing.

"Do you even care about your search for a sacrifice?" Em came up beside Angelos. "Or have you forgotten about that prey while you play with your pets?"

Lin didn't keep her smile to herself as Angelos snapped his head to glare at Em, his hand lashing out to grasp her throat and drag her to him. She let out a duck-like quack as he took her face in his hands. He started to squeeze, as if to press his palms together through her skull. He lifted, and Em was forced onto her toes. "What did you say?"

Em's eyes watered, and a tear tracked its way down her cheek. Unable to move her jaw, a squawk sounded in her throat. Lin's smile turned to a frown. She didn't much like the blonde ice

A PLAGUE OF SHADOWS   225

princess, and would happily kill her, but she disliked Angelos' management style even more.

Millimetre by millimetre, Angelos let Em's feet touch the ground again. "What do you say?"

"I'm sorry," Em said, her voice hoarse.

"Watch your tone, or you will be."

She rubbed her cheeks but stayed silent. Still, when Em shot her a look, Lin saw the fire flash in her eyes. *Not easily cowed, this one*. Lin realized she might need to reassess the ice princess.

"What prey?" Lin kept her tone even and faced Angelos with a bored expression, abandoning her ministrations of the gargoyle's wing.

He ignored her question and turned back to Em instead. "What news of the dhamphir?"

"You're hunting a dhamphir?" Lin said, her curiosity getting the best of her. "If it's that little snip of a thing that Jack brought to the woods, can I help suck the marrow from her bones?"

Angelos' fingers wrapped around her throat this time, before she even had a chance to snarl. He brought the other hand to her cheek. Her nostrils flared, but she stayed silent as his eyes when completely black and inky tendrils oozed from the fingers that touched her face.

"Why I hunt anything is my business." His breath was sour in her nose, and she kept her inhales shallow and small. "Do you understand?"

Lin's jaw clenched, and she nodded, albeit slowly.

"Good." He removed his fingers from her throat, one by one. As Lin's heels came to rest on the ground again, she came to a decision: Angelos had to die...after he woke Night.

"No sucking marrow from her bones," he continued. "I need her for the ritual to free Night."

"If you need her, let's go get her," Lin said, craning her neck.

"One problem," Em said. "Matteo doesn't let her out of his sight. "And she seems to be going a little mad, being cooped up in an invisible cage."

"Matteo?" Lin shrugged. "I'll take care of him. Two birds, one stone. And a little madness isn't always a bad thing."

"It is in a vampire when it's caused by hunger." Em's voice lowered and her eyes went vacant for a few moments before she returned to the present. "You should know. And we don't drink from vermin."

"Do you feel sorry for this little dhamphir?" Lin asked, a taunt in her voice, her lips in a snarl.

"No, what I *feel* is concern about Angelos' plan. If he wants to use her, he needs to extricate her. In one piece I'm assuming." She lifted her eyebrow at him, and he tipped his head in confirmation.

"So? It still doesn't matter if she's a little mad."

"If she snaps before we get her, the other vampires will kill her. They're already on edge."

Angelos turned away from them towards the gargoyles. "Maybe we can create a diversion, something to draw Matteo out."

IVAN SHIFTED HIS FEET apart, gently bending his knees, and reached behind his back, all in one fluid movement that be-

A PLAGUE OF SHADOWS   227

lied his size. His hand found the grip of his pistol as the darkness in front of them thickened into form.

"I want her," the shadow said as it stepped into the light, coalescing into the form of the priest as Angelos emerged from the pocket of darkness where he had been lying in wait.

Ivan didn't need to ask who 'her' was. Apparently neither did Matteo because he glanced at the dhamphir. She stood at the bottom of the stoop leading to the palatial mansion the Necrophagos called home, its simple facade hiding an expansive, opulent interior.

Matteo jerked his head, and Ivan paused, not drawing his gun but not removing his hand either.

"Angelos," Matteo said, stepping between the girl and the man. "I already told you, you can't have her." His voice was strong and even, perhaps drawing power from being so near their home base. But Ivan knew *near* didn't count for much.

Ivan looked over Matteo's shoulder at the man still dressed in priest's clothing, then scanned the street where inky shadows pooled despite the streetlamps. The road was empty, except for the three of them, and the dhamphir behind, but sniffing the air, he sensed something else. Not a gargoyle. Something much more feral. Ivan's jaw clenched as the scent dredged up memories of pain and blood. The werewolf was back.

Ivan's keen eyes scanned the street, following the tendrils of darkness. He realized he wasn't imagining the deepening shadows as he watched them swirl around Angelos' feet. He glanced up sharply at the man, who peered back at him, his chin lifting imperiously, and Ivan's lip curled in a precursor to a snarl.

A ghost of a smile passed over Angelos' lips then he slid his gaze to Matteo, taking a step towards the nosferat. "I can if I can take her." He shifted his eyes to the woman before coming back to focus on Matteo. "I'm merciful," he said, his eyebrow quirking. "As is tradition, I ask three times. Then I kill you and take her. Since I've already asked once, nicely, this is your last warning: next time you refuse me, you die."

Matteo held his ground as Angelos took another step closer. Ivan, however, shifted...there was not tradition between vampires and whatever this creature was. His muscles tensed as they fought against all the alarms of his preternatural defence system that were telling him to flee or to prepare for a fight he wouldn't win. As he cracked his neck, trying to let go of the tension, Angelos shifted his gaze to him. "You might want to tell your pit bull to back down."

Matteo tilted his head, then jerked it again. "Down," the nosferat said.

Ivan ground his teeth together as he bit back his response, using the self-control he'd learned over the years. He forced his body into a stillness his mind didn't feel. He sniffed the air again, and this time caught a whiff of decay, like the smell that lingered long after the battle was done. The werewolf wasn't alone. There were gargoyles out there.

"Why?" Matteo asked, not taking his eyes off the Messenger.

Angelos canted his head. "Why?"

Matteo breathed deeply, his shoulders rising and falling with the movement. "Why do you want her? She's just a dhamphir." He waved a hand towards the woman, who took a step down in response. Matteo snapped his head to look at her, giving it a sharp shake. She stopped, confusion written on her face. Ivan watched Matteo's fingers play at the hilt of his sword. Despite checking Ivan's reaction, Matteo obviously wasn't as comfortable

A PLAGUE OF SHADOWS   229

with the man's presence as he tried to appear. "She can't fight, she can barely even hunt for herself yet."

"And who's fault is that, keeping a raptor in a cage?" Angelos slid a half step towards the dhamphir in question. The shadows pooling at his feet followed him, oozing along the asphalt as they contravened the physics of light.

"It's not safe for man nor beast out on the streets these days with nasty things lurking in the shadows."

The tendrils around Angelos' feet writhed at Matteo's baiting. Ivan wondered if Matteo even saw them, as adrenalin spiked through his own blood, then Matteo's fingers finally wrapped around the hilt of the short sword sheathed under his long jacket. He followed Matteo's lead and loosened the clasp holding his gun in its holster.

"Are you sure you want to do that?" Angelos said, tipping his head to the side, his gaze landing somewhere over Ivan's shoulder.

Ivan's stomach twisted as an irresistible itch between his shoulder blades forced him to turn around. Two women stood in the street behind him. One was a vampire, pale, thin and kitted out in black leather, with her long black hair falling straight over her shoulders, reminding him of the ghouls in the Japanese horror flicks Em liked. The other....

"Fuck. I hate when I'm right," Ivan said as he took in the other woman, the toned muscles of arms and legs clearly defined under her tight clothes. Her strong jaw clenched and unclenched as if itching to sink her teeth into something. The chiselled bone structure of her face led him to her eyes: wild brown eyes that glinted with red even in the low lighting of the night time street. "Werewolf."

He turned sideways, trying to simultaneously keep the women and Angelos in sight, all while inching towards the door of the mansion. He didn't want to be here when the wolf shed its human skin.

"Enough of this." Angelos sighed, the shadowy tentacles writhing as he spoke. "I want her. Night needs her."

"Which is it?" Matteo asked, his tone still baiting. Angelos' lips thinned, but Matteo continued. "Do you want her, or are you just a puppet for Night?"

Angelos' eyes narrowed and nostrils flared. The air crackled and hissed with static in the pause before the man responded. He didn't say anything. Instead, the fingers of his left hand twitched against his thigh, stirring up eddies in the darkness that clung to him. From out of the lane behind him, another shadow emerged with a rustle of wind in the otherwise calm night. Stepping into the weak halo cast by the streetlight, the slate grey shadow resolved into a gargoyle with blood from some recent kill still dripping from its gory maw.

Ivan managed to stand fast, despite the fear that gnawed its way through his gut, like an animal trying to free itself from a leg-hold trap. The gargoyle crouched beside Angelos, its shoulders hunching as it stretched a pair of large, leathery wings, like a giant, demonic bat.

"Wings," Matteo whispered. Ivan shifted at the tone of Matteo's voice, a disconcerting mix of fear and reverence.

"Do you like what I've done with your gargoyles?" Angelos said, running one hand along the creature's head.

Ivan scanned the street, wondering what other new horror might descend on them. It was giving him a headache trying to

A PLAGUE OF SHADOWS

look at them all at once. And then the bloody dhamphir shifted, like she wanted to pet the gargoyle too.

Matteo broke free of his reverie at the movement and stepped up the stairs to the mansion, his back to the door, herding the dhamphir behind him. Ivan breathed a sigh of relief and did the same.

Angelos stepped towards them, stopping at the fence line. "You're not going to invite me in for a drink?"

Matteo's hand reached for the door behind him. "Somehow I think that would be unwise."

Angelos took a step back, towards the gargoyle. It snapped its teeth as a tentacle of darkness reached towards it. The Herald hissed and swatted at the shadowy tendril before turning back to them. "Perhaps it's unwise not to. There are dark times ahead, with Night coming." Then the man turned away, followed by a swirl of feathery darkness.

CHAPTER THIRTY-ONE

MINA SIGHED AND TURNED over. Again. Her internal clock told her it was mid-day outside. A time for all good vampires to be asleep. But she couldn't sleep. Every time she closed her eyes, she saw the young man's body in the park, mauled by gargoyles, and god knows what else. Except when she looked at the face, it was Dale's she saw. Either that, or she felt the beat of leathery wings pulse across her eardrums, or heard the screams of her niece and nephew as their father was torn to shreds. The sickly sweet-sour smell of incipient decay filled her nostrils.

Mina huffed and swung her feet out of bed. Her sketchbook lay open on her desk, the lurid colours muted in the half-light of her room. She thought about picking it up, finding zen through pen and paper. Instead, she shook her head, trying to clear her senses. She needed to get out. Pulling on a pair of jeans and a sweater, and grabbing up her jacket and boots, she headed up the stairs.

When she reached the top, Mina paused, her breath catching in her throat when she saw the figure flowing through a kata. She leaned against the door jamb and watched Jack. Mesmerized by his fluid movements, the ebb and flow of his muscles over his back and arms, the disquieting images were dispelled from her mind, temporarily at least.

Jack flowed into the next movement of his personal kata, not matching any martial art she knew. Mina sighed.

A PLAGUE OF SHADOWS 233

"Are you just here to watch, or did you want something?" His level voice carried across the empty Sanctuary.

Mina took a few steps towards him. "Just here to enjoy the view." Her lips quirked into a smile as she noted the split-second hitch in his flow at her words. Then the moment passed, and he moved into the next series of movements.

Mina went to stand by his shirt. His momentum slowed, and his head turned in her direction more than the moves required. It was as if he was using her as his spotting point. Mina's eyebrow arched. The corners of his lips started to lift into a smile, and her heart hiccoughed as she glimpsed what he would look like if he let that full-on smile out. Then she was left wondering what it was that always came to quash the smile as his lips fell into their usual neutral. His movements slowed further, and Mina bent down to pick up his shirt as he walked towards her. She leaned back against the pillar, holding the shirt behind her when he reached out for it.

"Say please." She watched a spark light deep in his black eyes.

Instead, he took a step closer, his muscled shoulders a handsbreadth away from her chin. The thought crossed her mind of what he would do if she licked away the bead of sweat that had settled in that divot below his Adam's apple. Instead, she took a deep breath in and cocked her head to look up at him.

The hand that had been reaching for the shirt came to rest on the pillar behind her, while the knuckles of the other graced her jaw before he ran his thumb across her cheek. "I see you've almost recovered from Dar's thrashing. That was fast."

"Too fast?" Her breath caught in her throat.

He shook his head, his hair falling over his eyes. "Unnaturally fast. But normal for a vampire."

"Good." Mina reached up to push the lock of hair out of the way, tucking it behind his ear, wishing he would smile. "I wouldn't want you to think me any more strange than you already do."

"Strange isn't necessarily a bad thing." His hand left her cheek, dropping to her shoulder, and Mina let out the breath she'd been holding. He tipped his head down, bringing his lips closer to hers. "Can I have my shirt?"

Mina rocked up on her toes and leaned in. "You didn't say please." Her lips whispered over his. Jack reached behind her with the hand that had been on the pillar, trying to grab his shirt. His eyes didn't leave hers as she shifted it to her other hand.

"I thought we agreed this would be a bad idea."

"I agreed to no such thing." She arched an eyebrow then deked to the left, before slipping the other way, taking his shirt with her. She glanced over her shoulder and almost wavered at the heat in his gaze. Instead, she turned back around and headed down the staircase, her pulse hesitating until she heard his footsteps following her. She didn't stop until she'd reached her bedroom door. She cracked it open then leaned against the door jamb, waiting for him to catch up, his shirt dangling from her fingertips.

Mina barely had a chance to look up at him, into eyes that still smouldered, before his lips were on hers. He leaned into her, and she pressed her torso against his, her free hand reaching up behind his neck.

A small groan escaped when he pulled his lips from hers, pushing away from her. She dropped her forehead to his chest. *What now?*

Jack's fingertips came to her chin, lifting her face up so he could lock his eyes on hers.

"Am I invited in?" he said, his breath whispering over her cheek.

She raised her eyebrows and gave him a grimacing smile. "Yeah, you're invited in." She turned into her room, throwing his shirt over the back of the chair.

DAR LAY ON THE FLOOR of the vaulted main room of the Sanctuary and gazed up at the faux sky rendered in shards of glass, pondering the meaning of life and of death. He'd been lying there in a half meditative state for almost an hour. He sighed inwardly when he heard the creak in the stairs, followed by footsteps padding across the floor. He continued to stare at the stained-glass ceiling, willing Bee to go away.

Instead, she lay down next to him. He tried to ignore her, but soon the weight of the silence became too much.

"What do you want, Bee?" He sensed her cringe at the edge in his voice, but he didn't care. Apparently neither did she, at least not enough to leave him alone with his mood.

"We need to talk about Mina," she said.

"Do we have to?" His voice rasped over the knot in his throat. He wanted to rub the tiredness out of his eyes, but his arms refused to do his bidding.

He sensed her turn her face towards him, but he continued to stare at the universe of glass. He'd known her a long time, almost as long as Jack. He knew she wouldn't leave him alone until they talked.

"She's different," Bee said. "And she's never told us the story of how she came to be."

He didn't look at her, just kept looking at the fake stars, without really seeing them. "We're all our own unique little snowflakes," he said. "Each with our own creation story."

Bee shifted beside him, joining him in his contemplation of the ceiling. "You know what I mean," she persisted, regardless of whether or not he wanted to hear it. "She learned to fight too easily."

"She's a quick study."

"She accepted life as a vampire awfully quickly."

"She's a pragmatist."

Bee let out a huff. "She senses things, knows things she shouldn't." Bee rehashed the details of their encounter with the gargoyles, the two vampires and the young priest.

"I've heard all this," Dar said.

"She knew one of them wasn't a vampire. How could she know that? All I felt was a sense of 'vampire', and I've been one for centuries."

Dar arched an eyebrow; that detail had been left out of last night's hurried tale. He had no comeback, so they continued to lay in the hush of the large empty space.

After a few minutes of silence building between them, Bee turned her head back to him. "She could be dangerous."

For the first time since she'd laid down beside him, Dar turned to look at her. "So could I."

Bee's eyes narrowed, drawing out crow's feet around them, and her lips pursed together. Dar smiled – Jack wasn't the only one who would do what was necessary to protect the conclave if it came to that. He looked back up at the stars and sighed.

And it is coming to that.

DAR LAY IN SILENCE after that, alone with his thoughts, though Bee stayed beside him. Then he realized that he didn't want to be alone with his thoughts. He opened his mouth to speak but was cut off by footsteps on the stairs. Mina and Jack from the sounds of it. He didn't like the tension that ran between them when they were near each other, but, even more, he worried about the looks Jack gave Mina when he thought no one was watching. It could upset the precarious peace necessary for a tribe of predators to live and work together. And it definitely upset his plans for the future of the conclave.

Dar glanced at Bee out the corner of his eye, then breathing in deeply, exhaling heavily, he sat up.

Mina and Jack froze in their transit across the room. Jack's hand rested lightly on Mina's back.

Dar scowled at that hand, even though he couldn't actually see it, then looked at Mina. "We need to talk."

She straightened, pulling herself ever so slightly taller. "Do we?"

He stood up, in a single movement that was disturbingly fluid, like a spider unfolding its legs. He didn't allow himself to think about how it appeared to others. He slowly stepped towards her, forcing himself to feel the solid floor with each footfall.

Mina sidestepped away from him, from Bee, even from Jack. "I think it's time you told us how you were made," Dar said.

Mina crossed her arms over her chest. "I thought you'd know that, being vampires yourselves."

"Tell me anyway." Without intention, he found his voice deepened, slowed. He made it compelling.

Mina looked at him for a long minute, her lips pressed together. "I imagine like the lot of you. A bastard vampire attacked me, sucked my blood, and almost killed me. Then, somehow, I ingested his blood before he left me for dead. After that, my life became a little more fucked up. Isn't that how it works?"

"Usually there's some choice in the matter."

"I didn't choose for him to bite me. What else is there to know?" Her hands came to her hips and her chin jutted towards him.

Dar blinked slowly as he caught a glimpse of what Jack saw in her. But he also saw the danger, a wild card with a stubborn streak.

"You're different," he said, keeping his tone even, forcing his face to relax. "You can do things the rest of us can't, and I'm trying to figure out why."

Rather than responding in shock or confusion, he saw anger flit across her face as she tilted her head to look at Jack.

"You told him?" she said.

A burning sensation flared in Dar's chest as his own anger flashed through him like a wave of flame, flooding his body and causing his cheeks to flush. He turned to Jack.

"No, I—" Jack's hands went up, though whether in protest or protection, Dar didn't know.

"You knew?" He asked, his voice as hard and smooth as a blade.

A PLAGUE OF SHADOWS 239

"I...no, I didn't know anything for sure." Jack turned to Mina. "So there was nothing for me to tell."

Dar glared at Jack a second before returning to Mina. He took a deep breath and forced his muscles to relax. "Exactly what strange things can you do?"

Mina shrugged and dropped her arms to her sides. "I don't know." She looked from Jack to Bee then back at him. "I don't know what's normal for a vampire. My maker left me for dead, remember? So how should I know what's abnormal about me, let alone why."

"If she's a potential threat, we should get a warlock or witch to bind her," Bee said to him. She looked at Mina. "Sorry."

Dar stared at his hands, letting the silence fall as he contemplated the lines on his palms. Then he raised his head, shaking it. "No."

"At least until we know what we're dealing with." Bee stepped up to him.

"He said no," Jack said, shifting closer to Mina as he did. Dar's eyes tensed as he watched the small movement.

"I've seen too many lost to threats ignored," Bee said, peering at Mina, her lips tense, then she sighed. Her demeanour changed, and her voice softened as she looked towards the door. "Better safe than sorry, as they say."

"We always run a risk when we take in a new vampire that they'll have too much of their maker in them." Dar glanced back at Mina.

"We should—" Bee started again.

The cut of Dar's hand through the air silenced Bee, though he kept his eyes on Mina. "I'm not ready to condemn Mina yet."

"Maybe your judgment is clouded," Bee said, her voice barely audible.

Dar froze, a part of him wanting to strike her for her impertinence, another part fearing she was right. His head was heavy as he turned to look at Bee. "I said no." Facing Mina again, he continued. "However, you need to stay at the Sanctuary until we have a better idea why you're different. And how."

"But—" Mina started.

Dar cut her off. "I'll talk to Rhys. He may have some explanation. Until then you're off patrol."

"Seriously?" Mina stood up straighter and squared her shoulders. She gestured towards the door. "The gargoyles are still out there." She strode towards the door, then stopped, her hands came back to her hips. "And there's something else that stalks the night, whether or not you want to believe me." Her voice lowered. "Something far more insidious than the gargoyles." She looked at Bee. "And far more dangerous than me."

"How do you know that?" Bee asked. "You say this priest is some messenger, that a piece of knapped stone is somehow evil. But no one else feels it."

Dar silenced her with a look, his lips white with tension. Glancing down at the floor, his voice was quiet when he spoke. "Rhys does."

Mina shrugged her jacket on, then turned on Bee, getting up in her face. "How can you question that something wicked this way comes? You saw what it did to Mike."

"We don't know what attacked him," Dar said, trying to keep the churning in his gut out of his tone. He reached out to lay a hand on her shoulder.

A PLAGUE OF SHADOWS   241

Mina took a step back, shaking her head, dislodging his hand. "I didn't ask for this life, and I certainly didn't ask to be different." She looked at him, steadfastly ignoring Jack and Bee. "But I've accepted. I've adapted. And I'm willing to do my part to find this thing and protect those people out there who know nothing of any of this."

Dar said nothing. Instead, he returned her gaze with a hard one of his own. She recoiled from him, pulling further away.

"Fine," she said, slicing a hand through the air. "Fine, you don't believe me, you won't listen to me, and you don't trust me on your patrol. See if you can solve this riddle on your own." Then, before he could react with his dracul reflexes, she was out the door and into the setting sun.

Jack started to go after her, but Dar placed a heavy hand on his shoulder.

"Jack," he said, his voice steely and cold, brooking no disagreement. Jack stopped and turned to face him.

"If she chooses to stay, we protect her. If she chooses to leave, we let her. Either way, it's her choice. The conclave needs you." Dar's eyelids fluttered, and he unclenched his other hand, letting go of the fist he hadn't realized he'd been holding, his fingernails leaving indentations in his palms. He looked at Jack. "I need you."

CHAPTER THIRTY-TWO

MINA SHOVED HER HANDS into the pockets of her denim jacket and wished again that she stopped to change before storming out of the Sanctuary. The cold was muted by her vampire physiology, but it was still there, and the wind cut through her like a hundred small scalpels, letting the drizzle seep into her bones.

Luckily, she'd had an arsenal strapped to her body when she'd left, in preparation for going out on patrol. Other than that, all she had was her phone, with ID, credit card and a few bills slid into the case. She shoved her hands deeper. And found a couple of bobby pins she used to keep her hair off her face when she was painting. She'd left her rucksack behind, and with it, the keys to her old apartment, which she hadn't quite let go of.

Mina sighed and glanced up. The apartment she no longer called home. *But maybe Cam's turned up.* Her roommate – ex-roommate – still wasn't answering her texts or replying to voicemail. Stepping towards the road, she paused to see if there was a car coming along the empty street, as she wondered what she'd done to earn this cold shoulder. Just as she stepped into the street, she was stopped by a pitiful cry.

She tilted her head, trying to pinpoint the source of the mournful sound. She walked along the sidewalk, to the alley half a block down, and peered into the dark. Though fainter now, the sound was definitely coming from down there.

A PLAGUE OF SHADOWS   243

A thread of fear wormed its way through her gut as she entered the unlit alley. Any lights it had once had were burned out or broken, and the only thing that lit her way was residual light from the street behind her. Luckily her supernatural vision made the most of that little light.

"Here kitty kitty." The crying stopped for a second, and Mina worried she'd scared the poor thing away. But then it started again, sounding even more wretched. She pinpointed the source: underneath a dumpster. Mina took out her phone to use as a flashlight. Even with her vampire senses, she wasn't keen on facing whatever lurked down there without illumination. Getting down onto her knees, trying to avoid the grimiest parts of the asphalt, she peered underneath. A pair of large eyes stared back at her.

A pair of eyes in a face she recognized. "You're Mike's cat. The werecat."

The animal mewed softly in response. Mina reached in with one hand to coax the cat out, but it hissed as soon as she tried to scootch it forward.

"What? I'm just trying to help." Then the light from her phone fell on the cat's hind leg, which glistened wetly. Seeing that, her nose picked up a scent she'd missed, underneath the layers of reek from the dumpster.

"You're bleeding." Mina shifted, and the light flashed on something twisted around the cat's haunches. "Oh, you poor thing." Mina slid the phone into her pocket and flipped out one of her blades, then lay down, grime forgotten. Carefully, using her hands to guide her more than her sight, she cut the wire that wound around the cat's leg and removed it.

Expecting the cat to take off once it was free, Mina was surprised when it sat there unmoving. She took the time to run the knife blade along her jeans and slide it into its sheath, then examined the bloody wire in the dim light. She glanced back at the cat. "A snare. Someone tried to trap you." The cat stayed silent.

Again, Mina reached gently under the dumpster, prodding the cat to come out. Finally, it limped forward, making soft mewing sounds. Once she had it in her hands, she nestled it under her leather jacket to keep it out of the icy rain. It shivered against her torso, the blood that oozed from its leg seeping into her shirt.

"Come on, sweet thing, let's get you home."

After a stop at the corner store to pick up an antibiotic ointment she hoped was safe for animals and something resembling cat food, stared at the whole time by a pierced clerk with tie-dye hair, Mina was at her old apartment. She raised her hand to knock on the door, then dropped it, realizing that she already knew Cam wasn't there. Her blood told her it was empty.

The cat clung to her as she tried to extract its claws from her T-shirt. "Sorry, sweetie. If we're going to get inside, I need to put you down." Mina glanced at her shirt as she laid the cat on the floor, and was glad she still had clothes here, unless Cam had tossed them in a dumpster in a fit of pique.

Mina dug the bobby pins out of her jacket pocket, then bent one into a lever and the other into a pick. Sliding the lever into the lock and turning slightly, she then nudged the pins with the pick. She was never so happy for useless party tricks as when she heard the last pin click into place, and she was able to turn the lever to open the lock. The cat slumped into the apartment, listing to the injured side.

Before it could get too far, and either find a nook to hide in or bleed all over the floor, Mina scooped it up and headed to the bathroom.

FORTY-FIVE MINUTES and countless scratches later, Mina and the cat were cleaned, disinfected and bandaged. Both were wrapped in terry cloth, her in a robe and the cat in an old towel, much to the cat's very vocal chagrin. It made no secret of its displeasure as they lay on her bed.

Mina looked into the cat's golden eyes, which stared daggers at her. The cat snarled at her then settled into a low, continuous growl from deep in its belly. Mina listened to it for a while, throwing a pillow over her head in hopes of blocking it out. Finally, she gave up.

"Fine, if that wound opens again, don't come bleeding to me," she said as she gently unravelled the towel. Freed from its confines, the cat turned to lick its wounds.

Mina tsked. "You might not want to do that. I don't know if that ointment is good to eat." The cat looked at her but stopped. "How did you get those scratches, anyway, Cat? Fight with a dog twice your size?" It hissed in response. "And who would want to snare you? Psychopathic bastards." At that, it peered at her for a minute before turning a circle on the bed beside her and settling down.

Mina stared up at the ceiling, realizing that this room no longer felt like home. She was alone, except for a werecat that refused to Were, with no sign of her friend. Torn between fear that something had happened to Cam and worry that Cam was avoiding her because of something Mina'd done, she was unsure what to do. Part of her wanted to call the police but didn't see that going well: *'when was the last time you saw her', shortly after I became a vampire, officer*. Cam still didn't know about that secret.

Mina's eyes fluttered shut. In a half-awake state, she thought of Jack, of laying in his arms in her narrow bed, his chest rising and falling slow and steady, her flushed cheek pressed against his torso. Her mind turned to Dar and the haunted look in his eyes that lurked behind the warmth in his gaze, to Adeh and his hundred-watt smile, and even to Bee and her careful tutelage. A tear slid down her temple. She sniffled. Then she let out an 'oomph' as the weight of a rather large cat landed on her abdomen. She opened her eyes to find the cat's orange ones scrutinizing her.

After a minute, Mina looked away, letting the cat win the impromptu staring contest. She stroked along its back, and it started purring and kneading her belly in response. Tipping her head to the side, her gaze fell on the picture of Dale, Hana, Maggie and Liam. This year's Christmas card – all of them were kitted out in hideous sweaters with either reindeer antlers or elf ears on their heads. Mina reached out her free hand to run a finger over the picture. They looked so happy. So alive. So safe.

I should go see them. But I'd bring darkness down on them.

That was the last conscious thought Mina had before her eyes closed and she drifted into sleep, a purring werecat on her stomach.

MINA HEARD CRYING, a sound that tightened her throat. She tried to swallow past it but something sharp and cold against

A PLAGUE OF SHADOWS   247

her neck blocked the movement. She couldn't breathe. Opening her eyes, she expected to see a pair of golden ones peering into hers. Instead, a set of obsidian eyes stared back at her. She tried to look away, but found herself caught, consumed by the abyss behind the obsidian, unable to break free. The blade pressed more insistently into the flesh of her throat, a bead of wet trickling onto her pillow. Gathering all the will she could muster, she turned her head. Looking into the dark corners at the edge of her vision, she wished she hadn't.

Hana. Her sister-in-law lay in a rapidly expanding pool of blood, while Dale crouched over his wife's body, his face pale with shock. Maggie and Liam, sat beside him, wailing their grief.

"I told you what would happen," a soft voice said from the darkness. "You can still save them." The voice coalesced into one she recognized. "Join me," Cam said. "Join me and I'll give you the power to protect them." Cam stepped out of the shadows, but she was a ghost of the woman Mina knew, and her eyes were an oily black.

Mina shook her head, refusing to open her mouth in case she said yes. Tears formed in her eyes at the idea of her family tortured because of her. The voice changed, deepened, and the figure morphed into that of a blond priest. "If you don't, I'll kill you." The thought of death terrified her, but not as much as that of her family suffering. "After I kill them."

"No," Mina said, her voice barely a whisper, her throat tight with tears. The blade pierced her skin before it slid away. "No!"

Mina jerked out of sleep. Groggily, she wondered where she was, looking around at a room that wasn't her own. Then the cat nipped her hand, and the pieces came back together again. She'd come back to her old place, her old life, looking for shelter. Looking for Sanctuary.

Mina sat up, pondering what to do, but no answers were forthcoming. She glanced at the cat and came to a decision. Swallowing away the hoarseness in her throat, she got up and donned clean jeans and a T-shirt.

"If nothing else, you need to be fed." Padding into the kitchen, she was followed closely by the cat, which started to paw at her legs as she pulled out the can opener and tin of cat food. "Hey, watch the pants," she said, as a claw snagged. The cat stopped pawing and sat primly beside her until she placed the bowl in front of it, at which point it turned into a ravenous lion.

While the cat ate, Mina looked around the apartment. She opened the door to Cam's room, the cat now at her side, licking its paw to clean its face. The sick feeling that her friend was in trouble rose to haunt her again.

Nothing had been touched since she'd last visited. Mina searched the room for any sign that Cam had been there, however briefly, while the cat did a tour, sniffing and scratching and mewing and growling.

"Oh Cam, where are you?" Mina said, flopping onto Cam's bed and grabbing one of the plush toy animals she'd often teased her friend about – no adult, let alone a soon-to-be doctor should have stuffed animals. She hugged the toy to her chest and cried. After a minute, the mattress shifted as the cat jumped up beside her. When she felt its paw tap her arm, she lay on her back, and let go of the stuffie. The cat took its cue and hopped onto her stomach, with a bit more weight in the paws than expected.

A PLAGUE OF SHADOWS

"Oomph. You need to watch that this doesn't become a habit. I'm not a cat person." The cat turned around a few times before settling in. "I guess you don't care."

She stroked the cat gently, careful of its wounds. "So what do I do now, Cat?" she said. The cat chirruped and started kneading her stomach.

"Do I keep looking for Cam?" The cat looked at her, its tail swishing. She scratched it under its chin, and it closed its eyes and lifted its head, pressing its jaw into her fingers. "Leave the hunt for this Herald to the vampires that don't even believe he's real." The cat twisted its head away from her hand and lay it flat on her stomach, its wide eyes staring at her unblinking.

"Okay, you've had enough of my scritching your chin. How's this?" She moved her hand to the top of its head. Mina went back to her thinking out loud. "If I want to protect my family, old and new, I need to find the Herald and..." She looked at the cat, which still stared at her.

"That's kinda creepy, you know." It crept up her torso until its head was just beneath her chin. She stroked its whiskers with both hands. She realized she had no idea what to do when she found the priest-turned-demon.

"I need some sound advice." Mina mentally scanned through her options and ended up with only one name, but it was a good one. She sat up, dumping the cat onto the mattress, which resulted in a loud meow. "Sam."

CHAPTER THIRTY-THREE

"WHAT?!" SAM TURNED to her, almost dropping the tablet he had in one hand. Instead, he placed it gently down on the counter and peered at her through his frameless glasses, his head cocked as if trying to compute.

"Maybe I could get my job back," Mina said quietly, unsure what had made her suggest it in the first place. She glanced to where Nicole was working on a client. The cat sat by the door, where it had been relegated when Sam told her he couldn't have a cat in the shop, though he hadn't quite shooed it all the way out.

"You're fucking kidding me, right?" Sam said, his voice rising. Nicole popped her head up from her work, eyebrow arching, even though Mina was sure the familiar couldn't have heard her request. Sam glanced around, then grabbed her arm and dragged her into the back. "I can't have a vampire working in my shop."

Mina shrugged. "Why not?"

He turned away and was silent as he started the coffee maker going. Then he sighed, letting his shoulders drop, before turning to face her. Leaning against the sink, he stared at her. She stared back, crossing her arms over her chest.

"Why?" he asked.

She paused before answering, then her posture sagged a little. "I have nothing else to do. And I'm good at it."

"You were good at it." He shook his head and studied the floor. Finally, he raised his head and looked her in the eye. He

A PLAGUE OF SHADOWS 251

spoke slowly when he continued. "Can you really imagine working around blood all day?"

"It's just a little," Mina said, but his words planted a seed in her mind. She breathed in deeply through her nose and caught whiffs of blood from the customer out front. Her vision blurred for a second, and she exhaled trying to clear the scent from her sinuses. Her teeth ached, and she tried to think of the last time she'd fed. Days, it had been days.

Mina slumped into one of two chairs at the little table that took up a good chunk of the small space. Her head came to rest in her hands as she examined the overlapping circles left by years of coffee cups.

"Maybe Nicole will give you a drink when she's done." Sam sat down in the chair opposite her and leaned back. "What's really up?"

Mina glanced up at him without actually taking her head from her hands. She peered at him for a few seconds, then sighed and sat back.

"I have no life."

Sam's arms, his sleeves unbuttoned and rolled up to just below his elbows, crossed over his chest. "Just because you're one of the undead doesn't mean you don't have a life." He tipped the chair forward, his forearms coming to rest on the table. Mina leaned back, tipping her own chair onto its rear legs. Sam continued. "You have more than that; you have a purpose."

"I already had a purpose, creating art on nature's greatest canvas." She cocked an eyebrow, daring him to contradict her.

Sam studied his hands. "I love what I do, but I'd say keeping me, Nicole, your family, Cam, my brother...." He looked up at her. "Keeping them safe, that's a greater purpose. Though I understand if it's not what you want." He stood up at that and went over to pour himself a mug of coffee.

"It's not that." The front of Mina's chair clunked to the floor as she shifted forward. She traced one of the stains with her thumb before looking back at him. "They don't want me."

"What?" He turned towards her, mug in hand, leaning against the counter.

"The Athanatos. They don't want me."

"That doesn't matter."

"But—"

"But nothing. In the fundamental battle to save the world, it doesn't matter if you feel wanted."

"But they don't trust me." Mina frowned at him, and her voice was louder than she intended. "So screw them."

"Exactly."

"Huh?"

"Screw them. What they think doesn't matter. They don't know you." He came back to sit down across from her. "I do. I know you don't let what others think stop you from doing what's right."

Mina glared at him as she followed the circles on the table. "That was low," she finally responded.

Sam shrugged and took a sip of coffee, smiling at her over the rim.

"Besides, I don't know what to do," she said quietly to the table.

He opened his mouth to say something more when his phone vibrated. He pulled it out of his pocket and frowned, looking at the display.

"Rhys."

"Hmm, true. He might have some ideas."

"No, it's Rhys." He held up his phone. "He wants to stop by."

"Tell him I'll come there."

"He wants to see me." Sam scowled at her when she made a face. "I do have a life outside the shop and being dinner for vampires, you know."

"With Rhys?"

"Well, no." Sam stared at his phone for a second, his eyebrows pulling together in question, then he glanced at her. "Up for a walk?" he asked, standing up again.

"Remember the 'screw them'?" Mina said, though she followed his lead.

"Remember that I know you? Your curiosity will eat away at you if you don't come."

MINA KEPT HER ELBOWS in as she trailed Rhys into his apartment, afraid she might topple one of the piles of papers and books, setting off a domino effect that would bring the whole place down. Or that she'd trip on the werecat, who wove in and out between her ankles. Rhys turned his head back, speaking to her and Sam, who trailed her through the maze.

"I wasn't expecting our Mina." He shuffled some papers, revealing another chair. "I really just wanted to find Dar." Rhys straightened up but didn't turn around. "He's been ignoring me lately." Putting the papers down on his desk, he finally faced them. "I wonder sometimes if he's found a new librarian."

"He's stressed," Mina said, studying Rhys. His face was paler than normal, the bags under his eyes bluer. "Thinking he has to carry the weight of the night on his shoulders."

"He does..." Sam and Rhys both started. Sam stopped, and Rhys continued. "He does have a tendency to do that. Have a seat." He sat in a creaky wooden chair beside a desk piled high with papers. There was a cleared space where a pot of tea nestled, steam rising from the cup beside it. Rhys indicated a chair opposite that Mina hadn't noticed amongst the books.

A demonic yowl went up as Mina sat down and the werecat entered. The sound was followed by a streak of grey skittering up to the top of one of the piles. A shadow of a cat with green eyes stared daggers at the werecat, who plunked herself down in the middle of the room to lick her paws.

"Is that—" Mina stopped, as the grey cat shifted its hostile gaze to her.

"An ordinary house cat." Rhys shook his head. "Grey. Though I'm sure he thinks he's extraordinary." Rhys turned to Sam. "Tea?"

"No, thank you. I just had some coffee."

"Kids these days." Rhys smiled as he picked up his mug, taking a sip before speaking. "What can I do for you, Mina?"

"Well, I..." Mina slumped into the chair then quickly sat upright again when it started to teeter. "You wanted to talk to Sam." She looked over to her friend, who had his head tilted reading the titles of the books on Rhys' bookshelf.

"I wanted to talk to Dar." Rhys glanced at Sam, before returning to her. "Since he wasn't answering, I figured Sam was the next best thing." Mina's eyebrows scrunched together, biting back the question she had for Sam, as Rhys took another sip of tea before continuing. "Dar didn't send you for something specific?"

A PLAGUE OF SHADOWS 255

Mina shook her head. "Dar didn't send me at all."

Rhys sipped his tea. "Well, then, if you didn't want something, why did you come along with Sam?" he asked, with a waggle of the eyebrows and a smile at the corners of his mouth, as he reached down with his free hand to pat the werecat that sniffed at his shoes. The cat shied away, but then must have decided to allow it, since she rubbed the side of her face on his pants. "Likely not for my company, and definitely not for my tea." He smiled at her from behind his cup.

Mina's gaze travelled over the room, as she considered what to say, her eyes grazing over an old, sepia-toned picture on the wall. It took her a second to realize that it was Dar with a younger Rhys, by which point Sam decided to speak up. "They've had a falling out," he said from the bookcase. "You have a copy of the *Eldritch Covenant*?" He turned to Rhys, a look of mingled awe and horror on his face.

Rhys put his mug down on the desk and stared at Sam. "*You* know what the *Eldritch Covenant* is?"

"Yeah, what he said." Mina shifted her focus from Rhys to Sam, seeing her former boss in a new light.

Sam shrugged. "Interests outside of ink and vampire fodder, remember?" He turned away from the bookshelf and stepped over to Rhys' grey cat, which deigned to let him stroke its head while it continued to glare at the Were. "What did you want to talk to Dar about?"

"The blade, of course."

"I found it, the blade of Night," Mina said.

"The blade of the Evening Star."

"What?" she said.

"Technically the riddle says the blade of the Even Star."

Mina stopped her eyes from rolling, turning the look into a glance at Sam for support.

"Details are important," Sam said, shifting his gaze from her to Rhys, who was silent as he poured himself more tea.

"Ok, I found the blade of the Even Star."

"I know," Rhys said, before sipping his tea.

"You know?"

"Dar mentioned what you'd seen and asked me to check it out."

Sam arched an eyebrow at that, but she ignored him. Instead, she let her shoulders sag as she peered down at her palms. "And you don't believe me either."

"Quite the contrary. I do believe you." His voice deepened, causing Mina to look up. Wrapping the long fingers of both hands around his mug, he continued. "I just don't know why you see it, and none of the others do."

"What do you mean? Bee saw the blade." Hearing echoes of her mother's voice lecturing about posture, Mina sat up straight.

"For legendary creatures, you vampires can be quite literal," Sam said, shifting away from the bookshelf.

Rhys glanced at him as he blew on his tea, then took a long sip. "As he says. I mean, why can you sense the evil in this thing, but the other vampires can't? What's so special about you, Mina Sun?" He peered at Mina.

Mina didn't look either of them in the eye. She just shrugged and stayed silent, shifting in her seat until she remembered the precariousness of the chair. She rubbed at a smudge of India ink on her thumb as the silence in the room grew heavier. She glanced up to see Sam watching her, an expression on his face

A PLAGUE OF SHADOWS 257

she'd never seen before. She turned to Rhys and the werecat at his feet.

"Nothing," she said finally, when she couldn't take the silence anymore. "I'm Mina Sun. Orphan, former slacker student and wannabe tattoo artist, who was just trying to have some fun when I made the mistake of inviting some jackass vampire into my apartment." Her mind drifted back to that night.

"So you did invite him in." Rhys' voice was quiet, contemplative, as he looked into his mug.

"Yeah." Mina's voice rose and became harsh. "But I didn't ask to be made a vampire."

He glanced up at her. "I didn't suggest you did. What else do you remember?"

She bit her lip, before remembering that that was a bad habit for a vampire. "Funny, more now than right after it happened. I thought he was just a little kinky when he held my wrists and brought his teeth to my neck. I wasn't fussed." Mina's eyebrows drew together. "Then the bastard actually bit me." She looked from Rhys to Sam and back, her lips in a hard line. "I felt the blood dripping down my neck. That's when I got pissed. I kneed him in the groin and scratched at him. And when that didn't soothe my anger, or get him off me, I bit the bastard back." Mina's arms crossed over her chest. "As hard as I could. Teach him to bite a woman without asking."

"Hmm." Rhys looked at her as he sipped his tea and absent-mindedly pet the werecat.

"I think you drove home that lesson when you staked him in the heart," Sam said, calming Grey when it hissed at the werecat from its perch.

Mina glared at him, then shifted her attention to Rhys. "Hmmm what?" she asked.

"Perhaps that's what's different about you."

"What, killing your maker? I know, I've heard this before." Her jaw clenched as she stared at him.

"No." Rhys put his cup down. He pulled out a cloth and took his glasses off to clean them. "I mean, it's an unusual creation story. Usually, the vampire nearly drains the victim, then slices some blood vessel of its own to feed its blood to the person it wants to transform. So, you see my dear, you *are* special." He put his glasses back on and looked at her. "You're the vampire who created herself, in a way."

Mina's hackles raised. "I didn't ask for this. I was happy with my low-key life."

"Aren't we all," he said, his voice going quiet as he glanced at the photo on the wall, the one of him and Dar.

Mina's anger drained out of her as she shifted, feeling like she was intruding. Scuffling her feet, she tucked a wayward strand of hair behind her ear, glancing at Sam, who watched Rhys intently. Finally, Rhys looked back at them with his rheumy eyes.

After a second, Mina asked the question that had been niggling at her since Rhys said he believed her. "So, about this blade of...the Even Star, why do you believe me when no one else does?"

"Because I felt it too." He held her gaze as he spoke, then he pressed a button to wake up his laptop. "A heaviness in the air around it, pressing at my chest, constricting my throat."

"Did you hear it...them?" Mina asked.

Rhys' knotted fingers stopped moving the mouse. He looked sideways at her. "No, I didn't." He turned back to his computer. "What did you hear, my dear?"

A PLAGUE OF SHADOWS   259

"I'm not sure." Mina's eyes slid around the room, coming to rest on the werecat, who peered at her with its fiery eyes. She looked away, to see Sam staring at her. She turned back to Rhys. "A wail of voices. Without form; if there were words, I can't tell you what they were. Except in pain." She shrugged. "Other than that, I can't say."

"Hmmm."

"Would you stop with the 'hmmms', they make me nervous."

"What?" Rhys looked at her. "Sorry, that wasn't for you this time." He shifted the laptop so she could see the screen. A drawing of the blade stared back at her, right down to the silver dagger inlaid in the hilt, a little lopsided, four-pointed star.

The blade sat inside a golden circle, as if the circle was trapping it. Mina reached out to trace the circle, then her finger moved to the drawing underneath both of them. The thick top line had a dip in the middle, almost like the silhouette of a bird, then a thin line ran along the bottom. It looked like a bow. "What's this?" she asked, feeling a spark of recognition, though she couldn't imagine why.

Rhys leaned in to read the fine print on the scanned page. "I can't read this. But the circle..." He looked up. "The blade of the Sun."

A low yowl arose from beside Rhys' feet as the werecat hissed and backed up, bumping into Sam's legs. Rhys' cat responded in kind, hissing and spitting and leaping from its perch to one above the werecat's head.

"Doesn't look like a blade," Sam said, leaning over Rhys' shoulder. "Looks like a halo." Mina looked from the two of them to the image, her eyes drawn to the bird-like, bow-shaped drawing at the bottom. It niggled at something in the back of her mind though she couldn't put a pin in what.

"It may not, but it matches other sources," Rhys said, glancing at Sam. "It's what I wanted to mention to Dar. From what I've read, 'the blade of the Sun can destroy the blade of Night, if ever the keen knife of darkness is found.'"

"So it is the blade of Night." Mina shifted to look at him.

"Hmmph." Rhys grabbed his cat before it could make the mistake of pouncing on the Were.

"Details matter," she said, a smile working into the corners of her mouth. "So where do we find this blade of the Sun?"

"You can't," Rhys said.

"You're not going to tell me?" Mina crossed her arms and started to lean back, before remembering the ramshackle chair. "So you don't trust me either."

"It's not a matter of trust, my dear. It was lost to the world. Though even if it weren't, I'd say you probably shouldn't try to find it on your own."

Mina ignored the look Sam gave her at Rhys' words. "So what now then?"

Rhys pressed a button on his computer, and an unseen printer came to life near his feet. When it was done, he handed her the paper. "I suggest you visit the Smiths. Give them this. They're the experts on all things mineral, magical and murderous. If these two are magical blades..." He ran his thumb over the circle and the blade of Night. "Well, maybe the other one is too."

"The blade of the bird?" Mina looked at the printout. On it were the blade of Night, the circular blade, and the bow shape that plucked at her memory. She tilted her head to the side but couldn't jar the recollection loose. If she squinted her eyes, she

A PLAGUE OF SHADOWS 261

supposed she could see a double-ended sword. Finally, she decided she must've seen something like it in some cheesy B action flick.

CHAPTER THIRTY-FOUR

"WHERE DO YOU THINK you're going?" Dar asked, stepping in front of him as Jack shrugged on his jacket. Over Dar's shoulder, he noted the hiccough in the capoeira-like movements Bee was practicing, before she regained her flow.

"Out," Jack said. Dar arched an eyebrow; Jack arched one back.

"Are you going to search for her?"

Jack was tempted to ask who he meant by *her*, even though he knew exactly who Dar referred to. But he recognized that it wouldn't ameliorate either of their prickly moods. He shook his head as he took a step towards the right-hand alcove that lined the large space but said nothing.

"She knows where to find us if she wants to come back." Dar stepped in front of him, blocking his way. "So where are you going?"

Jack looked at Dar for a minute, pondering how to respond. He noticed the lines around Dar's eyes and the faint stress fractures across his forehead, and bit back his instinctive, snarky response. "To see the Smiths," he said instead.

"Why?"

"It's what Rhys told me to do...when you sent me as your messenger boy. Which he didn't appreciate by the way."

Dar ignored his commentary. "Why the Smiths?"

A PLAGUE OF SHADOWS 263

Jack scowled. "Because we need a new weapon against the gargoyles." He moved past Dar into the alcove, opening up a cupboard to reveal his knives and guns. Running his fingers over the assortment, he weighed his options. "Now that they can fly."

"He told you what we need?" Dar came to stand beside him, arms crossed over his chest. "Why didn't you tell me?"

"He didn't tell me." Jack picked up one of the guns and loaded a magazine of silver-filled hollow points. The other he loaded with the Smiths' new liquid lead rounds meant for gargoyles. He turned to Dar. "Sometimes I have my own ideas."

Dar leaned against the cupboard beside him, watching Bee instead of looking at him. "And what's your idea?"

"Kusarigama."

"Bless you." Dar raised an eyebrow.

Jack rolled his eyes as he glanced at Dar. "It's a weapon." He snugged a holster of blades onto his back, under his jacket. "I should go, before Finn thinks I've stood her up and decides to exact payment in flesh." Jack stepped back into the faint evening light of the Sanctuary. "Again. She doesn't like me very much anymore."

"I can't imagine why." Dar's lips formed into a wry smile.

Jack ignored the jibe and walked toward the door.

"Wait," Dar said. Jack paused. "Take Bee with you."

"Why?" Jack asked, shooting a look at Bee.

Dar shrugged a shoulder, his eyes sliding from Bee to the floor then to Jack. "She has nothing to do now that her student has quit. Besides, it's smart to be in pairs right now."

Jack regarded Dar for a few long seconds, before glancing at Bee, who looked at him in the same way. "I guess you're probably right."

JACK STALKED DOWN THE tunnel that led to the forge, steadfastly ignoring Bee. She'd stopped trying to strike up a conversation before they descended into the underground, so now the only sound was the dripping of water and the clomping of four angry feet. Jack paused, causing Bee to almost run into him.

"Why the sudden stop?" she said, her voice sharp.

"Probably nothing." He shook his head, trying to refocus his senses. "But we might not be alone down here."

"Thank god, maybe whatever it is will be better company." Bee pushed past him.

Jack laid his hand on her arm, ignoring the tensing of her muscles. "Look, I'm sorry. I know you did what you thought you needed to to protect the conclave."

"But you don't think it was the right to suggest we keep closer tabs on Mina, a vampire with strange abilities who has now run away?" She pulled her arm away.

Jack craned his neck, trying to stretch out the tension. He sighed and gave up. "Who knows what's right, right now?" He stepped in front of her again, finding the gap in the wall that led to the Smith's lair. "All we can do is muddle through and try to be ready for something we've no idea how to prepare for."

Pushing open the door to the forge, he was met by a wall of heat and a howl of anger.

A bone-jarring clang was followed by a rumbling shout. "Who dares come into my domain uninvited?"

"Pa!" An equally voluminous voice, only slightly higher pitched, echoed across the chamber. "Why are you being such

A PLAGUE OF SHADOWS 265

a cantankerous—" Finn stopped short of what she was going to say. "Something or other."

"Don't take that language with me, young lady."

"And don't take that tone with me. I'm a grown woman. I can invite a man to come by if I please." Her voice dripped with the sass and sensuality that Jack knew well. Then she turned to him and scowled. Seeing Bee over his shoulder, her scowl turned to a radiant smile. "Bee, come on in. Ignore my father." Turning back to Keagan, the parent she referred to, she glanced over her shoulder at Jack. "I suppose you can come in too, even though you're late." She looked pointedly at the elaborate clockwork set against the far wall.

Jack started down the staircase into the bowels of the underground lair, followed by Bee. "Maybe your clock's off."

"You come in uninvited and you insult my craftsmanship," Keagan said, but he took off his gloves nonetheless, and wiped his forehead with the cloth he took from his neck. "I might be only a Smith, but my clocks are never off."

"He's come about a weapon," Finn said.

"Isn't it always?" her father said from behind the cloth, the question clearly rhetorical.

Finn glanced at Jack, her chin lifting, the corner of her mouth rising, and her eyes shining. "No, not always."

"Hmm?" Keagan looked up, tucking the cloth into his back pocket. "So what is it this time, more magic bullets? Those seem to do the trick if you lot manage to ferret out a gargoyle and fire at it before it rips your heart out."

"No, no bullets this time." Jack shook his head, pulling a piece of paper out of his pocket. "Something new. A bladed weapon."

"Oh, my favourite." Finn's eyes shone bright, brighter than they had looking at him. She came up beside him, peering over his shoulder as he smoothed the paper on the workbench. Keagan scowled, his gaze travelling between Finn and Jack. Bee went to stand on the far side of the bench, beside the Smith, and looked at what Jack had drawn.

"What is it?" Keagan asked, his thick finger tracing the lines of the drawing.

"A kusarigama." Jack looked up at the master Smith. "Basically, a sickle attached to a chain."

"What's this spiky bit at the other end of the chain?" Finn asked.

"The weight."

Bee looked from the drawing to Jack. "Why? What's it good for?"

"The weight helps the chain travel when you throw it. I just thought the spikes were a nice touch."

"No, I mean this kusari...thing. Why not just use a sword or a bullet?"

"I used something similar against riders on horseback a long time ago. It has a greater reach and cuts a broader swathe as things are flying past you." Jack glanced at the others around the table. "Or above you."

"Why do you need that in the city?" Finn dropped her hand on Jack's shoulder, and looked at him like she used to, when they were just friends. "Not so many horses in the city. More's the shame."

"You haven't heard, then? The gargoyles have spread their wings."

CHAPTER THIRTY-FIVE

IVAN DUCKED TO GRAB his gun from where it sat on his coat and kept hold of the sword he'd been sparring with in his other hand. He ran up the stairs two at a time, with speed and lightness of step despite his hefty build. His sparring partner, Adam, made a lot more noise as he followed, even though he was much scrawnier.

What had drawn his attention was the bang of the front door slamming open, and now Matteo's incensed roar cascaded along the cold marble and warm wood of the mansion. At the top of the stairs, Ivan's mind struggled to digest the scene before him.

There was a wolf in their midst. A werewolf. Unable to find a blessed person to bless their home, the only thing keeping out interlopers was the menace of the Necrophagos, a patchwork of spells from dark fairies and warped warlocks, and a steel-reinforced, solid wood door. Usually, the strength of the vampires themselves was more than enough, without the other protections. But now that door was torn half off its hinges. Matteo stood between his new pet vampire and the canid's fangs, rapiers drawn. The nosferat's face was even paler than usual, the only colour from his red-rimmed eyes and the blue lips pulled back in a growl. The wolf snarled back at Matteo, its muscled torso pulsing as it panted and its bones cracking as it readjusted the shoulder it had clearly used to break open the door.

Ivan slid to a stop beside Matteo, with Adam coming up on his other side, as a figure stepped up to the doorway, but stayed on the far side of the threshold.

"Angelos." Matteo spat the name out like a viper spewing venom. Ivan shifted away as he tried to think of a plan that ended with him surviving this incursion. He glanced between Matteo and the man, adjusting his position to better prepare for whatever Angelos might do. But so far, the Herald of Night did nothing. Ivan wondered if the creature cloaked in the priest's skin couldn't cross the threshold or chose not to.

"Why are you disturbing me?" Matteo finally asked, his voice calmer.

"I've already told you," Angelos said, as he stepped through the doorway, past the broken jamb, answering Ivan's unspoken question. "I want her." He pointed at Camellia.

Ivan looked sidelong at the dhamphir. She was almost as pale as Matteo, despite being newly turned. He pressed his lips together. He didn't understand the science of being a vampire, since there weren't many vampires willing to subject themselves to study, himself included, but one thing he knew from personal experience was that the vampiric strain would feed itself at the expense of the host. She was starving.

He turned back to Angelos as the man continued to speak. "Will you give her to me or do I have to take her? This is the last time I ask."

Matteo didn't answer the question. Instead, he asked one of his own. "How did you and your vermin get past my door? The wards still hold."

Angelos' eyes shone like oil in the dimly lit foyer. "I was invited, of course."

A PLAGUE OF SHADOWS   269

Ivan took a small step sideways to avoid the rapier that came dangerously close to his thigh as Matteo tensed beside him; Adam and the dhamphir shifted away on the other side.

Matteo glanced at Ivan, then at Adam and his pet, then past them to the vampires that had arrayed themselves on the grand staircase leading from the upper floor. "Impossible. None of the conclave would dare."

"Oh, but I would." A voice of warm caramel and spice drifted down the stairs.

Ivan's head spun as he snapped it around. "Em," he whispered, a shard of ice lodging in his gut, as his often partner, not quite friend, descended. The vampires on the staircase parted, turning to stare, as they pressed into the wall to avoid the long sword Em held in one hand. None of them took a step forward to stop her. Maybe it was the gun she gripped in her other hand, or those she had holstered on either hip, maybe the daggers snugged into her thigh-high boots. She sashayed down the stairs.

"Emily," Matteo said, his voice deathly flat.

"Why?" Ivan asked, more to himself than to her, but she still answered.

"Night is coming." Em shrugged, her lustrous blond hair cascading over her shoulders. "Already the beat of gargoyle wings thrums through the night sky. All I've ever wanted was to be on the winning side."

A weariness settled in Ivan's bones. *Em, so easily swayed by powers that would only use her.* She'd always wanted to win in their sparring; sometimes he'd let her just to avoid the seething that followed. *Maybe I shouldn't have done that.* Something moved in the shadows behind her...Jin shifting slightly as he drew his short sword and lunged at her. *Not the right move if you want to survive the night*, Ivan thought. Em casually drove her sword back, sending it into Jin's abdomen. His sword clattered down the stairs, landing at Camellia's feet. A squawk escaped the dhamphir's lips, but, untutored in fighting, she let it lie there.

Meanwhile, Em twisted her sword and pulled it slowly from Jin's gut, effectively disemboweling him. Without the support of Em's blade, his body tumbled down the stairs to join his sword.

Camellia stared at Jin's body, her feet shuffling back to avoid the pool of blood and bodily fluids that seeped towards her toes. Beside him, Matteo snarled, his face contorting before he forced it back into some semblance of human.

"You believe the things he says?" Matteo kept his swords down as Em came to stand beside his dhamphir. "I thought you were smarter than that."

Em holstered her gun, her blade dripping Jin's blood on the marble, and took hold of Camellia's arm. She gripped it so tight, Ivan saw a grimace pass over the woman's face and smelled the blood drawn by Em's fingernails digging into flesh. Then Em stepped up to Matteo, dragging the woman with her, getting closer than Ivan would have dared, given the look on Matteo's face.

"Bite me," Em said, staring at Matteo, as the dhamphir tried to pull away, which just caused Em to grasp more tightly. "Seriously, bite me," Em said, tipping her head to the side, exposing her neck. "I want to be a nosferat, as promised." She scanned the gathered conclave, still and silent after Jin's death. "I can see you've promised others the same. Well, I've been patient. Now it's time to pay up. Bite me." Matteo didn't rise to the bait, and Em stepped back. "All promises and no follow through." She

A PLAGUE OF SHADOWS 271

dragged Camellia with her to stand between Angelos and the wolf. "Your turn," she said, tilting her head, exposing her neck to Angelos.

"Not now," the man said, his voice sharp. Angelos stepped beside her, replacing her hand with his on the dhamphir's arm. The woman pulled harder, finally showing some fight as she put her body weight behind her efforts to get away from Angelos and Em. But it was not enough.

Ivan shifted his grip on his sword, unsure what to do. The werewolf turned its red-brown eyes on him, causing him to pause.

Angelos turned to Matteo. "I told you I would have her. Now I give you another choice. Join me or die."

Ivan jaw clenched as he glanced from Angelos to Matteo. He didn't want to serve this creature, but neither did he want to die tonight. Hc could see Matteo play over the same scenarios. After a few long seconds, his rapiers, which had been singing during the exchange, came to rest beside his thighs. Angelos' chin lifted as he watched. Ivan didn't count himself much of a judge of character – if he were, he wouldn't be here – but he suspected the priest didn't trust Matteo any more than the nosferat did him.

Matteo returned the expression, his lips forming into a thin and tense smile. "How may I serve...Night?"

CHAPTER THIRTY-SIX

A DROP OF WHAT MINA hoped was water snaked down her neck, from somewhere or something overhead that she didn't dare look at. She paused to listen for signs of pursuit. She couldn't hear any sounds except the skittering of the underground denizens as they made way for her.

Or made way for whatever was tracking her. Mina was back in the deep belly of the underground, searching for the Smiths. And she felt the weight of an unseen predator at her back, with no means of escape.

Beside her, the werecat howled, a constant, low, grumbling growl.

Mina crouched to pet the cat and felt that its fur was standing on end.

"I know, I feel it too," Mina whispered. "Bloody Sam, having to work."

Unable to go back, she went forward until she hit the next T, where she once again cursed that she hadn't paid more attention when Jack and Bee brought her here last time. Her supernatural vampire skills didn't extend to navigation. Having nothing that pointed her one way or the other, she turned right.

"Bugger," she swore under her breath as she faced yet another dead end. She turned and slumped against the wall, heedless of whatever grime and muck she was getting on her jacket.

A PLAGUE OF SHADOWS   273

The cat, silent now, eyes wide, clawed at her legs. Then Mina heard the sound that had spooked it. A shuffle rather than a skitter emanating from the passage they'd just come from.

Mina coiled, tensing her muscles for fight or flight. Preferably flight. From a runner's crouch, Mina grasped the cat in one hand before launching herself down the other end of the T, past the opening to the passageway, past whatever was following her. She didn't look as she flew by, not wanting to know what was going to kill her.

She ran full-tilt along the tunnel, turning by instinct at the next few intersections. Not stopping until she found herself faced with a door.

A door that clearly belonged to the Smiths, given the hammer and anvil and the stylized flames.

I don't remember this door. She lifted the horseshoe knocker and dropped it as gently as she could muster against the door, then swore again as the sound of metal on metal echoed along the tunnel. She leaned her right ear into the door, but no sound came from the other side, not even the sound of hammer on anvil. Instead, her other ear flexed at a scrabble from the tunnels she'd just run through.

Mina rapped the door again, harder, not caring how much noise she made since she was trapped between a well-crafted metal door and an unknown pursuer. The definite slap of feet running on slick concrete ricocheted off the tunnel walls towards her and the cat.

She lifted the knocker again and repeatedly banged the door with it while her other hand loosened the knife at her hip from its sheath.

With her knocking still unanswered, she turned to face her fate, back pressed against the door, knife in her hand.

And tumbled backwards into empty space, while the cat pulled off an acrobatic move, its four paws landing on her solar plexus before vaulting itself over her head as she fell.

The door slammed back in place and a bar dropped down to keep it shut a second before something heavy struck the other side. The metal complained, but the door held.

"What in Heph's name were you doing coming through Hell's gate?"

Mina spun up into a crouch, knife still miraculously in hand, to face the owner of the voice. Breathing deeply, her brain started to function and take in what she saw.

Keagan, the Smith, and his daughter, Finn.

She filled and emptied her lungs in rapid, panting breaths before finding her voice. "Huh?"

"And what do you think you're doing bringing that thing into my forge?" The Smith indicated the werecat with the end of his hammer, which he swung around with ease, the flame tattoos on his bare arms undulating. The cat peered at him before lifting a leg to scratch behind its ear.

"Pa, be polite. This place has been without a forge cat for far too long. Not since Ma...." Finn stopped, tucking a stray lock of fiery red hair behind her ear.

"That ain't no forge cat." Keagan stared at the cat for a minute before turning around and heading down the steep stone stairs that led into the belly of the smithy. "It's a Were."

"You know?" Mina asked. Keagan didn't say yes, but he gave a small nod. "How?"

"Just look at it," he said without looking back.

A PLAGUE OF SHADOWS 275

Finn, meanwhile, crouched to the cat, offering a hand to be sniffed, before lifting it into an embrace and speaking in a tone of voice that didn't match her weightlifter's physique. "I don't care. You're just so soft and cuddly, yes you are."

"You're a woman grown, Finn," Keagan said, turning to grimace at his daughter, before continuing into the pit of the forge.

Finn stared after him. "Funny how you're so selective about seeing that," she said, barely audible to Mina, still on her knees at the woman's feet. Remembering she was there, the younger Smith reached a hand to Mina to help her up. Mina hastily sheathed her blade and took the proffered hand. "Since you're here, you might as well come down and tell us why."

By the time she and Finn arrived at the bottom of the long flight of stairs, Keagan had stripped off his gloves and poured himself a drink.

"So why did you bring that thing crashing into my door?" the Smith asked, before taking a swig of the dark, frothy beer.

Mina glanced up the way they'd come. "The gargoyle?" She realized that the word didn't sit well in her gut.

Mina shifted as Keagan peered at her over his beer mug. "That wasn't a gargoyle," he said.

"What was it then?"

He took another couple chugs of beer before wiping the foam from his mustache. "If you don't know what it is, I don't suppose you know why a werewolf is chasing you?"

"A what?" Mina glanced quickly at the cat that sunk further into Finn's arms.

"Why would a werewolf chase you through Hell's gate?" Finn asked, seemingly talking to the cat.

While her mind digested the thought of being pursued by a werewolf, Mina asked a trivial question. "Why do you call it Hell's gate?" Other than being really high and covered in carved flames, Mina didn't see anything particularly hellish about it.

"It's the entrance for uninvited guests," Finn said, momentarily pausing her cooing over the cat. "If you come through that door, you're in for a hell of a reception."

Keagan scowled at his daughter, or the cat, Mina couldn't tell. "That's not the actual reason," he said, then turned back to Mina. "Though it is for the unwanted visitor."

Mina finally turned to what Keagan had said. "How do you know it was a werewolf? Do Smiths have some sixth sense, like vampires?"

He nodded towards a screen to his left. "Triggered the security camera. Checked that as soon as I got my beer."

"Oh." Mina looked at the still displayed on the screen. A mass of muscle and ash brown fur filled the image, its lips pulled back to reveal vicious fangs.

"So what were you doing at Hell's gate?"

"I don't know anything about a Hell's gate, or the werewolf. I was just trying to find you." Mina shrugged. "I couldn't remember how we got here last time."

"Why didn't you get one of the others to bring you?" Finn said, without looking at her.

"They were busy," Mina said, peering at the screen, pretending to study the werewolf.

The Smith crossed his arms, causing his biceps to bulge even more. "What brings you here?"

Mina reached under her coat. The Smiths both stiffened then relaxed when she pulled out the piece of paper with the

A PLAGUE OF SHADOWS   277

drawings on it. The cat jumped out of Finn's arms and tried to pounce on the paper, before coming to sit by Mina when she was unsuccessful at snagging it.

"This." Mina handed the paper to Keagan. "Rhys thought maybe you could tell me about it."

He wiped his hands on his apron before taking the paper and gently unfolding it. His eyes flashed to her face before returning to the drawings. The Smith whistled.

"The blade of Night. I never thought I'd see that again."

Mina glanced from the paper to Keagan. "You know what it is?"

Keagan nodded. "Don't sound so surprised."

"It's just that it was a mystery to everyone else. Until I saw it."

"You've seen it?" His bushy eyebrows raised, crinkling his freckled forehead. He looked back at the paper and traced a calloused thumb over the circle before travelling to the bow-like drawing at the bottom.

It was her turn to nod. "At the museum. But it's not the one I've come to ask about. It's these other ones." Mina leaned over the table, stepping close to Keagan, pointing to the circle. "Rhys says this is the blade of the Sun." Keagan stiffened beside her, and she glanced from him to Finn. "You know it?"

Finn nodded. "One of the three blades of the Heavens: Star, Sun, Moon. We do know our weapons lore. But they're a myth."

"Like gargoyles?" Mina gave a harsh laugh. "Like me? And, as I said, I've seen the blade of Night, or the Even Star as Rhys calls it."

"Really, can you show me?" Finn asked.

Mina shook her head. "You might not want to see it. It's...evil."

"It's stone," Keagan said, shoving the paper into her hands. "Sorry. We can't help."

"Speak for yourself." Finn shot a sharp glance at her father.

Mina's jaw tightened as she smoothed out the paper onto the table again. "Rhys said the blade of the Sun had been lost. But that you might also know what this is." She stabbed at the bow-shaped image and again felt that tug of familiarity. "I'm looking for anything that might stop this Herald from bringing some creature called Night to Earth."

Keagan crossed his arms over his chest. "How can you vampires expect us to help you if you don't tell us anything?"

"I—" Mina looked from him to Finn, her shoulders lifting in a small shrug.

Finn lay a hand on her father's forearm. "We already knew about the Herald and the impending descent of Night through the netherworld rumour mill. Even if Dar didn't deign to share." She turned her attention to Mina. "I already told you what it is."

Mina drew her eyebrows together, giving her head a small shake, as if that might jog something. "No?"

"The blade of the Moon. A crescent blade. Well, two to be exact. See this arc?" She ran her finger along the upper edge, with the dip in the middle. "Two curved blades. There's a grip here in the centre, as well as one behind each cutting edge." She traced the lower arc in the drawing. Keagan coughed beside her. She looked at him but continued. "It's said to have a blue glow, harnessing moonlight itself." She pulled over the tablet sitting at the end of the table, closing the program that showed a Da Vinci-like sketch. She tapped in some words then turned it around to show a more detailed painting.

Mina gasped when she saw it.

"Beautiful, isn't it?" Finn sounded wistful. "But it's also lost. Having travelled the length of the Middle East in the Middle Ages, it crossed over into China. Then all mention of it stopped."

"It's not lost," Mina said, not taking her eyes off the image. She knew exactly where it was: hanging over the fireplace in Dale and Hana's study. A family heirloom, her sister-in-law had said.

The cat growled, her eyes trained at the door they'd come in through, a second before a rattle of metal cascaded down the smithy walls.

Mina peered up into the dark reaches. "Will the door hold?"

"Oh, my door will hold," the Smith said. "However, you can't leave the way you came." He turned to glare at Hell's gate and picked up a hefty pair of tongs with his free hand. "Finn, show her the way out while I go deal with our uninvited guests."

"I HAD A VISIT WITH Mina," Rhys said, tossing a piece of the scone he wasn't eating at an already over-stuffed pigeon. "And Sam."

"Is that why you've been calling me?" Dar sat at the far end of the bench, hands on knees, face taut. Rhys couldn't remember a time when he'd seen him so drawn.

"Partly," he said, leaving out the part about being worried. He threw another morsel to the bird that strutted towards him, chest puffed. "She told me how she was made."

"Like other vampires, I imagine."

"So you didn't ask her before you kicked her out?"

"I asked. She didn't answer." Dar stared at the pigeon. "And I didn't kick her out. She left."

"No, you just clipped her wings."

Dar didn't rise to the bait. "What did she want?" he asked instead.

"She didn't want anything. I wanted to talk to someone about our riddle, and you haven't been answering my calls." Dar didn't say anything, so Rhys continued. "So I called Sam, and she tagged along. But she was curious about what to do about the blade of Night."

"Of the Even Star?" Dar turned his head sharply. "What did you tell her?"

"What could I?" Rhys looked into Dar's brown eyes, flecked with sparks of red. "This riddle is a conundrum wrapped in an enigma cloaked in a mystery, and the key's been lost to the ages."

"If only the werecat would un-Were, maybe she could give us some clue as to the old man's mind," Dar said. "What he meant by it. Have you considered that he was just mentally ill, like so many denizens of the street?"

Rhys shook out his napkin, dislodging the last crumbs of scone for the pigeon, then used it to pat his clammy forehead. "Oh, no. He wasn't crazy. That's the other reason I was calling...they're not the old man's words."

"What?"

"They're part of a longer riddle: Dark blade of the Even Star, piercing the heart of the Sun."

"That's what the man said."

"Remember the other piece." Rhys arched an eyebrow at Dar then continued. "Rends the pitch vault of Hell, sundered by the blooded Blade, the prison of Night unlocks, at the break of Day."

"That makes no sense," Dar said, turning to him.

A PLAGUE OF SHADOWS 281

"I know." Rhys took a deep breath, letting his shoulders sag as he let it out in a huff. "You know I don't believe in prophesy."

"'It's hokum', and I quote." Dar shooed the pigeon away with a none-to-gentle nudge of his foot as it came looking for its next morsel.

"Yes." Rhys switched into his professor's voice. "Any resemblance of prophecy to actual events can be explained by realizing they are long lost tales told in the arcane rhythms of ancient tongues, passed through a millennium of broken telephone wire. Or by words generalized enough that eventually gullible minds mould them to fit present circumstances." He paused, watching the pigeon strut. "However, in this case, I may be wrong."

"Why do you say that?"

"Mina may need protection."

"What? Why? What does she have to do with this riddle?"

"Mina *Sun*. 'The heart of the sun.'"

"Oh." Dar peered at him with those eyes, that look that meant his mind was churning behind that smooth face. "You think?"

Rhys shrugged. "I still have no idea what it means. It could be some jewel somewhere. It could refer to some ritual. What the Herald needs to do to wake Night or how to stop him...I honestly don't know. But it's also possible it's not entirely a coincidence that the threads of time brought Mina Sun to us now. She might be the key." He stood up, causing a flutter of pigeons. "If she is, she's in danger." Dar came to stand beside him, and Rhys turned to him, tilting his head slightly. He lay his hand on Dar's smooth cheek and felt the muscles of Dar's jaw clench. Dar grabbed his wrist and drew it slowly away, his lips tight. Rhys stepped back.

"By the way," Rhys said. "*She* bit Luca when he drained her. That's how she was made."

CHAPTER THIRTY-SEVEN

DAR LAY PRONE ON THE floor in the centre of the Sanctuary. It seemed to be his new favourite place, at least when it was like this, empty and hushed. Looking up at fake stars, with the cool marble against his back, it brought to mind the open-air courtyards of his second life. The life after he was taken from his family but before he was turned. Except there were no fevered bodies entwined in the shadows. But in the ripples of memory there were also no worries.

He pressed his eyelids shut, blinking away the distractions of the past, and instead turned his mind to his conversation with Matteo. The nosferat had waylaid him as he wandered the alleyways, his shoulders slumped with apprehension. He hadn't made his usual offer this time – to turn Dar into a nosferat, rather than waiting for time to do it, which would happen soon enough. Instead, he'd shared information on the whereabouts of the gargoyles and the Herald. Asking nothing in return. Nothing except that Dar decimate the gargoyles and stop the Herald. And now he couldn't decide whether to trust the information since he certainly didn't trust Matteo. He always thought it funny that *don't look a gift horse in the mouth* and *beware of Greeks bearing gifts* both came from the same tale.

Dar heard the front door open and slowly close, and sighed. The sun was just climbing over the horizon. He'd sensed the tentative rays even before they had started to shine, bringing to life the tessellated night sky that comprised the dome of the Sanctuary's ceiling. The diffused light hadn't reached the floor of the cavernous space, so he was still swathed in dusk. Not for the first time he wished that the makers of the building had chosen a daytime scene.

Soft steps shuffled through the entryway, pausing at the threshold.

"Why were you following me?" he asked. The footsteps stopped. Silence followed. He craned his neck, turning his head towards Jack and Bee. "I asked you a question."

"You've been acting strange lately," Bee said, not moving from her place against the wall.

Jack stepped towards him. "I'm worried about you."

Dar gave a short, sharp laugh then looked back up at the stained-glass ceiling. "That could be taken in more ways than one."

"You can take it however you like, old friend," Jack said, coming to crouch beside him. "But Bee's right. You're acting strangely."

Bee came to stand behind Jack. Jack continued. "And then you have a rendezvous with Matteo, without backup, without telling one of us." He waved his hand over his shoulder at Bee. "What were you talking to him about anyway?"

Slowly Dar drew his gaze away from the stars overhead and turned back to his oldest adepts. His oldest friends. He shifted onto his side, curled and pushed up until he was sitting cross-legged.

"There's something you should know." He breathed into his lower back, pulling strength from the solidity of the floor. "I've had more than one conversation with Matteo over the years."

A PLAGUE OF SHADOWS   285

"What?" Bee came to one knee beside Jack. "Why? What could you have to say to him?" she asked, her voice sharp.

Dar looked down at the palm of his right hand as the thumb of his left traced the long life line from his wrist to the base of his index finger. "Matteo is wicked, with little remorse or empathy." He followed the head line back across his palm. "But not the worst thing we've faced in the past. And, unfortunately, I'm certain we'll face worse in the coming days." He looked up at them. "Night is coming. The Herald is already here, making way for her."

"You believe Mina?" Bee said.

She spoke without judgment or rancour, Dar noticed, and nodded in response. *That's good. She's flexible.*

"You think we'll need Matteo's help?" Jack said, his tone betraying none of his thoughts. *Also good, waits to process before making up his mind.*

"We may have no choice," Dar said aloud.

"Why? What did he say?"

Dar looked back at his hand, tracing the heart line this time, as he formed his thoughts into words. "He confirmed the identity of the Herald: the young priest."

"So you don't believe Mina," Jack said. "But you believe him."

Bee huffed, a coarse laugh, and shook her head. "And what makes you think you can trust him?"

"Nothing." Dar breathed deeply, his whole torso rising and falling. "But, in this case, I do." He realized it was true as he said it.

Jack sank into half lotus. "Do you believe what Mina said about the blade?"

"Yes." Dar glanced at Bee, before coming back to Jack. "But not because of what Matteo said. Rhys also thinks the blade at the museum is the blade of Night. And that if we find the Herald, if we stop him, we can stop Night from coming." Dar circled his shoulders and tipped his head from side to side, cracking his neck. "It explains what happened to Father Pietro."

"What do you mean?"

"The Herald had already taken the priest. The messenger of Night killed Father P."

"I don't suppose Matteo told you where to find this Herald or how to stop him?" Bee asked.

Dar glanced from her to Jack. "No," he said, the lie heavy in his mouth, as he shook his head and looked back at his hands. "Rest up. Tomorrow night we ferret out where he's hiding."

After they left, Dar lay back on the floor and shoved his hands into his pockets. His fingers worried at the piece of paper Matteo had given him. He didn't actually need it anymore, the address burned into his brain. He supposed he should have given it to Jack or Bee.

Suddenly he sat up, not wanting to be alone anymore. *Rhys*. But he couldn't go there. If he did, Rhys would see through him like glass. He'd be caring and concerned and comforting. Dar's canines ached at the thought of Rhys' comfort and realized his old love might not make it through alive. Dar didn't need anything else weighing down his soul.

AS THE SUN PEAKED IN through cracks around the blinds in Sam's bedroom, Dar realized that it was Monday, the only day

A PLAGUE OF SHADOWS

287

the shop was closed. He traced a lazy finger over the arm draped across his hip and along the tattoos that ended at the wrist. He intertwined his fingers through Sam's and brought that wrist to his mouth, sinking his fangs in and closing his eyes as he took a deep draught of sustenance. Fortifying himself for what lay ahead, so he told himself. He pulled his fangs out, something he couldn't imagine doing if it had been Rhys' wrist, though Rhys had also kicked him out of his bed years ago.

Sam shifted against his back. "Penny for your thoughts?" he asked, his lips whispering over Dar's neck.

Dar's ear twitched. Sam's heartbeat was slightly too fast, even given their recent exercise, and his skin was slightly too warm: Sam was sick, and Dar hadn't even concerned himself with that when he'd shown up at his door. His eyebrows pulled together in a frown.

"You're burning up," he said.

"You know I am." Sam's voice was throaty in his ear as he ran a hand down Dar's arm.

Swatting the caressing hand, Dar shifted away. "You know what I mean."

"I'm fine, just that bug that's been going around. But you're avoiding the question."

"What?"

"Penny for your thoughts."

"That's not a question." Dar twisted to face him, turning away from the shards of daylight that pierced into the back of his skull. Placing a hand on Sam's shoulder, he pushed him down into the pillows, letting out a small smile that quickly dropped from his lips. "I wouldn't burden you with my thoughts for all the money you have."

"Would be a cheap burden, given that I spend all my money on expensive clothes and outrageous Scotch." Sam ran his thumb along Dar's jaw and over his lips before dropping his hand to Dar's arm. Then he fixed his gaze on Dar's eyes. "Seriously, whatever it is, you don't have to bear it alone."

Dar heard Sam's thready pulse and felt guilty at disturbing him. He broke the look as his stomach clenched. "It's...I'm just worried."

"I can see that."

"There's a tide of evil coming our way."

"I know." Sam lay his palm against his cheek, trying to turn Dar's head back to face him. "But there's always evil, Darius. You should know that. Just sometimes it comes in like a lamb, wearing a business suit, sometimes a lion carrying a bomb."

Dar closed his eyes, not wanting to burden Sam with Night or nosferatu. His shoulders hunched to bring his lips to Sam's cheek. "I know...*in niz bogzarad*."

Sam twisted his head to look at him. "Bless you?"

Dar smirked. "It means 'This too shall pass'. You're right." He rolled off to sit on the edge of the bed. "I'm just not sure who will live to see that." He sighed, pulling his heavy shoulders back. Coming to a decision, he looked at Sam. "If anything happens to me, will you watch after Rhys...and Jack?" Dar reached down to pick up his pants. "Sorry, I really didn't mean to burden you," he said.

"You didn't." Sam ran a hand along his spine. "You don't have to go, you know. I have all day."

"The work of a vampire never ends." Dar cast a wry smile at him over his shoulder.

A PLAGUE OF SHADOWS 289

Sam's face remained serious, his eyes shining in the dusky room. His hand came to rest on Dar's thigh.

Dar grabbed his wrist and brought the hand to his mouth, running his lips over the palm.

"Really, I need to go. And don't put too much store by my mental meanderings. A long life leaves lots of time for melancholy." He pulled his shirt over his head, then leaned over and gave Sam a quick kiss.

"Call me in a few days?" Sam said, as Dar pulled on his shoes and grabbed his jacket.

"Count on it," he said, not turning around, forcing a smile to his lips in the hopes that it would colour his words.

CHAPTER THIRTY-EIGHT

RHYS AWOKE TO GREY licking his eyebrow. Perhaps that was why he'd been dreaming of his mother, long dead, and the thumb-and-spit polish she'd apply to his cheeks before sending him off to school. Or perhaps he was feeling maudlin.

He gently shoved the cat away and shifted onto his side. In indignant response, Grey started kneading his back, with claws, and growling. Rhys turned back to the cat and stroked his head. "What is it, Grey?"

The cat meowed and jumped off the bed, looking at him, clearly expecting him to follow. He peered at the clock on the bedside table. *Not even midnight*. He was too groggy for midnight, but the medications tended to do that.

The cat mewed again and walked a few paces down the hallway before sitting and staring at him. Rhys sighed.

"I'm coming, Grey. The drugs, they make me slow. Old age is no time to get sick." Rhys pulled the covers back and swung his legs out of bed, sliding his feet into his slippers. He grabbed his glasses from on top of the book he'd been reading before bed: *Agricultural Practices in Extremadura from the Bronze Age to the Present Day*. Even he found the book soporific, which was exactly why it was at his bedside lately.

He flipped on the light in the hall, and followed the cat, taking a detour into the kitchen to get a drink of water. The drugs also left his mouth dry.

A PLAGUE OF SHADOWS 291

Grey protested loudly at the delay, compelling Rhys to find him. It was when he picked the cat up from its station by the front door that he noticed the envelope. His mouth went dry again as he looked at the crisp cream paper, holding Grey tight to his chest. He stared at it for a long minute, unsure whether he wanted to read whatever letter it contained. But if he didn't, he wouldn't sleep for thinking of it, and it would just be there in the morning. With a sigh, he bent his stiff knees and cranky hip, putting the cat down and picking up the envelope.

Rhys ran his thumb over his own name written in a hand he knew intimately.

Dar. He found his way to the armchair and sat down heavily. At one time, the envelope would have caused a trill of pleasure to course through his nerves. Now his stomach fluttered with nausea – he was too old for secret love notes in the middle of the night.

Grey jumped up on his lap, and Rhys absentmindedly pet the cat's head as he stared at the envelope. Turning it over, he slowly slid his thumb under the flap and pulled out a piece of paper, in matching cream, folded neatly into thirds.

Rhys tucked the envelope under Grey's haunch and unfolded the letter. A slip of paper floated out and came to rest on his thigh. He picked it up, the letters and numbers floating in his vision before he recognized it as an address. A building somewhere near the water, on the far side of the river. He slipped this into the envelope and turned to the writing, its crisp, delicate stroke giving him a sense of foreboding.

My dearest Rhys, there are dark days ahead, for me regardless of whether or not I stop the Herald from calling down Night.

Rhys tried to swallow the lump forming in his throat. Grey kneaded his abdomen with his paws, claws retracted, and started a chirruping purr. Rhys ran a hand along the cat's back, out of training more than conscious thought. The hand holding the letter shook, and he scanned through the fine script. Somehow, he reached the end.

You are the heart, the soul, the conscience in my unnaturally long life. But I know to keep you safe, I have to let you go. And you me.

Yours always, Darius

"Oh Darius, what have you done?" The cat poked its head between the paper and his chest. Laying the letter, envelope and address carefully beside him, he clutched Grey to him and buried his face in its soft fur. The cat nuzzled its whiskers up into the crook of his neck. After a few long minutes, he breathed through the knot in his throat, and took out a tissue, wiping his eyes and blowing his nose.

He picked up the letter again. Whatever Dar said, Rhys recognized it for what it was: a suicide note. If nothing else, the request to give the address to Jack *if* Dar didn't contact him made it clear: he didn't expect to come back from whatever he was up to. Grey squawked when he put him down, hovering around his ankles. At his desk, he picked up his phone and found a number he'd never had to actually use before.

"Hello, Jack," he said when the call was answered. "Dar needs you."

A PLAGUE OF SHADOWS

JACK SLAMMED HIS PALM into the brick beside the door, then dismissed the sting with a shake of his head and a wave of his hand as he glanced around, his face turning red.

"Fuck!" He stared at his phone. Between what Rhys had said of Dar's letter and what he had left unsaid, Jack was sure that not only did Dar know the location of this Herald, but he was headed there now. And that he didn't expect to return, well, he trusted Rhys' judgment on that. "Damn it, Dar."

We're supposed to be in this together. Jack glanced at the people around him, giving him a wide berth after his outburst. Sliding his phone into his pocket, he went back into the club to find Bee. After scanning the main dance floor, he headed up to the mezzanine and finally found her in a corner, having a 'conversation' with the shapeshifter she had cornered. The shifter – a lizard boy by the looks of him, smooth and angular and slightly green – was not likely high enough in the netherworld to know the whereabouts of Night's messenger. But he and his ilk were all they had. Werewolves and warlocks and midges might know but wouldn't be keen on sharing...if he and Bee could locate some. The shifter was struggling to maintain human form under Bee's interrogation. Jack sympathized, given Bee's techniques included applying not-so-gentle pressure to his bits and bobs with one hand while grasping his throat with the other. Jack realized that might be contributing to the green cast of his skin. As he approached, Jack caught a few words of what Bee said, something about the shifter's jewels if he dared do that with his forked tongue again.

Bee looked over, as if she felt his eyes on her, and gave him a questioning look. He glanced at his phone, at the text that had followed Rhys' call, then raised his eyes and shook his head.

Nothing, he mouthed, then turned away to appear to scan the club, even though he'd already done that. A quiet night. The only not-quite-human denizens were the shapeshifter and a giant pixie he'd strong-armed earlier and gotten nothing out of. Knowing there wasn't anything more to be gained here, Jack made his way out to the street. Once out of the cacophonous club, he pulled out his phone again and mapped the address Rhys had relayed.

Fuck, just as I thought. He groaned. It was a warehouse in a deserted section of the dockyards, slated for razing, on the other side of the river. He hated that dark expanse of sluggish water, waiting to drag him under into a nightmare world of wispy, watery creatures. Nevertheless, he raised his hand to hail a cab.

"Hey, where do you think you're headed to?" Bee asked, her strong fingers grabbing his arm and pulling it down. Jack stared at her, his mind not coming up with something to say to put her off.

"You know I'll just follow you if you don't tell me," she said finally.

Jack sighed. As parsimoniously as possible, he relayed the message Rhys had told him. He hoped so much was lost in the game of broken telephone and Rhys' reticence to share the details of the letter that it didn't pique her curiosity. As he spoke, Bee's eyes narrowed, and he saw his hopes dashed. When he finished, she crossed her arms over her chest.

"And you were going to be just as pig-headed and foolish as Dar, and go off to rescue that selfish ass on your own?" She stood there staring at him, her index finger tapping out a beat on her arm.

A PLAGUE OF SHADOWS 295

"I..." Jack cast his gaze around, searching for the right words to explain. "Yes." He looked at her with what he hoped was contrition.

"Well, let's go save the damn fool then," she said, raising her hand.

A cab pulled up in front of Bee. Jack headed around the other side and slid in beside her. She turned her head sharply towards him when he gave the address of the Sanctuary, her eyebrow raised in question.

"There's something I need to pick up first."

CHAPTER THIRTY-NINE

ANGELOS GRASPED HIS right wrist with his left hand, fighting the urge to reach out and break Emily's fingers. She sat beside him in the back of the car, her long fingernails drumming against the sides of the leather seat. He scowled. Over-eagerness led to errors.

I should have left her back at the warehouse instead of Lin. But Angelos needed foot soldiers, and someone needed to stay with his prize, Camellia. He didn't trust the gargoyles alone with her. Even if he didn't exactly trust Lin, she did have a way with the beasts. And whatever he decided to do with the blade, he still needed a vessel...and a sacrifice.

In the driver's seat sat one of Matteo's brood, Adam; vouched for by Em, he'd seemed eager to join the cause. He knew the winning side when he saw it, but then they were the type of creatures whose loyalty was bought by power. *A pack of animals I'll have to cull when all this is done.* Matteo himself sat on Em's other side. He didn't trust him anywhere except in his sight. In front of Angelos was one of his own, Kian, a werewolf long in the service of Night.

So not really my own, he thought. Her dark brown eyes, set in the angular lines of her human face, stared at him in the rearview mirror. From the twitching muscle at the side of her jaw, she seemed ready to snap Em's fingers off with her teeth.

A PLAGUE OF SHADOWS   297

Angelos reached his right hand out and placed it on Em's. Bloodshed would not advance his plans.

"Tell me again your part in tonight's caper."

She sighed then turned towards him before looking back out the window and re-starting up her drumline with her free hand. "We've already gone over it. I won't fail you."

He gripped her hand harder. "Humour me."

She pouted at him but used her free hand to talk, which at least removed it from Kian's seat. "I go to the women's washroom just before the entrance to the exhibit, along with your...pet." A rumble rose in Kian's throat. Em smiled. "I keep everyone else out while she does her thing." Em waved her hand in Kian's direction. "Then I run screaming towards the exhibition, followed by a seemingly rabid hell hound. Signalling you to do your smash and grab of the dagger and run with the horde to the nearest exit."

She turned away, laying her hands on Kian's seat. Mercifully her fingers stayed where they were.

"And then?" Angelos glanced back up at the rear-view mirror. Kian's eyes sparkled, and slowly, carefully, she ran her tongue over her teeth, from canine to canine. He wasn't sure what that meant in werewolf body language, but he thought it might mean he'd have to let her eat Em at some point.

"And then I join the crowd fleeing this terror made flesh. And hopefully for her, she can find a way to get out of Dodge before they shoot her hide full of holes."

"There's something I don't understand about the plan," Adam said, having remained silent for the entire drive.

"Your task is to drive the getaway car, not to understand," Angelos said. "You can do that, yes? Em said you were a great driver."

Adam peered at him with his black eyes before continuing. "Usually we stay on the down-low. Not showing ourselves. So the vampire hunters and demon slayers don't find us. What happens to that anonymity when you let a werewolf loose in a crowded museum, with security cameras?"

"Honestly?" Angelos stared at him in the mirror. "I don't care. Let the gargoyles fill the sky and werewolves stalk the streets. And let the vampires rule the dark when Night descends upon the Earth."

Angelos watched the slow smile spread across Adam's face, the wicked grin reaching his eyes.

Em started drumming the seat again, then stopped. "Get ready to rumble folks. We're here."

ANGELOS LEANED ON A cane that he didn't need. However, the magic infused in it by the witch who'd pointed him to the blade, now that was useful. It gave an extra oomph to any strike. He'd felt the power himself, once, before he'd killed the witch, and taken the cane.

Standing in front of the blade again, the pull of the sweet song of death lured him in. A shard from the obsidian crypt that encased Night, it had a natural lust for blood, seeking out those who would wield it to greatest effect. He wanted to reach out and touch it, run his fingers along its multi-faceted surface. But he forced himself to be good, to delay gratification.

As he waited for the signal from Em, he pretended to read the large history of the site where the artifacts had been found, while in fact he watched the crowd ebb and flow, judging how

A PLAGUE OF SHADOWS 299

it would move in the moment of panic. He glanced at Matteo, standing by the gold and jade armour. The nosferat scowled at him, looking demonic, not bothering to pass as human. Angelos' lips thinned; he had more important things to do than teaching a recalcitrant nosferat a lesson in obedience.

He glanced at his watch and frowned. The museum would close soon. He felt the eddy of energy behind him as someone stepped towards him, separating from the flow.

"Interested in the Aztecs, Father? I guess you must be. This is your second time through after all."

Angelos looked to the source of the question: the docent. For a moment he was confused, then remembered that he'd kept the clerical accoutrements – priests were still given deference – and had donned them for tonight's enterprise.

Forcing the scowl from his face, he inclined his head towards the man, contorting his expression into a mockery of benevolence. "I believe it's always good to know our past, lest we repeat it."

"True," the docent said. "I guess I just don't expect the violence and the blood sacrifice to be your thing, being a priest and all."

"You'd be surprised at what some priests go in for," Angelos replied. He stopped his foot from tapping, instead tapping the cane rhythmically on the floor. He glanced at his watch again.

"Oh, I...I suppose," the docent stammered. "I should let you be. You'll never get through the exhibit again before closing if I don't."

Angelos relaxed his shoulders down his back as the docent backed away. To keep up appearances, he moved to the next sign, leaning in as if absorbed in every detail but checking his watch once more. He ran his hand over the dragon's head carved into the handle of the cane.

He was about to turn and head to the bathrooms, to give Kian an extra impetus to transform, when the screaming started. Em truly had a great set of lungs, among her other assets, even if she wasn't his type. People began to stream past him just as he picked up Kian's wolfish snarls and growls amongst the screams. The docent rushed to find the source of the commotion.

Angelos changed his grip on the cane he'd gotten past security and took aim at the glass of the display case as the alarm sounded, adding to the general riot of noise. He found his swing stalled by a resistance that shouldn't be there. He tilted his head sideways to look first at the fingers that had latched onto the cane then into the confused eyes of the docent.

"Father?" the man said, letting go.

Angelos stepped back, shifting the cane to his other hand, his nostrils flaring in anger at the impertinence of the man. In a swift, circular motion, he bashed the docent's skull in, blood and brain spattering up the wall. He followed through on the swing, and a shatter of glass fell onto the docent's crumpled form. Angelos reached in and wrenched the blade from its supports. For a second, the breath was stolen from his lungs, sucked in by the dark depths, before it came back with a rush of electrifying power. Recovering, he wiped the blood off the head of the cane and slid the dagger into a pocket. Then he joined the stream of people fleeing towards the emergency exit, adding a hobble to his steps and leaning on the superfluous cane. He looped an arm through Matteo's as the vampire strode past him towards the exit. "Help your crippled brother to the door." He smiled at the

A PLAGUE OF SHADOWS 301

snarl that flashed across Matteo's lips before the nosferat caught himself.

As they approached the door so did the security guards, attempting to search those who passed. The world slowed, and his senses heightened. With nothing else for it, he kept hobbling, shifting the cane slightly in his hand, getting ready to fight his way out if needed. But the guards were focused on what was happening behind him.

The sounds of terror from the exhibition hall had quieted, and the snarls and panting of a sated werewolf were imperceptible to human ears. The guards looked at each other before taking off at a slow jog in that direction. As they reached the door, he heard a tearful voice behind him.

"It's...a monster." Softened by a rumbling burr of a Scottish accent, it was still a voice he knew: Kian.

Passing outside into the night, it wasn't long before the padding of bare feet came up behind him.

Disentangling himself from Matteo, he glanced back to see Kian come down the steps, clothed in a wrap dress and nothing else.

"Did you get what you came for," she asked, looping her arm through his. "Do we have what we need to raise Night?"

He slipped his other hand into his jacket and a shiver passed through him as it landed on the hilt of the blade. "Yes, I got what I needed."

"Mmm, yes, so did I," she said, holding her hand up in the moonlight. A bracelet of gold and green stones circled a wrist that had been bare before.

"Kian."

"What, do you really want it to look like all that was taken was a little, old blade? I think that bitch vampire went shopping too."

Angelos couldn't really argue with that logic.

CHAPTER FORTY

FROM THE DARK, ELECTRIC buzz in his blood, Jack knew he'd found the right place. He would have known even if the lights hadn't been blazing. He glanced over his shoulder but couldn't see Bee. She'd gone off in the other direction as they tried frantically to find this warehouse among the maze of similar buildings.

Turning his attention ahead again, he jogged towards the building. For a second, he contemplated calling Bee before dismissing the thought: Dar didn't have the time. He started to run, covering the ground faster than any human could have managed. There was a hiccough in his step as he considered doing some recon. But that was displaced by 'fools rush in' just as he leapt up onto the loading dock using his superhuman forward momentum, skidding to a halt millimetres before the threshold of the open door.

Gargoyles circled at the edge of a halo of light, and he cursed himself for not taking the few seconds to let Bee know he'd found the place. The gargoyles had been busy spreading their strain; there were now six of them, all arrayed around Dar. Jack's heart caught in his chest before racing ahead.

Dar was a blur of motion in the centre of the circle, a blade in one hand, gun in the other. Something about that tableau niggled at the base of Jack's brain, but there was no time to puzzle it out now. Somewhere in the shadowed corners, other things lurked, unfamiliar things that left a jumble of sensations filling his blood, his nostrils, his ears, with a buzzing so loud it was like being in the middle of a hive.

But it was the gargoyles that drew his attention: though still awkward, they were growing into their wings, learning how to harass their target – in this case, Dar – while avoiding projectiles and mid-air collisions. Still, with his flowing, cat-like movements, Dar had already taken one down. A statue stood to Jack's left, its mouth drawn into a frozen snarl. Another was seriously wounded, limping lowly through the air with a damaged wing and leaden feet. That still left four behemoths of muscle, teeth and talon.

Jack grabbed the leaded scythe at the end of the kusarigama in one hand; with the other, he clutched the chain just below the weighted, spiked ball. He made sure the chain, also heavily leaded, was ready to unfurl. Bobbing back and forth, he watched the ebb and flow, looking for an entry point. Finally, he was able to dart through a gap in the aerial formation and slid in beside Dar.

Dar stopped, letting his weapons drop for a fraction of a second. Up close, Jack noticed the blood soaking his left sleeve, and the awkward way he stood on his right leg.

"What are you doing here?" Dar asked, his face flat, showing no relief at getting reinforcements.

"Head's up," Jack said, as he spun around so his back was covered by Dar's. He flipped the scythe in his hand, taking aim at the wing of the nearest gargoyle as it swooped down on him. "You didn't think I'd let you have all the glory, did you?"

"You weren't supposed to know I was here at all," Dar said, followed by the report of his gun firing and a gargoyle howling.

A PLAGUE OF SHADOWS   305

Jack let the scythe fly. "Yeah, about that. We need to talk about your failure to communicate." The scythe carried the chain over the gargoyle's shoulder blade and looped around. Jack yanked to catch the blade on bone, tearing the leathery wing. A howl ricocheted through the rafters. "Keeping something like this from the conclave...not okay."

"Perhaps not now," Dar said, and Jack felt Dar's sword arm ready for a swing.

"Perhaps not now," Jack repeated, grabbing the chain with both hands. The rough metal grated over his palms as he yanked with all his body weight, the angry gargoyle threatening to pull him off his feet as it reared and thrashed. The creature suddenly dropped, feinting, sending Jack off-balance as it lashed out with its equally deadly feet. Jack ducked, but a talon grazed his cheek. Blood welled up along the cut, but there was no time to tend to it as the creature reared back again. Then it dove, driving the pointed barb at the end of its wing into his thigh. Jack fell hard on his knee but took the chance to slide the leaded blade out of his leg sheath.

The gargoyle spun around, forcing Jack to go with it or lose his hand to the chain of the kusarigama, not a wound he'd heal from. The tension on the chain eased when he stepped towards the creature, and he unlooped it from around his hand, while continuing forward, letting his momentum drive the blade through the leather skin and into the gargoyle's chest. The gargoyle started to snarl, and Jack gave the chain a quick shake to loosen it from around the creature's wing. Its snarl became a hideous scream, cut short when its throat turned to stone.

He heard another shortened howl followed by a dull thud, like a wet slab of clay, as a third gargoyle fell. The final one beat its wings furiously as it tried to retreat into the rafters. Dar took aim, though his arm shook, and fired.

Click. Dar's gun was empty. The gargoyle perched itself in the rafters on the far side of the warehouse, out of reach of swords.

And the kusarigama, Jack realized. *Next one gets a longer chain.* "No more ammo?" he asked, looking over at Dar, his eyebrows coming together. He pinpointed the incongruity he'd felt earlier: Dar never used guns, only blades, a peculiarity Jack had never understood. He opened his mouth to comment but snapped it shut again at seeing Dar's state.

Dar shook his head, breathing heavily with his hands on his knees, his normally tanned skin pale. He'd lost a lot of blood from the various cuts and abrasions, shallow and deep.

Dar looked back at him. "How did you find me?"

"If you don't want to be found, don't leave a note saying where you'll be." The gargoyle chittered from its perch. Something small shifted in the shadows.

"Rhys." Dar's chest heaved.

"Why did you even think to come out here on your own?"

"You know." Dar's eyes shone. "The end is near for me, one way or another." He looked at the ground, his hands still pressing into his knees. "This way you don't have to kill me." A low growl rose from the gargoyle, and they both looked up at it.

"You should have told me."

"To have you charge in after me, be the hero and save the day?" He graced Jack with a lopsided smile. A whooping cough tumbled from the rafters. "I'll flip you to see who goes up there after it."

A PLAGUE OF SHADOWS 307

Jack grinned and waved the scythe end of the kusarigama in its direction. "After you. I don't want you to have all the glory, but you can have most of it."

"What is that thing anyway?" Dar asked as he stood up straight, indicating the kusarigama with the back of his bloody hand, still gripping his sword.

"A peasant weapon for a nomad boy."

The shadows shifted again, and the buzzing in Jack's ears increased. They both went silent, glancing around to find the source as they sunk into a fighting stance, back to back.

A vampire appeared out of the shadows, her olive skin an unhealthy grey except for the dark circles under her eyes, eyes which had a wild look to them. Jack felt the tug of some memory as the woman canted her head to the side to shift her unblinking gaze from them to the gargoyle. His eyes narrowed as he searched the recesses of his brain.

"Our new vampire," Dar said, shifting his blade in his hand.

"Matteo's new vampire." A wave of nausea passed through Jack's gut.

"The one we've been searching for. It might not be too late to save her."

"Oh, it's too late," another voice said from the shadows behind the woman, a voice that sent slivers of ice down Jack's spine.

"Lin."

"Hello, my Chagodai." Her sinuous tone turned hard. "Always the hero."

Jack flipped his knife in his hand, getting ready to throw it, but Lin knew him too well. She drew the young vampire in front of her, shielding herself from his strike, a hand around the woman's throat.

"I don't think the messenger of Night will be happy if you kill his sacrifice before he does," she said. The false smile slid from her face as she raised her other hand. "And I've had enough of your heroics." In the same moment, Dar spun around to step in front of him.

Before he even saw the crossbow, the bolt was embedded in Dar's chest.

Jack watched in shock as Dar fell, seemingly in slow motion, looking for all the world as if he were just slipping down to his knees to pray.

He lifted his gaze from Dar on his knees to Lin and stepped forward to charge at her. He blinked as he saw, over Lin's shoulder, that Bee had finally found them. Her eyes flicked over the scene, then, in a flash of metal, a blade left her hand. Lin snarled as the knife lodged itself in her back just below her shoulder blade. Turning, she bowled over a shocked Bee and fled into the night, dragging the new vampire with her. The gargoyle followed with a thump of wings. A hundred other skittering shadows trailed them into the darkness.

Jack sunk to his knees beside Dar, placing his hands on either side of the crossbow bolt, not wanting to pull it out, unable to push it through. He knew the poison from the silver tip and ashwood shaft was already spreading through Dar's blood, and the pale pallor of Dar's face had turned a sickly grey. Still, Jack gripped the shaft with bloody fingers and pressed his lips together, his nostrils flaring.

"Too late," Dar said, with a red smile, placing a crimson hand on Jack's, as he shook his head. "I get the glory after all." The smile dropped from his face. He grabbed Jack's jacket and looked at him with his fierce brown eyes. "Look after Rhys. And Mina." He

A PLAGUE OF SHADOWS   309

glanced over Jack's shoulder, his eyes losing their focus. "And Bee. And Jack."

Bee came to kneel beside him, her hand on his back, as the light faded from Dar's eyes.

CHAPTER FORTY-ONE

MINA STOOD AT THE GATE without speaking. She watched Jack, where he sat on the steps of the Sanctuary, rhythmically running a blade across the whetstone laid along his left thigh, apparently not caring what passersby thought. Or wayward vampires. If he'd noticed her presence, he gave no sign. He kept his eyes on task, his hair falling across his face. Not wanting to surprise him, which might cause his hand to slip, she stayed silent and just watched. It was almost meditative, trance-like. But the trance was broken when he held the dagger up to examine it, flipping his head to get his hair out of his face. The silver-embellished knife caught a glint from the rising sun. He ran an oiled cloth along the blade, still not acknowledging her.

The gate creaked as Mina entered the yard. Apparently, she hadn't been uninvited. As she stepped closer, she recognized the weapon as the dagger Dar always carried with its distinctive whorls.

She sat beside Jack and watched the rising sun as he finished tending to the dagger. Sliding it back in its sheath, he laid the sheathed blade across his lap, his hands on his knees, and lifted his head to the sun.

Mina glanced at the knife, then looked at him out the corner of her eye for a long minute before speaking. "I'm sorry."

A PLAGUE OF SHADOWS 311

There was an even longer pause before Jack spoke, leaving her to wonder how angry he was at her. Finally, his head shifted her way, though he didn't quite look at her.

"He was the one who found me, you know, after I escaped from Lin...and other things," he said when he finally spoke, laying a hand on the hilt of the dagger, and wrapping his fingers around it. "He took me in without knowing what she might have wrought within me." He looked at her with his black eyes shining like deep wells of ink. "As he said, it's always a risk."

Mina placed her hand on his, feeling the tension with which he grasped the knife. "I—"

Jack stood up abruptly, and she followed, not willing to let go. His eyes bored into her when he spoke. "Now he's dead because of me."

Mina inhaled sharply. She laid her forehead on his chest, placing her hands on his hips. Her chest constricted as an icy fist clutched at her heart. She breathed through the tightness, then hugged him in an unreturned embrace. "No, it's not your fault," she whispered into his T-shirt, closing her eyes.

Finally, his arms wrapped around her and she felt the stubble of his jawline on her cheek and the length of the sheathed knife on her back.

Because it's mine, she thought, as they became haloed in the golden rays of the sun.

His chest rose and fell against her, and she sighed, happy to just stand there in the rising sun forever. He breathed into her hair, lifting the strands, then his lips moved against her ear. "You're right." He pulled back to look into her eyes, running a thumb along her jawline. "It's Lin's."

Mina's mouth moved as she tried to find the words to explain that that wasn't what she meant but his lips were on hers before she could speak.

FOR MOST OF THE DAY, they'd just lain in Mina's small bed, still mostly dressed, limbs entwined, silent in their own thoughts. She wanted to ask about Jack's relationship with Dar; she hadn't realized it ran so deep. But she bit her tongue, unwilling to disturb their mutual melancholy.

But at some point, mid-afternoon, the caress of Jack's hand through her hair became a tilt of her chin, which led to a whisper of his lips against hers. Which led to him lifting her T-shirt over her head as she straddled his hips. Which led to her lips leaving a trail down his torso.

After they'd worked through some of their disparate sadness, they lay with limbs still entwined, but a lot more undressed. Mina dozed fitfully, but whenever she woke, it was to find Jack awake, absentmindedly running a thumb over her chin or a hand along her thigh.

Finally, she woke to find herself alone in the bed, but she knew she wasn't alone in the room even without opening her eyes: the subtle beat of wooden drums and brass percussion that was Jack's signature played through her blood. She sensed the sun was near setting and shifted to face the room. Propping herself up on her elbow, she frowned as Jack rifled through the paintings on her desk.

"These are really good," he said without turning. He lifted one of the watercolours so she could see what had caught his at-

A PLAGUE OF SHADOWS 313

tention: a rough portrait of Dar in Payne's Grey. Mina swung her legs out of bed and went to stand beside him.

"Thanks," she said, as a matter of habit, taking the painting from him and placing it with the rest. She used to love that shade, but now it seemed to be the only colour she could paint in. She placed her hand on his hip, turning him towards her. "We should get dressed. I imagine there are more important things to discuss than my paintings. The conclave needs to decide what to do next."

Placing his hands on her head, he pressed his forehead to hers. Swallowing loudly, he nodded, then pulled away.

"There's no discussion." He picked up his clothes and started to pull them on. "We find Lin. We get justice for Dar."

Mina paused, her fingertips on the door to the wardrobe. She collected herself, grabbing a clean pair of underwear from the darkness within.

"Revenge...do you really think that's the priority?" she said, not turning around, as she pulled on the underwear.

"Do you have a better idea?"

"Yes, find the Herald." Mina turned to look at him, but his expression was hidden underneath the T-shirt he was pulling over his head. She reached for her own shirt. "Maybe grab the blade." She shrugged into her T-shirt. "Get this new weapon Rhys says might help kill the Herald and stop Night from coming."

"New weapon?" Jack asked. Mina spared a glance over her shoulder at his question. He sat on the bed and had paused in the middle of pulling on his socks.

"I...I've been busy, investigating. A blade of the Moon. The Smiths say there's three: sun, moon and star."

"You talked to the Smiths?"

"Yeah?" It came out more a question than she wanted. She turned back to the wardrobe and dug out a pair of jeans. "All three were thought lost to the world."

"Three."

Mina charged ahead, ignoring his flat tone. "But the blade of the Even Star was found...Dar and Rhys both agreed." She paused, staring into the dark recesses of the wardrobe. "And I know where this moon blade is."

"You *have* been busy," he said, an edge to his voice replacing the flatness. Her bed creaked as he stood. "Doesn't change the fact that Lin killed Dar."

"I know." Mina slid her left leg into the jeans to join her right then shimmied them up her thighs. "But I think he'd agree that protecting people from Night is more important than avenging his death," she said.

"You didn't know him."

She finally turned to face him, boots in hand. "I knew him well enough to know that." She glared at him as he threaded his belt through the loop on the sheath of Dar's dagger.

He looked up at her, his face stony. "Lin killed Dar. What has this Herald actually done?" he said, stalking out of the room, leaving her with her mouth agape.

Seema slunk through the open doorway, coming to twine herself through Mina's ankles. She absentmindedly picked up the cat, once again forgetting that there was a person in there somewhere. "It's not what he's done but what he's planning to do."

A PLAGUE OF SHADOWS 315

MINA STOMPED UP THE stairs after Jack, letting her boots do the talking as their thudding resonated across marble and through wood.

"What gives?" a voice behind her said, just as she reached the top of the staircase and entered the main space. She glanced over her shoulder.

"Some of us were asleep," Adeh continued as he pulled a T-shirt on over his bare torso. The sight alone made her shiver. Even if her vampire body felt the cold less keenly, the damp still seeped into her bones. She zipped up her leather jacket all the way to her chin as she grimaced.

"Sorry." She walked more quietly to the armoury nestled in the arcade at the side of the hall, where Jack loaded himself down with enough weaponry to fight a small army. Or draw the attention of even the most reluctant cop. Arms crossed over her chest, she glared at him. Soon others followed Adeh up the stairs. Simon, Sha, Bee, Tana, Alex. Their numbers had dwindled in her short time with them.

"Don't you worry you might be stopped?" Mina asked when he didn't turn around. "The police have stepped up their patrols, what with all the deaths lately."

He looked up at her, then at the others, who were all grim-faced. "I don't plan to stand still long enough to be noticed by law enforcement," he said, as he checked one of the guns before sliding it into his holster.

"What are you going to do?" Adeh asked.

"Find Lin. Avenge Dar."

"Judge, jury and executioner?" Mina asked.

"What did you think our legal system entailed?" He slid a couple of knives into sheaths strapped to his legs. "This is the law of the netherworld."

Mina looked at the floor, not having an answer for that. Bee stepped into the arcade, opening the cupboard with the silver darts and throwing stars. She started secreting these on her person before tossing a bunch of inlaid ash stakes into a hip quiver.

"You're joining him in this?" Mina asked her. "What about the Herald? What about Night's blade?" A presence came up behind her. Glancing over her shoulder, she smiled at Brett. He placed his hands on her shoulders as she turned back to the vampires. "What about the weapon that can stop him?"

"Your weapon can wait," Bee said. "Right now, we have business to take care of." She strapped a belt with sheathed knives to her waist then slid another pair into her boots.

"It's not *my* blade. Dar believed me. Rhys believes me. And he found this crescent blade thing...the blade of the Moon. Kinda goes with Night, don't you think?"

The others drifted away from her, following Jack and Bee's lead, arming themselves to the teeth, a decimated platoon heading into battle.

"Rhys showed it to me. And I know where it is." But they ignored her and kept arming themselves. Mina huffed. "I didn't know Dar as long—"

"No, you didn't," Bee said, with Jack remaining taciturn.

Mina persisted. "I didn't know him as long as you, but he put all of you, all of them..." Mina waved her hand towards the door "... before himself. I don't think that would change now."

"Dar wasn't just my leader, he was my friend." Bee looked at her with narrowed eyes and a set jaw. "If it were one of us, he'd

A PLAGUE OF SHADOWS

317

do exactly what we're doing now." With that, Bee strode out the doors into the setting sun, trailed by the rest of the conclave.

Jack peered at her. "You're not coming?" he asked, though his tone was more statement than question. She shook her head, and he opened his lips as if to speak. Instead, he turned and followed the others.

Mina trotted after them, then stopped at the threshold as they trudged down the steps. She watched until they disappeared into the gloaming, pondering what to do now, all by herself.

"What are you going to do now?"

She jumped at the voice over her shoulder. Brett came to stand beside her; she'd forgotten he was there. She shrugged, placing a hand on his strong shoulder. "I...." Truth was, she didn't know. She might be able to steal Hana's blade, but she had no idea what to do with it. If she fought the Herald and whatever creatures of Night he'd recruited, she'd probably die. "I..." she started again but was saved from finishing as Sam came running up, breathless. Mina cocked an eyebrow. "You don't run."

Hands on his knees, he struggled to catch his breath as he held up a finger. "Wait. One. Second." It came out as a croak.

Mina walked the narrow path to the gate and laid a hand on his back. "Come inside, and I'll get you a drink."

They joined Brett and went into the Sanctuary. It was quiet as the grave. They were alone. Except for the werecat, she remembered, as the creature wound around her ankles.

"Where are the others?" Sam said after he'd caught his breath.

"Gone to avenge Dar," Brett said, his face more serious than Mina had ever seen it.

"They haven't heard then?"

"Heard what?" Mina asked, realizing it must be something big for Sam to have run without being chased.

"The blade's been stolen," Sam said, running a thumb over his familiar tattoo on his neck. "At least, I think it's the blade everyone's been asking after."

"What?! How do you know?"

"How do you not? It's all over the news. And the netherworld rumour mill." He stood up, drew out his phone and swiped the screen."A blade at that Mayan exhibit...stolen" He held it out for Mina to see.

"Aztec," Mina said as she gaped at the footage, chills spreading from her toes to the back of her neck. "They didn't even try to hide themselves, or what they are."

"That's Mark, yes?" Sam said. "The young priest that's missing."

"But why would a priest want an evil blade?" Brett said.

"He's not the priest anymore," Mina said, turning away from the video to pull together her own arsenal from what remained in the armoury. "He's the Herald of Night."

"The one you all have been talking about?" Brett asked. "The one who's trying to bring this creature Night back to our plane of existence from wherever she's been banished?"

"Yeah." Mina glanced up from checking the magazine she held.

"So, what are you going to do?" Sam asked.

"Find Finn." Mina slid the magazine into her gun.

"Finn?"

Mina nodded as she turned to a cupboard holding a couple of short blades. "There's another blade. Three of them actually, but one is lost. The other now stolen." She regarded the dagger

A PLAGUE OF SHADOWS

319

in her hand without really seeing it. "The third is at my brother's house."

"What?" Sam gawked at her.

"Your brother has a magic blade?" Brett asked.

"My sister-in-law, and I doubt she knows there's anything special about it, other than it's really old." Armed with as many weapons as she could muster without feeling completely conspicuous, Mina turned back to Sam and Brett. "Finn knows a thing or two about this 'crescent blade'. And unlike her father, she seems willing to help. And if I run into problems, like my brother's changed their codes, she has the skills to help me break and enter."

"Right." Sam nodded, his tense lips showing his disapproval. "Um, why not just ask instead of this criminal escapade?"

"'Hey, Sis, I'm a vamp now. Would you lend me your priceless family heirloom? I can't guarantee it won't be immolated, but I'm sure it'll get covered in blood.'" Mina cocked an eyebrow at him. "Shall I go on?"

Sam rolled his eyes but didn't respond.

Brett stepped forward from where he'd been leaning against the nearest pillar. "You do know what I do during the day, don't you?"

Mina turned to him, her head tipping to the side as she wracked her brain for the answer. His lips twisted into a wry smile. "No?" she said.

"Security. Holistic penetration testing for paranoid rich folk."

"English?" Sam asked.

"I'm contracted to break into people's homes and tell them what their vulnerabilities are."

Mina's mouth dropped open, but before she could say 'you're shitting me', Sam spoke.

"You're just like a donkey, full of layers." He smiled at Brett.

"I don't think you mean donkey," Brett said, an eyebrow lifting. He stepped up to the cupboard and picked up a gun, checking it over as if he'd done it many times before.

"That's where you go when you get all dressed up?" Mina gave him a lopsided smile.

"I have a life outside the conclave," he said, his voice soft.

"Are you sure you want to get involved in this..." She peered at Sam. "...criminal escapade?"

"Sure." Brett nodded, his face returning to grimness.

"Not me," Sam said, his voice quiet again. "I think I'll go check on Rhys."

Mina glanced down, feeling cautious claws on her calves. "And what about you, Cat? What are you going to do?" The cat rowled then took off out the still open door. "Okay then."

CHAPTER FORTY-TWO

"IT'S EMPTY," Bee said.

Jack glanced at her, her skin gleaming in the light of the near-full moon. Her jaw was clenched and her voice tight as she stared at the dark building. It was possible there was someone, something, there despite the lack of light, but he knew she was right: the warehouse was devoid of life, other than completely normal rats and spiders. He kicked a stone at his feet, sending it skittering across buckled asphalt. Maybe Mina was right. Maybe he was being selfish seeking revenge. Still, his blood itched, beyond the normal sense of vampires nearby. His skin prickled, as if something crawled underneath it. There was a thrum against his eardrums, which could have been the hubbub of the city, but sounded a lot like the echo of powerful, lingering magic. And when he opened his mouth halfway and breathed in, there was a metallic tang in air that tasted almost like blood.

"We should probably still check it out," Adeh said from behind his other shoulder, then stepped past him towards the desolate building.

Bee looked at Jack; he shrugged and followed Adeh. "Since we came all this way." He drew his gun despite the emptiness he sensed. As a vampire, his eyes picked up any available light, and with moonlight seeping in through all the broken windows in the warehouse, he easily made his way across the threshold and through the open space.

It was still littered with statues of gargoyles contorted in the rictus of a painful death. Even though he tried not to look, his eyes were drawn to the centre of the space, to the dark stain on the concrete.

Adeh and Sha walked over, somehow knowing that that was the spot where Dar had died. Bee went to join them, while Jack made a circuit of the first floor, telling himself he hadn't had a chance to do it the previous night, caught in the midst of a melee. There were claw marks on the walls and scuff marks on the floors that spoke of a much larger horde than what they'd faced last night. He forced himself to cast his mind back, and recalled the skittering of unseen creatures following after Lin as she'd disappeared into the darkness.

"There were more than gargoyles here."

Jack startled at the voice behind him, echoing his own thoughts. Taking a deep breath, he turned to see Bee's shining eyes on him.

"Yeah," he said, then continued on his circuit, until he came to a staircase that led up to a second floor, the layer of dust on its treads disturbed by recent traffic. He glanced at Bee, and she gave him a sharp nod. He squared his shoulders, then headed up the stairs, pausing halfway when a stair creaked under him. He listened for sounds of attack from above, even though his preternatural senses told him nothing was up there. But there was still something that itched in his blood so badly his teeth hurt.

Raising his gun, he peeked his head over the top of the stairs, turning around to look for anything waiting to lop his head off. He shot a glance at Bee and shook his head. "Nothing." His voice was hushed even to his ears.

A PLAGUE OF SHADOWS   323

She took the stairs two at a time to pass him and step out into the open space. Reaching the top, Jack scanned the area. It wasn't any more protected than the floor below, all the panes of glass gone from the windows, but it offered an impressive view of the downtown and its constellation of lights. There'd be condos here in a year, he was sure.

Bee toured the perimeter while he rifled through the scattered detritus of life gathered in the middle of the large space, encircling a portion of wall that had escaped demolition. Shifting around to the other side, he saw that, at some point, someone had started a fire up here. Squatting down, he guessed it wasn't that long ago, the remnants of the blaze not yet turned to dust. A clattered sounded, followed by swearing, as Bee kicked something metal by the window. Jack looked up to see if she was okay, but the wall was in between them. He tipped his head as he looked at the wall.

"Bee," he said, as he stood up and stepped closer to the wall.

"What?" she shouted from the far side, apparently still cranky at kicking something.

"Come here." His voice was even as he spoke, interrupting a stream of soft curses. "Please." He heard her heavy boots clomp across the floor.

She came to a stop beside the piece of wall, facing him with her hands on her hips. "What's gotten into you?" She stepped towards him, lifting her leg high to clear a piece of rubble. "You sound like Rhys."

Jack slid his eyes slowly from her to the wall, jutting his chin in its direction. She followed his gaze.

"Oh." Bee didn't say another word for a minute as she took in the charcoal marks that covered the wall. "What do you think it is?" she asked, finally breaking the heavy silence.

Jack stepped towards the wall, and his skin prickled like a sunburn. "Writing," he said. "In some arcane language I've never seen before." Still, he was sure it was writing of some kind, with symbols that looked like Egyptian hieroglyphs, but weren't. There were harshly drawn lines and cross marks, scratched so strongly it was as if someone was trying to extirpate the section of wall completely. Some of the symbols had been rubbed out, leaving smudges of grey that were overdrawn with more charcoal.

"I wish we had Rhys here." Jack nodded at the wall. "He might be able to give us a clue."

Bee slid her gun into its holster and reached for something else. "We have the power," she said, taking a step back as she brought her phone up. Jack looked away, avoiding the flash, as she snapped a photo. She swiped the screen, sending the image. "We'll see if he's up."

Jack peered at Bee for a second, wondering at the slight widening of her eyes if she'd the same thought he had.

"See if he's still willing to help us, after what happened to Dar," she said, picking her way back across the debris to the stairs.

ANGELOS SAT IN THE chair of bones, so like a throne, and decided he liked it. He ran his hand over the contorted carvings on the arm rest, and scowled as skin flaked off onto his lap. He lifted the hand to examine it in the candlelight. Lesions and

A PLAGUE OF SHADOWS 325

scabs. *These weak forms.* His gums ached, and he tasted metal as he pressed his lips into a tense line. Running his tongue along his teeth, he noticed a few were loose. *That's what I get for taking a human.* He gripped the obsidian blade that lay across his lap, and heard the voices trapped inside howl through his blood. He let their tortured tones comfort him and took solace in its song that spoke of power untapped. Then the knuckles began to throb, and he loosened his grip.

Sitting alone, he watched his stolen subjects as they shifted nervously, unsure in their new reality. Except Matteo. A cold flame of anger flared in his chest: the vampire didn't fidget, didn't bow his head. Instead, he held himself stiff and glared at Angelos. There was strength in his stance. Under the planes of the ghostly visage, he could see the classic lines and handsome features Matteo had once possessed, and an idea wormed its way into his brain.

Angelos beckoned the dhamphir to him. Camellia, the one Matteo had been so protective of. He'd planned to give her to Night. *But plans change.*

"Come, it's time for dinner." He pitched his voice low, modulating its frequencies towards seduction but not into compulsion...yet. She came without hesitation. Matteo shifted, and Angelos smiled, his eyebrow cocked. Keeping his eyes locked on Matteo, he let that smile lick over his lips as the woman sashayed up the few stairs to his new throne. He glanced sidelong at her. She stopped in front of him, one foot half lifted off the ground, as if unsure what to do next.

"Kneel."

She complied, but there was a brief spark in her eyes, even if it burned out quickly. *Maybe there's hope for her yet.* As she came to her knees, she tipped her head down, causing her dark curls to cascade over her rosy cheeks.

He cast his gaze lazily around the room. Most of the vampires kept to the shadows, including Em. She pretended to stare steadfastly over his shoulder, but he caught the momentary glances she threw his way, filled with fire. His body responded even though she wasn't his type.

On the other side of the room, the werewolves who were not out prowling sat hunched in a pack near the wall, wearing their human forms uneasily so close to the full moon. There was always one looking his way, like prey watching a potential predator. Every now and then one of them snapped at the gargoyle that crouched to their right. The gargoyle glared at them or at the floor. Beside it, Lin stared at him, careful to keep her face as expressionless as marble and her eyes as empty as the void.

Sitting there, Angelos realized two things: he didn't trust Lin any more than Matteo, and, after lifetimes of living in the shadow of Night, it was his time to be ascendant. He caressed the blade, causing heads to pop-up momentarily before looking away, not wanting to be picked.

Who should I kill first? he thought, and the blade sang in response. He took a shuddering breath in and checked himself – none of these creatures deserved to be a sacrifice. Again, the blade vibrated under his fingers, as if responding to his thoughts.

A light touch on his knee brought his attention back to the woman in front of him. She looked at him with her big brown eyes, full of hunger. Angelos ran his fingertips across her red lips, pulling at them to expose her fangs. He drew his hand away, and she rocked forward. He could almost smell her need. *But what to do with such hunger?* He smiled at the thought.

A PLAGUE OF SHADOWS

"Angelos." Matteo's voice was like a whip in the hushed room. "Aren't you supposed to be doing something more important? Like bringing the reign of Night back to the Earth."

Angelos glared at Matteo, but reminded himself to not harm the man, or the body, strong and whole and preternatural. "I decide what's important and what's not." Matteo took a half step forward at that, but Lin shifted in front of him.

"I hate to agree with the rat—"

"Then don't." Angelos' jaw was tight as he suppressed the snarl.

"Night is waiting." Lin was not quelled, as if she didn't understand the power he held in his hand.

Angelos looked at the dhamphir at his knees, rather than Lin, as he spoke. "She's been waiting for millennia. So what if she waits another night." He glanced up at Lin. "The sacrifice is not ready and the moon is not full."

He returned his attention to the woman in front of him. "I wonder what happens when a vampire feeds from a priest turned Herald," he said, as he rolled up the sleeve to his shirt. "What dark magic might we brew in this empty vessel?" With his other hand, he grabbed the tumble of mahogany curls, placed the exposed arm close to her mouth. "Feed." He let out a ragged gasp as her greedy lips clamped onto his wrist, and her fangs sunk through flesh.

He sighed and slumped back in his throne, letting his gaze travel the room through half-closed eyes, leaving everything slightly out of focus. He watched the vampires watch him as the dhamphir sucked the life from this body. He felt its weak heart slow and the pulse become thready. Sweat sheened its skin. And it was entirely too Teutonic for his tastes, its blond hair and blue eyes at odds with the thing he was inside. His hooded eyes, still unfocused, trawled the room to find the figure much more like his own. Long and lean limbs, with a face of sharp angles, aquiline nose and chiseled jaw. Angelos straightened up. *It's time.*

"Enough," he whispered, his voice rough. The dhamphir either didn't hear him or chose to ignore. He grabbed her dark curls in the fingers of his other hand, the grip strong despite the blood loss, and yanked her head back to an unnatural angle. "I said enough." He held her there for a second until the fear came alive in her eyes.

Then he returned his focus to Matteo, who dropped his glamour of a moment ago, and slid back into nosferat form: all angles and pale skin and bloodshot eyes.

"That's right. Show me the monster inside." Angelos rose from the throne of bones and stepped down from the dais, the dark blade still in his hand. Matteo eyed him warily but didn't flinch. But Angelos passed him and looked at Lin, who regarded him with careful blandness. The only sign of what she might be thinking was the thinning of her lips and the tense hand on the gargoyle's head. He stopped between the two former alphas and turned so he could assess them both. Matteo had shifted so he could see him over his shoulder.

Angelos inhaled, and they both tensed. "It's a long night tomorrow," he said, the human voice warped as he called up powers deep and dark. "Sleep." The word resonated, and he watched as, one by one, from weakest to strongest, the vampires and the werewolves and finally the lone gargoyle slumped to the floor.

He stepped over to Matteo, blinking when the heavy eyelids opened, and the blurry gaze tried to focus on him. "You're

A PLAGUE OF SHADOWS 329

stronger than I expected. Good." He drew the blade and ran the flat along his palm, watching Matteo's eyes widen a fraction.

"Don't worry, I won't harm you," he said, crouching down over the vampire. "No. I need that body intact if I'm going to wear it."

CHAPTER FORTY-THREE

ONCE AGAIN MINA STOOD in the dark outside her brother's house. The night was quiet and deep, the tentative nocturnal sounds muffled by a blanket of late-season snow.

"Can we get going on this caper?" Finn said, drawing Mina's attention to her. Her cohort's arms were wrapped around her chest, her hands in her armpits. "I'm not much use as a lock pick if I can't use my fingers." She huffed out, staring cross-eyed at the stray strand of curly, red hair she was trying to dislodge from her face. All she succeeded in doing was creating a cloud of condensation.

Mina looked away, back at the house. "Just making sure they're actually asleep." Shaking her head to dispel the maudlin thoughts that threatened to take over, she stepped into the empty street, where the pressure of her boots turned the wet snow to slush. She glanced back to see that Finn followed, with Brett bringing up the rear, scanning the street as if he were their bodyguard. She nodded to the driveway, where a square patch of black asphalt contrasted with the white snow. "And Hana's still at work."

"I'm sure we could take care of them if needed," Finn said.

Mina stopped, causing the Smith to bump into her. "This is my family. We won't be 'taking care' of them."

Finn's mouth opened and closed like a fish before she answered, her voice a rough whisper. "That's not what I meant. We

A PLAGUE OF SHADOWS   331

could explain. You could glamour them, or whatever it is you vampires do."

Mina's eyebrows pulled together, and she gazed at Finn, who tilted her head and stared right back.

"They've been a bit remiss in your education, haven't they?" Finn turned away and trudged through the wet snow to the front of the house.

Mina glanced down at the obvious footprints and hoped the mist would turn to rain and wash them away before the theft was discovered. Joining Finn at the door, she kept her voice low, as she crouched to pick up a smooth rock at her feet. "What do you mean?"

"With the right training, even as a dracul, you could charm the pants off a priest." Finn stopped, her eyes narrowing. "Which isn't always that hard, depending on the priest, but still...."

"Enough of the chitchat," Brett said, cramming onto the small porch. "We have a job to do."

"Right." Finn turned to the door, bending to look at the lock.

"Shove over," Mina said, coming to stand beside Finn. She placed her fingers over the keypad.

"Wait." Finn grabbed her fingers, and Mina felt the woman's pulse. Despite participating in a break and enter, it was slow and even. "What if they've changed it?"

"They haven't."

"How do you know?"

"It's been their anniversary since they bought the house, same as the alarm." Mina punched in the first three numbers. "No reason for them to change it now." Still, she paused before pressing the final number.

"Then why bring me along? I could be home by the fire."

"In case they'd changed it."

"But...."

"You two are going to wake the neighbours," Brett hissed.

"Dale could never remember." Mina punched in the last number. "He wrote it on the bottom of that rock." She nodded down to the smooth stone. Closing her eyes, she willed her assumption to be right, then pressed the key to enter the number. Her ears twitched as an alarm sounded. Then she breathed deeply, calming her nerves. The door had clicked. The sound was an ambulance two blocks over.

Exactly two blocks...how do I know that? But reflections on her unnatural senses would have to wait, so she turned away from that and carefully swung the door open. "Wipe your feet," she whispered.

"You're stealing from him...do you think he'll care about dirty floors?" Brett said, though he did as she asked.

"If we leave no trace, the longer it will take for them to discover it's gone."

Finn touched a finger to the side of her nose and followed suit, then started tiptoeing to the left.

Mina lay a hand on the woman's arm and gave her a questioning look. "Where do you think you're going?" She pitched her voice low.

Finn shrugged, lifting the hand with the burglar's bag she carried. "It's obvious the study is over here," she whispered then kept walking.

Mina startled as the bulk of Brett's torso pressed against her shoulder. He tipped his head so his lips were next to her ear. "She's right," he said, his breath lifting the hairs against her neck, before he went after Finn, his footsteps nearly silent despite his solid physique.

"Yes, but...it's *my* brother's house." Mina sighed then followed them to the study.

"SO, SOMEONE KNOWS THIS blade is worth something," Finn said, hands on her hips, burglar's bag at her feet, as Mina entered the room.

"Shhh," Brett remonstrated again.

Mina pulled the door mostly shut, then turned to the Smith. "But this is the blade of the Moon, right?" She stood in front of the weapon. Though it still looked a bit like a bow, the allusion to a crescent moon was clear now that she knew what to look for – the luminous whorled steel and the elegantly arcing blades on either end. On the other side were a pair of hand holds, as well as the one in the middle that gave the weapon the appearance of a bird's body in the drawing, the blades showing up as wings.

"Oh yes." Finn's tone was reverential. "And someone knows it's more than just a family heirloom," she added in a theatrical whisper, before crouching down to her bag.

"Why do you say that?"

Finn beckoned her over to the wall, using the tool she'd pulled out of her bag to indicate something that meant nothing to Mina. "This."

Mina nodded slowly, her eyes shifting between Finn and the blade, then shook her head.

Finn rolled her eyes, then used the tool to point at Brett. "Ask him, he's the professional." She turned back to her examination of the space between wall and weapon.

Brett leaned in to get a look, then let out a low whistle. "That's professional grade."

"Care to explain?" Mina said.

He stepped back to join her as Finn continued her study. "It's an alarm, triggered by weight. We lift this blade up...." He turned his gaze to Mina. "Well, let's just say we won't have to worry about being quiet."

Mina went over to Finn. "But you can disable it, right?"

Finn tipped her head to the side and made a noise which didn't actually answer Mina's question.

Brett leaned towards Mina. "The best thing for it might be to get ready to run. The calibration would have to be spot on, with the blade being so light."

Finn turned to peer at him, her eyes narrowing as something rumbled along the street outside. She glanced back at the blade.

As Brett went to stand beside Finn, a thread of possessiveness flared in Mina's veins. He looked from Finn to the blade, not sparing a glance for Mina. "Are you thinking what I'm thinking?"

"Maybe." Finn crouched down to reach into her bag again.

"Would someone care to enlighten me what you're thinking? This is my brother's house, after all."

Brett's gaze travelled over Finn's red curls before meeting Mina's eyes. "There might be a wider margin for error. This may be professional grade." He nodded at the display before casting his eyes around the room. "But this is not a museum. It's not an art gallery. It's a house in a busy residential neighbourhood. With kids."

A PLAGUE OF SHADOWS   335

"So?"

Finn popped up from her bag, holding an unsharpened sword. "So, if it were calibrated too finely, the garbage truck would set it off." She flipped the blade over in her hand. "Here, catch."

Mina barely had time to realize Finn was tossing her the blunt sword before she snatched it out of the air to keep it from clattering on the floor. "What the hell are you thinking?" she hissed. Peering at Finn, Mina considered she might have to re-evaluate her assessment of the Smith.

"You *are* special, aren't you? Catching that without warning? I can see why Jack's intrigued."

Mina just glared at her.

Finn raised an eyebrow and shrugged a shoulder before turning back to the wall. "What it means is that we just need to get close enough in weight." She turned to Mina. "So what do you think?" When Mina gave her a questioning look, Finn nodded to the blade in her hand. "Is that close enough?"

Mina tested the weight of the blunted blade and glanced between it and the one on the wall. She'd never held her sister-in-law's family heirloom, nor really heard the story of how it had come into her possession, only that it had been in the family for years. "Yes?" she said, looking from Brett to Finn. "But we still might want to be ready to run."

CHAPTER FORTY-FOUR

JACK HESITATED AT THE door to the brownstone, realizing it was only the second time he'd been there without Dar. His hand was poised over the solid wood, fingers curled, as he willed himself to knock.

"He said he'd help," Bee said, leaning in behind him, her voice soft, barely audible over the rumble of traffic.

"I know." Jack's fist finally contacted the door, as an unpleasant mixture of grief and guilt gnawed at his stomach. "It still doesn't feel right."

"That's not going to wake a guard dog, let alone an old man." Bee stepped past him and grabbed the knocker. It was torn from her hand as the door opened.

"I'm not that old, and my hearing is fine." Rhys peered at them then turned around and trundled back into the dim apartment, pulling a cloth from the pocket of his housecoat to clean his glasses. Jack glanced at Bee, who had the grace to look abashed. But Jack sympathized: when you were immortal, it was easy to think anyone older was infirm. He followed after Rhys, who was still in his pyjamas, blue stripes with paisley amoeba crawling up in between the lines, his hair wild. He'd had never seen him so unkempt; usually Rhys was the picture-perfect example of a proper, albeit slightly eccentric, English professor.

In the living room, Rhys shifted the cat from its place in his armchair to the floor, resulting in a disgruntled meow followed

A PLAGUE OF SHADOWS

by hissing as it eyed the two vampires accusingly. Jack ignored it; instead the assortment of flower arrangements on the small side table caught his attention.

Rhys followed his gaze. "From people who knew about...." His voice broke. He coughed into his sleeve then picked up a mug that emitted an aroma of bracing mint and sweet fennel. Jack tried to think of something to say as he watched Rhys, the man's watery blue eyes gazing at the flowers. But Rhys continued before Jack could form his grief into words.

"I appreciate the thought, though I don't know what I'll do with a bunch of dead flowers." He put the mug down and picked up a box, running a hand over it. "Now, our Sam, on the other hand, he apparently knows a bit about grief." Rhys frowned and slid the box top open to reveal a selection of packaged teas.

Bee moved beside Jack, and Rhys shifted his attention to them.

"But you're not here to talk about people's discomfort with death."

"We could come back," Jack said.

"What?" Rhys shut the box quickly and placed it back on the table. "No, you can't."

"You're not going to help us?" Bee asked.

Rhys arched an eyebrow. "Don't be daft. Of course, I'm going to help. I wouldn't have told you to come otherwise."

"But you said...." Bee canted her head in confusion. Jack commiserated.

"I said you can't come back *later*. You need to know what you're dealing with right now." Rhys turned to his computer, the signs of grief temporarily fading away as he slid into his comfort zone. He pulled up a copy of the image Bee had sent onto his laptop, the one from the warehouse with its arcane writing and strange symbols. "Where did you find this?"

Jack shifted forward in his chair to get a better look at Rhys' screen. "The warehouse where...." He glanced at Rhys.

"Ah," the man said, coughing into his sleeve. "What were you doing there? I don't think Angelos is hanging around a derelict warehouse when he's taken over the local Necrophagos."

"What?" Jack squinted at Rhys.

"Don't you keep up on the supernatural rumour mill at all?"

"I...I've been preoccupied," Jack said. "We were at the warehouse to find Lin, to—"

"To exact revenge." Rhys peered at him, his face blank. "Really? You have greater concerns right now." He turned back to the computer screen. "See this?" He ran his finger along an area where a number of symbols had been rubbed out and new ones written over top.

"Smudge marks? Mistakes?" Jack glanced at Rhys, who responded with a wry smile before turning back to the image.

"No." He shook his head. "Alterations. I've been telling you there's a ritual to wake Night."

"Really?" Bee shifted from where she leaned against the wall, her eyebrows raising.

"Well, I told Dar. I wasn't sure about the wording." He turned his gaze to them, and Jack was taken aback by the fire there. "This is it." He shook his head again, returning to the screen. "But it's not. Someone's changed it."

"Changed it how?" Jack asked, a thread of fear twisting in his gut.

"I don't know exactly. But I only know of one person...one creature who could."

"Angelos."

Rhys nodded. "Angelos. The Herald." He turned back to face Jack. "He's the one you need to stop, not Lin."

When Jack didn't respond, Bee spoke. "We'll take that under advisement. But right now we should go." She turned towards the door, and Jack stood to follow.

But Rhys wasn't done yet. "If he's going to perform this ritual, whether it's to wake Night or do something worse, there are two optimum times: at the dark of the moon or—"

Jack finished for him. "Or when it's full."

"Tonight," Rhys added.

There was a hiccough in Bee's stride but she didn't stop until she was outside. At the door, Jack turned to Rhys. "You'll continue to help us?" He realized he liked the man and wanted to give him a purpose without Dar.

Rhys huffed, a harsh laugh, peering at him over his glasses. "Of course. You still need me," he said. "Maybe even more now." Then he closed the door and Jack was left staring at the wood.

MINA GLANCED OVER HER shoulder at the sound of a siren. Even though the blade was in a soft guitar case, slung over her torso, and its theft probably hadn't been noticed yet, it weighed on her. Brett had gone to work, without sleep, and Sam had turned her out when she and Finn had shown up at the tattoo shop, wanting nothing to do with her criminal escapades.

But they needed somewhere to pause, discuss what came next, and the Sanctuary was out of the question; she was still too angry at Jack. The apartment had become a dark spot in her mind, tainted by worry and guilt. So, now she stood rapping a brass knocker against the door of a brownstone. Somewhere along the way, the werecat had picked up their trail and now wound its way through her ankles. Mina lifted the knocker to strike again when the door swung open. She chided herself for getting lost in her thoughts, instead of hearing the soft footfalls approaching. What if she were somewhere else, and it wasn't an old man on the other side of the door.

"Back so soon?" the aforementioned old man said, looking down at the housecoat he was tying up. "I already told you, I'm not deaf."

"Sorry?"

Rhys' eyes darted up to her as he pulled the housecoat around himself more tightly. "Mina, and young Finn."

Mina glanced at the Smith in time to catch the grimace in response to Rhys' words.

"Not so young, old man." Finn frowned. "I'm older than she is." She raised an eyebrow at Mina. "If we were counting in human years."

Mina turned back to Rhys. "We found it." She swung the case off her shoulder, almost bonking the cat on the head. It let out a disgruntled yowl and took off into the apartment.

"Found what?" Rhys rubbed his eyes before focusing on the case.

"The blade of the Moon, of course."

"The what? Wait, come inside." He ushered them into the hall then, after looking both ways down the street, closed the door behind them. Squeezing past them, he led them into the living room. It was the same controlled, catalogued chaos Mina

A PLAGUE OF SHADOWS   341

remembered, the only thing different the wilting flowers on the side table.

"I'm sorry, we don't have to be here," she said, her gaze fixed on the flowers.

"'Course we do," Finn said, taking a seat opposite Rhys. "We need to know what to do with this thing."

"No, we can come back," Mina started, lifting the case to sling it back over her shoulder.

"Don't be ridiculous," Rhys said, giving her a hard look. "You can't pique my curiosity and then leave. Show me what you've found."

"The blade of the moon." Mina unzipped the side of the case after laying it flat on the floor. The werecat sniffed the air above it then backed up, its lips pulled back.

"I'm not sure I know that one," Rhys said, but his measured words told her his brain was churning. She flipped open the lid to expose the brilliant steel and dark ebony handle of the double-ended crescent blade. "Ah, the third part of the drawing of blades."

Finn leaned forward in the chair, stopping as it started to tip. "The Sun, lost forever. The Even Star, in our enemy's hands apparently. But we have the Moon."

"We just don't know what to do with it," Mina said. "How do we make a magical weapon...phah...magic itself?"

"Are there magic moves to go with the magic sword?" Finn added.

Rhys pulled his glasses off and started cleaning them with a kerchief from his pocket. "Who said anything about magic?"

"What?" Mina glanced from him to Finn. "But we need a weapon that can stop Angelos."

"And we have that." He put his glasses back on and peered at her. "We have an exceptional weapon." He nodded at the blade.

"That's not a lot."

"No, but get it into the hands of an exceptional fighter, and maybe it's enough." He sighed. "Or if it is magic, hope that it decides to wake at the scent of blood."

"There's no special incantation? No potion?"

"I'm not a witch, my dear. If I were, I'd be one that waved his wand and everything was clean." His smile was lopsided as he glanced around, then he turned back, serious again. "But it is likely Angelos will try whatever he plans tonight."

"Why tonight?" Mina asked, glancing to her left, at the werecat, who'd started a low growl.

"The full moon," Finn said. "When the fabric between worlds is thin."

Rhys nodded. "The full or the dark, as I told Jack and Bee when they were here earlier." Mina opened her lips to say something though she wasn't sure what. Rhys continued as if he hadn't noticed. "They're hunting for him, I hope. Or they're still stubbornly going after Lin. But they'll likely find Angelos all the same." Rhys' eyes were penetrating, like shards of cold glass as he gazed at her. "He needs three things: a vessel, a sacrifice and the blade."

"He has the blade." Finn toyed with a curly lock of hair, her pale lips pulled into a frown.

"And he likely already has a vessel."

"So all he needs is a sacrifice?" Mina said, followed by a heavy sigh. She slipped the blade back in the case. "And that's easy enough to come by. There are a thousand people who wouldn't even be missed until it was all over."

A PLAGUE OF SHADOWS 343

Rhys shook his head. "No, this sacrifice is in exchange for Night. It needs to be someone worthy."

"Any ideas?" Mina turned as the werecat spit and hissed and arched its back. Werewolf mythology came back to her – the full moon – but the cat kept its form and Rhys continued.

"Some." He squinted at Mina for a second before his gaze found the werecat, who had settled down but stared right back at him, her face angry, if a cat could be angry. "Some."

"Like the last remaining member of an ancient line of royal werecats." Mina recalled what Rhys had told her when he'd first seen the cat.

"Something like that." He was quiet for a minute, his attention turned back at her. "Take the blade to Jack, or even better, Bee. And hope they're good enough to fight him."

CHAPTER FORTY-FIVE

A WHIFF OF ODOUR SNAKED amongst the tombstones on a whisper of wind, sickly sweet, almost rotten like overripe cantaloupe. Condensation from each exhale hung heavier than it should have in the crisp, clear night air. Ivan found it hard to get the deep breath he needed to calm his pulsating nerves and clear his head. Besides himself, Em, Adam and a few others stood in a wide circle near the centre of the graveyard.

Between them, by the low crypt, stood the triad at the centre of the night's proceedings: the shivering woman, arms wrapped tight around her torso; Lin, who'd reluctantly torn herself away from her gargoyle, though it still lurked in the shadows somewhere; and the priest, still wearing clerical vestments, even though he now wore Matteo's skin. Though he looked younger, less skeletal. Ivan shivered, telling himself it was the wind that had picked up.

None of them looked particularly pleased or at ease. Angelos reminded Ivan of a drug addict, fidgeting and twiddling his fingers, his eyes – brown now, like Matteo's – shining. It was out of the ordinary for a man who didn't move a finger without thinking about it, though maybe the man was uncomfortable in Matteo's skin. Lin looked as if she'd tasted something sour, her neck tense, her lips pursed and her face ghostly, almost translucent. The woman Matteo had turned, breaking his own rule against

A PLAGUE OF SHADOWS 345

creating new vampires, well, she just looked confused, a little scared, and very hungry. *Camellia.*

"What's are we doing here?" she asked, wrapping her arms more tightly around her skinny torso. She'd fed earlier, not from the priest-turned-Matteo this time, but she still licked her lips and swallowed obsessively. "Can't we go back inside? Maybe I can wait in the car." Her voice was lost in a gust of wind.

"Hush, child," Angelos said, his voice still his own. "It'll all be over soon." He removed his jacket and draped it over the woman's shoulders, seeming almost chivalrous if it weren't for the flare of icy anger in his eyes. He stepped back to the grave marker where he'd focused his attention, though Ivan couldn't see what was so special about that one.

"It's cold," she smiled a weak smile at Angelos before another shiver passed through her. "No matter what, I can't get warm."

"Stop whining," Lin said, her voice sharp, causing the woman to take a step back. "It's unbecoming in a vampire," she continued, her voice softening when Angelos' gaze flashed her way before it turned back to the satchel at his feet. He pulled something out, placing it on the crypt. A metal cup, Ivan saw. He looked away as Lin continued. "And, as he says, you'll be done here soon enough."

Ivan shivered, and had to admit he agreed with the girl, but didn't say anything. He craned his neck and peered over his shoulder at some sound, but it was just the wind in the trees. He glanced towards Em. Even with the distance between them, he could see her eyes were shining, fixated on Angelos, as a length of chain came out of the bag and joined the goblet. Her tongue poked out between her fangs; the muscles on the side of her neck strained to see what the Herald was doing as the man reached into the bag again, muttering words in a language Ivan didn't understand, and was sure he didn't want to.

Lin's gaze homed in on the herald, her eyes narrowing, her head tilting. The vein on her temple ticked her impatience, so like Matteo in some ways, perhaps part of the reason for their decades' long feud. "What *are* we waiting for? I've better things to do than stand around doing nothing."

Angelos stood up and stopped muttering as something flashed in his eyes, and Ivan was glad he wasn't on the receiving end of the stare. "Really? What better things do you have to do than this?" he said, pointing at Lin with a tapered length of wood he'd pulled from the bag, almost like a wand, or stake. "Go back to rummaging in the woods, digging for voles and vermin to feed on?" He waved the wand around, its smooth surface catching the moonlight. "What do you plan to do without Night exactly?" He placed the wand beside the other items on the crypt.

"I don't know," Lin said, her words measured. "Maybe whatever it is you're planning to do without her, since it seems like you're not planning on waking her."

The night went still as she spoke, the wind died down, even Ivan's heart stopped beating. Angelos stopped reaching into the satchel, and stared straight ahead, not looking at her. For a handful of seconds, Ivan thought he wasn't going to respond to her accusation. But finally he spoke, his voice as even as hers, but so glacial it caused a shiver to travel up Ivan's spine into his hair.

"Whatever do you mean?"

"I know what you're saying," Lin said. "At least enough to know the words aren't the right ones."

Angelos scoffed. "There are many ways of saying the same thing. And I've learned many things in the years of exile. Like

A PLAGUE OF SHADOWS 347

how to strengthen the spell to call up Night." He went back to his bag. "As for the wait, I need one more person to join us."

"Who?" Lin asked. Ivan's lips tightened at her tone; he didn't sense that this Angelos, whatever he was, liked to be challenged. And was a lot more dangerous than appearances led one to believe.

"You'll find out soon enough." The Herald gave her an angelic smile that set Ivan's teeth on edge.

"And why should I trust you, skin-stealer?"

"You shouldn't," Angelos said. "But we're all here for one purpose: Night is coming. And we need to make way."

"Then why are you changing the words to an incantation written by Night herself? Altering an ancient ritual?" Lin stepped towards Angelos. Ivan's hand went to the handle of his gun, though he wasn't sure who he'd shoot if the two of them went at each other's throats. He relaxed his grip on the handle.

Angelos didn't take her bait. "Just because it's old doesn't mean it's right." He turned back to his collection of items and beckoned to her with Matteo's long fingers. "Come."

There was a fraction of a second's hesitation before Lin made her way over to his side, with her herky-jerky nosferat movements, like a sped-up stop-motion film. The wind rose again, causing Ivan to shiver.

Lin came to stand nose to nose with the Herald for a second, her head moving side to side, lips open as she sniffed at the man. Then the priest grasped the back of her neck and pulled her head in close, his lips a hair's-breadth from her neck. "Does smelling me like a dog make you trust me anymore?" He pushed Lin away, ignoring her angry eyes and tense lips.

A woman scorned, Ivan thought.

But Angelos didn't see or didn't care. "Enough," he continued. "As you say, we have more important things to do." He scanned the circle of watchers, his gaze resting on Em, before returning his attention to Camellia. Then he crouched down, reached into the bag and pulled out the shining black dagger with an undulating edge.

The obsidian blade that had been stolen from the museum. Ivan let out an involuntary gasp. Seeing it in the moonlight, it gleamed in a way it hadn't in the candlelight, like it had found its atmosphere. Somewhere, it plucked at a thread of memory, shrouded in the dust and blood of long-ago battles. The Herald ran his fingers along the edge.

Em rocked onto her toes, more keen than Ivan for whatever was next, while the girl looked even more confused than before, having no idea what was coming. But then again, neither did he.

He'd heard Night was coming. But only the priest – the Herald who now walked in Matteo's skin – and Lin seemed to have any idea what that meant, and neither of them were much into sharing. Ivan scanned the rows of graves, shining silver in the moonlight, and the denuded, forlorn trees, shivering in the breeze. But there was no sound, other than the odd rustle of some creature scurrying for shelter.

Makes those creatures smarter than us. Smarter than me.

Angelos looked at the cloudless sky. Lin picked up and put down the items on the gravestone, until she came to the cord which she kept in her hands, winding and unwinding it through her fingers.

"Camellia," Angelos said, his voice more resonant than a moment before. The girl stepped towards him, her lips moving as if to speak, but no words came. He beckoned her forward. She tore

A PLAGUE OF SHADOWS   349

her other foot from the ground. A wayward tear rolled down her cheek as she took another step. *Maybe she does have an idea of what's coming*, Ivan thought, his chest constricting as he himself realized what would happen next.

Finally, the woman stopped and found her voice. "Please."

The Herald looked at her. "Come." His voice resonated with power.

"I told you, I want to live."

"Ha." Angelos' laugh was mirthless. "And you will." He stepped towards her, the obsidian blade, held casually in his hand, belying his words. "I'm not going to kill you. I need you alive."

"Oh." The girl's lips twitched. She took a tentative step forward. Then another until she was facing the man, her back to Lin. Angelos smiled at Camellia, placing his hands on her shoulder, then ran his hands down her arms. He glanced up at the moon as a whisper of wind snaked through the cemetery. Ivan shivered.

CHAPTER FORTY-SIX

A STILLNESS ENVELOPED the old cemetery, its headstones faded, its names forgotten. Jack crouched low on the rooftop of a bodega across the street, far enough outside the perimeter of holy ground to keep from disturbing any wards. He glanced at the frosty sky, the stars shimmering like shards of ice, the momentary thought of winged gargoyles passing through his mind. Beside him, Bee squatted, gun already drawn, as she peered over the edge of the roof.

"Do we go in?" she whispered.

Jack, keeping his eyes on the events transpiring in a clearing ringed by cracked mausoleums, shook his head. "Not yet." He craned his neck and shifted forward, trying to get a better look at the group, counting numbers and taking names. He couldn't see the priest anywhere, the one Mina said was the Herald of Night, though it was hard to tell for sure; even with a vampire's vision, it was a long way and, although skeletal, the trees impeded clear sight. One form he was certain of: Lin. She did nothing to hide herself amongst headstones and bare branches, almost seeming to relish the light of the full moon on her face. Hanging low in the sky, it was ripe and flush and so bright it hurt his eyes.

A rough circle of guards was arrayed around the three figures in the middle, including Lin. The other woman picked at a snag in his memory; he felt he should know her but couldn't place her. Squinting, he recognized the ashen face of the final figure.

A PLAGUE OF SHADOWS   351

"Matteo's down there," he said to Bee.

"Yup. What do you think he's doing?"

Jack's eyebrows pulled together, his eyelids tensing as he tried to see what the nosferat was pulling out of the bag at his feet. His ears twitched as he tried to hear what the man was saying to Lin.

Jack glanced at Bee. "No idea. You?"

Bee's gaze slid from him to the scene below and back, her mouth opening then closing. "I hate to say it, but there's been mention of a ritual."

"Wha—" Jack stopped at the crunch of gravel behind them, disconcerted that he hadn't heard the door in his forward focus. He spun in his crouch towards the source of the sound, letting out the breath he'd been holding when he saw Mina standing there. Then he cursed, not bothering to keep it quiet, as Finn stepped up beside her.

Another set of footsteps, louder, trudged up the stairs and Brett appeared, coming to stand by Mina. Rounding out the merry band, the werecat insinuated itself amongst them, winding itself around Mina's ankles, making an endless chirring sound, its tail flicking back and forth with vigour.

"You've come to help us after all?" Bee asked.

"What are you all doing here?" Jack asked, shifting to stand. If it weren't for Bee's hand landing on his shoulder, he would have exposed himself to eyes from the cemetery.

Mina's gaze left Bee's face to travel to Jack's before looking over both their shoulders at the cemetery beyond. "I've come to stop the Herald. Angelos."

"He's not down there," Bee said.

"He has to be." Mina's head canted in question, and she came to crouch between them, the cat jumping up on the ledge in front of them. "Are you sure?"

They all turned their focus back to the cemetery, the cat included, its chirring turning to a low mrowl.

"Pretty sure," Jack said, his voice pitched low again. "How did you find us?" Mina shifted beside him.

"You forget," she said, the breath of her words whispering over his jaw. "I can hear your song. A whirlwind tempo of wood, leather and brass."

Jack turned to look at her, but she was watching the scene below. He tore his eyes away, back to whatever was happening in the cemetery. He couldn't see the third person anymore, the woman he should recognize. That thought niggled at him as Mina moved beside him.

"I've come bearing gifts," she said, lifting off the case she had slung over her shoulders. She lay the case on the rooftop and unzipped it, opening it almost reverently. "A weapon."

Bee shifted, unable to resist a new weapon. Jack half turned, trying to keep an eye on the scene below while getting a look at what Mina had in the case.

Bee reached out her fingers to run them along the dark handle. "What does it do?" she asked.

Mina looked up at her. "It cuts things."

"I think she means, what's its power?"

Mina shrugged. "Rhys didn't know. It might just be a blade."

"It's not any blade," Finn hissed, crouched behind Mina. "It's one of the triad: the blade of the Moon, the blade of the Sun, the blade of the Evening Star...or Night, as you've come to call it."

A PLAGUE OF SHADOWS 353

"If it's related to the blade the priest has, maybe it's evil," Jack said, then glanced down to the clearing. There was movement. Something was happening. He stood, no longer having Bee's hand on his shoulder to stop him showing himself and giving away their position to anyone who might be watching. "We should go," he said.

"What? We can't leave." Mina's face was angry as she stood up to stare at him.

"They're up to something down there." He stepped towards the stairwell.

"Wait," Mina said, her voice full volume. He turned towards her. She held out the blade to him. "Take it. Rhys said if we gave it to an exceptional fighter, it might be enough to kill Angelos."

"He's not there," Bee reiterated. "Besides, Jack's not the best fighter here."

"I'm pretty sure he is...I mean, the Herald, I'm sure he's down there somewhere." Mina paused as the cat sat at her feet and glared at him. "I can feel him. And Lin. And Em and Ivan, and others I don't know."

Seconds ticked past in silence, the others staring at her. Finally, Jack stepped towards her, laying his fingers on the wrist that held the blade. She shook with the fury of her conviction as her dark eyes lifted to gaze into his.

"Bee's right," he said. "She's the best fighter."

Bee scoffed. "No, I'm not." She shifted towards the roof edge.

"Don't be modest, Bee," Adeh said.

"I'm not," she said, half turning. "She is." She nodded at Mina, then hopped up onto the ledge and stepped off into darkness.

Beside Jack, Mina gasped, then she sighed, her shoulders slumping. He stepped away from her, turning to follow Bee.

"What are you doing?" Mina grasped his arm, trying to pull him down.

"What I came here to do. Avenge Dar." Then he stepped off the edge.

CHAPTER FORTY-SEVEN

MINA CREPT THROUGH the gravestones, making barely any sound on the crunchy, frozen ground, the only mark of her passing the condensation of her breath in the air. Behind and beside her, her ears picked out the soft footfalls and ragged breathing of the others. Her blood was buzzing; too many vampires in one place to pick out a single thread of song. At her feet the werecat padded silently, except for a rapid, low-frequency purr that was too loud to Mina's ears. The cemetery was rendered all in shades of grey in the moonlight: pewter, dove, slate, charcoal.

Just ahead, Jack came to a stop behind a mossy grave marker, flint and olive grey. Mina crouched beside him, feeling his warmth waft towards her in the cool night. She shivered, and shifted closer, her anger at him not enough to keep her warm or keep her away. And she was glad that his path, and that of the others, had led them to the same place. He glanced at her, his eyes shining in the dark, then they both turned their focus to the gathering in front of them. Mina watched as the werecat slunk around the gravestone and hunkered behind another one 20 paces ahead. Mina wanted to tsk, to admonish the cat to stay back. She didn't want it to startle the Necrophagos into precipitous action, never mind becoming a snack for a gargoyle. But, beyond not wanting to make any noise, however small, she knew the cat would do what it would do.

Mina peered around the stone, trying to catch a glimpse of what was going on. But the circle of vampires drew tighter around whatever nefarious ritual they were working. And one of them stood directly in her line of sight. She slid the case off her shoulder again, unzipping slowly, silently. A crunch of frozen, dead grass to her left caused her to turn her head sharply, but nothing was lurking in the darkness between the gravestones, other than Bee crouching behind another one a few metres back. Mina returned her attention to the case, drawing out the bow-shaped sword, its two blades matte in the moonlight. She gripped one of the handles like she would a normal sword, but knew it was wrong.

I have no idea how to use this thing. Mina sighed and caught Jack looking at her. She shrugged and laid the unusual blade down on the case, drawing her gun instead. The cat came padding back, sitting itself beside the case, and peered at her with its keen, golden eyes. Mina glanced at it, but her attention was pulled away as the breeze came up.

Mina's senses were dulled by the cold and muddied by the number of creatures convening on the cemetery, but as the wind lifted, she caught a familiar scent: lavender and rosemary. *At this time of year?* she thought, but that thought was torn away by the inhuman growl that followed. She adjusted her crouch, pulled out a dagger to go with her gun. The behemoth in front of her – the one called Ivan, she realized, who'd tried to collect her the night she met Jack – rocked on his feet as he shifted away from the scene. The move revealed the bloody scene beyond. It took Mina a minute to process what she was seeing, then a wave of horror passed through her.

"Cam." The whispered name came out hoarse, as if her voice had been torn from her.

"HOLD HER," ANGELOS said, his voice redolent with power. Ivan couldn't refuse and took a half step towards the trio at the centre of their circle, his hand on his gun. Before he could even blink, Lin whipped out a silver chain that she quickly looped through the woman's elbows before pressing her knee into the woman's back. Some tension left Ivan's shoulders. Meanwhile the Herald drew out his obsidian blade. Ivan didn't want to look at it, but he couldn't turn away. A voice inside called to him. It sounded almost like—

"What? No! You said...." Camellia's eyes went wide, and she started to struggle, apparently finding some life left inside. But Lin's grip on the chain only tightened, keeping the woman close. A spark flared in Camellia's eyes, a fire Ivan hadn't had for a long time, then she aimed her heel at Lin's foot. But Lin was too fast for that.

"I'm true to my word." Angelos stepped towards her. "I'm not going to kill you. I'm going to transform you."

The woman struggled against the chain even though the silver wasn't touching flesh. She created a gap between her and Lin, but Lin still kept a tight rein on the chain. The woman glared at Angelos. She didn't seem to trust the priest anymore than Ivan did. His nostrils flared as he watched her hopeless rebellion.

"I never asked to be transformed in the first place," she said, then jabbed an elbow into Lin's ribs. But the move had no force, bound as she was, weak as she was.

Angelos hissed. "Matteo said you were willing."

"I willed to live." She lifted her chin. "When you, he, whatever, bit me. Yeah, I said I wanted to live."

Angelos contorted Matteo's face into a smile that was all his own. "Good enough."

"I...but I...." The woman looked around at a circle of stony faces. A creature, small and soft, like a rabbit in a snare, twisted in Ivan's gut. He squashed it. She wanted to live...but so did he. He forced his face into the impassive mask worn by the rest; they'd all made the choice in their own way.

Her shoulders slumped, and the Herald took a step towards her, the black blade in one hand, the wooden stake in the other.

Lin held the free end of the chain in one spidery hand as she stepped around to the other side of the headstone. Ivan couldn't imagine how she was withstanding the sear of silver on her flesh, but her face was smooth, showing no signs of pain. In fact, her eyes shone in the moonlit night. Angelos stepped up to Camellia until they were almost nose to nose. She took a step back. At the same instant, Lin looped the loose end of the chain around the woman's delicate neck and pulled back. Camellia fell over the stone, her back arched. She didn't go down easily. She kicked out, her left heel catching Angelos' knee as he came forward. Ivan knew from experience, that with Matteo's body, the kick would smart but it certainly wouldn't hobble the Herald.

Instead it made him angry. Through gritted teeth, the man said something in a language Ivan didn't understand, but he got the gist. He looked at the woman's exposed neck and shifted from one foot to the other. He glanced to his left, where Adam stood with his back towards the proceedings, seemingly bored, then to his right, where Em watched intently, her mouth half

A PLAGUE OF SHADOWS 359

open. Ivan looked back to the scene. In the struggle, the woman's shirt had lifted, barely covering her breasts, and her abdomen glowed in the moonlight.

Lin knelt on the ground, her torso against the gravestone, and pressed her cheek to the woman's head. Lin's lips moved against the woman's ear, but for once Ivan's unnatural hearing failed him. The woman stopped kicking and turned her wide eyes to Lin. A visible shiver passed through the Camellia. He didn't need to hear the words to know, whatever the Herald said, she was not surviving the night.

Without any preamble, Angelos drove the stake up under the ribs on the woman's left side. As the sliver of wood pierced the skin, the Herald started uttering guttural words in an arcane language that made Ivan's skin crawl.

As he watched, the woman stared at the Herald, whose eyes shone, and bucked her hips, causing thick blood to seep out around the stake. Lin pulled the cord tighter, and the woman's struggles slowed.

Ivan's jaw clenched as he was overwhelmed by reek of the viscous blood; he could almost see it, black vines carried on the breeze, snaking along the ground. He pulled himself up straight, tilted his head back, up to the clear night sky, and breathed deeply. He tried to map out the constellations of his childhood in the stars above that winked in and out between the inky tendrils that threatened to overtake his field of vision. As a wave of dizziness passed through him, he righted his head, but that didn't help.

The Herald kept muttering, faster, louder, deeper. Then the tone of his words changed, and the cadence shifted. Lin let go of the chain and stared at him, and the expression of white-hot rage on her face sent shivers down Ivan's spine. But Angelos paid her no mind, he just kept at his chanting.

Until Lin grabbed him. Shoved him. "Those are not the words." Her words were muted, garbled, as if they were travelling through water. Heavy heartbeats pulsed through Ivan's ears.

"They're close enough." The Herald's whispered words carried across the graveyard. Ivan tipped his head back again to look up at the stars, trying to not think about how he would survive the night. Then the stars disappeared.

CHAPTER FORTY-EIGHT

"CAM." MINA STOOD UPRIGHT. Jack froze at her voice. There was a pause in the universe, a hiccough in time. Mina gazed at the scene in front of her, stock still. The other vampires stared at her. Even the cat didn't move, not so much as a swish of its tail.

No one moved. Except him. He turned to her, his head cocked, his brows pulling close, as his brain clicked together pieces in a dizzying rush. He realized where he'd seen the woman before: Mina's roommate. Then the world returned to normal speed as he stayed trapped in a warp of slowness.

He reached out as Mina side-stepped the meagre protection of the headstone, exposing herself to the Herald, Lin, and whatever else lurked in the shadows, but his hand grasped air.

He leapt over the stone to grab her as she left his side, heading towards the circle of Necrophagos, but his limbs felt like they were bound by the dark strings of an unseen puppet master.

His voice stuck in his throat as he tried to shout out when she ran ahead, gun drawn.

He tried to stop her rushing to her death, but failed. He watched as a slow, lopsided smile spread across Matteo's face. Something was wrong. His gut told him something was very wrong. Then Matteo turned, and Jack saw the black blade in his hand. His attention returned to Matteo's expression, to the sneer of icy certainty on the lips and the wicked gleam in the black eyes...obsidian eyes. And then it struck Jack like lightning, the shock leaving him breathless. *That's not Matteo.*

Just as his breath returned, the world around him started moving again. He glanced over at Bee to find her engaged with a pair of werewolves. They were twice the size of a normal wolf, and with a glint of unnatural intelligence and commonplace malevolence in their eyes. He'd been so focused on the target of his revenge he hadn't noticed when they'd joined the fray. Bee was holding her own, so he turned to the rest of the field. Ahead of him, Mina's charge had been stalled by Em, while Ivan stood by and watched, gun in one hand, sword in the other. To his other side, Adeh and Sha were fighting a pair of Necrophagos stronger and faster than them.

Jack leapt forward to join the fight, expecting Ivan to stop his progress, but the large vampire didn't move. Instead it was Adam who stepped in front of him, pulling a gun to augment the blade he already held. Jack slued to the side, slicing his blade across and down, catching the edge of the man's wrist. He was rewarded with a snarl and a slice to his own thigh. He spun, sinking down, his leg circling around to knock Adam's feet out from under him. The other vampire fell back, hitting his head on a grave marker. Jack prepared to finish the fight, but the man's body went limp, so he spun back to the centre of the action.

In the minute his attention had been elsewhere, Mina had bested Em, who now knelt on the ground, with a bloody hand clutching at her abdomen, her face pale as a ghost. Jack glanced at Mina, who was once again striding towards Herald, her cheeks flushed as if she were drunk.

Jack took off towards her but slowed as she froze a few metres in front of him. The Herald stepped behind her friend,

A PLAGUE OF SHADOWS 363

whose face was an ashen olive grey that contrasted with the red blood soaking her shirt. He held the obsidian blade in one hand, pressed tight against the woman's throat, a weird cup in the other. And when the man spoke, in a voice that wasn't Matteo's, it confirmed Jack's belief that this was somehow Angelos. At that moment, it seemed like he could hear nothing else, not the breeze in the trees, not the rustle of the fighters beside him, not his own heart beating.

"Someone willing to give up their life for a friend. How quaint." The blade slid casually across the woman's throat. "Too bad it's too late." He held the chalice to the woman's neck to catch the blood that oozed out and muttered unintelligible words that caused goosebumps to raise across Jack's body. A flicker of movement to his right caught his attention. Lin, looking livid. Stalking towards Angelos.

"No!" Mina's ragged scream tore at the air, drawing his attention back. She started running again, and the Herald paused, taking a step back, away from her and her fury.

"Mina!" Jack shouted, chasing her across the uneven ground, sword in one hand, gun in the other. But he couldn't get to her.

Mina slid to a halt beside the bleeding woman, gun pointed at Angelos' chest.

"Cam," she whispered, as she pressed the fingertips of the hand that held her dagger to the woman's face. Judging by Mina's expression, she knew what he knew, somewhere deep down: this was one vampire who would not heal from these wounds.

Angelos stepped towards her. Mina turned to him with a feral snarl that tore at Jack's heart and pulled the trigger.

Jack stopped short. Angelos paused to look at the blossom of red on his chest. Jack held his breath, waiting for the Herald to fall. Then Angelos raised his head, snarled and grasped Mina's wrist, bending her arm. Jack raced forward again, cut to the quick by her cry of pain.

"Stop," Angelos said, his voice flat, as he twisted harder. The gun fell from Mina's hand, and she had no choice but to follow the torquing of her body until her back was against his chest and the obsidian blade was pressed to her throat.

Jack froze.

"Good boy."

"Those were not the right words," a voice to his left said. An all too familiar voice. Jack glanced over, despite not wanting to look away from Mina, but he saw that Lin's eyes were not focused on him. She stared at Angelos as she stood over the woman lying on the gravestone, the cup held in her bloody hands. She tipped the vessel forward. It was empty.

Jack glanced at Cam's face, at the blood smeared across her lips, and realized what Lin had done.

"What have you done?" Angelos asked, his voice livid. "Answer me." His tone became deep and resonant. Compelling.

"I gave it back to her. Time to complete the ritual." She stepped towards Angelos. With the Herald's attention on Lin, Jack took the opportunity to lunge forward, not having any solid plan other than getting Mina out of Angelos' grasp.

As he moved, he saw Lin spin towards him, saw her red lips and the dark circles under her eyes. What he didn't see was her sword, not until it was buried in his shoulder up to its hilt. He looked at it, his forehead furrowed, and felt the sting of silver.

"Stay out of this, Chagodai," Lin snarled. His eyes lifted to look at her rabid face, contorted in anger. Then his gaze travelled to Mina. "Sorry," he whispered.

Lin kept the blade in his shoulder, giving it a twist that brought him to his knees as she turned back to Angelos and continued. "Complete the ritual. As it was intended. Perform the sacrifice. Wake Night. And pray she'll forgive you."

Angelos glared at her, pure fury in his eyes, and Jack watched the calculations being performed in the creature's brain. The seconds ticked slowly away, in time with the blood that pulsed from his shoulder as the night waited for a response.

Finally, he sneered. "You think it's as simple as that. Fine." He arched an eyebrow. The blade scraped up the skin on Mina's neck until it was right under her jaw. Jack made an involuntary jerk towards her, which only resulted in a searing pain from the sword that pinned him. Angelos leaned in until his lips almost caressed Mina's cheek. "But first, to complete the ritual I need a sacrifice. We can't keep Night waiting after all."

THE DARK BLADE SCRAPED along Mina's throat. Her nostrils were filled with the scent of Cam's blood, and a tear slid down her cheek.

I'll never know what Cam's song sounded like. A flame ignited in her chest, flickering in time with Jack's heartbeat as the blood oozed from the wound on his shoulder. The flame grew to fill her gut. She shook her head – this was all wrong – then stopped as the blade drew a bead of blood across her neck. She heard its voices flood her head, yearning to get out. A snarl formed on her lips.

"No." The rough word was barely more than a whisper. She dropped her blade, the only weapon she had left, then spoke again, louder. "No, the monster says I should kill you."

"With what? You dropped your only weapon." Even though she couldn't see him, the sneer was clear in his tone.

"Not my only weapon." The fire burned bright at that. There was a minuscule slackening of tension in his arm, but it was all Mina needed. She slammed the heel of her now empty hand into the elbow that held the blade, forcing it to slide past her neck. As he tried to move it back into a kill position, she leaned her head forward and sunk her teeth as hard as she could into his hand. He howled, more in fury than pain, but in that split second of distraction she drove her heel into his foot. Which gave her the opening to break the weakened lock on her other arm and twist out of the hold. As she did, his rage took over, and he recovered enough to slice at her with the obsidian blade. A wave of nausea flooded through her, and the fiery beast inside flared, reaching towards the tortured song of the blade. Off kilter, she slipped to her knees, tumbling forward. Somehow, she got her shoulder tucked and somersaulted into a crouch, with the presence of mind to grasp for her dropped dagger, before she had to fall back to avoid having her head sliced off by the black blade. But she used the opportunity to drive her feet up into Angelos' abdomen.

Only he wasn't there when her feet should have made contact. She found him on the other side of her. Anger surged from deep in her belly. She turned back over, onto hands and knees, eying him warily, trying to suss out his next move. But he moved like lightning. Even faster than Matteo had, though the limbs still had the herky-jerkiness of the body's former owner. On the

A PLAGUE OF SHADOWS 367

other hand, she was sluggish and clumsy, overwhelmed by the fire in her stomach and the cold song of obsidian that rang in her veins. She shook her head, trying to dispel the voices and expel the monster that gnawed at her insides. *But you are the monster*, a hoarse voice said.

Mina smiled as another blossom of blood formed at his shoulder. She'd rather it was her bullet that hurt him, but this would do. The smile dropped and bile rose in her throat as she choked on her glee. But he barely looked down at the wound before advancing on her again. Mina's fingers tightened around the sticky handle of her short dagger, and she wished she'd stuck with that damned crescent blade, even if she had no idea how to use it. She scanned the ground for her gun, but it was behind Angelos. She sighed and stepped towards him. So far, the bullets had done little to slow him down anyway.

Beyond the Herald, beyond her gun, was Jack, his face ashen as a gargoyle sunk its talons into his torso, careless of Lin's sword still lodged in his shoulder.

"Aaarghhh!" Deep inside, the beast of flame and acid flared again, and Mina charged at Angelos, hardly feeling it as another cut opened on her arm from a strike she never saw coming.

CHAPTER FORTY-NINE

SEEMA WATCHED THE SCENE unfold in front of her, pacing back and forth, crouching so low the hairs on her belly brushed the frozen ground. A growl rose around her, and she pressed lower before realizing that it was coming from her. She watched Mina run and kneel beside her friend. She watched Jack get stabbed. She watched Angelos take a bullet to the chest and keep moving as if nothing happened.

Glancing up at the darkening sky, she saw the full moon fading, as if behind a black curtain. Looking around, she saw all the other Athanatos struggling against an enemy of teeth and shadow. Her gaze travelled down beside her, to the blade of the Moon, abandoned by Mina. She snorted out a breath of air. Clearly the girl had no clue how to wield it, a weapon from a long-lost culture from a bygone age, and had left it despite it being a better weapon than a dagger or a gun. But then Seema knew how to use it.

If she had hands again, she could pick it up and carry it into battle. But then she'd also be able to pick up other things. Other weapons to hold high as battle fire boiled her blood. Weapons like the blade of the Sun. Seema shied away from the cold steel, a low keening sounding from her gut. She looked back at Mina, Mina who'd been kind to Mike, Mina who'd saved her. Blood splattered the ground all around her and covered her flagging right arm. The keening in Seema's gut stopped. Instead, she

A PLAGUE OF SHADOWS 369

hissed and spat and growled, wishing herself large and human, but was unable to make it happen. Her growl turned into a howl as she thought of all the things she'd failed to do: defend her family, protect Mike. *And now I'll fail to help Mina. And Night will win and take the day away.*

The howl turned into a yowl of pain and pent-up rage that reverberated through her bones. Her claws scratched at the earth as electric shocks of anger pulsed through her from tail to whiskers. Her stomach clenched, her body arched, as if her belly were trying to disgorge all she'd eaten since she was last human. When she was consumed by a hollow, hacking cough and an empty all-over ache, she realized what was happening. *I'm finally turning.*

She wouldn't have chosen to transform in the heat of battle, especially after so long as a cat. But better now than over a field of her friends' corpses. Her back twisted, her neck craned at an angle unnatural for woman or beast. Her bones felt like they were being torn apart at the joints and her pelt flayed from her flesh.

She'd always hated this part, but after a lifetime of not changing, her body had become fused to its feline form. As eyes turned her way, drawn by the demonic howl from her contorted body, she also remembered the vulnerability. Another thing she hated. The sounds of the world became warped and muddied, the images skewed sideways and dimmed, and the scents muted. Her yowl turned to a hoarse cry of pain from a ragged voice unused for a lifetime. A final jolt of agony racked through her limbs as her bones lengthened and skin stretched. She tried to scratch the pain away, but her claws had retracted into nails. Finally, she collapsed, naked on the cold, muddy ground.

Panting, breathing through her teeth, she glanced up and knew she couldn't take any time to let her body recover. She saw Jack's dark eyes widen, before his awed smile twisted into a grimace as he was carried off by a gargoyle, its claws digging into flesh. Then her gaze shifted to Mina. Mina who was on her knees in front of Angelos.

Get up...get up now. She forced her aching limbs and her rusty joints to do her will. The long fingers of her right hand reached out and grabbed the crescent blade while the other three limbs pushed her to standing. Then she strode across the cemetery, her movements jerky for the first few steps until her muscles remembered their ancient training. The blade swept in arcs around her, naked except for the scant cover of her wavy hair, too long and now streaked with grey. Her steps still as silent as a cat, she approached Angelos as he gloated over Mina.

MINA STAGGERED UP IN a desperate, dizzy lunge at the Herald. Then she stopped short, gazing at the black blade embedded in her shoulder, eyebrows pulled together in a question. She dropped to her knees again, hair falling in her face as she hung her head.

Cam's dead. Mina squinted over the shoulder of the Herald. *But she's a vampire, she'll heal*, she tried to tell herself as she stumbled and fell to her knees, bruising something when she hit the frozen ground. Her hand lost hold of the dagger, slick as it was with her own blood.

The song from the obsidian blade swelled, the weight of its melancholy pressing on her chest to the point she couldn't

A PLAGUE OF SHADOWS 371

breathe. *And my soul will be consumed.* When the blade was pulled from her shoulder, she slumped forward, her hands on the icy mud. A roar filled her ears, drowning out the howl of voices escaping from the bloodied blade of the Even Star.

The monster inside, the one that made her a vampire, was angry with her. *My blood*, it wailed. She shook her head, and the black blade disappeared from her narrowing field of view. Stars filled her vision. *At least if I die, the monster dies too.*

But so do Jack and Cam and the others, another voice said. She ignored it. Instead, she lifted her face to meet Death, eyes closed, not wanting to see the Herald's obsidian eyes gazing on her with malevolent glee as he killed her. She waited for the keen bite of the blade piercing her heart.

But the strike didn't come. The blade remained at his side, and his gaze was focused over her shoulder. His eyes were full black, glinting like the blade as a sneer played at his upper lip. Tendrils of black fog, like ink in water, snaked along the ground from around his feet. Mina shied away as one brushed her hand, and its brief caress caused her skin to blister. She grit her teeth and forced herself to reach through the tentacles of darkness to grab her dropped dagger. The ink burned like acid, and her frozen fingers struggled to grip the handle. When she grasped it, she drew her hand back, expecting it to be covered by red welts; instead, she only saw lines of shadow barely visible in the dimming moonlight.

She tried to stand, but the world tipped sideways, forcing her to stay on all fours for a few more seconds. She breathed deeply, into her ribs, still waiting for the stabbing pain of the obsidian blade piercing her back to reach her heart.

But the pain didn't come, and the ground stopped spinning. She stumbled to her feet, reeling away from Angelos, who still ignored her. But he had sunk into a fighting stance. Mina mirrored his posture. When he didn't react to her, she turned her head slowly, keeping the ground steady, to look at what had diverted his attention.

A woman strode through the graves, her movements shifting from stiff to fluid as she walked. A cascade of long, wavy hair, sable brown to match her walnut skin, shimmered over her torso. Otherwise she was stark naked, and her skin gleamed where it caught the wan light of the shadowed moon. The bow-shaped blade in her right hand flashed as it wove arcs of light, brighter than the moon, around her.

The blade of the Moon.... Mina's mouth gaped in awe, before the sounds of fighting crashed in on her again as the voices from the blade of Night faded. *But who's the woman?*

"What are you?" Angelos asked, his voice warped and his face contorted. But it wasn't just a flash of anger that made him seem more demonic. His neck extended and fangs grew longer. His dark eyes widened under a bony forehead. His voice was heavy with compulsion, but the woman stayed silent as she drew closer, seemingly uncowed by the transformation that made Mina's skin crawl. The woman glanced at her, her eyes flashing gold, before returning her attention fully to the hellish Herald.

Mina's mouth dropped open. "The cat," she whispered. She watched in stunned silence as the woman slid her leg out to try to catch Angelos', the crescent blade flowing towards his knee.

But he had the speed of the nosferat body he possessed and the flexibility of the demon he was turning into, and easily dodged her movement.

A PLAGUE OF SHADOWS 373

"I ask a question, you answer." His voice rippled with anger so powerful Mina struggled to stay upright against the shock waves. He spun in toward Seema's guard as she flowed into her next position. Mina's sticky fingers flexed on her own dagger, preparing to re-join the fight. But the Were moved so fluidly, flicking the blade so deftly, that Mina couldn't discern its path as it blurred through the air, slicing the Herald in the side.

He snarled and stabbed at the Were, but she was no longer there. Though when Mina locked eyes on her, she saw a scarlet line along the woman's bare arm.

"Tsk. Never let your anger determine your next move." There was a rasp to the woman's voice when she spoke, accompanied by a lilt.

"What are you?" he asked again, his tone more strident, but less quaking with power. As he spoke, he lunged at the Were again, the speed causing an eddy in the air. Mina lashed out with her own knife, aiming for where she thought he would be. A howl and the fresh tang of blood in her nose told her she'd hit something, but he still swirled towards Seema.

"I am nothing but teeth and talons." Seema moved again, little more than a distortion of moonlight. "Rending the darkness to let in the light."

"The agents of Night wiped out your kind." Angelos spun towards where Seema had been but was hobbled by the new cut along his thigh – Mina's knife had found its target, though not exactly where she would have liked. As he turned, he left his back exposed to her, and Mina took a step towards him to strike again while his attention was on the Were. Instead, she was rewarded with another numbing cut from the dark blade, while nearly losing an ear to the crescent blade. Something about wisdom and valour ran through her head as she took a step back. She deked to the side, just in time to avoid the flash of blue light that flew past her head. The blade of the Moon, she realized, as she looked back to the pair of fighters.

"Not all." The Were stood over Angelos, a sneer on her face and her chest rising and falling quickly. The crescent blade pressed against his neck, blood oozing from a long gash across his chest. "And you are no Night."

Mina wondered why he still had his head. The Were's nostrils flared as her eyes glistened in the brightening moonlight. Her jaw was tense when she spoke. "My mother always said, to forgive is to set yourself free." Her hand twitched, and a line of blood appeared on his neck. "But my mother is dead. So why should I listen to her, instead of the voice that seeks vengeance for Mike?" Angelos didn't speak, he just glared at her.

And in the silence, Mina realized it was quiet all around her; the sounds of fighting had died away. She wanted to turn around, assess the damage, but couldn't tear her eyes away from the pair.

Then Angelos snarled and lunged at the werecat with the ordinary blade in his hand. In a blur, his head was neatly severed from his body, an arc of blood spatter following the path of the moon blade. Mina closed her eyes just in time.

Wiping the blood from her face, she heard a small cough behind her.

"Cam," she whispered as she spun around.

CHAPTER FIFTY

"CAM." MINA STUMBLED towards her friend's body, no longer draped over the tombstone. Instead, Lin had one of Cam's arms around her narrow shoulders as she tried to drag her away, but Cam was a dead weight.

Nearly a dead weight. Mina froze for a second as her friend's legs moved ever so slightly of their own volition and her eyes fluttered as her head lolled back and to the side. "She's not dead." The hard lump in Mina's throat ached as she swallowed. Mina scrambled over the bloody gravestone, brandishing her dagger, and finding her voice again. "Let her go!"

Lin turned halfway, a sneer contorting her smooth face. "Or what, you'll prick me to death?" She turned more fully towards Mina, exposing the obsidian blade she held in her free hand.

Mina stopped, almost stumbling with the suddenness of it.

Lin shifted it so the point pressed just below Cam's ribs. "I'm pretty sure I can stab her in the heart before you do that, no matter how strange you are."

Mina's stomach clenched, and her fingers tightened on her dagger. She opened her mouth to speak, without knowing what to say. The ground crunched beside her. Taking her eyes off Cam for a spare second, she saw the werecat, still human, still naked, still with the wicked crescent blade in hand, dripping blood on the frosted ground. She sensed Bee come up on her other side. She looked back at Lin, forcing a sneer onto her own lips.

"I think you're outnumbered." She watched Lin's eyes dart left, right, calculating. Then Lin whistled, causing Mina to pause.

"Whistling won't help."

Lin suddenly dropped Cam to the ground, letting her go rather than stabbing her. Out the corner of her eye, Mina saw Bee's gun come up. In the same second that she heard the click of the gun, she saw the brown hulk of a werewolf slide in front of Lin. The bullet sunk into its muscular torso, but its only reaction was a sneer of its upper lip, exposing a vicious, bloody canine. It growled but shuffled back rather than charging.

It took Mina a second to realize what it was doing, figuring it out at the same time as Bee.

"Fuck!" Bee's exclamation was shocking from someone who almost never swore.

"It's guarding her retreat," the werecat's soft voice said.

"We need to go after her," Bee said.

But Mina didn't listen. Instead she crouched to pick up her gun from where it had dropped when Angelos attacked her, then went to kneel beside Cam. Her friend's eyes were closed again, but they moved under the lids. Laying her hand on her chest, she felt the heart beating, albeit thready and weak. "No, we need to tend to our wounded."

"We need to kill that thing."

Mina turned her head sharply to see a blue arc of light coming towards her. Towards Cam. A surge of fury coursed through her as she propelled herself into Seema's legs. Before she even had time to think, her dagger pressed at the woman's throat.

"I didn't fight to save her life so you could take it." Flecks of spittle flew from her mouth as she spoke, but she didn't care. What she did care about was the spark of fear in Seema's eyes and

A PLAGUE OF SHADOWS 377

the tension in the corded muscles of her neck. Mina shifted back, drawing her dagger away.

"What are you?" Seema's voice was a whisper as her arms came up beside her head, palms exposed, having let go of the blade of the Moon. Mina got off her and stepped back to Cam before letting her gaze find Bee.

"We need to go after Jack." Bee stared down at her, arms crossed over her chest.

"What about Jack?" A hollow pit grew in Mina's tumultuous stomach.

"We can still track him." Bee's voice was even, but strong.

"Jack?" Mina stopped in shock for a minute, her brain not computing, then glanced around. Jack wasn't amongst the few faces. And she couldn't hear his blood song. "What do you mean?"

"I think Mina is right," Seema said, her voice gravelly. "We should tend the wounded." The werecat shrugged her wiry human shoulders into the jacket Brett gave her, nodding towards him, before returning to peer at Mina. The blade was back in her hand, but she made no attempt at Cam. "It's better to live to fight another day than pursue a fool's death."

"Jack's gone?" Mina's voice barely left her chest.

Bee either didn't hear or ignored her, focusing instead on the Were. "And who are you, to have any say?"

"I'm the one who just slew the Herald who thought to become Night. None of you even understood the words he said." She shook her head, wrapping the scarf Sha had given her around her hips. "What do they teach you nowadays?" She looked up. "Besides that, Jack is long gone, probably dead."

Mina stood up straight. "What happened to Jack?" Her voice reverberated across the hushed cemetery. No one met her gaze. Except Brett, whose eyes were sad.

"After Lin stabbed him...." He shifted his stance, looking away before returning to her. "He was carted off by a gargoyle." He crouched down beside Cam and threaded an arm under her shoulders.

"Gargoyle." Her voice was quiet. Jack was gone. But maybe not dead. "I want to go after Jack too."

"I told you, your Jack is likely dead, or will be soon." Seema didn't even turn as she spoke so casually of Jack's death.

Mina glared at the woman's back. "No, I don't believe that. If a gargoyle spirited him away, it means—"

"It means it wanted to eat in peace," Seema said. The blood left Mina's face, and her world tilted again.

"That's enough from you," Bee said. The Were turned around, her mouth dropping open when her gaze fell on Mina. But instead of speaking, she turned and walked along the path Lin had taken, peering at the ground. After a heavy silence, Bee continued. "Jack is still alive. We go after him."

"No." Mina shook her head. After lifting her gaze and squaring her shoulders, she continued, louder. "No. Our first priority is to tend our wounded." She scanned the ragtag group. Blood still oozed from a series of long cuts on Bee's thigh. Sha supported Adeh, though he still stood despite the ashen cast to his skin. Her gaze travelled to the bodies of the Necrophagos and the werewolf that had met their ends. It was amazing that their side hadn't lost anyone. Except Jack. But she willed herself to believe he was still alive. "Jack would agree."

A PLAGUE OF SHADOWS 379

"Jack isn't here to give his opinion," Bee said, though her tone was less strident.

Mina ignored her, instead turning to Cam, cradled in Brett's arms. She walked over to them, and crouched beside Cam, pushing damp curls off her face with a bloody hand, and was rewarded with a weak moan. Brett looked at her then hefted Cam up off the frozen ground. He returned her sad smile. "Let's at least get her and Adeh back to the Sanctuary," she said. "Then we'll go hunt for Jack."

"You can't bring her to the Sanctuary." Bee's voice was stony, brooking no argument.

"What? But—"

"No. We have no idea what he did to her, and we don't have the numbers to watch our backs."

"I don't want to kill her, but Bee's right," Adeh said, his voice weak, as he shifted towards Bee. Mina glanced from him to Sha, who looked away.

"Fine. I'll take her somewhere else."

Bee stepped toward her. "We need you."

Mina waved her dagger at Cam. "So does she. It's my fault she's in this state at all." She sighed and wiped her dagger on her pants before sheathing it. "I'm taking her home with or without you."

"I can help." Seema had come back from whatever she'd wandered off to do. Mina glared at the werecat-turned-woman. "Don't worry. I've decided not to kill her."

Mina clenched her jaw, studying the woman. Noting that the blade was back in the case, she offered her hand. "Mina."

"I know." The woman tilted her head sideways and looked at Mina's hand. Realizing it was still covered with blood, Mina rubbed it on her jeans.

"That's usually an opening for you to give your name."

"Oh, I thought you knew. You can call me Seema, all my friends do." She tipped her head the other way, her eyes glazing over for a second. "Though I suppose they're all dead now. But you can still call me Seema."

A wail started up from the far side of the cemetery. Police coming to investigate the ruckus. Brett started walking, with Seema beside him.

"Whatever we do, we can't stay here." Mina turned away from Bee and wove her way through the gravestones under the light of the full moon, heedless of whether the others followed or not.

DID YOU ENJOY A PLAGUE OF SHADOWS?

IF YOU ENJOYED THIS book, I would really appreciate it if you left a review. Not only do reviews help me get the word out about my books, they also inspire me to keep writing.

Want to find out what happens next? The third book series will be released in 2019. Sign up to my mailing list over on my website to be the first to know when it's out.

About the Author

Author of the Bloodborne Pathogens dark fantasy series, C. Rene Astle gained a love of fiction, fantasy in particular, and a voracious appetite for story literally at her mother's knee, being read The Hobbit and Chronicles of Narnia as bedtime stories - because those are the types of stories her mom wanted to read.

From her father, she got an enduring curiosity about the universe, earned shivering in the dark beside a telescope on cold, Canadian winter nights waiting to witness some celestial event.

Now she fits in writing between her day job, gardening and getting out to enjoy supernatural British Columbia.

Read more at www.creneastle.com.

Made in the USA
Middletown, DE
10 July 2019